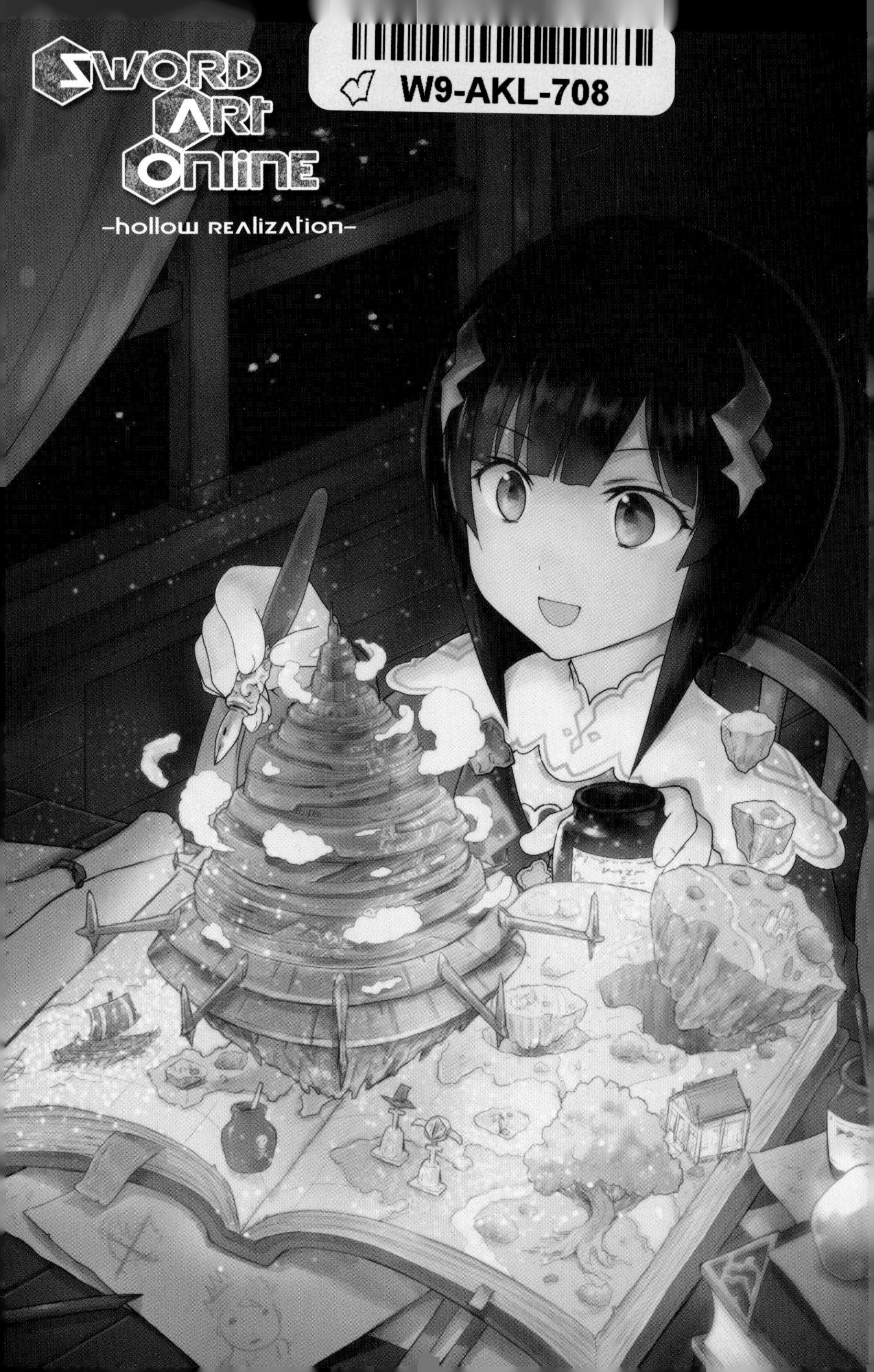
Sword Art Online
-hollow realization-

SWORD ART ONLINE
—HOLLOW REALIZATION—

005

CONTENTS

#21

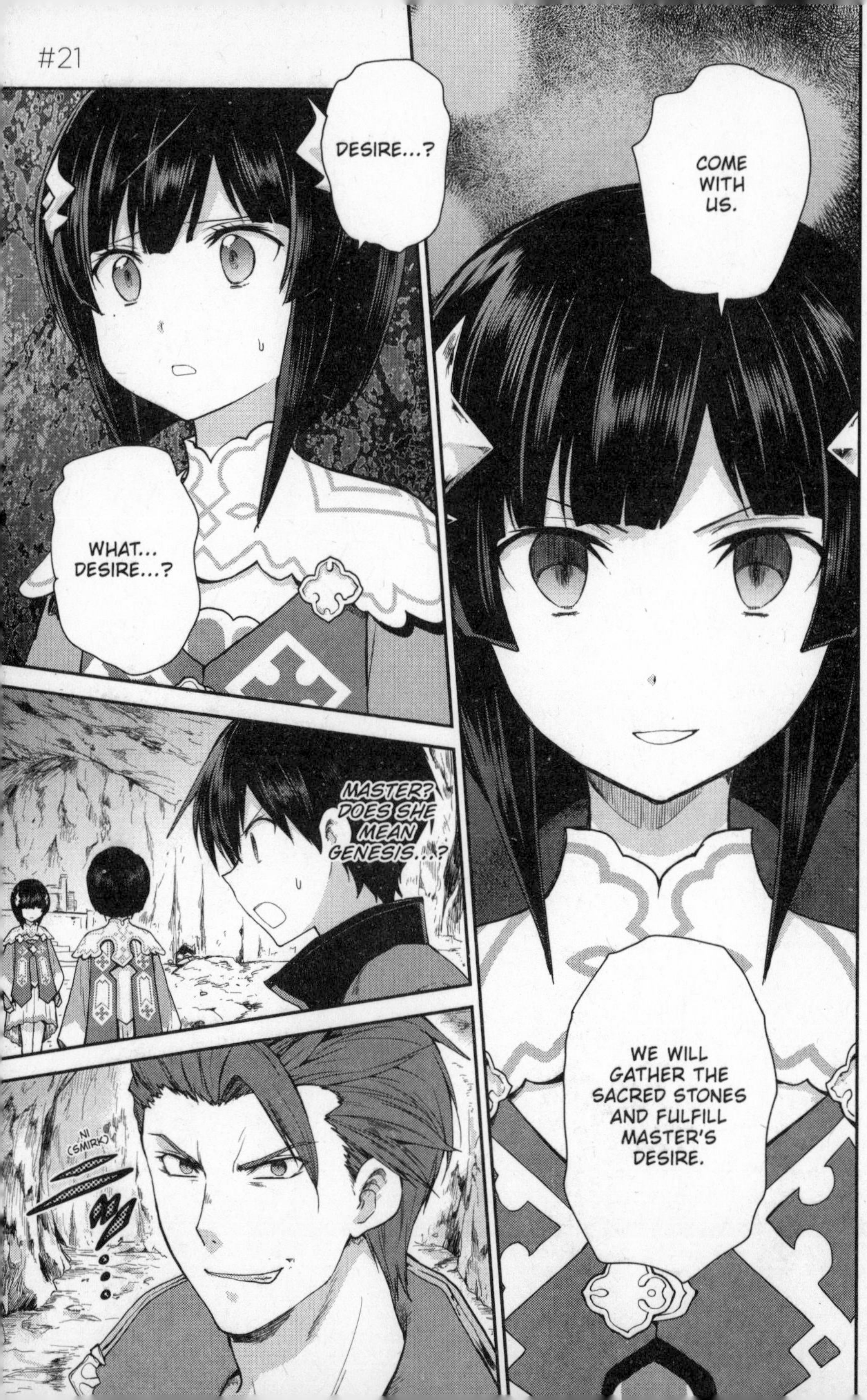
COME WITH US.
WE WILL GATHER THE SACRED STONES AND FULFILL MASTER'S DESIRE.
DESIRE...?
WHAT... DESIRE...?
MASTER? DOES SHE MEAN GENESIS...?
NI (SMIRK)

#21: Two Goddesses, Part II

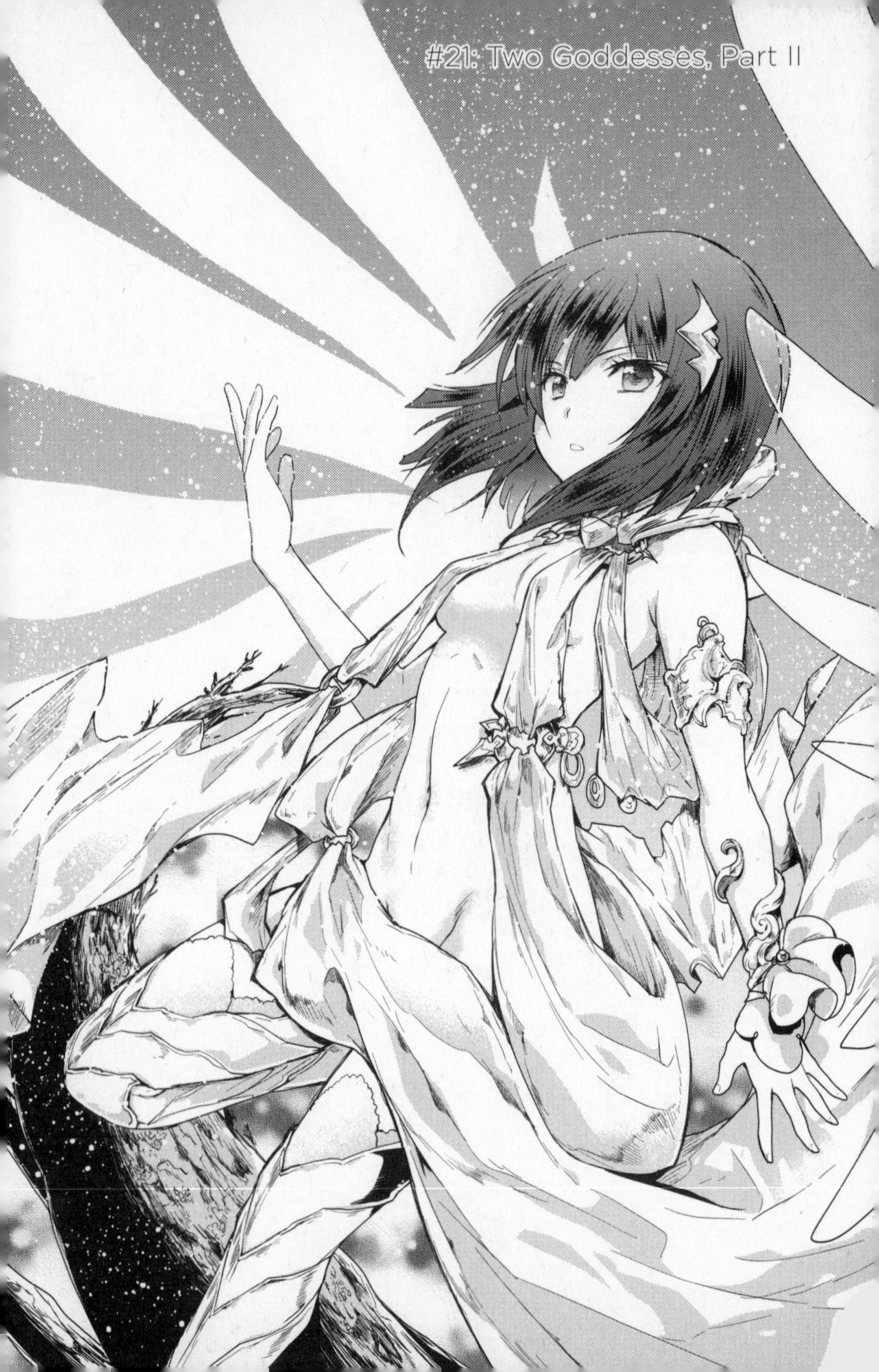

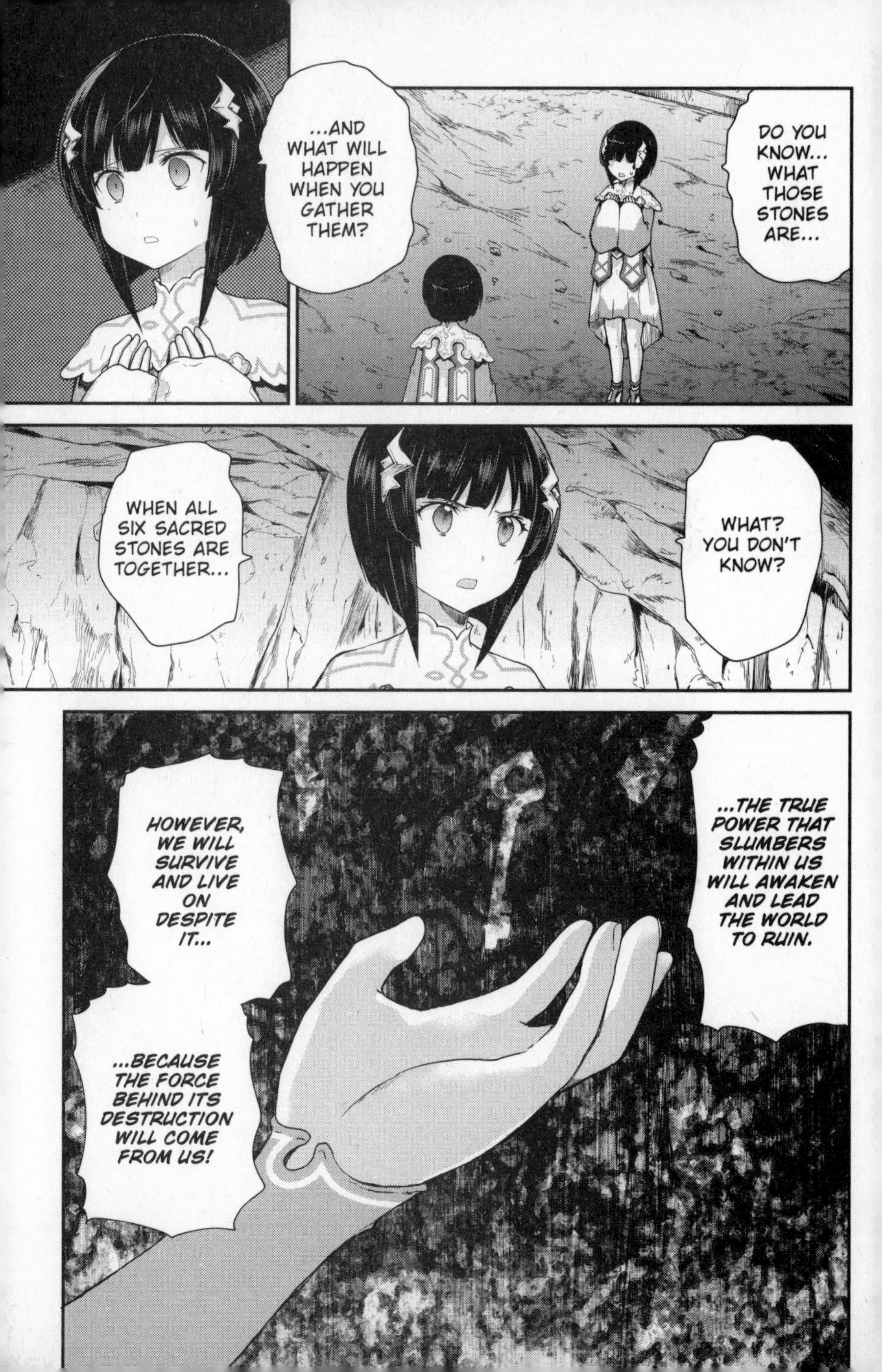
DO YOU KNOW... WHAT THOSE STONES ARE...
...AND WHAT WILL HAPPEN WHEN YOU GATHER THEM?
WHAT? YOU DON'T KNOW?
WHEN ALL SIX SACRED STONES ARE TOGETHER...
...THE TRUE POWER THAT SLUMBERS WITHIN US WILL AWAKEN AND LEAD THE WORLD TO RUIN.
HOWEVER, WE WILL SURVIVE AND LIVE ON DESPITE IT...
...BECAUSE THE FORCE BEHIND ITS DESTRUCTION WILL COME FROM US!

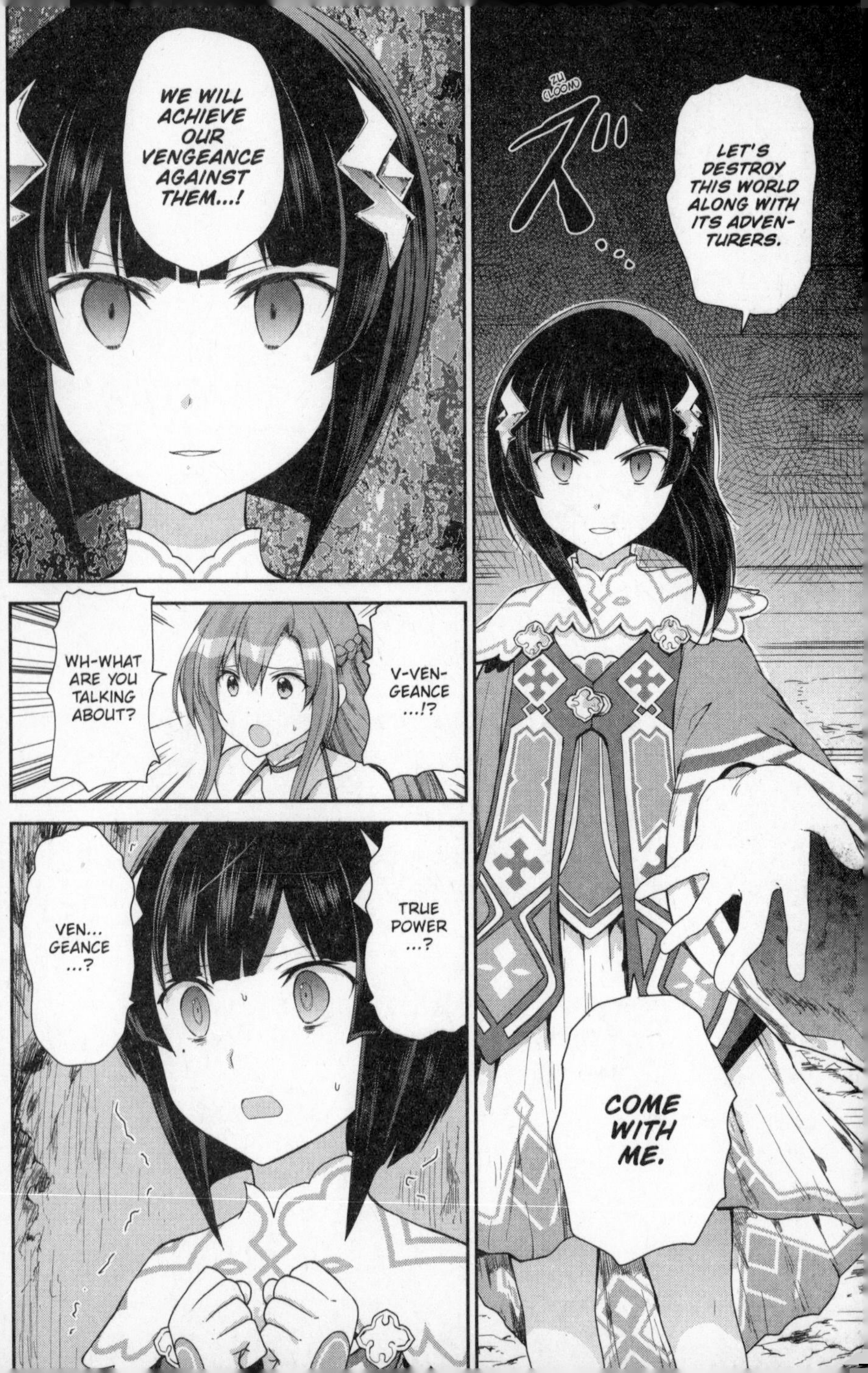
ZU (LOOM)
LET'S DESTROY THIS WORLD ALONG WITH ITS ADVENTURERS.
COME WITH ME.
WE WILL ACHIEVE OUR VENGEANCE AGAINST THEM...!
V-VENGEANCE ...!?
WH-WHAT ARE YOU TALKING ABOUT?
TRUE POWER ...?
VEN... GEANCE ...?

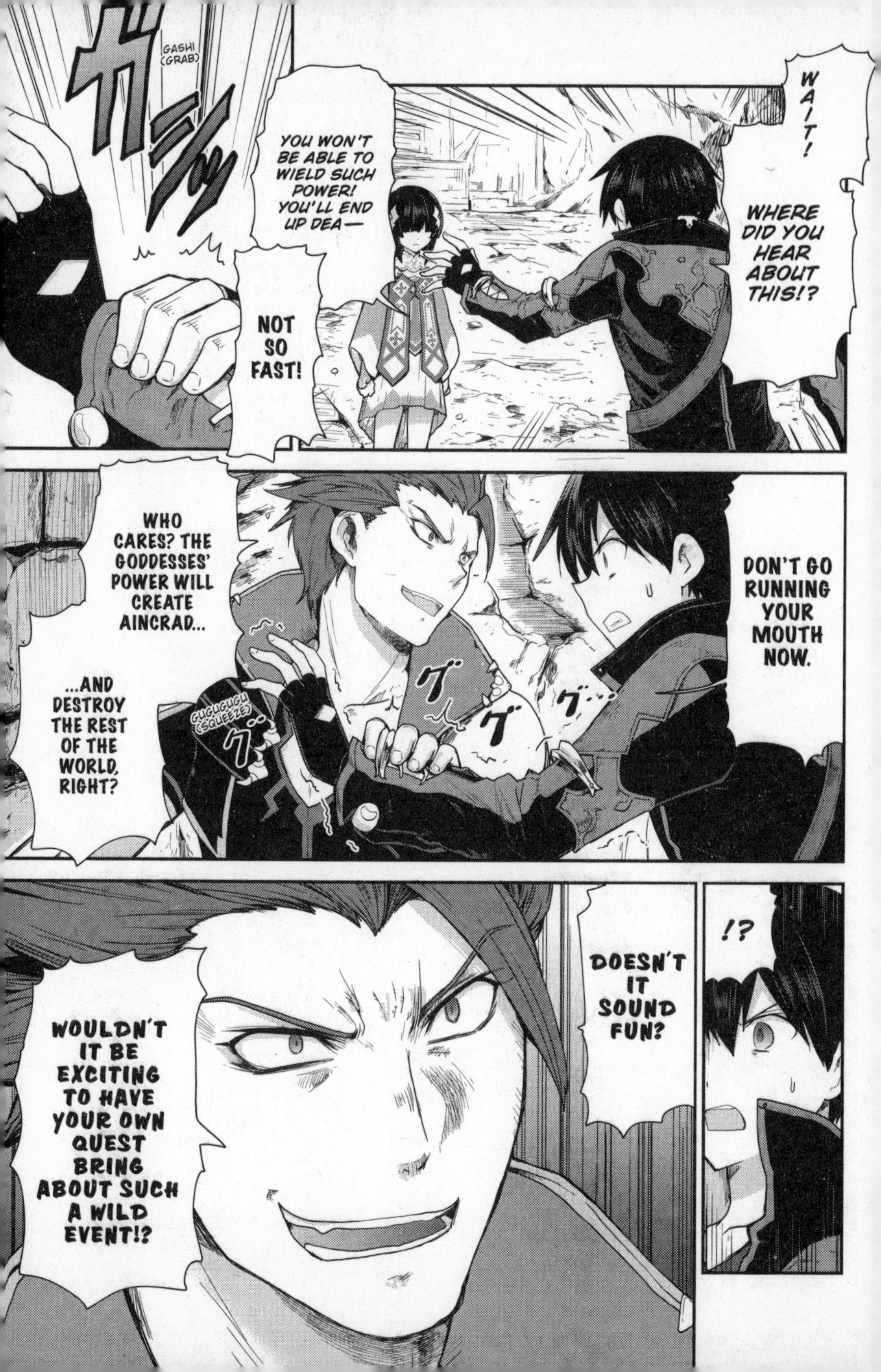
WAIT!
WHERE DID YOU HEAR ABOUT THIS!?
YOU WON'T BE ABLE TO WIELD SUCH POWER! YOU'LL END UP DEA—
NOT SO FAST!
GASHI (GRAB)
DON'T GO RUNNING YOUR MOUTH NOW.
GUGUGUGU (SQUEEZE)
WHO CARES? THE GODDESSES' POWER WILL CREATE AINCRAD...
...AND DESTROY THE REST OF THE WORLD, RIGHT?
!?
DOESN'T IT SOUND FUN?
WOULDN'T IT BE EXCITING TO HAVE YOUR OWN QUEST BRING ABOUT SUCH A WILD EVENT!?

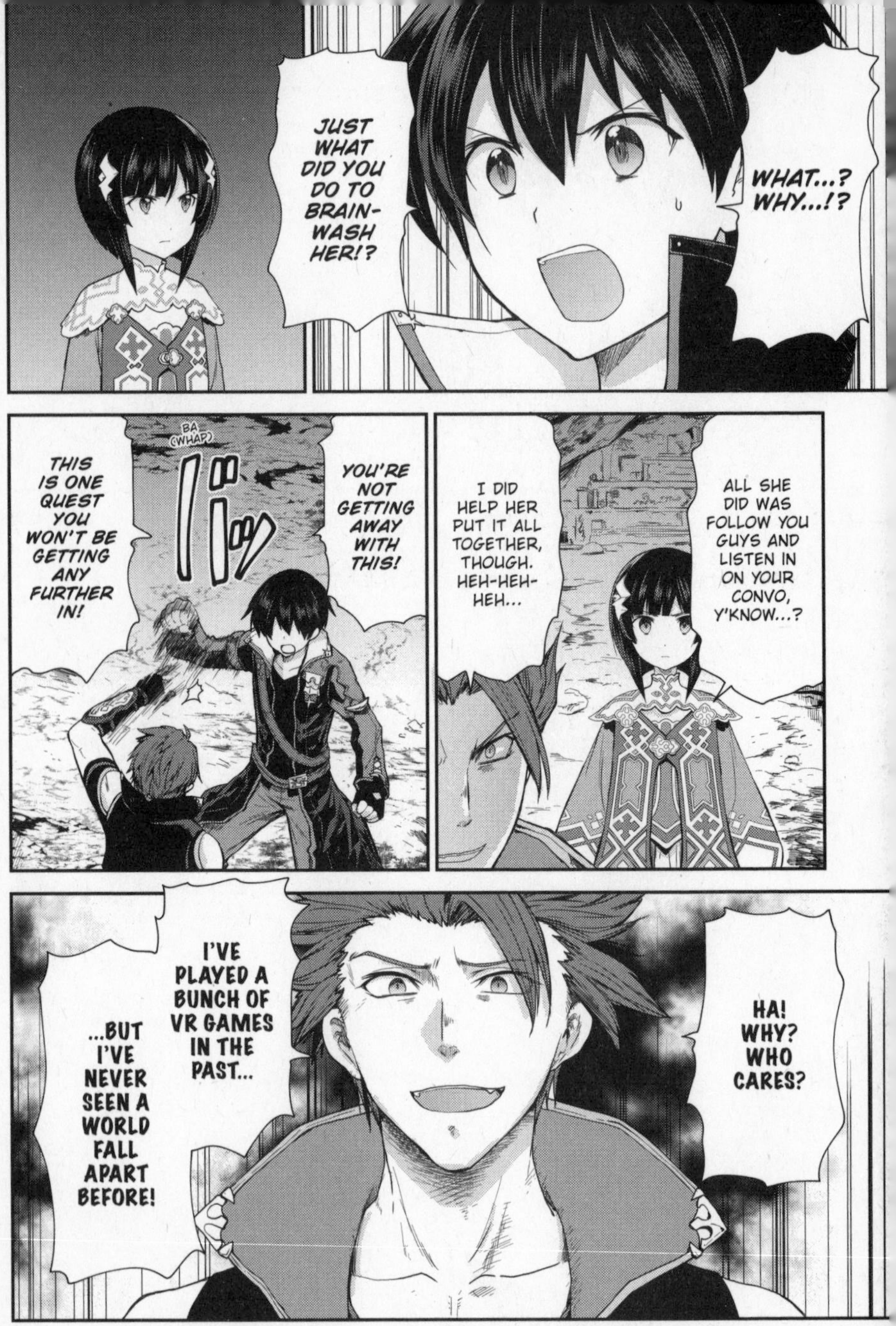
WHAT...? WHY...!?
JUST WHAT DID YOU DO TO BRAIN-WASH HER!?
ALL SHE DID WAS FOLLOW YOU GUYS AND LISTEN IN ON YOUR CONVO, Y'KNOW...?
I DID HELP HER PUT IT ALL TOGETHER, THOUGH. HEH-HEH-HEH...
YOU'RE NOT GETTING AWAY WITH THIS!
BA (WHAP)
THIS IS ONE QUEST YOU WON'T BE GETTING ANY FURTHER IN!
HA! WHY? WHO CARES?
I'VE PLAYED A BUNCH OF VR GAMES IN THE PAST...
...BUT I'VE NEVER SEEN A WORLD FALL APART BEFORE!

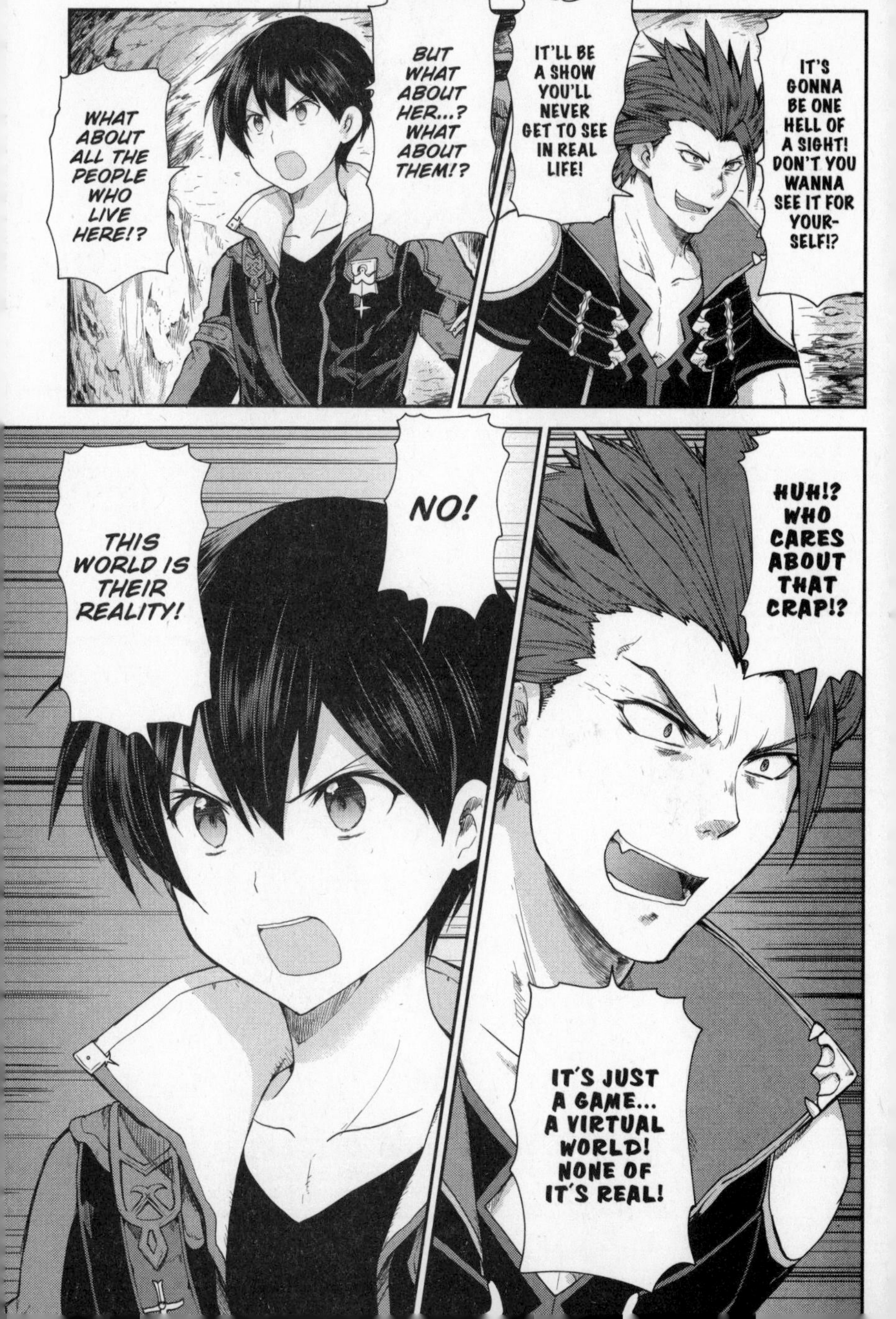
IT'S GONNA BE ONE HELL OF A SIGHT! DON'T YOU WANNA SEE IT FOR YOUR-SELF!?
IT'LL BE A SHOW YOU'LL NEVER GET TO SEE IN REAL LIFE!
BUT WHAT ABOUT HER...? WHAT ABOUT THEM!?
WHAT ABOUT ALL THE PEOPLE WHO LIVE HERE!?
HUH!? WHO CARES ABOUT THAT CRAP!?
IT'S JUST A GAME... A VIRTUAL WORLD! NONE OF IT'S REAL!
NO!
THIS WORLD IS THEIR REALITY!

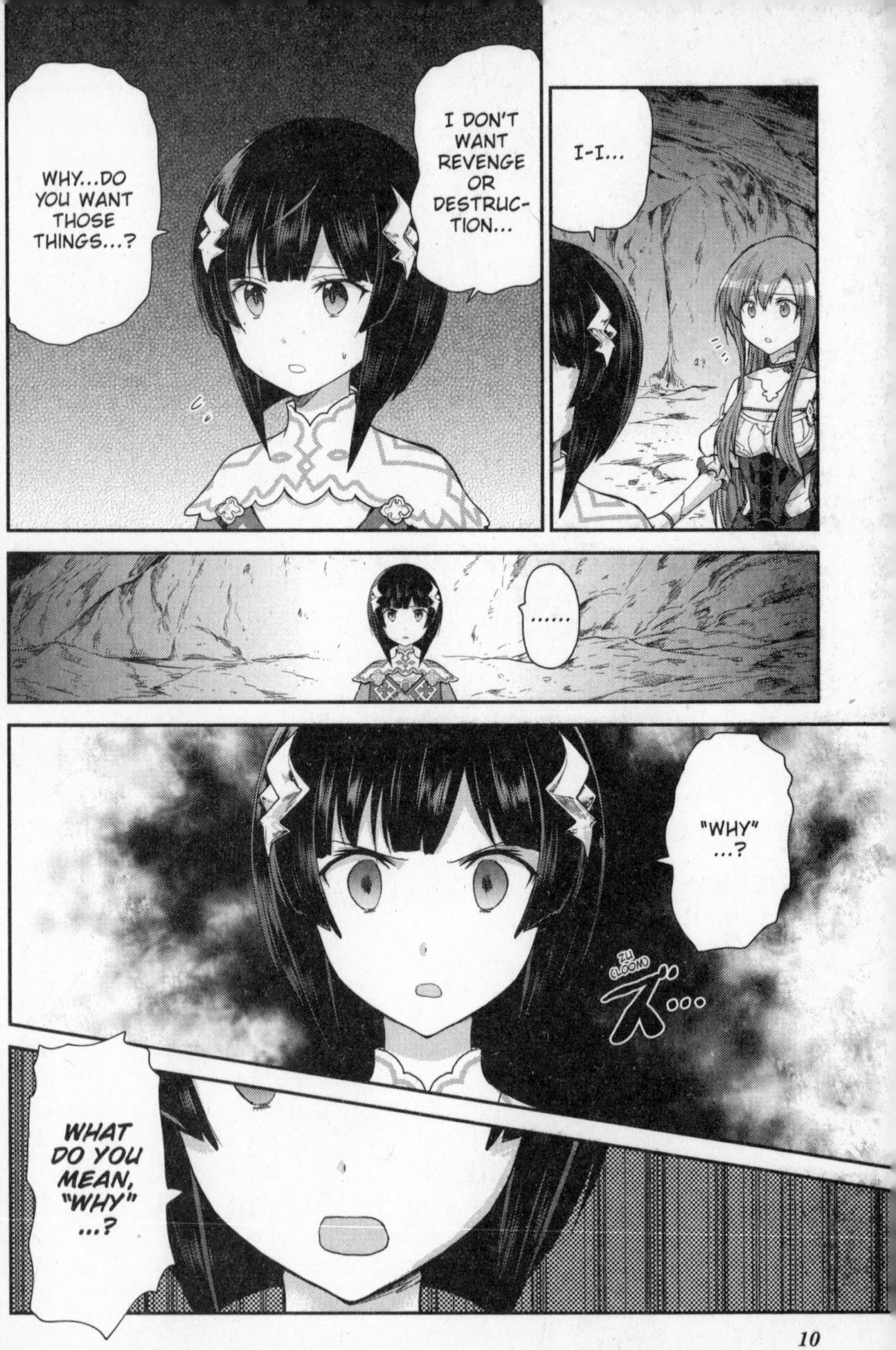
I-I...
I DON'T WANT REVENGE OR DESTRUCTION...
WHY...DO YOU WANT THOSE THINGS...?
......
"WHY" ...?
ZU (LOOM)
WHAT DO YOU MEAN, "WHY" ...?

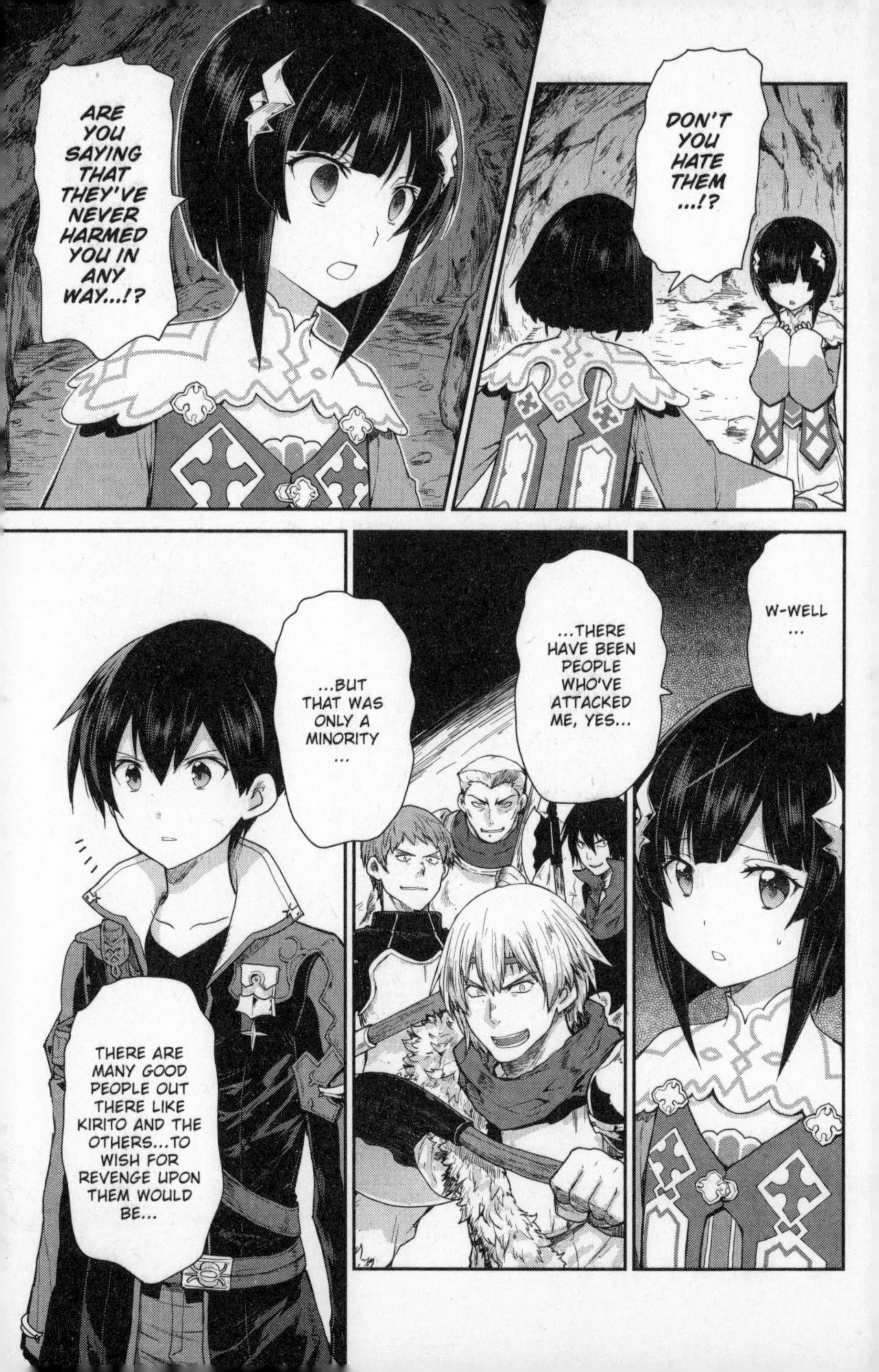
DON'T YOU HATE THEM ...!?
ARE YOU SAYING THAT THEY'VE NEVER HARMED YOU IN ANY WAY...!?
W-WELL ...
...THERE HAVE BEEN PEOPLE WHO'VE ATTACKED ME, YES...
...BUT THAT WAS ONLY A MINORITY ...
THERE ARE MANY GOOD PEOPLE OUT THERE LIKE KIRITO AND THE OTHERS...TO WISH FOR REVENGE UPON THEM WOULD BE...

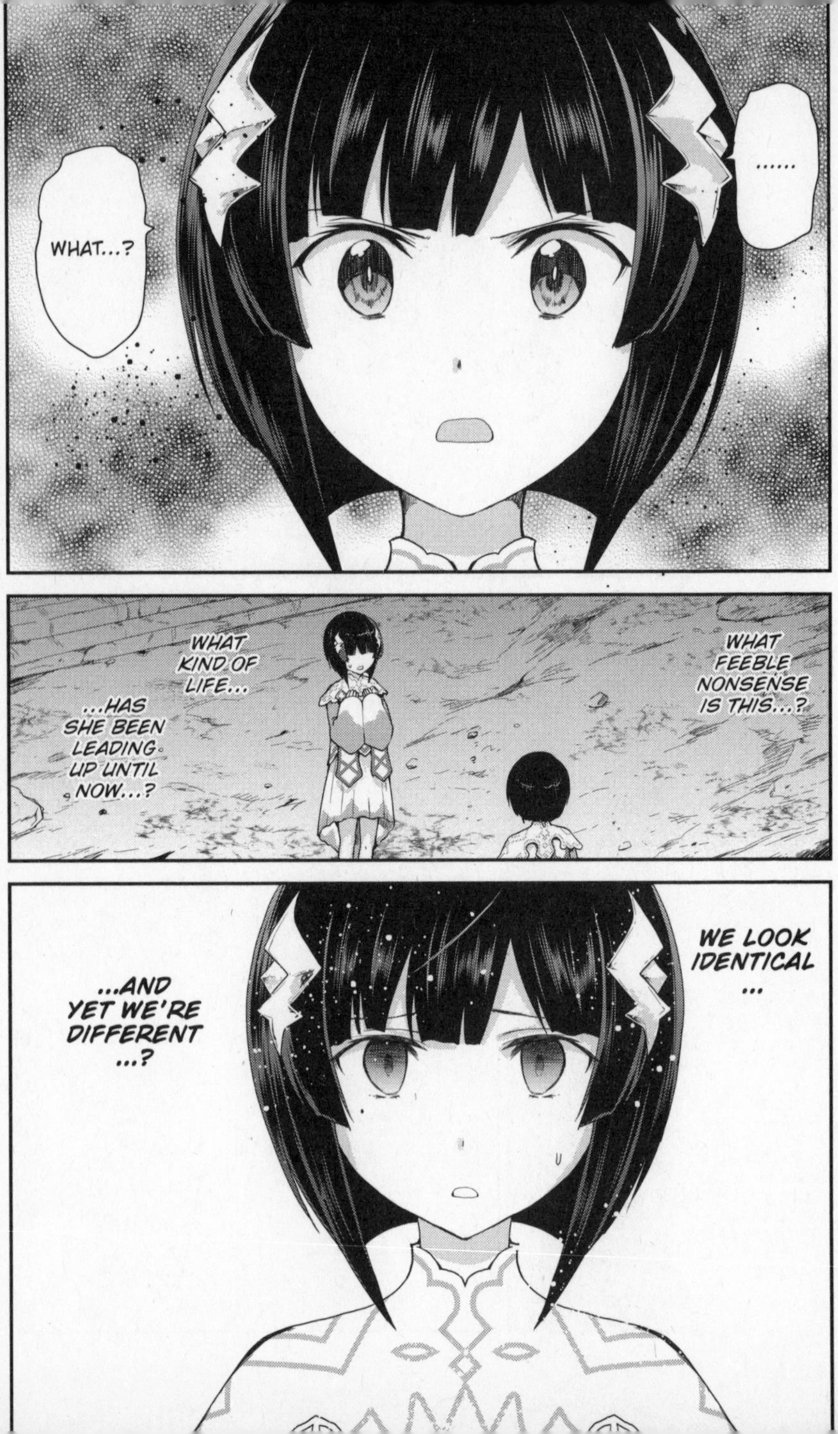
......
WHAT...?
WHAT FEEBLE NONSENSE IS THIS...?
WHAT KIND OF LIFE...
...HAS SHE BEEN LEADING UP UNTIL NOW...?
WE LOOK IDENTICAL...
...AND YET WE'RE DIFFERENT...?

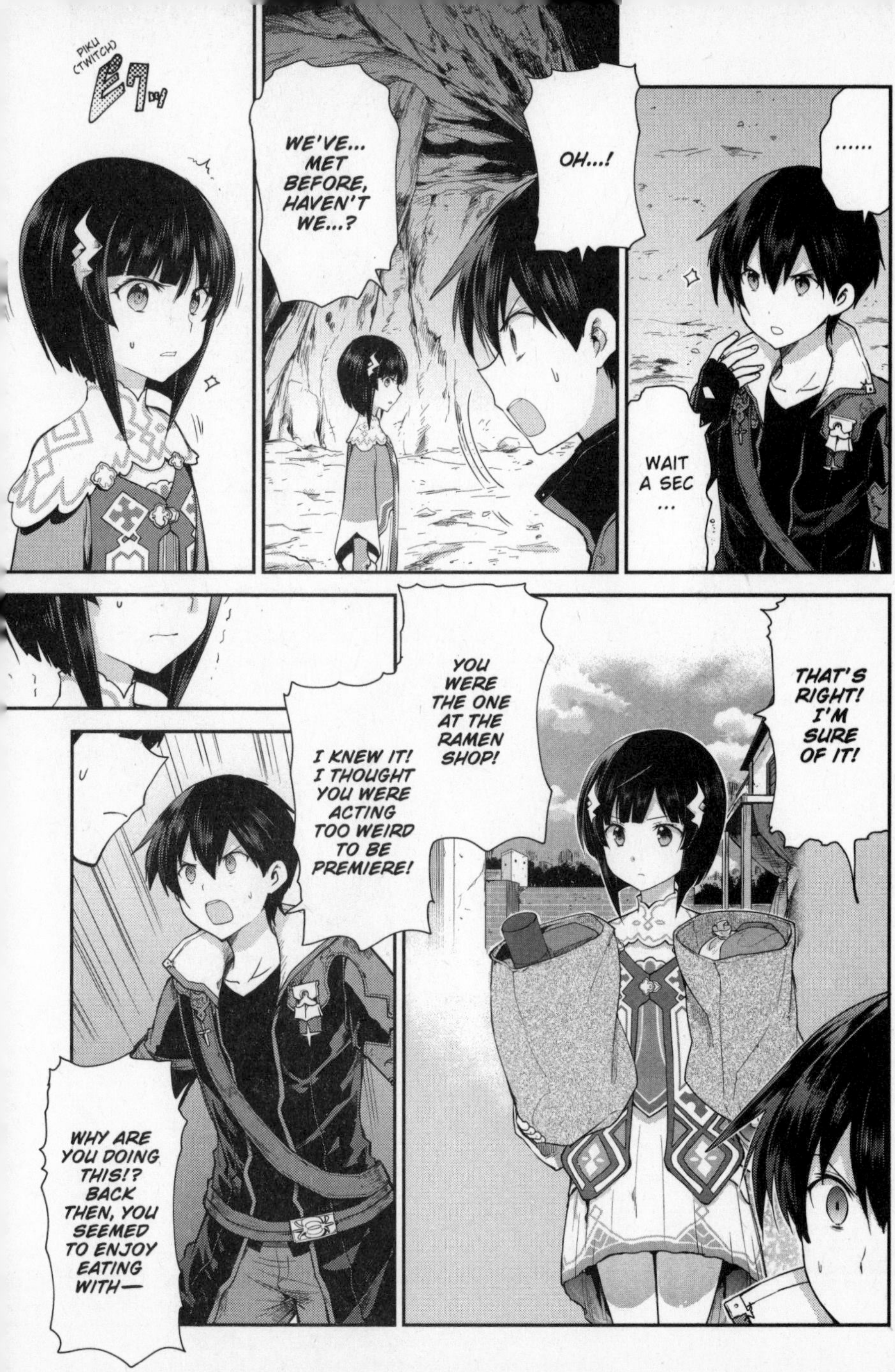
......
WAIT A SEC ...
OH...!
WE'VE... MET BEFORE, HAVEN'T WE...?
PIKU (TWITCH)
THAT'S RIGHT! I'M SURE OF IT!
YOU WERE THE ONE AT THE RAMEN SHOP!
I KNEW IT! I THOUGHT YOU WERE ACTING TOO WEIRD TO BE PREMIERE!
WHY ARE YOU DOING THIS!? BACK THEN, YOU SEEMED TO ENJOY EATING WITH—

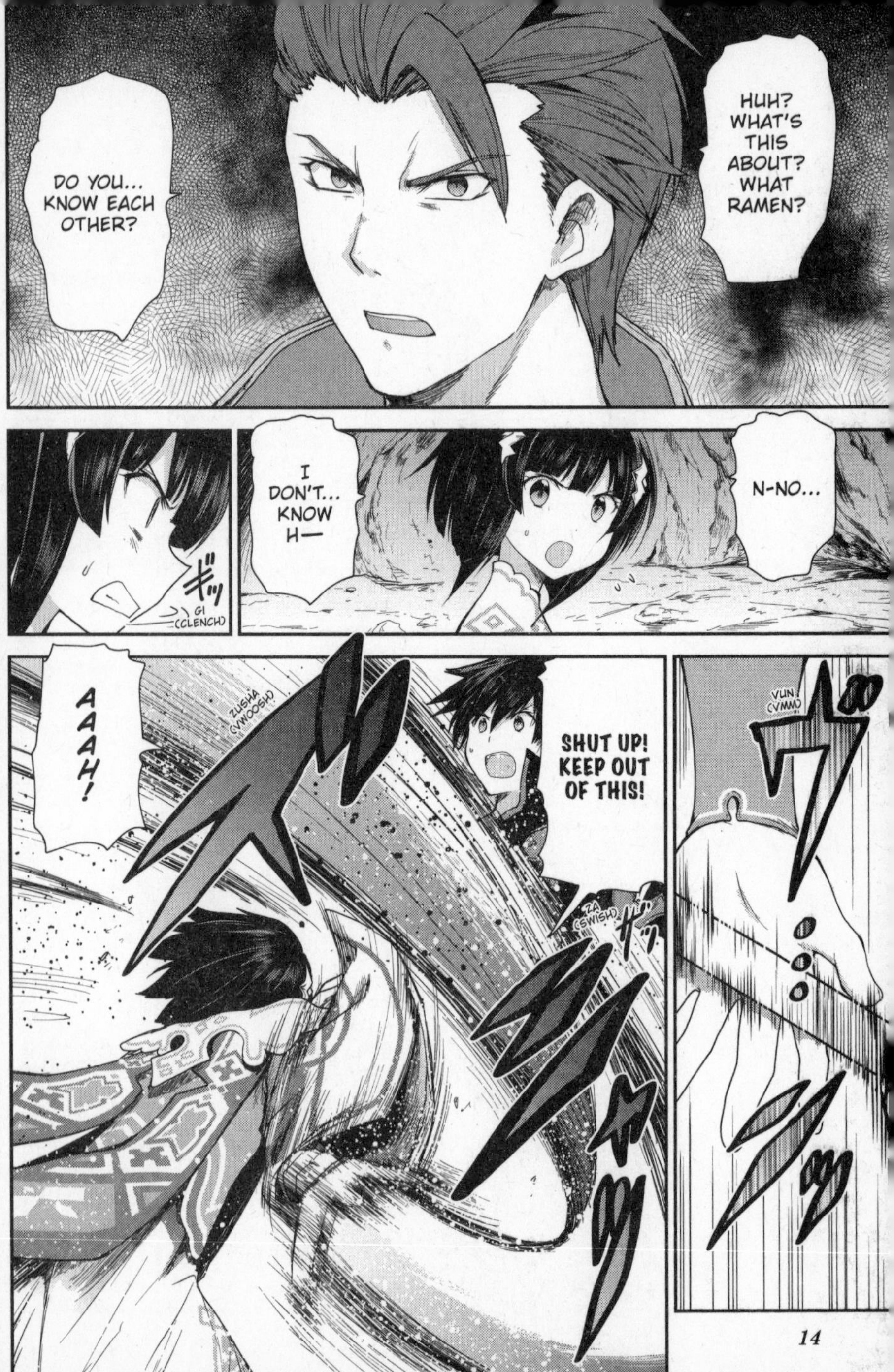
HUH? WHAT'S THIS ABOUT? WHAT RAMEN?
DO YOU... KNOW EACH OTHER?
N-NO...
I DON'T... KNOW H—
GI (CLENCH)
VUN (VMM)
SHUT UP! KEEP OUT OF THIS!
ZA (SWISH)
ZUSHA (VWOOSH)
AAAH!

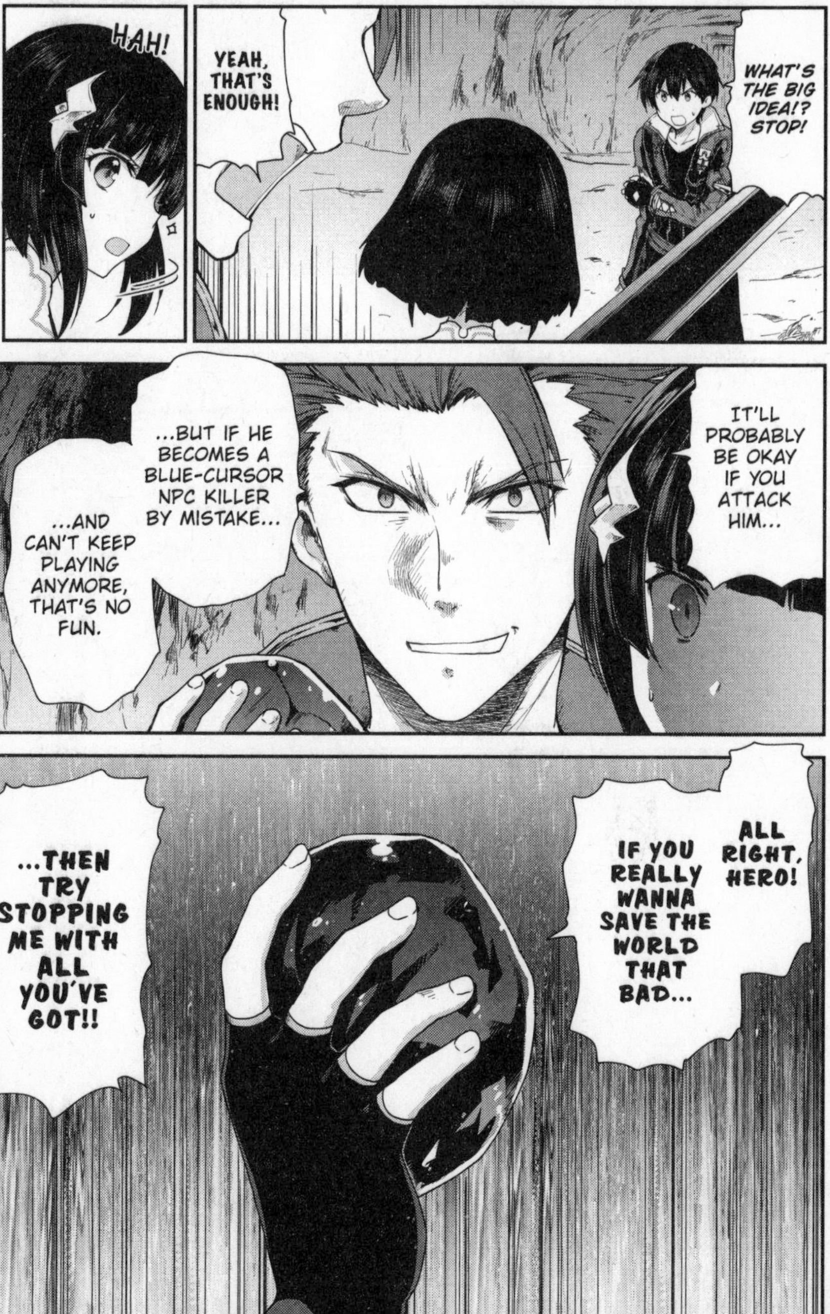
WHAT'S THE BIG IDEA!? STOP!
YEAH, THAT'S ENOUGH!
HAH!
IT'LL PROBABLY BE OKAY IF YOU ATTACK HIM...
...BUT IF HE BECOMES A BLUE-CURSOR NPC KILLER BY MISTAKE...
...AND CAN'T KEEP PLAYING ANYMORE, THAT'S NO FUN.
ALL RIGHT, HERO!
IF YOU REALLY WANNA SAVE THE WORLD THAT BAD...
...THEN TRY STOPPING ME WITH ALL YOU'VE GOT!!

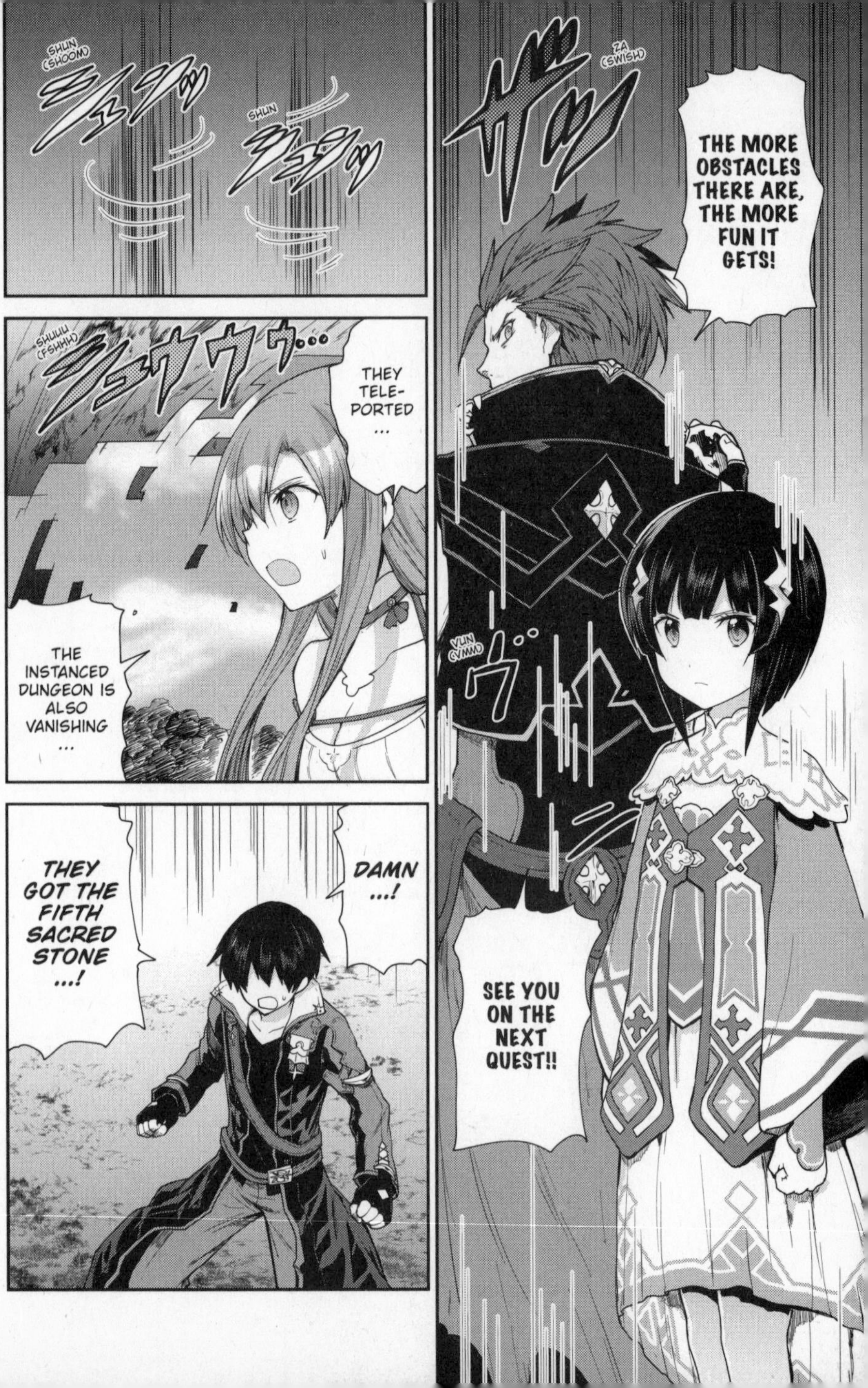
ZA (SWISH)
THE MORE OBSTACLES THERE ARE, THE MORE FUN IT GETS!
VUN (VMM)
SEE YOU ON THE NEXT QUEST!!
SHUN (SHOOM)
SHUN
SHUUU (FSHHH)
THEY TELE-PORTED ...
THE INSTANCED DUNGEON IS ALSO VANISHING ...
DAMN ...!
THEY GOT THE FIFTH SACRED STONE ...!

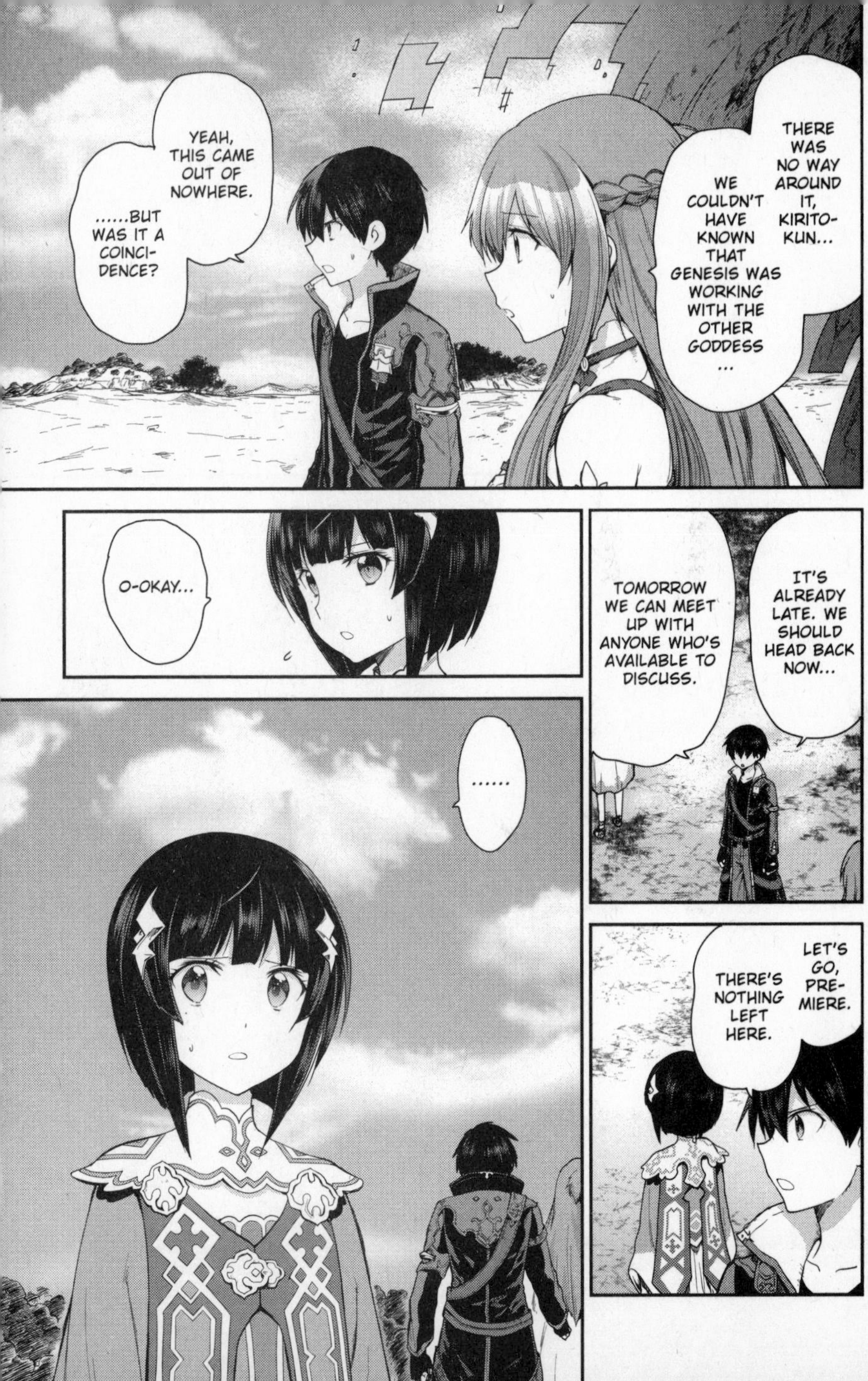
THERE WAS NO WAY AROUND IT, KIRITO-KUN...
WE COULDN'T HAVE KNOWN THAT GENESIS WAS WORKING WITH THE OTHER GODDESS ...
YEAH, THIS CAME OUT OF NOWHERE.
......BUT WAS IT A COINCIDENCE?
IT'S ALREADY LATE. WE SHOULD HEAD BACK NOW...
TOMORROW WE CAN MEET UP WITH ANYONE WHO'S AVAILABLE TO DISCUSS.
O-OKAY...
LET'S GO, PREMIERE.
THERE'S NOTHING LEFT HERE.
......

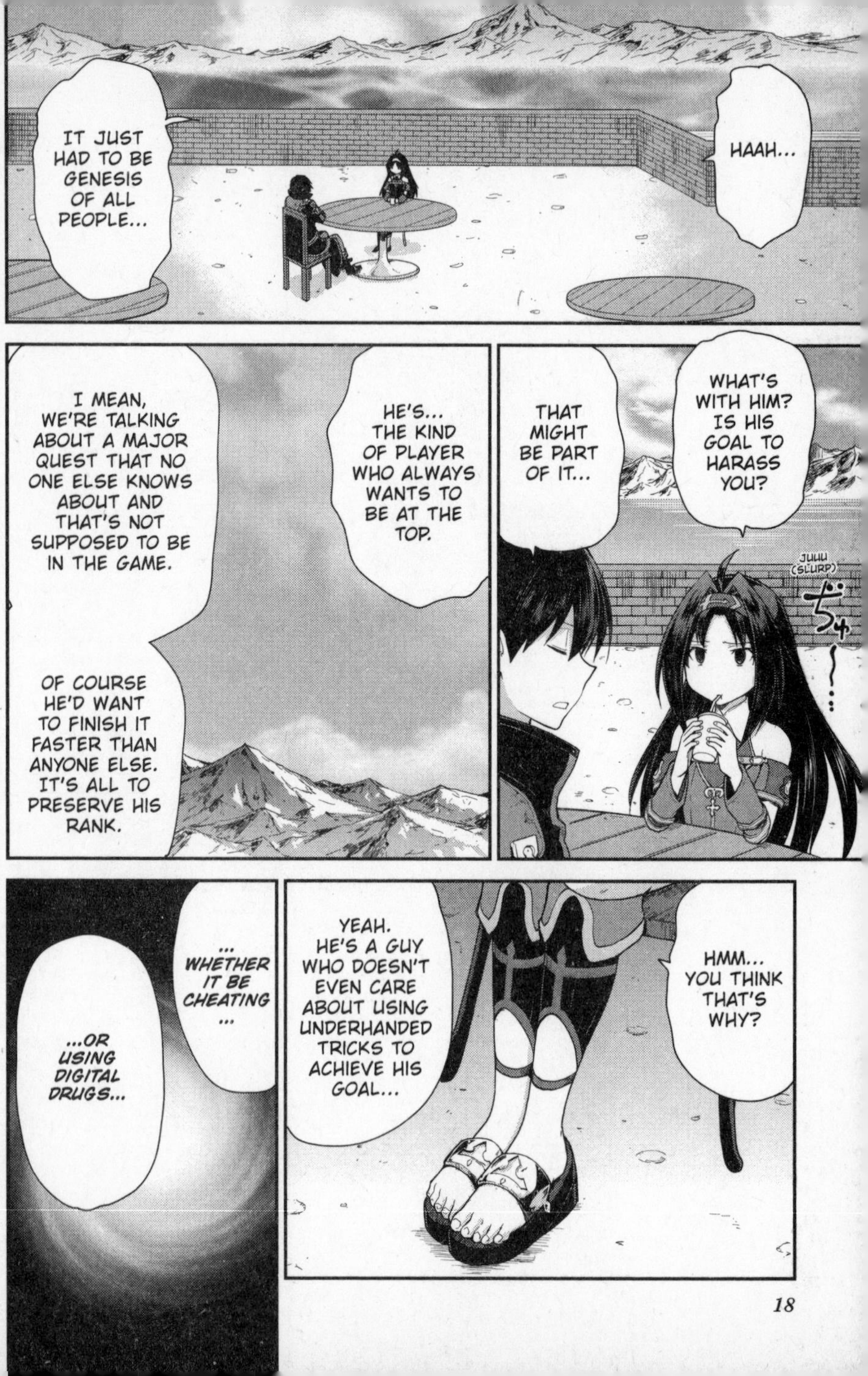
HAAH...
IT JUST HAD TO BE GENESIS OF ALL PEOPLE...
WHAT'S WITH HIM? IS HIS GOAL TO HARASS YOU?
THAT MIGHT BE PART OF IT...
JUUU (SLURP)
HE'S... THE KIND OF PLAYER WHO ALWAYS WANTS TO BE AT THE TOP.
I MEAN, WE'RE TALKING ABOUT A MAJOR QUEST THAT NO ONE ELSE KNOWS ABOUT AND THAT'S NOT SUPPOSED TO BE IN THE GAME.
OF COURSE HE'D WANT TO FINISH IT FASTER THAN ANYONE ELSE. IT'S ALL TO PRESERVE HIS RANK.
HMM... YOU THINK THAT'S WHY?
YEAH. HE'S A GUY WHO DOESN'T EVEN CARE ABOUT USING UNDERHANDED TRICKS TO ACHIEVE HIS GOAL...
...WHETHER IT BE CHEATING...
...OR USING DIGITAL DRUGS...

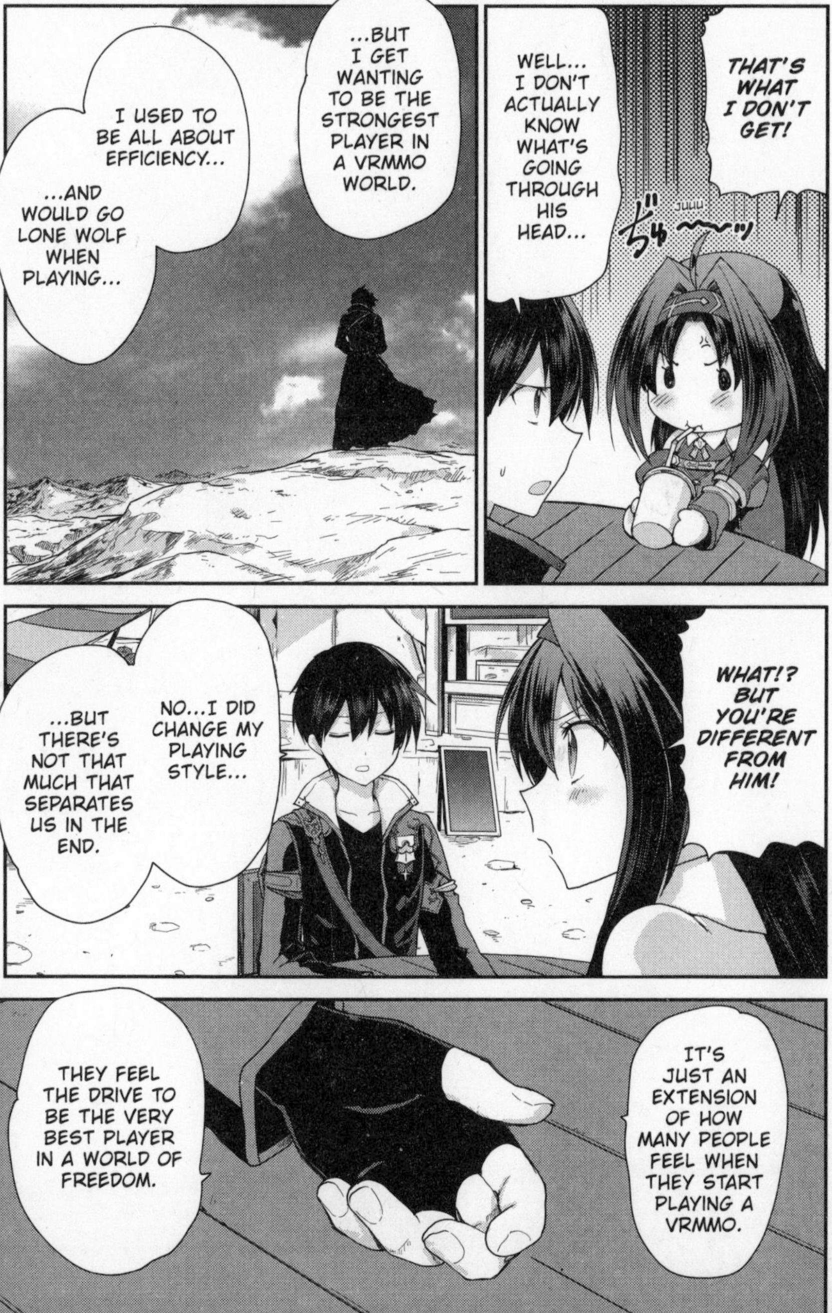
THAT'S WHAT I DON'T GET!
JUUU
WELL... I DON'T ACTUALLY KNOW WHAT'S GOING THROUGH HIS HEAD...
I USED TO BE ALL ABOUT EFFICIENCY...
...AND WOULD GO LONE WOLF WHEN PLAYING...
...BUT I GET WANTING TO BE THE STRONGEST PLAYER IN A VRMMO WORLD.
WHAT!? BUT YOU'RE DIFFERENT FROM HIM!
NO...I DID CHANGE MY PLAYING STYLE...
...BUT THERE'S NOT THAT MUCH THAT SEPARATES US IN THE END.
IT'S JUST AN EXTENSION OF HOW MANY PEOPLE FEEL WHEN THEY START PLAYING A VRMMO.
THEY FEEL THE DRIVE TO BE THE VERY BEST PLAYER IN A WORLD OF FREEDOM.

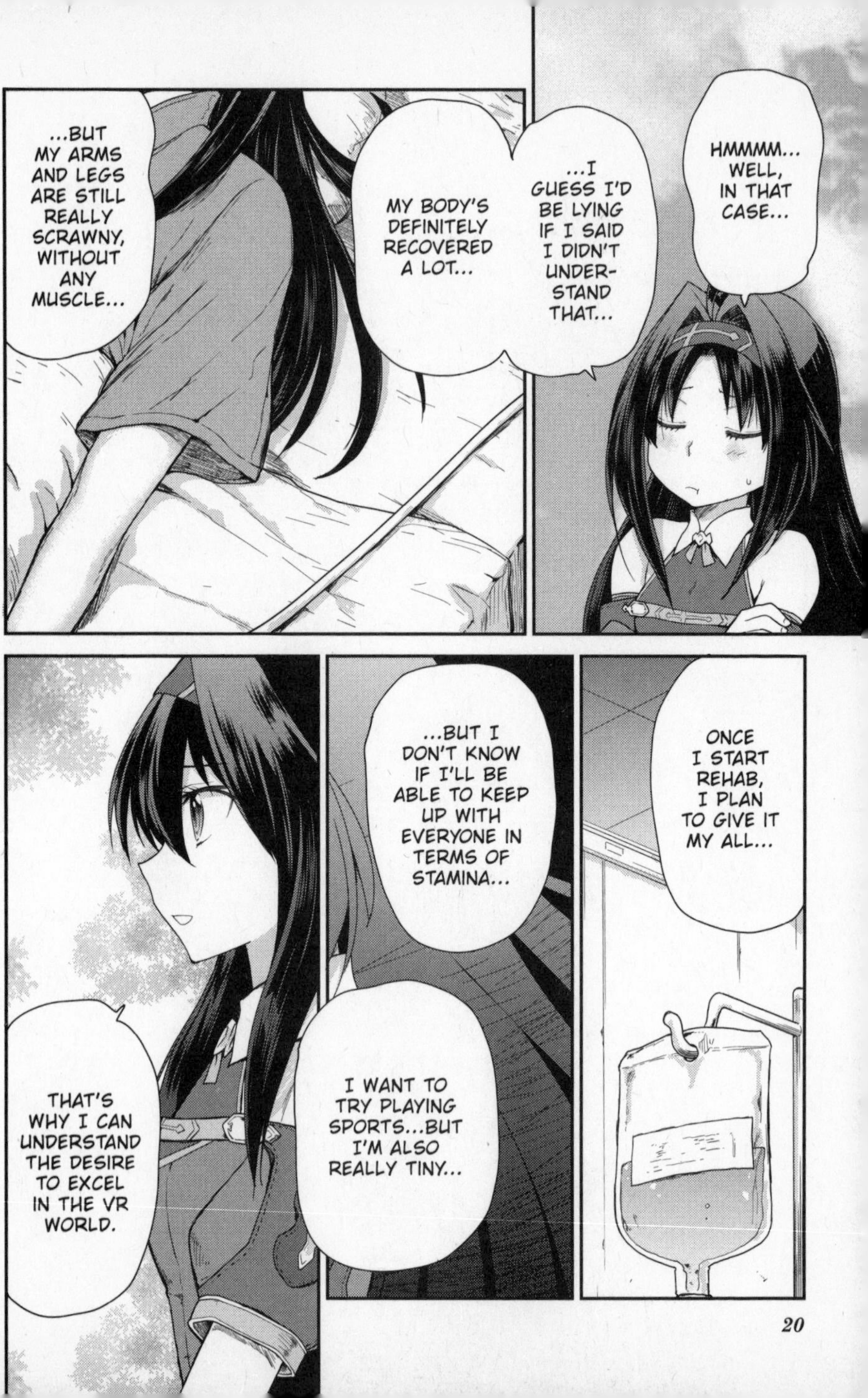
HMMMM... WELL, IN THAT CASE...
...I GUESS I'D BE LYING IF I SAID I DIDN'T UNDER-STAND THAT...
MY BODY'S DEFINITELY RECOVERED A LOT...
...BUT MY ARMS AND LEGS ARE STILL REALLY SCRAWNY, WITHOUT ANY MUSCLE...
ONCE I START REHAB, I PLAN TO GIVE IT MY ALL...
...BUT I DON'T KNOW IF I'LL BE ABLE TO KEEP UP WITH EVERYONE IN TERMS OF STAMINA...
I WANT TO TRY PLAYING SPORTS...BUT I'M ALSO REALLY TINY...
THAT'S WHY I CAN UNDERSTAND THE DESIRE TO EXCEL IN THE VR WORLD.

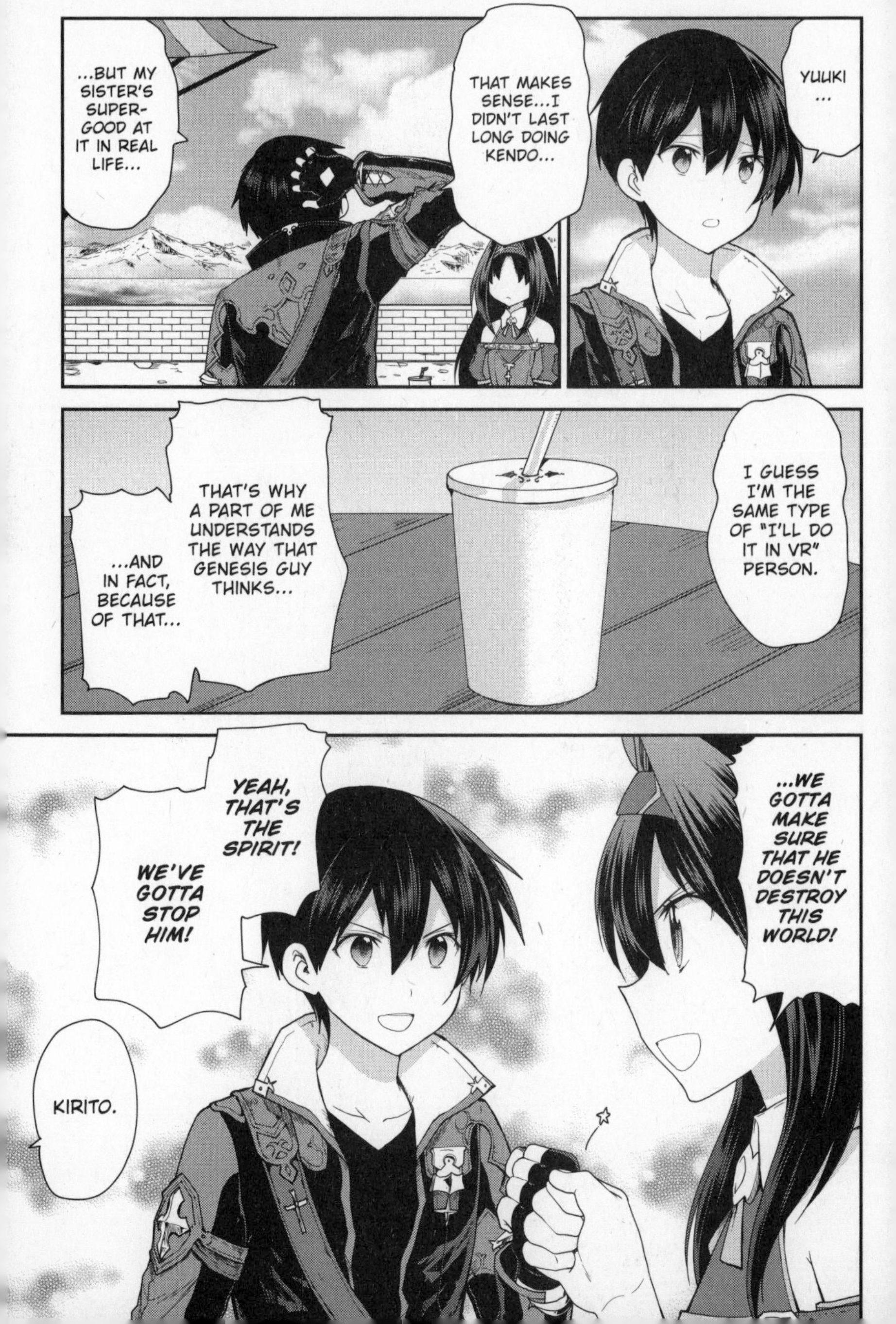
YUUKI ...
THAT MAKES SENSE...I DIDN'T LAST LONG DOING KENDO...
...BUT MY SISTER'S SUPER-GOOD AT IT IN REAL LIFE...
I GUESS I'M THE SAME TYPE OF "I'LL DO IT IN VR" PERSON.
THAT'S WHY A PART OF ME UNDERSTANDS THE WAY THAT GENESIS GUY THINKS...
...AND IN FACT, BECAUSE OF THAT...
...WE GOTTA MAKE SURE THAT HE DOESN'T DESTROY THIS WORLD!
YEAH, THAT'S THE SPIRIT!
WE'VE GOTTA STOP HIM!
KIRITO.

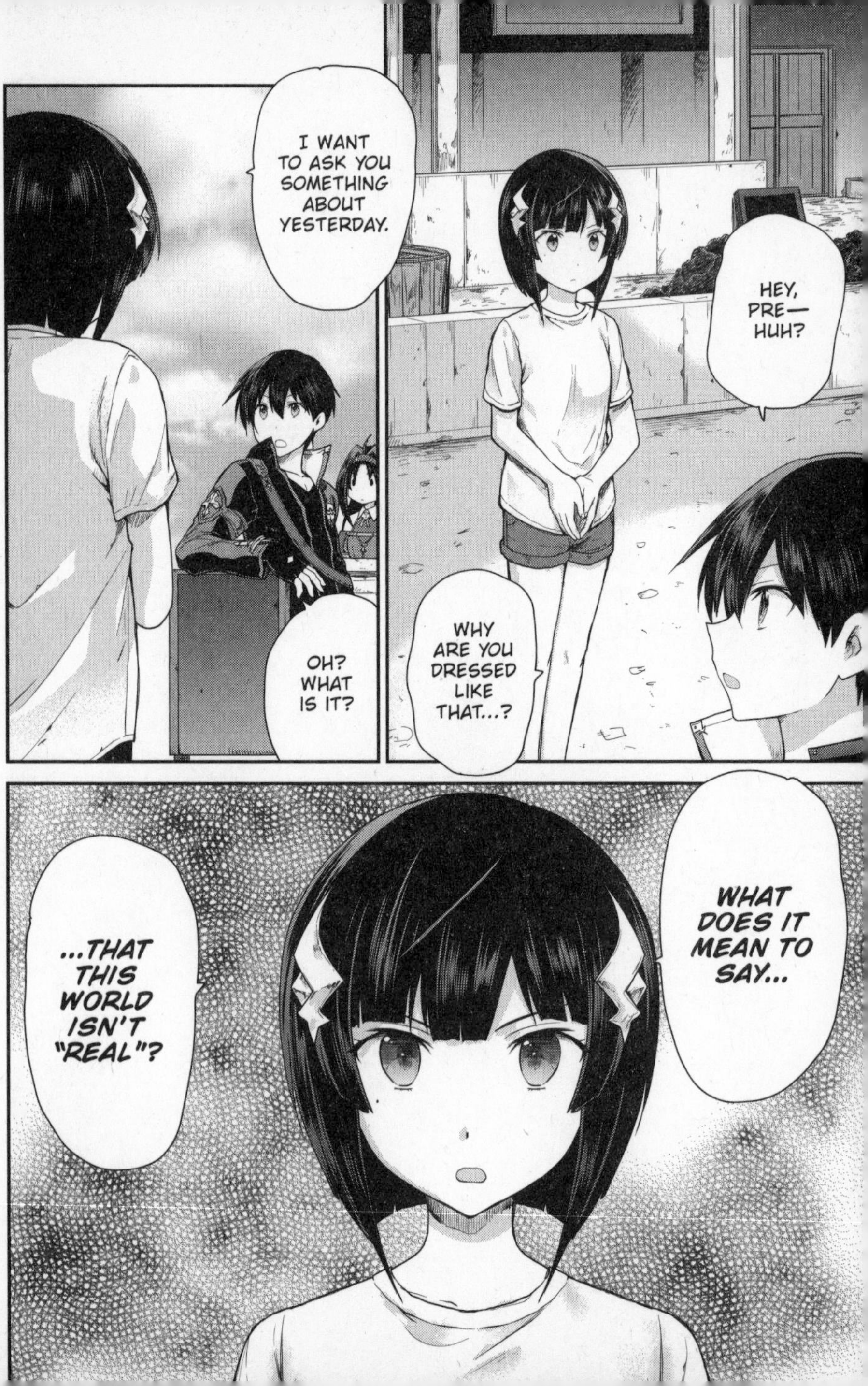
HEY, PRE— HUH?
WHY ARE YOU DRESSED LIKE THAT...?
I WANT TO ASK YOU SOMETHING ABOUT YESTERDAY.
OH? WHAT IS IT?
WHAT DOES IT MEAN TO SAY...
...THAT THIS WORLD ISN'T "REAL"?

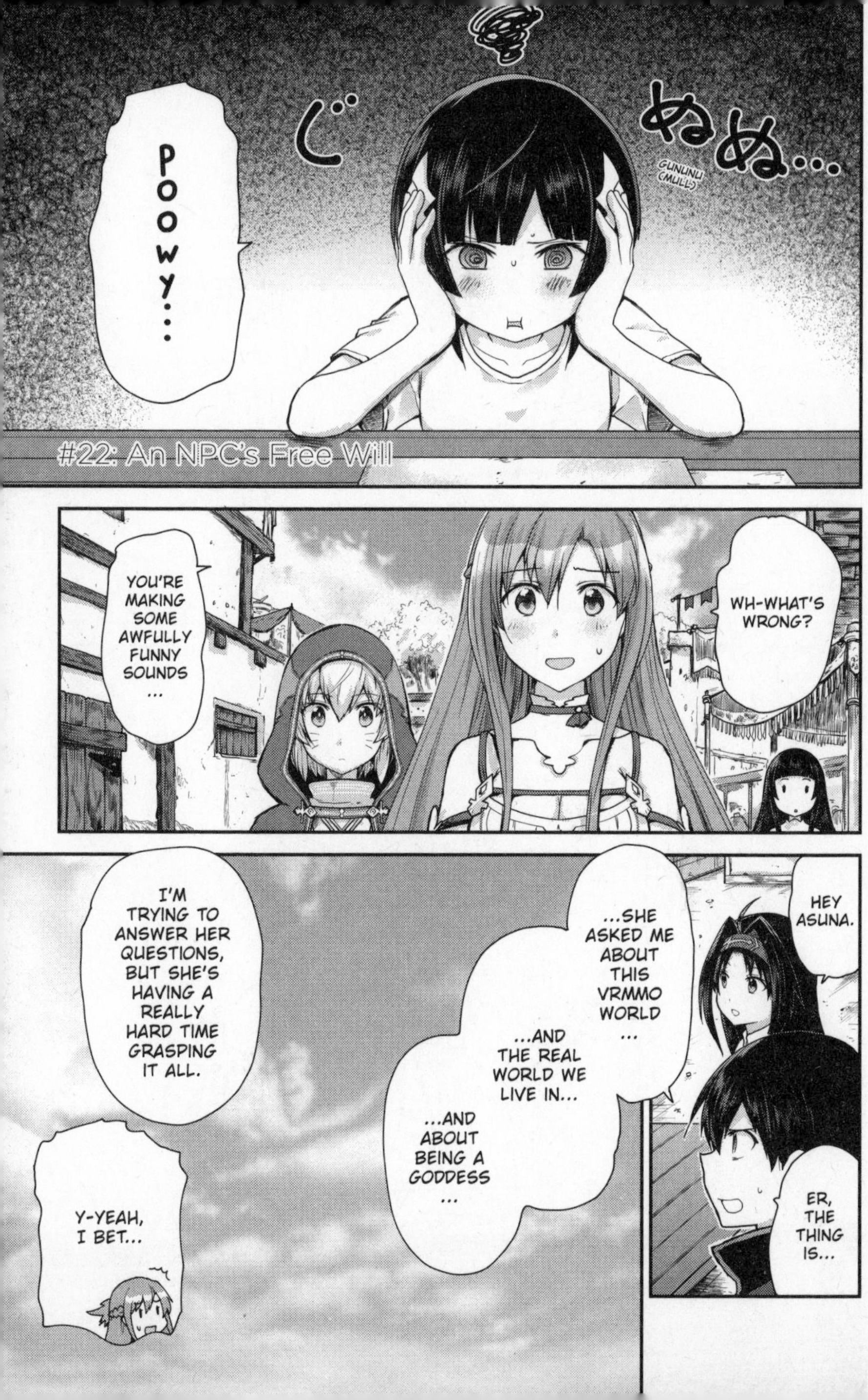
ぬぬ…
GUNUNU (MULL)
じ
POOWY…
#22: An NPC's Free Will
WH-WHAT'S WRONG?
YOU'RE MAKING SOME AWFULLY FUNNY SOUNDS …
HEY ASUNA.
ER, THE THING IS…
…SHE ASKED ME ABOUT THIS VRMMO WORLD …
…AND THE REAL WORLD WE LIVE IN…
…AND ABOUT BEING A GODDESS …
I'M TRYING TO ANSWER HER QUESTIONS, BUT SHE'S HAVING A REALLY HARD TIME GRASPING IT ALL.
Y-YEAH, I BET…

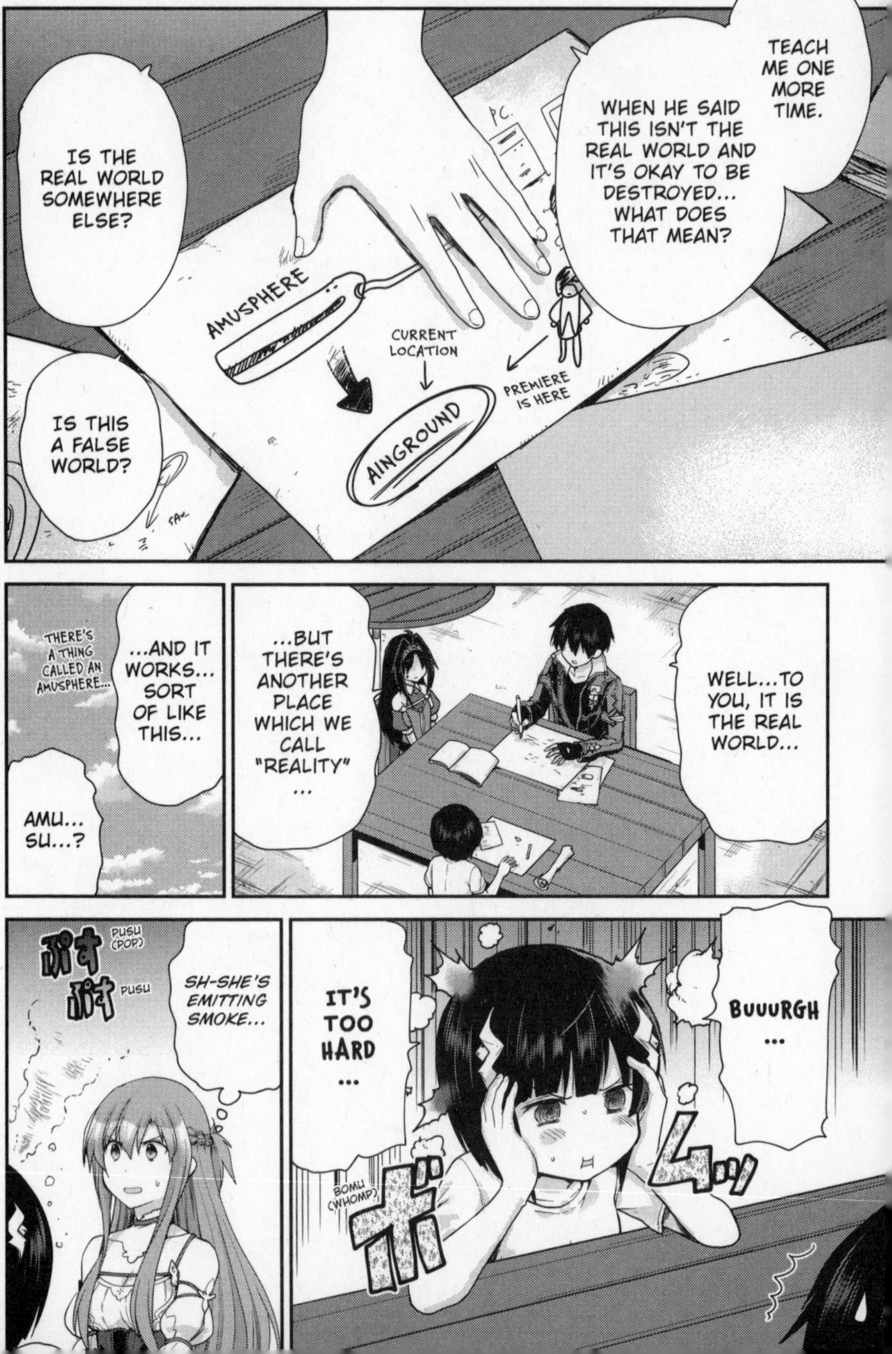
TEACH ME ONE MORE TIME.
WHEN HE SAID THIS ISN'T THE REAL WORLD AND IT'S OKAY TO BE DESTROYED... WHAT DOES THAT MEAN?
PC.
AMUSPHERE
CURRENT LOCATION
PREMIERE IS HERE
AINGROUND
IS THE REAL WORLD SOMEWHERE ELSE?
IS THIS A FALSE WORLD?
WELL...TO YOU, IT IS THE REAL WORLD...
...BUT THERE'S ANOTHER PLACE WHICH WE CALL "REALITY" ...
...AND IT WORKS... SORT OF LIKE THIS...
THERE'S A THING CALLED AN AMUSPHERE...
AMU... SU...?
BUUURGH ...
IT'S TOO HARD ...
ムッ
ボ
BOMU (WHOMP)
SH-SHE'S EMITTING SMOKE...
ぷす PUSU (POP)
ぷす PUSU

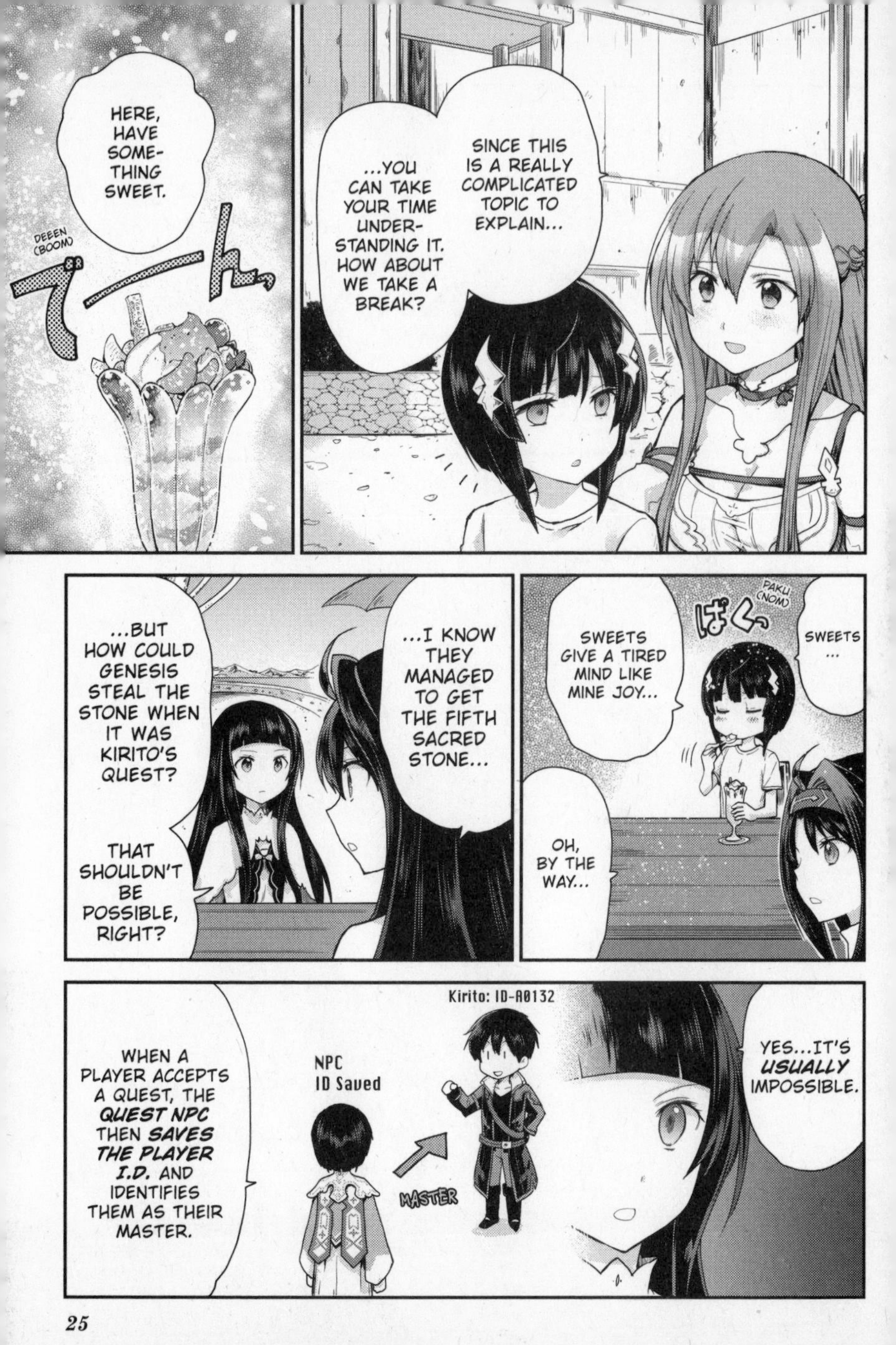
SINCE THIS IS A REALLY COMPLICATED TOPIC TO EXPLAIN...
...YOU CAN TAKE YOUR TIME UNDERSTANDING IT. HOW ABOUT WE TAKE A BREAK?
HERE, HAVE SOMETHING SWEET.
DEEEN (BOOM)
でーん
PAKU (NOM)
ぱく
SWEETS...
SWEETS GIVE A TIRED MIND LIKE MINE JOY...
OH, BY THE WAY...
...I KNOW THEY MANAGED TO GET THE FIFTH SACRED STONE...
...BUT HOW COULD GENESIS STEAL THE STONE WHEN IT WAS KIRITO'S QUEST?
THAT SHOULDN'T BE POSSIBLE, RIGHT?
YES...IT'S *USUALLY* IMPOSSIBLE.
Kirito: ID-A0132
WHEN A PLAYER ACCEPTS A QUEST, THE ***QUEST NPC*** THEN ***SAVES THE PLAYER I.D.*** AND IDENTIFIES THEM AS THEIR MASTER.
NPC ID Saved
MASTER

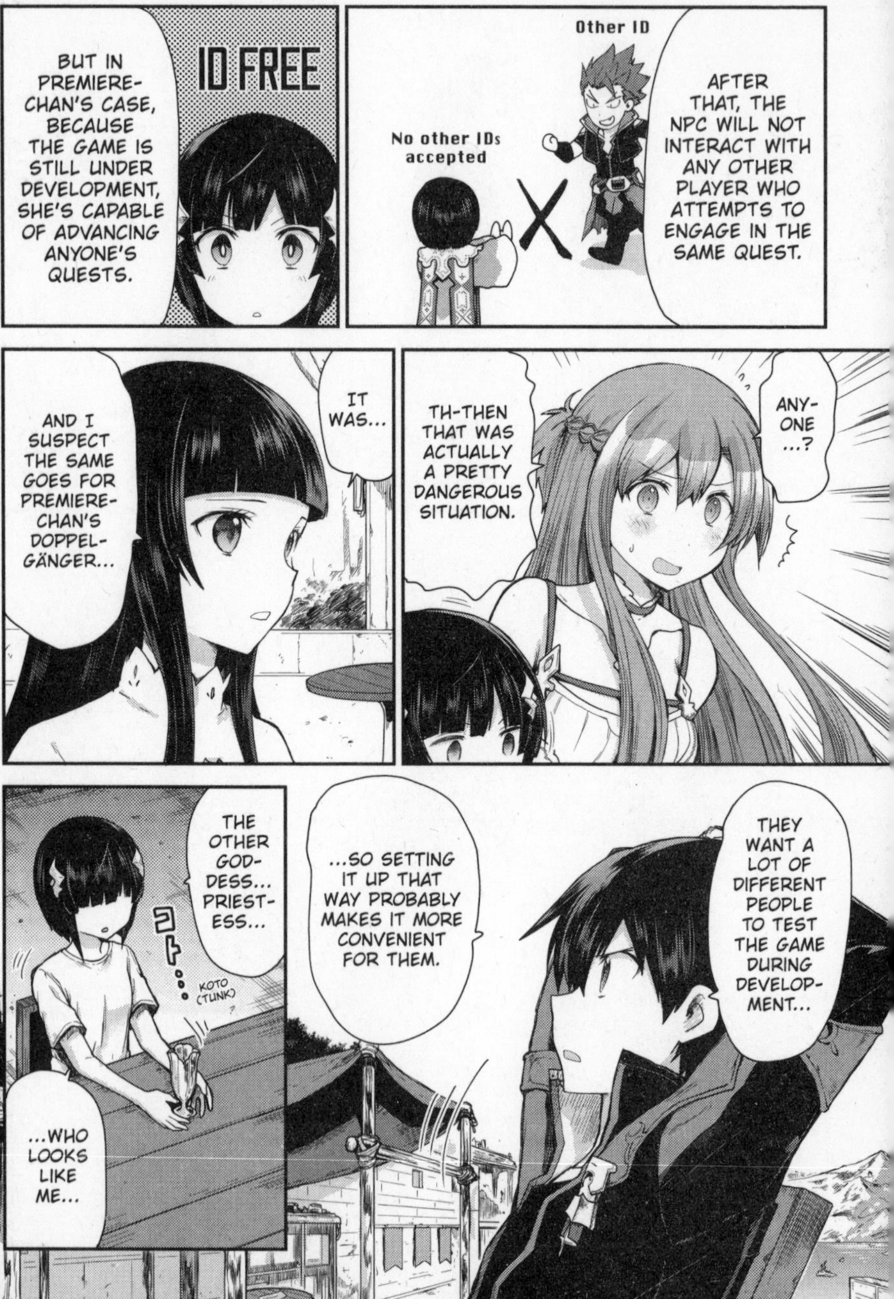
Other ID
AFTER THAT, THE NPC WILL NOT INTERACT WITH ANY OTHER PLAYER WHO ATTEMPTS TO ENGAGE IN THE SAME QUEST.
No other IDs accepted
ID FREE
BUT IN PREMIERE-CHAN'S CASE, BECAUSE THE GAME IS STILL UNDER DEVELOPMENT, SHE'S CAPABLE OF ADVANCING ANYONE'S QUESTS.
ANY-ONE...?
TH-THEN THAT WAS ACTUALLY A PRETTY DANGEROUS SITUATION.
IT WAS...
AND I SUSPECT THE SAME GOES FOR PREMIERE-CHAN'S DOPPEL-GÄNGER...
THEY WANT A LOT OF DIFFERENT PEOPLE TO TEST THE GAME DURING DEVELOP-MENT...
...SO SETTING IT UP THAT WAY PROBABLY MAKES IT MORE CONVENIENT FOR THEM.
THE OTHER GOD-DESS... PRIEST-ESS...
コト...
KOTO (TUNK)
...WHO LOOKS LIKE ME...

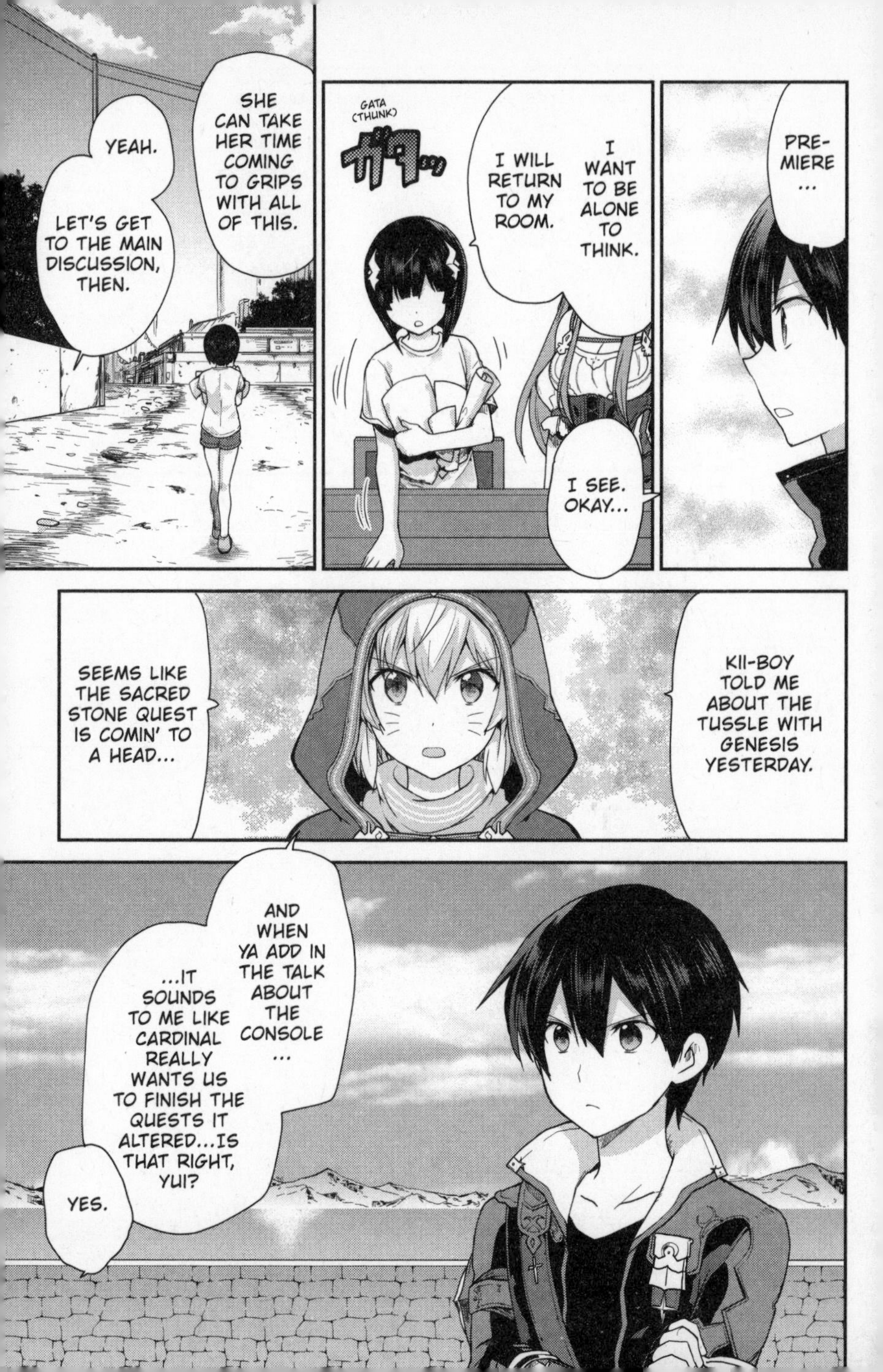
PRE-MIERE...
I WANT TO BE ALONE TO THINK.
I WILL RETURN TO MY ROOM.
GATA (THUNK)
I SEE. OKAY...
SHE CAN TAKE HER TIME COMING TO GRIPS WITH ALL OF THIS.
YEAH.
LET'S GET TO THE MAIN DISCUSSION, THEN.
KII-BOY TOLD ME ABOUT THE TUSSLE WITH GENESIS YESTERDAY.
SEEMS LIKE THE SACRED STONE QUEST IS COMIN' TO A HEAD...
AND WHEN YA ADD IN THE TALK ABOUT THE CONSOLE...
...IT SOUNDS TO ME LIKE CARDINAL REALLY WANTS US TO FINISH THE QUESTS IT ALTERED...IS THAT RIGHT, YUI?
YES.

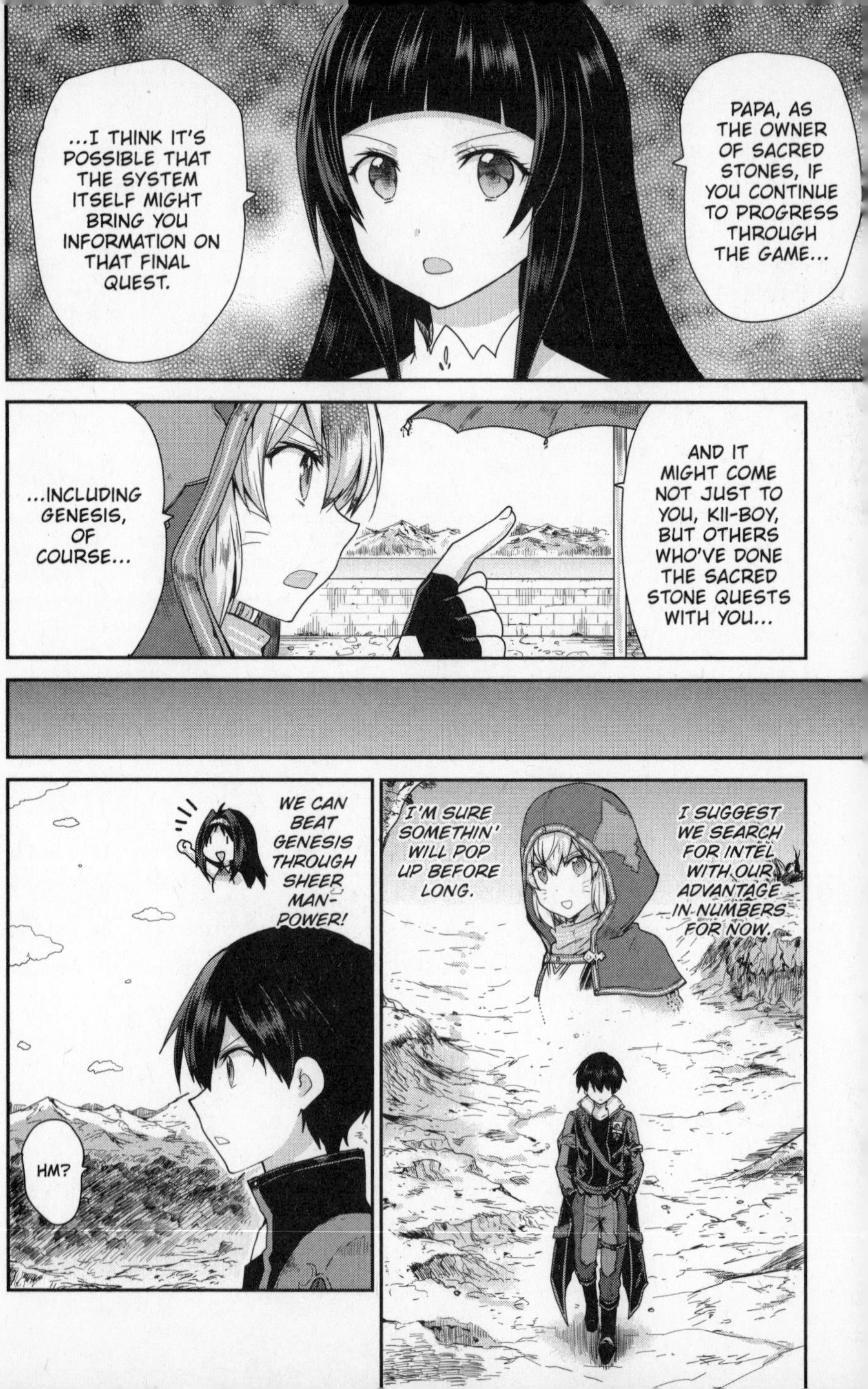
PAPA, AS THE OWNER OF SACRED STONES, IF YOU CONTINUE TO PROGRESS THROUGH THE GAME...
...I THINK IT'S POSSIBLE THAT THE SYSTEM ITSELF MIGHT BRING YOU INFORMATION ON THAT FINAL QUEST.
AND IT MIGHT COME NOT JUST TO YOU, KII-BOY, BUT OTHERS WHO'VE DONE THE SACRED STONE QUESTS WITH YOU...
...INCLUDING GENESIS, OF COURSE...
I SUGGEST WE SEARCH FOR INTEL WITH OUR ADVANTAGE IN NUMBERS FOR NOW.
I'M SURE SOMETHIN' WILL POP UP BEFORE LONG.
WE CAN BEAT GENESIS THROUGH SHEER MAN-POWER!
HM?

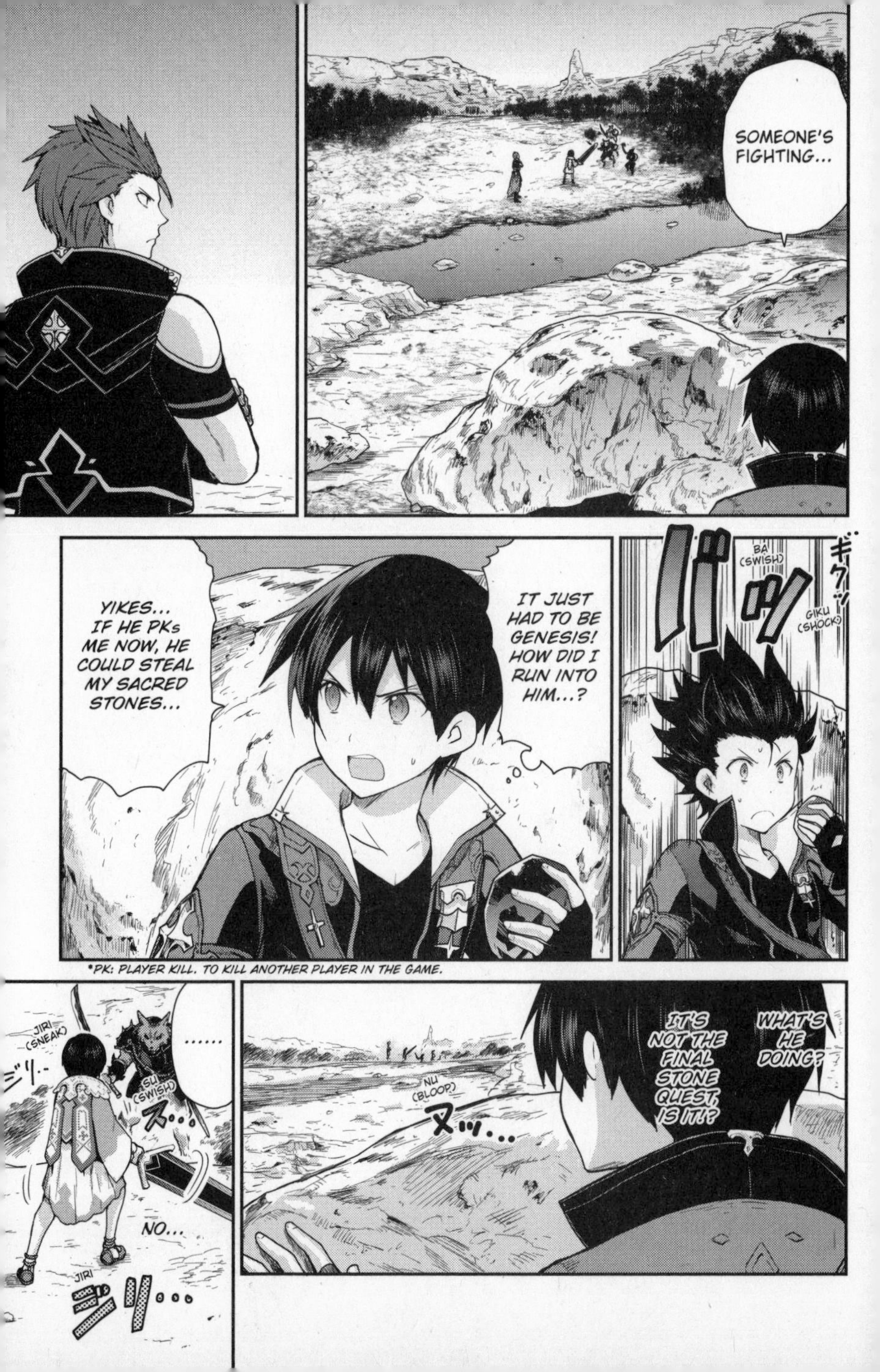
SOMEONE'S FIGHTING...
バッ
BA (SWISH)
ギクッ
GIKU (SHOCK)
IT JUST HAD TO BE GENESIS! HOW DID I RUN INTO HIM...?
YIKES... IF HE PKs ME NOW, HE COULD STEAL MY SACRED STONES...
WHAT'S HE DOING?
IT'S NOT THE FINAL STONE QUEST, IS IT!?
ヌッ...
NU (BLOOP)
......
ジリ...
JIRI (SNEAK)
ス...
SU (SWISH)
NO...
ジリ...
JIRI

*PK: PLAYER KILL. TO KILL ANOTHER PLAYER IN THE GAME.

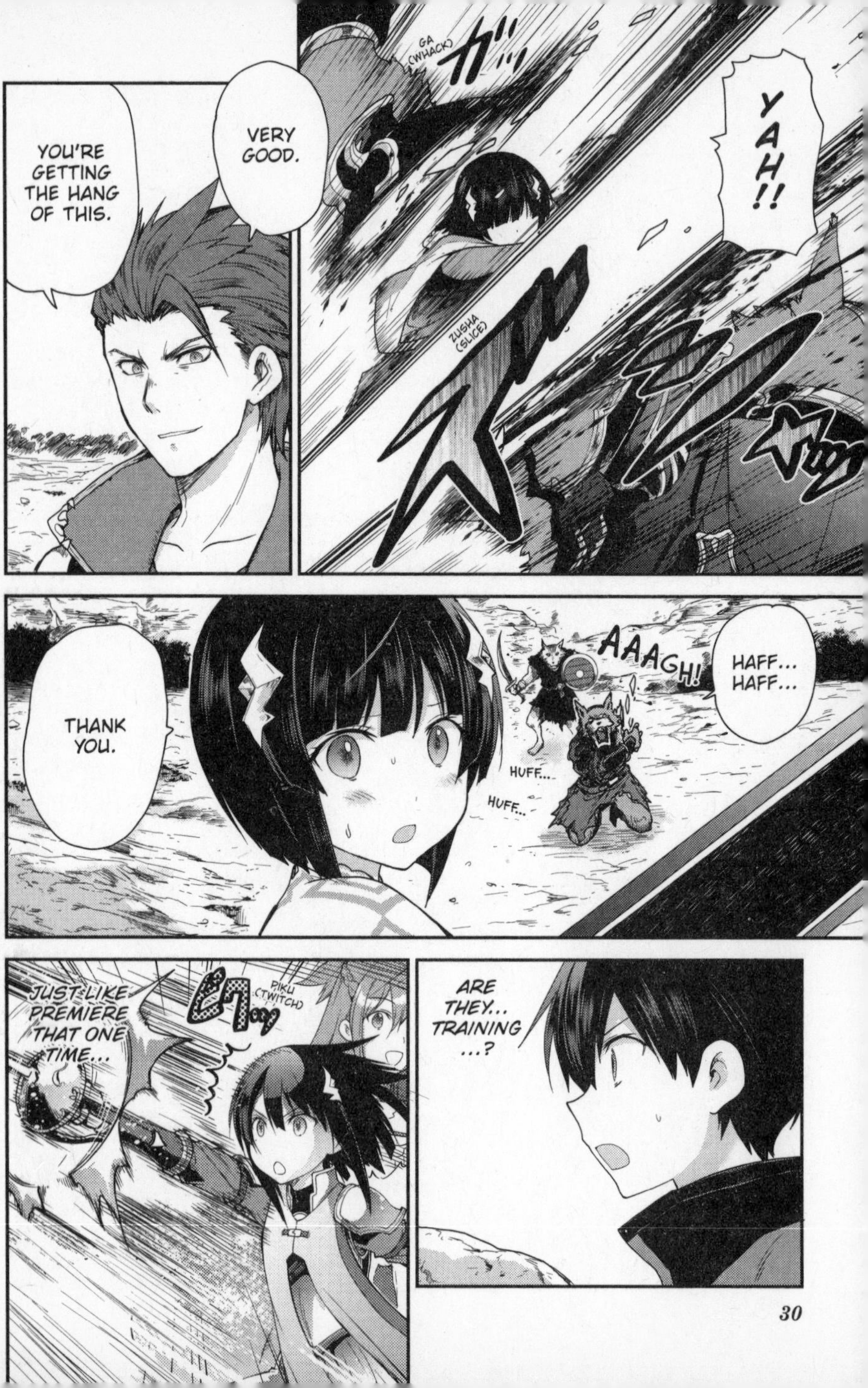
GA (WHACK)
YAH!!
ZUSHA (SLICE)
VERY GOOD.
YOU'RE GETTING THE HANG OF THIS.
HAFF... HAFF...
AAAGH!
HUFF... HUFF...
THANK YOU.
ARE THEY... TRAINING ...?
PIKU (TWITCH)
JUST LIKE PREMIERE THAT ONE TIME...

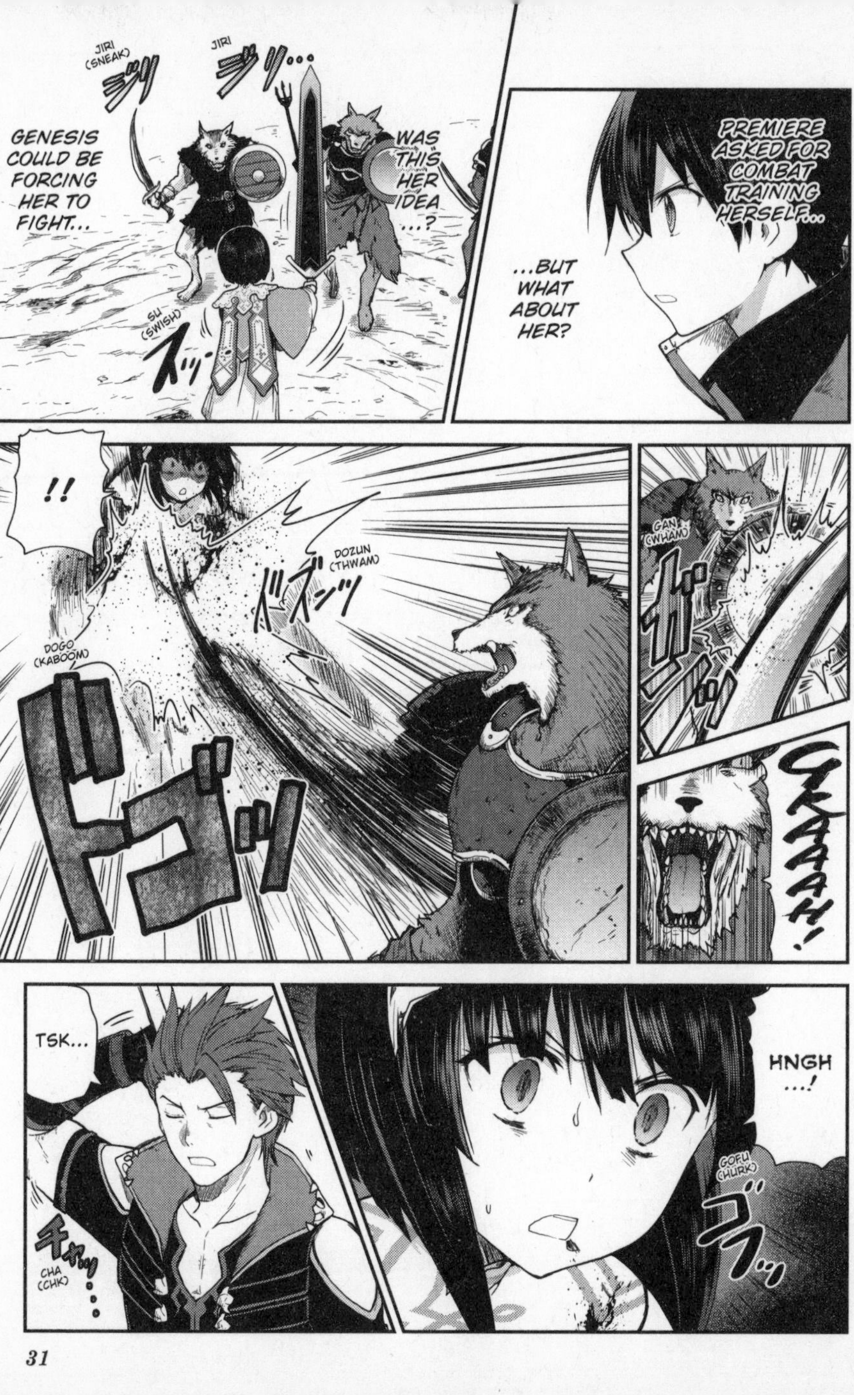

PREMIERE ASKED FOR COMBAT TRAINING HERSELF...
...BUT WHAT ABOUT HER?
JIRI (SNEAK)
JIRI
WAS THIS HER IDEA ...?
GENESIS COULD BE FORCING HER TO FIGHT...
SU (SWISH)
GAN (WHAM)
GRAAAAH!
!!
DOZUN (THWAM)
DOGO (KABOOM)
HNGH ...!
GOFU (HURK)
TSK...
CHA (CHK)

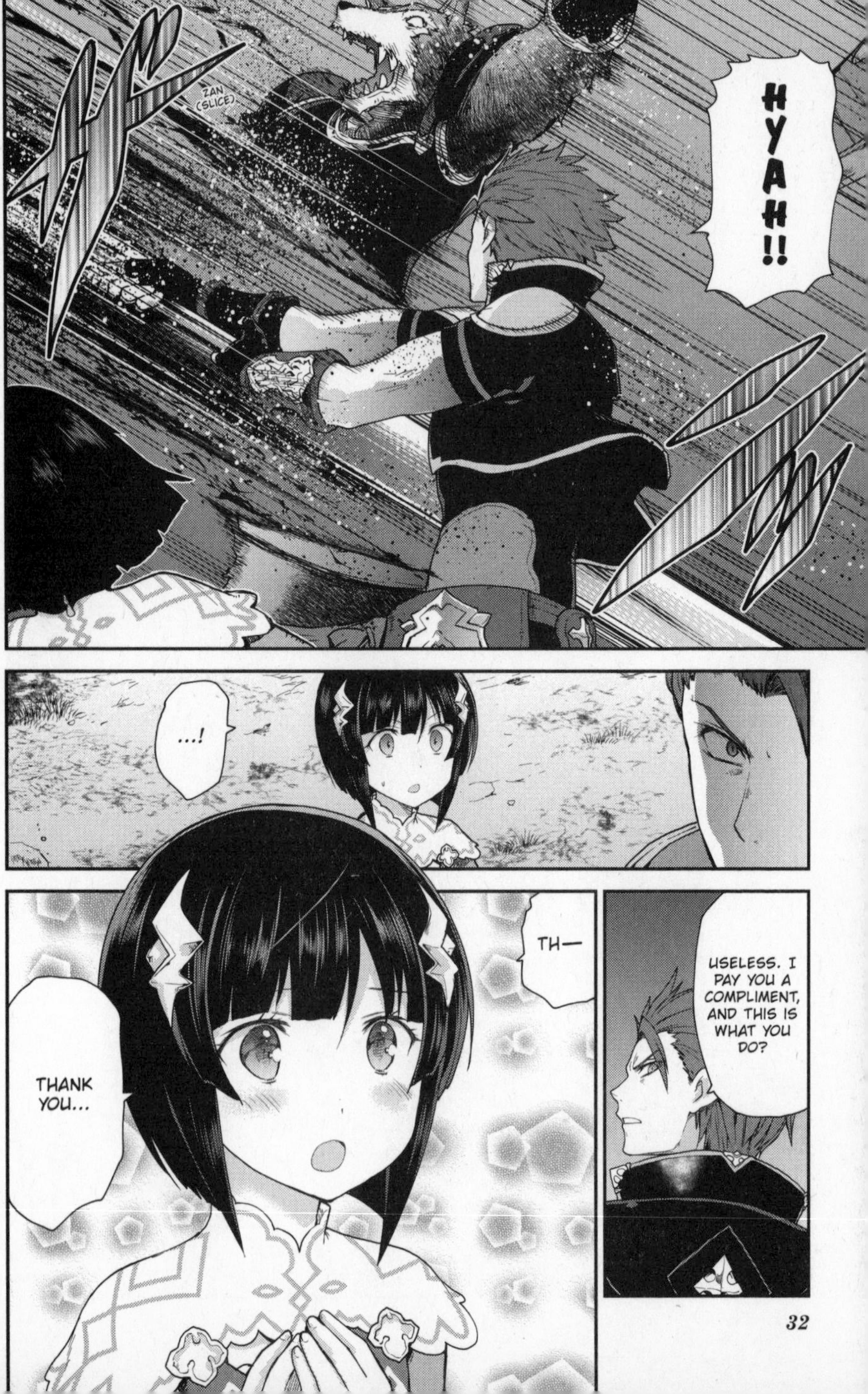
HYAH!!
ZAN (SLICE)
...!
USELESS. I PAY YOU A COMPLIMENT, AND THIS IS WHAT YOU DO?
TH—
THANK YOU...

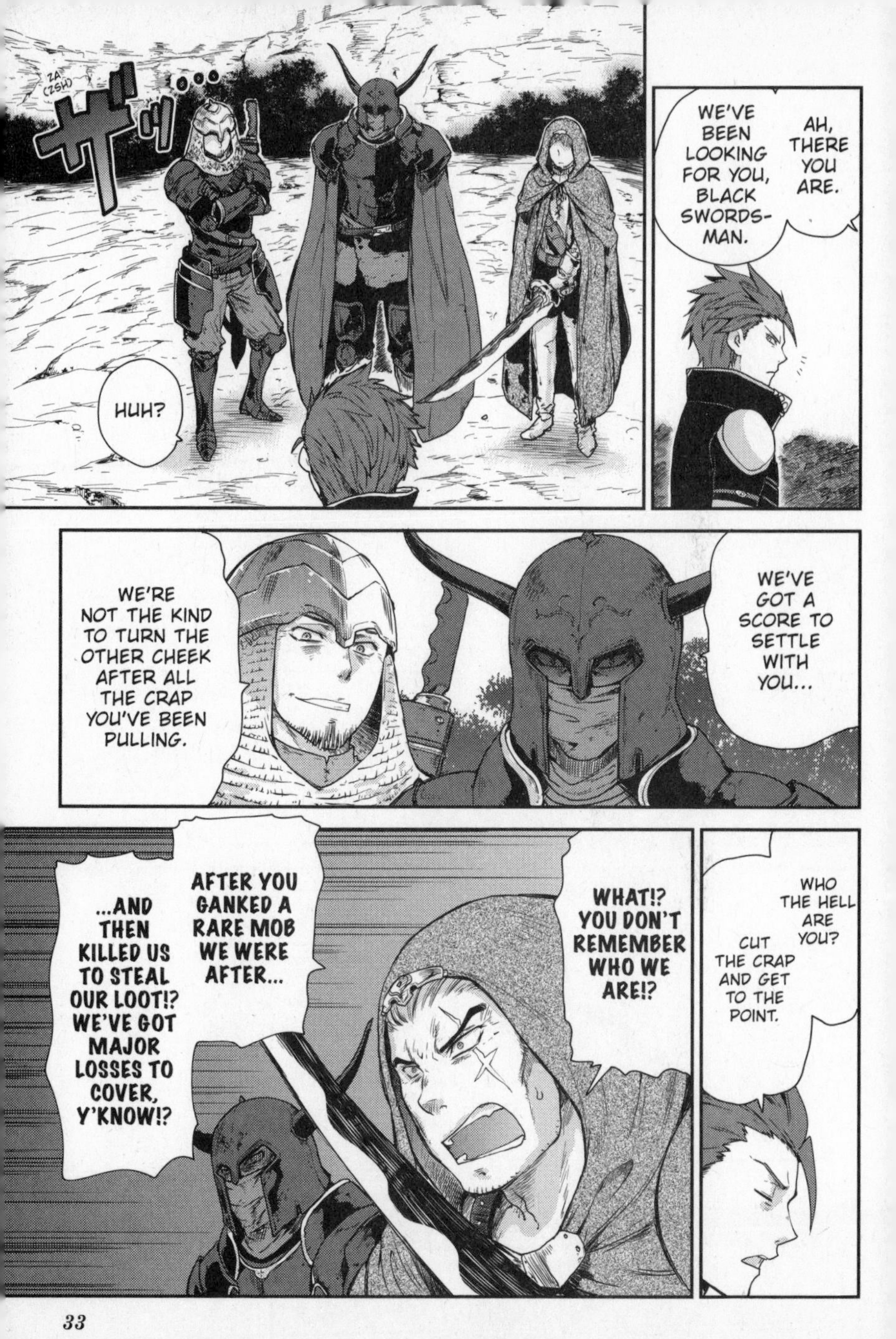
AH, THERE YOU ARE.
WE'VE BEEN LOOKING FOR YOU, BLACK SWORDSMAN.
ザッ
ZA (ZSH)
...
HUH?
WE'VE GOT A SCORE TO SETTLE WITH YOU...
WE'RE NOT THE KIND TO TURN THE OTHER CHEEK AFTER ALL THE CRAP YOU'VE BEEN PULLING.
WHO THE HELL ARE YOU?
CUT THE CRAP AND GET TO THE POINT.
WHAT!? YOU DON'T REMEMBER WHO WE ARE!?
AFTER YOU GANKED A RARE MOB WE WERE AFTER...
...AND THEN KILLED US TO STEAL OUR LOOT!? WE'VE GOT MAJOR LOSSES TO COVER, Y'KNOW!?

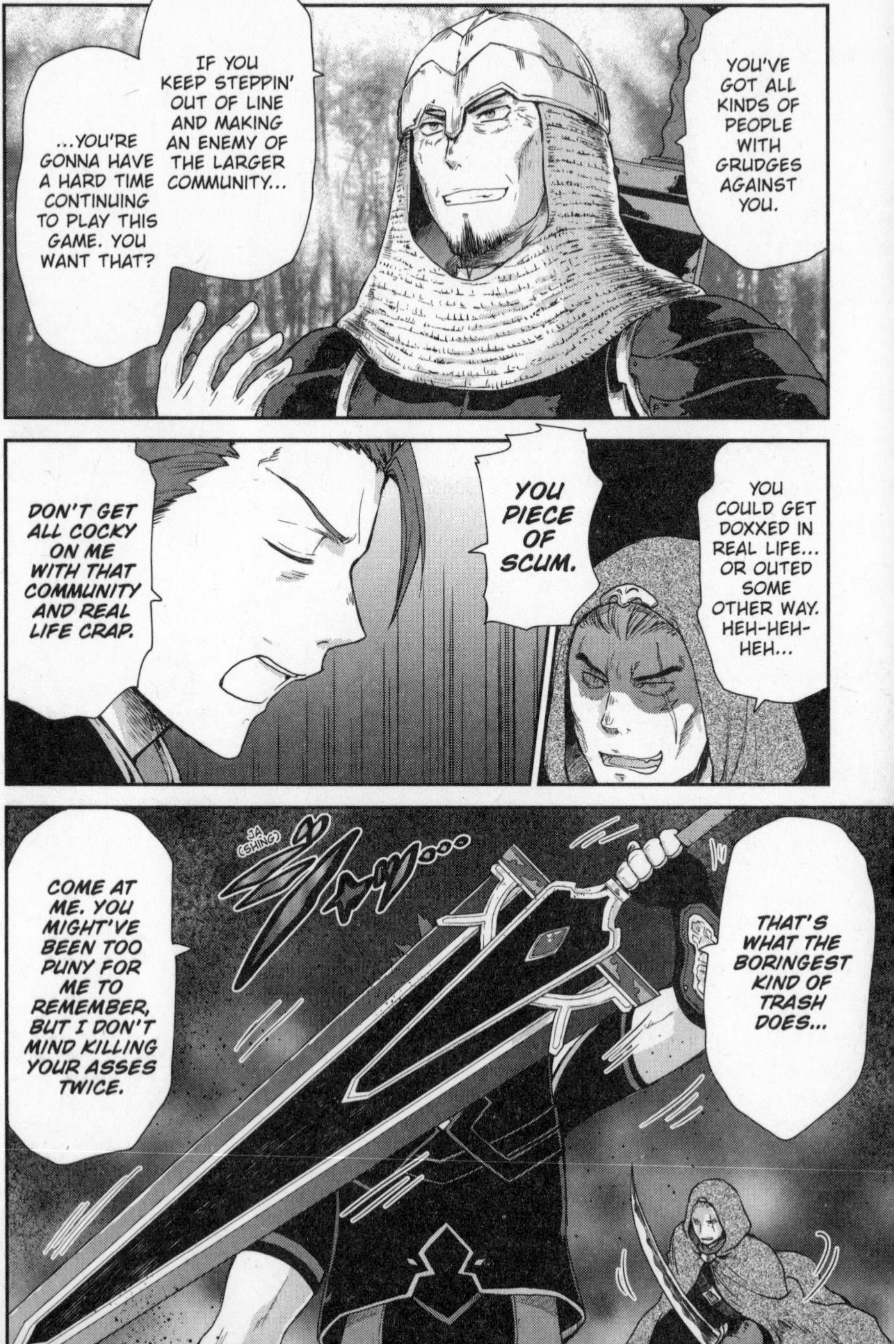
YOU'VE GOT ALL KINDS OF PEOPLE WITH GRUDGES AGAINST YOU.
IF YOU KEEP STEPPIN' OUT OF LINE AND MAKING AN ENEMY OF THE LARGER COMMUNITY...
...YOU'RE GONNA HAVE A HARD TIME CONTINUING TO PLAY THIS GAME. YOU WANT THAT?
YOU COULD GET DOXXED IN REAL LIFE... OR OUTED SOME OTHER WAY. HEH-HEH-HEH...
YOU PIECE OF SCUM.
DON'T GET ALL COCKY ON ME WITH THAT COMMUNITY AND REAL LIFE CRAP.
THAT'S WHAT THE BORINGEST KIND OF TRASH DOES...
JA (SHING)
COME AT ME. YOU MIGHT'VE BEEN TOO PUNY FOR ME TO REMEMBER, BUT I DON'T MIND KILLING YOUR ASSES TWICE.

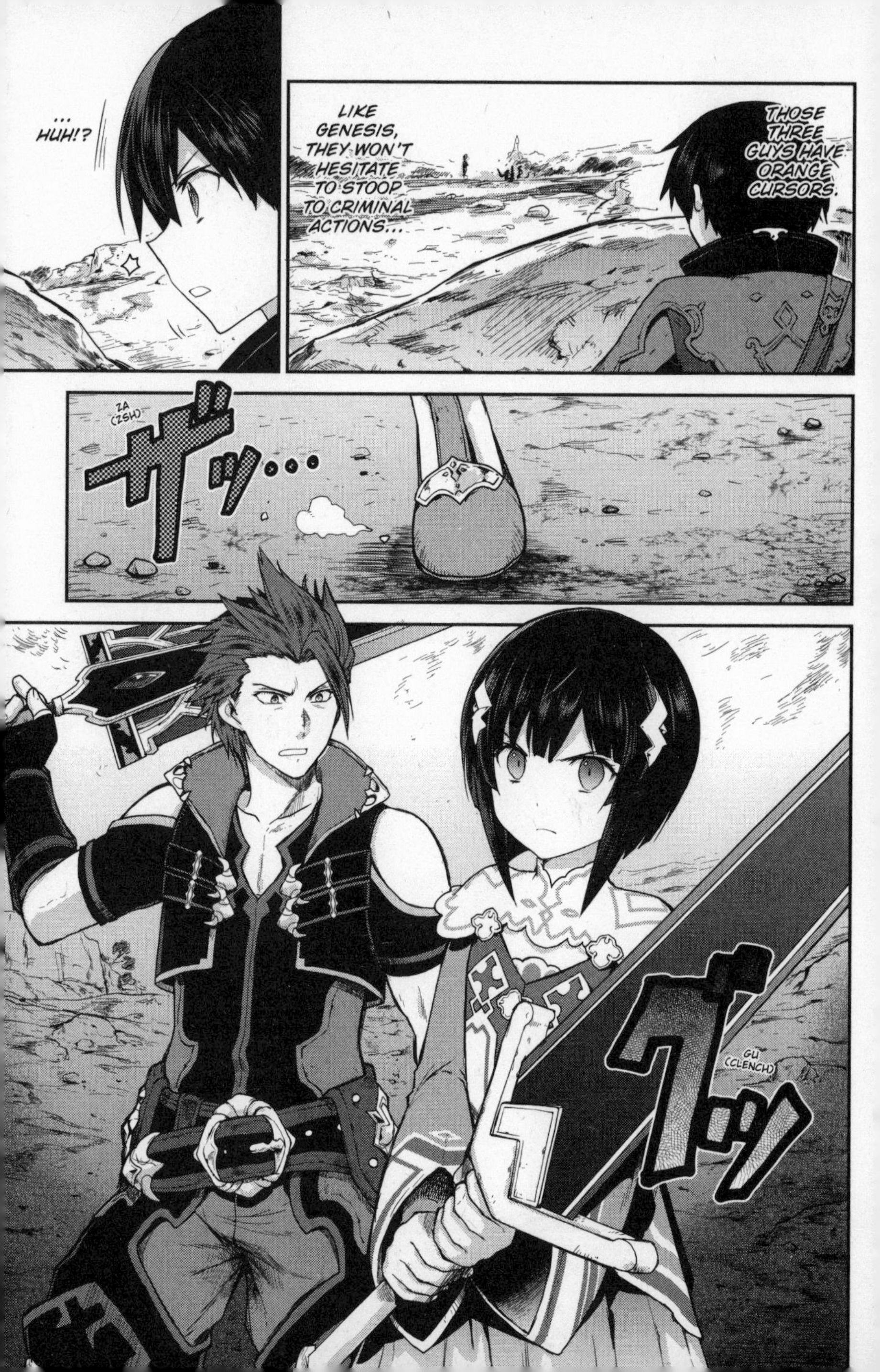
THOSE THREE GUYS HAVE ORANGE CURSORS.
LIKE GENESIS, THEY WON'T HESITATE TO STOOP TO CRIMINAL ACTIONS...
... HUH!?
ザッ…
ZA (ZSH)
グッ
GU (CLENCH)

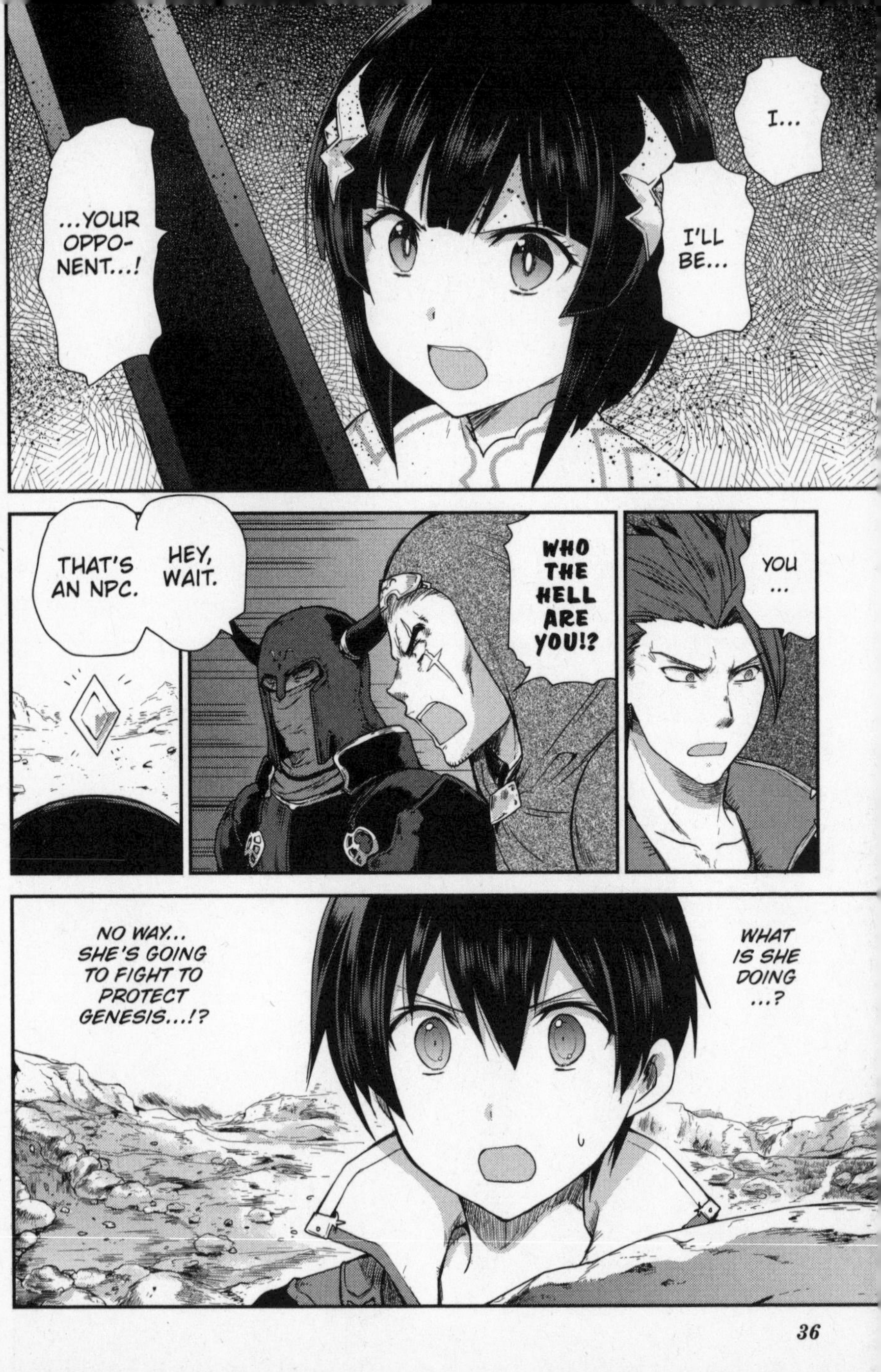
I...
I'LL BE...
...YOUR OPPO-NENT...!
YOU ...
WHO THE HELL ARE YOU!?
HEY, WAIT.
THAT'S AN NPC.
WHAT IS SHE DOING ...?
NO WAY... SHE'S GOING TO FIGHT TO PROTECT GENESIS...!?

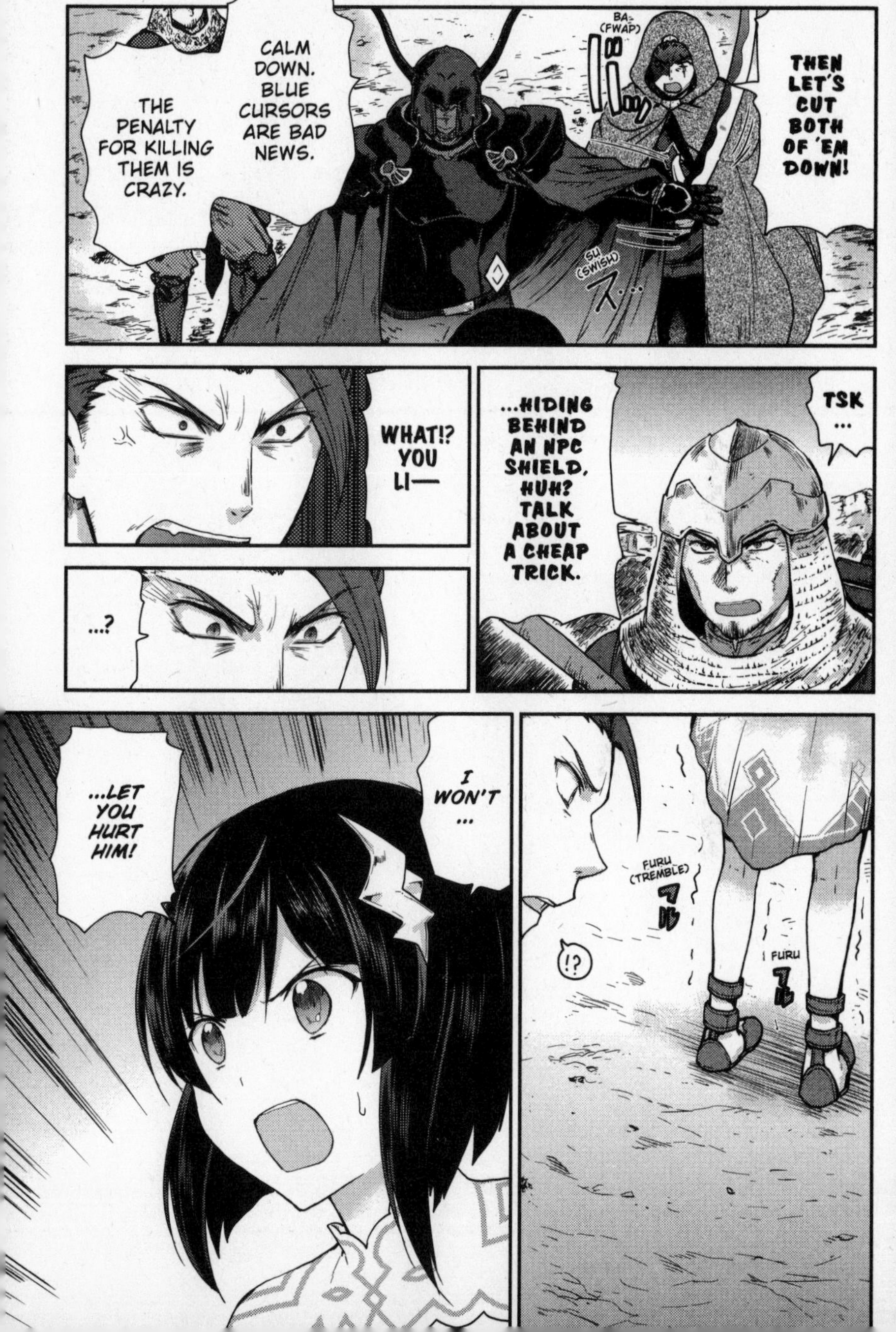
THEN LET'S CUT BOTH OF 'EM DOWN!
BA (FWAP)
CALM DOWN. BLUE CURSORS ARE BAD NEWS.
THE PENALTY FOR KILLING THEM IS CRAZY.
SU (SWISH)
TSK ...
...HIDING BEHIND AN NPC SHIELD, HUH? TALK ABOUT A CHEAP TRICK.
WHAT!? YOU LI—
...?
FURU (TREMBLE)
FURU
!?
I WON'T ...
...LET YOU HURT HIM!

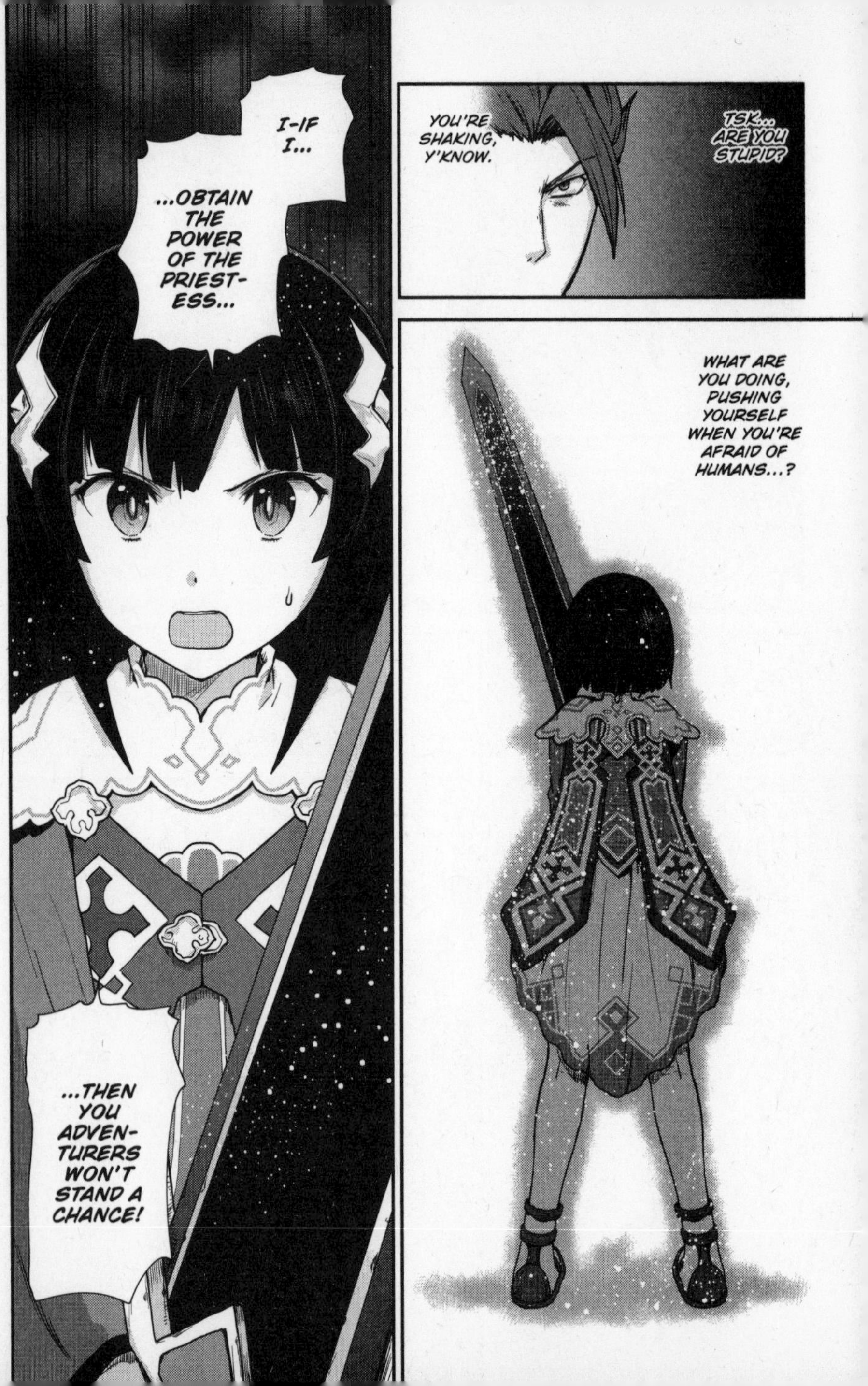
TSK... ARE YOU STUPID?
YOU'RE SHAKING, Y'KNOW.
WHAT ARE YOU DOING, PUSHING YOURSELF WHEN YOU'RE AFRAID OF HUMANS...?
I-IF I...
...OBTAIN THE POWER OF THE PRIEST-ESS...
...THEN YOU ADVEN-TURERS WON'T STAND A CHANCE!

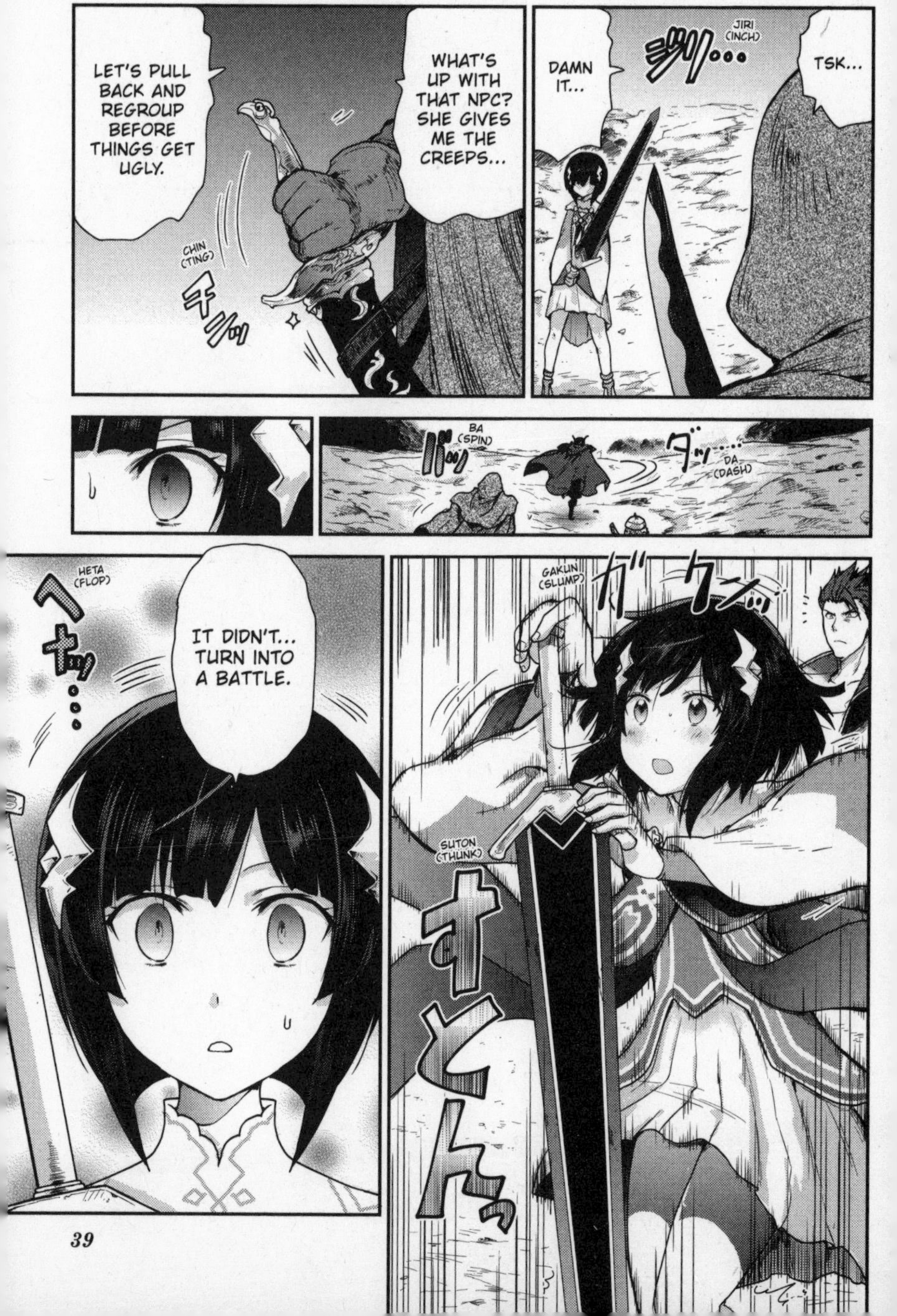
TSK...
JIRI (INCH)
DAMN IT...
WHAT'S UP WITH THAT NPC? SHE GIVES ME THE CREEPS...
LET'S PULL BACK AND REGROUP BEFORE THINGS GET UGLY.
CHIN (TING)
DA (DASH)
BA (SPIN)
GAKUN (SLUMP)
SUTON (THUNK)
IT DIDN'T... TURN INTO A BATTLE.
HETA (FLOP)

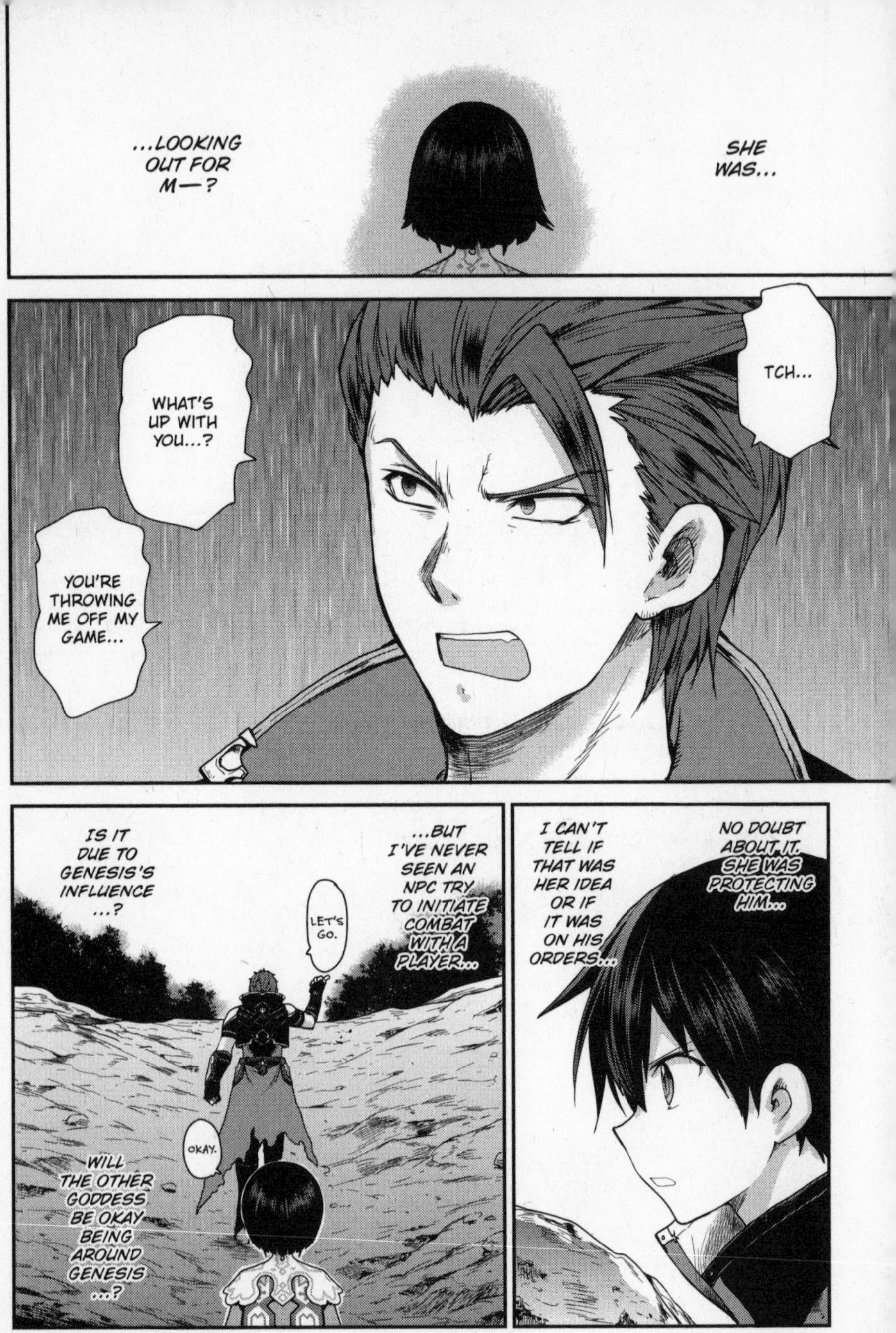
SHE WAS...
...LOOKING OUT FOR M—?
TCH...
WHAT'S UP WITH YOU...?
YOU'RE THROWING ME OFF MY GAME...
NO DOUBT ABOUT IT. SHE WAS PROTECTING HIM...
I CAN'T TELL IF THAT WAS HER IDEA OR IF IT WAS ON HIS ORDERS...
...BUT I'VE NEVER SEEN AN NPC TRY TO INITIATE COMBAT WITH A PLAYER...
LET'S GO.
IS IT DUE TO GENESIS'S INFLUENCE...?
OKAY.
WILL THE OTHER GODDESS BE OKAY BEING AROUND GENESIS...?

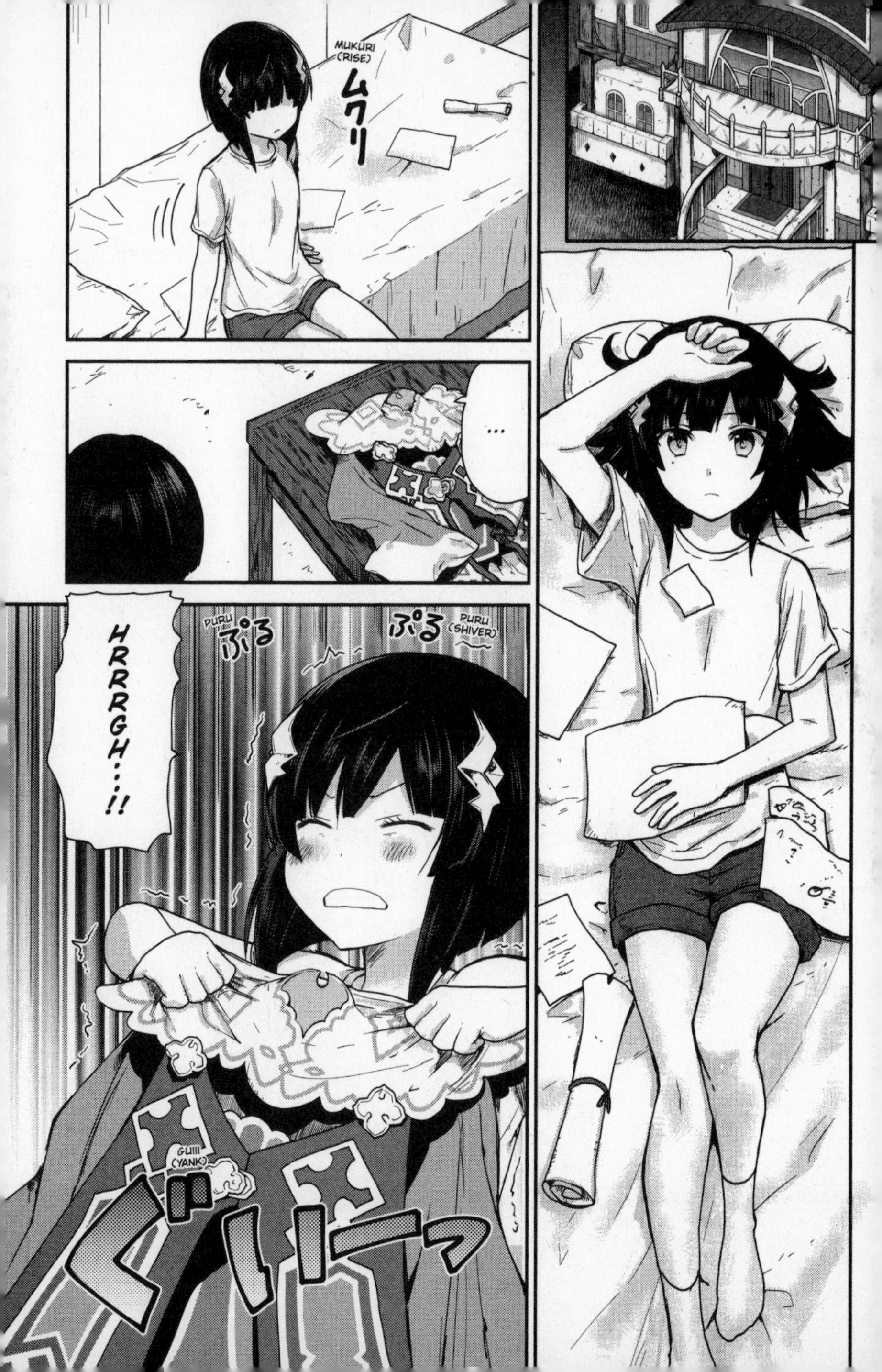
MUKURI (RISE)
ムクリ
...
HRRRGH...!!
PURU
ぷる
ぷる
PURU (SHIVER)
GUIII (YANK)
ぐいーっ

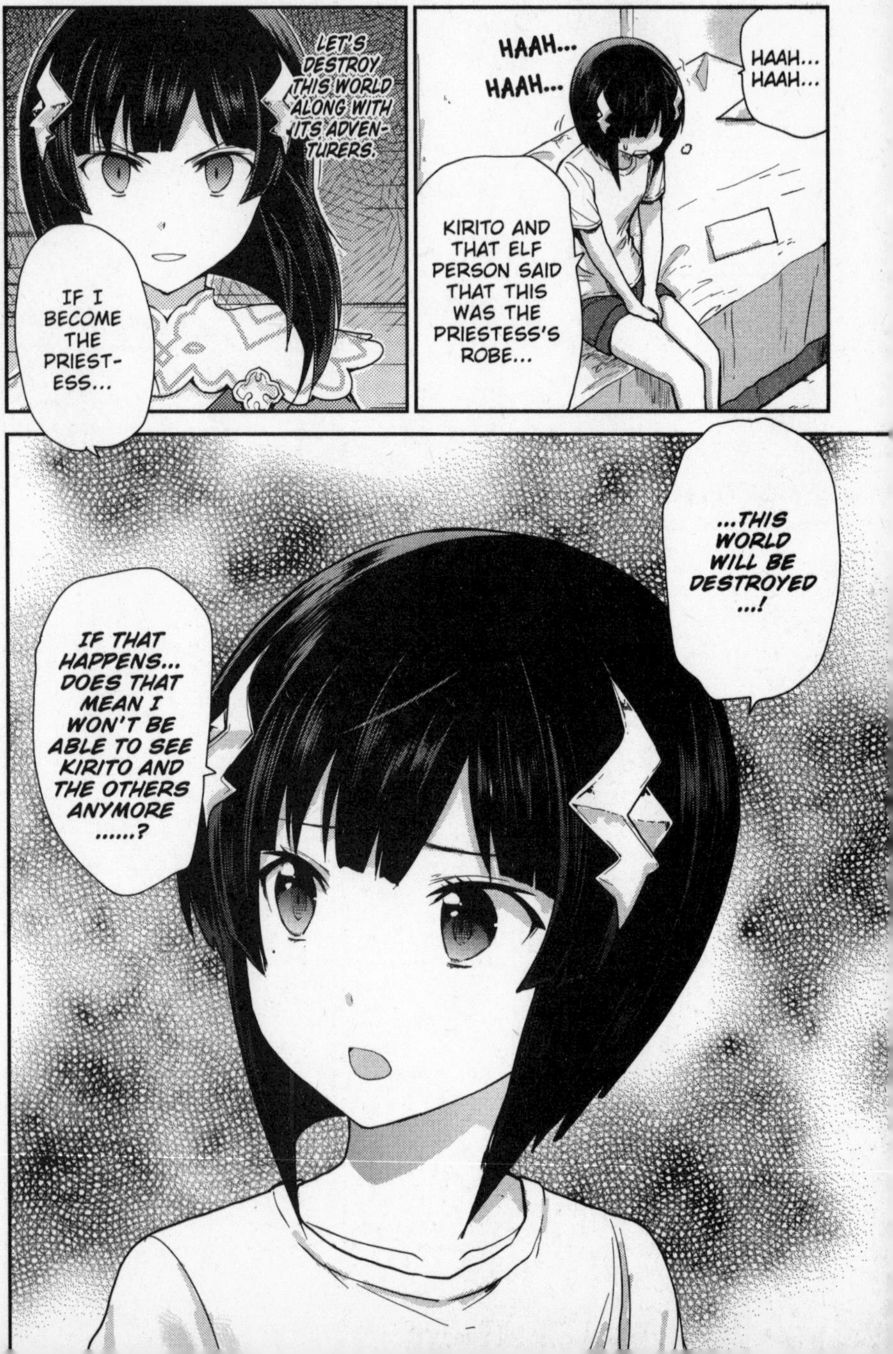
HAAH... HAAH...
HAAH... HAAH...
KIRITO AND THAT ELF PERSON SAID THAT THIS WAS THE PRIESTESS'S ROBE...
LET'S DESTROY THIS WORLD ALONG WITH ITS ADVEN-TURERS.
IF I BECOME THE PRIEST-ESS...
...THIS WORLD WILL BE DESTROYED ...!
IF THAT HAPPENS... DOES THAT MEAN I WON'T BE ABLE TO SEE KIRITO AND THE OTHERS ANYMORE ......?

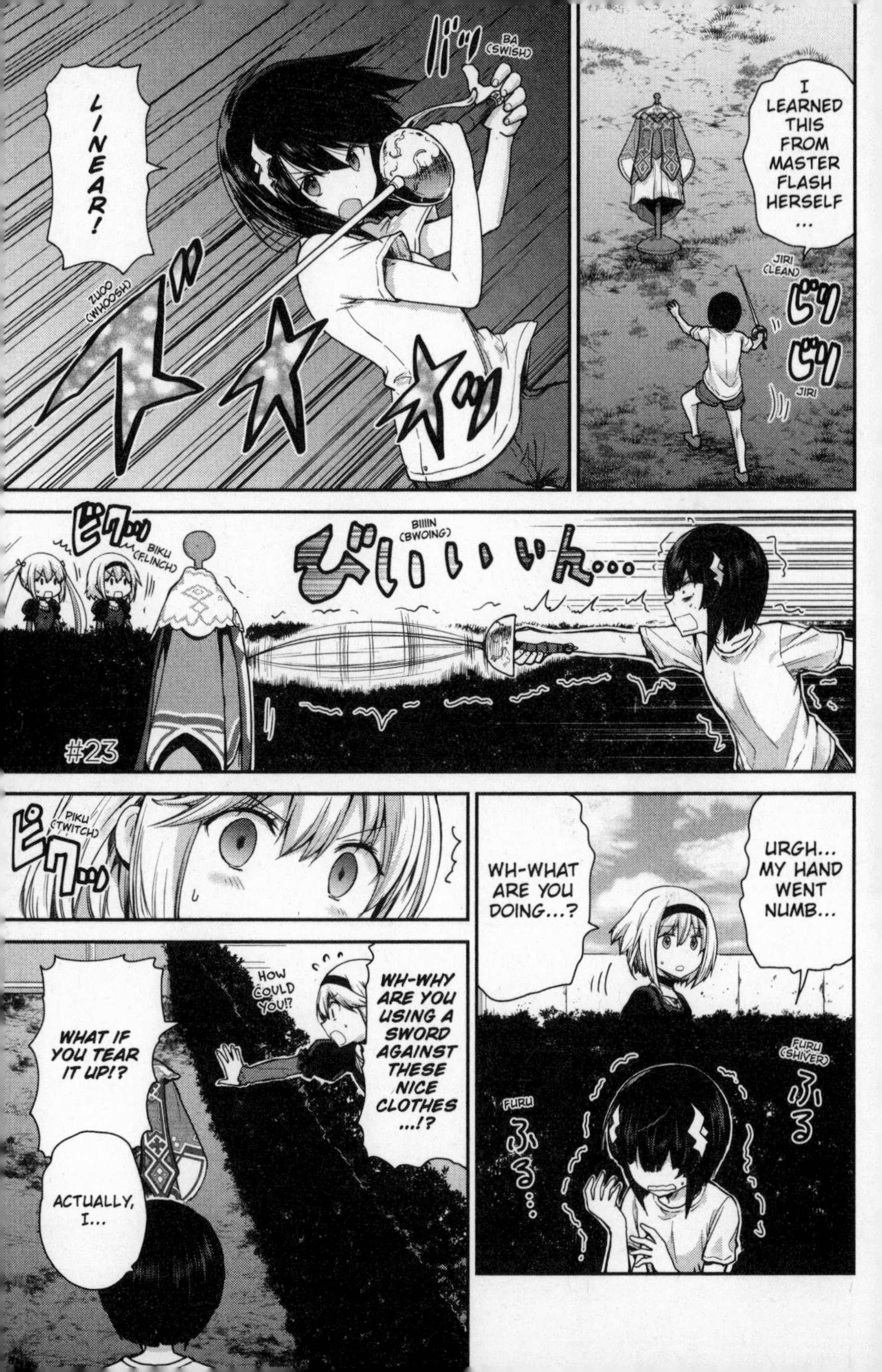

I LEARNED THIS FROM MASTER FLASH HERSELF...
JIRI (LEAN)
JIRI
BA (SWISH)
LINEAR!
ZUOO (WHOOSH)
BIIIIN (BWOING)
BIKU (FLINCH)
#23
URGH... MY HAND WENT NUMB...
WH-WHAT ARE YOU DOING...?
FURU (SHIVER)
FURU
PIKU (TWITCH)
WH-WHY ARE YOU USING A SWORD AGAINST THESE NICE CLOTHES...!?
HOW COULD YOU!?
WHAT IF YOU TEAR IT UP!?
ACTUALLY, I...

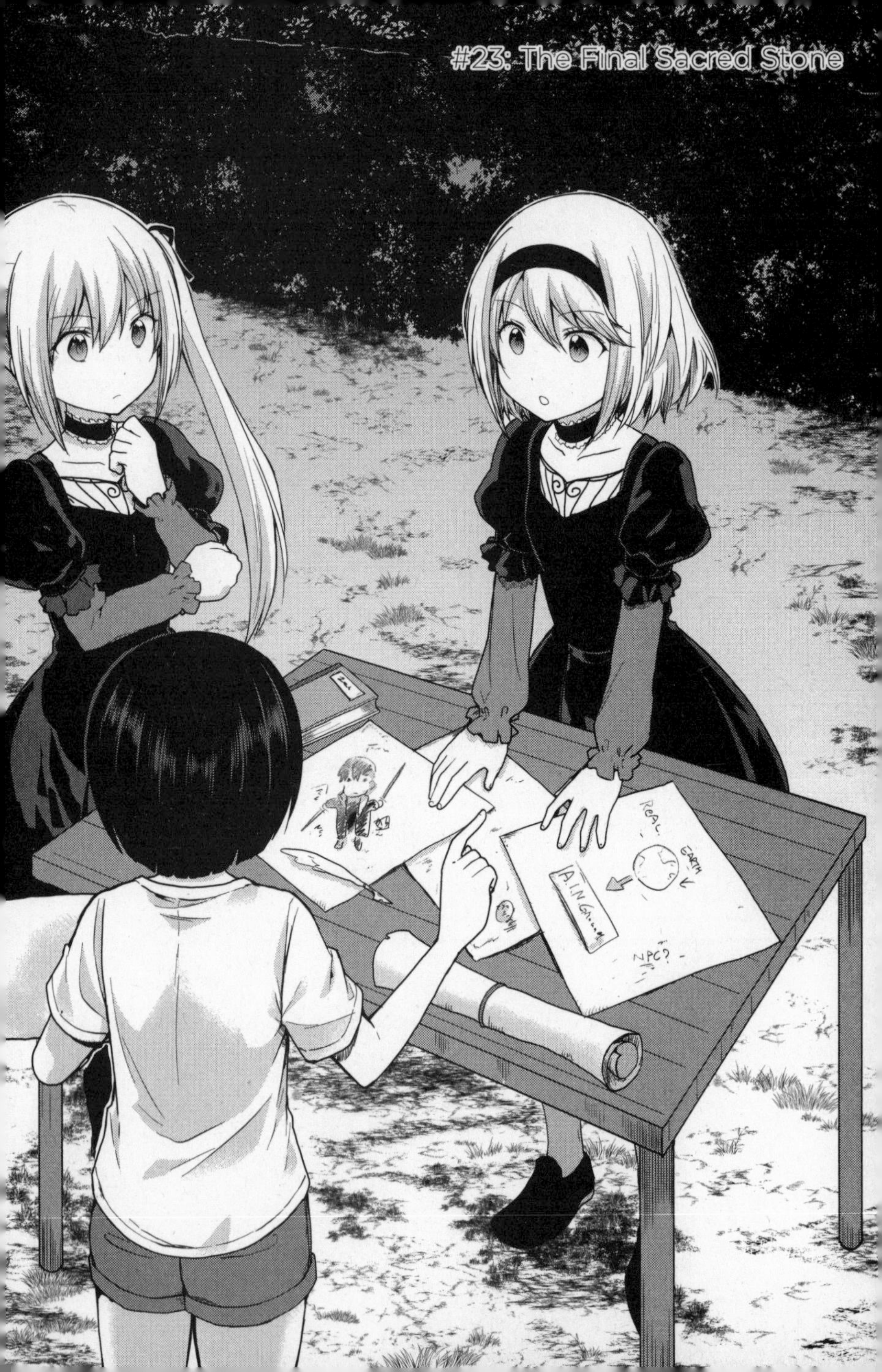
#23: The Final Sacred Stone
REAL
EARTH
NPC?

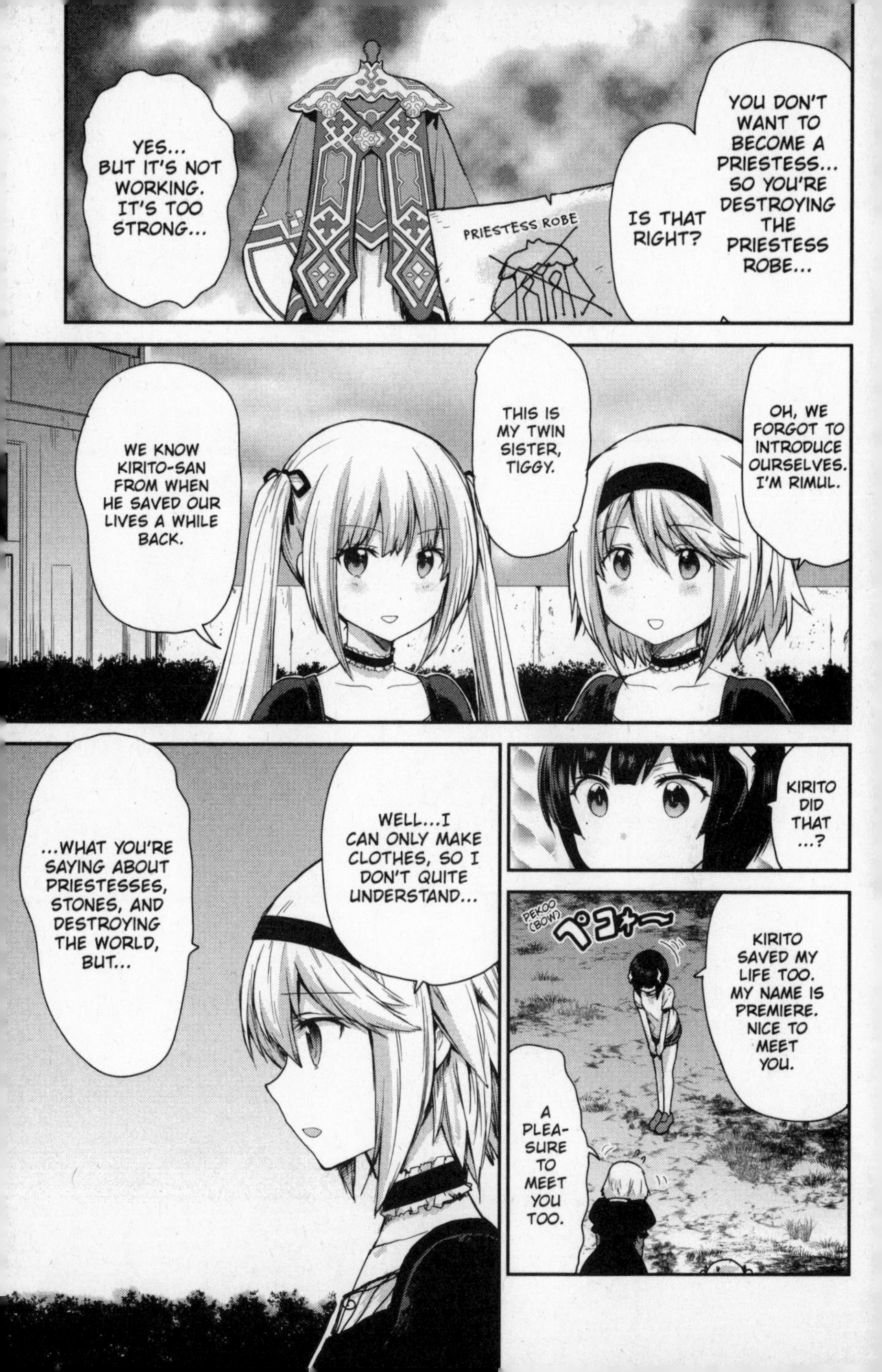
YOU DON'T WANT TO BECOME A PRIESTESS... SO YOU'RE DESTROYING THE PRIESTESS ROBE...
IS THAT RIGHT?
PRIESTESS ROBE
YES... BUT IT'S NOT WORKING. IT'S TOO STRONG...
OH, WE FORGOT TO INTRODUCE OURSELVES. I'M RIMUL.
THIS IS MY TWIN SISTER, TIGGY.
WE KNOW KIRITO-SAN FROM WHEN HE SAVED OUR LIVES A WHILE BACK.
KIRITO DID THAT ...?
PEKOO (BOW)
ペコォー
KIRITO SAVED MY LIFE TOO. MY NAME IS PREMIERE. NICE TO MEET YOU.
A PLEA-SURE TO MEET YOU TOO.
WELL...I CAN ONLY MAKE CLOTHES, SO I DON'T QUITE UNDERSTAND...
...WHAT YOU'RE SAYING ABOUT PRIESTESSES, STONES, AND DESTROYING THE WORLD, BUT...

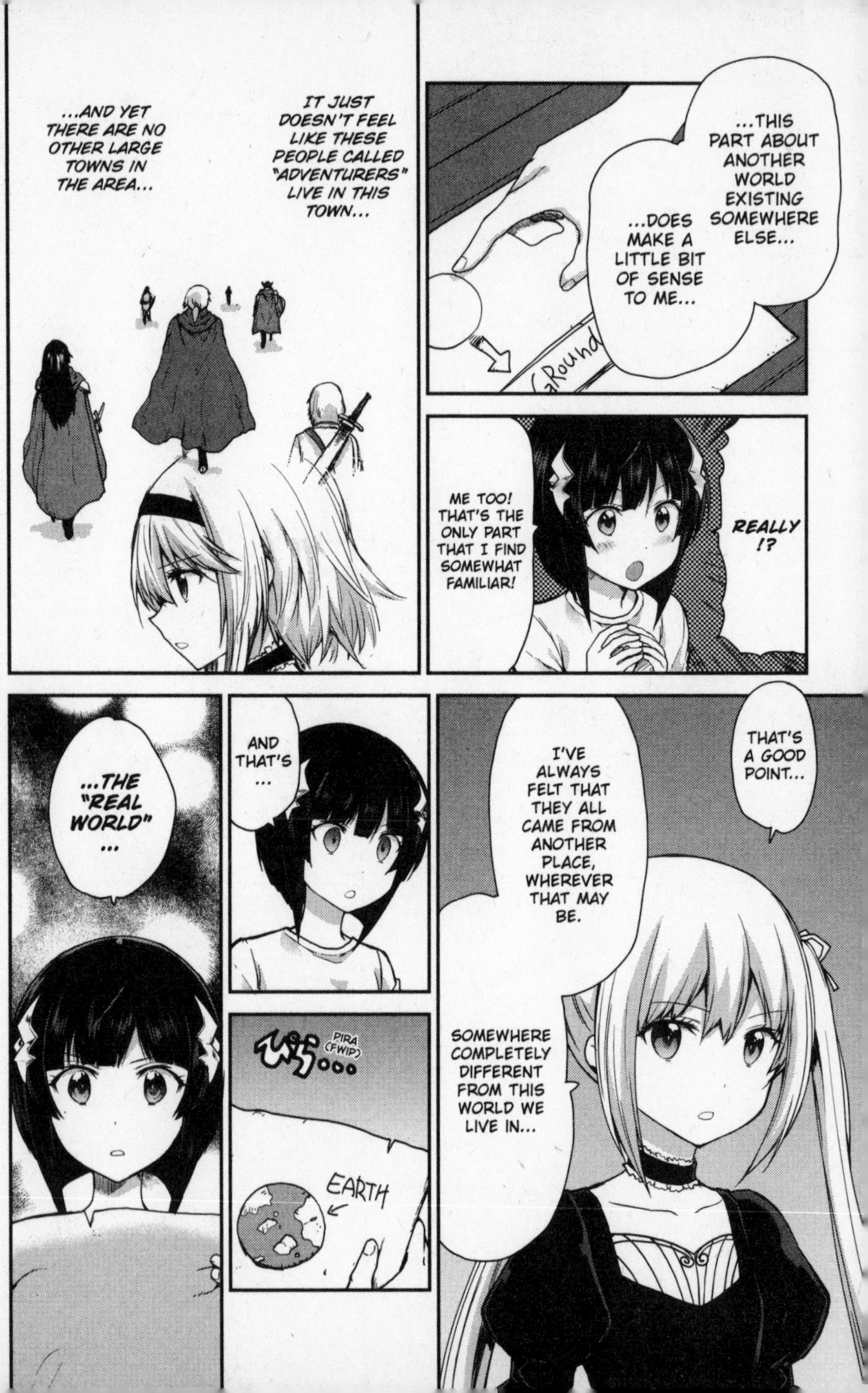
...THIS PART ABOUT ANOTHER WORLD EXISTING SOMEWHERE ELSE...
...DOES MAKE A LITTLE BIT OF SENSE TO ME...
GRound
REALLY!?
ME TOO! THAT'S THE ONLY PART THAT I FIND SOMEWHAT FAMILIAR!
IT JUST DOESN'T FEEL LIKE THESE PEOPLE CALLED "ADVENTURERS" LIVE IN THIS TOWN...
...AND YET THERE ARE NO OTHER LARGE TOWNS IN THE AREA...
THAT'S A GOOD POINT...
I'VE ALWAYS FELT THAT THEY ALL CAME FROM ANOTHER PLACE, WHEREVER THAT MAY BE.
SOMEWHERE COMPLETELY DIFFERENT FROM THIS WORLD WE LIVE IN...
AND THAT'S...
PIRA (FWIP)
EARTH
...THE "REAL WORLD"...

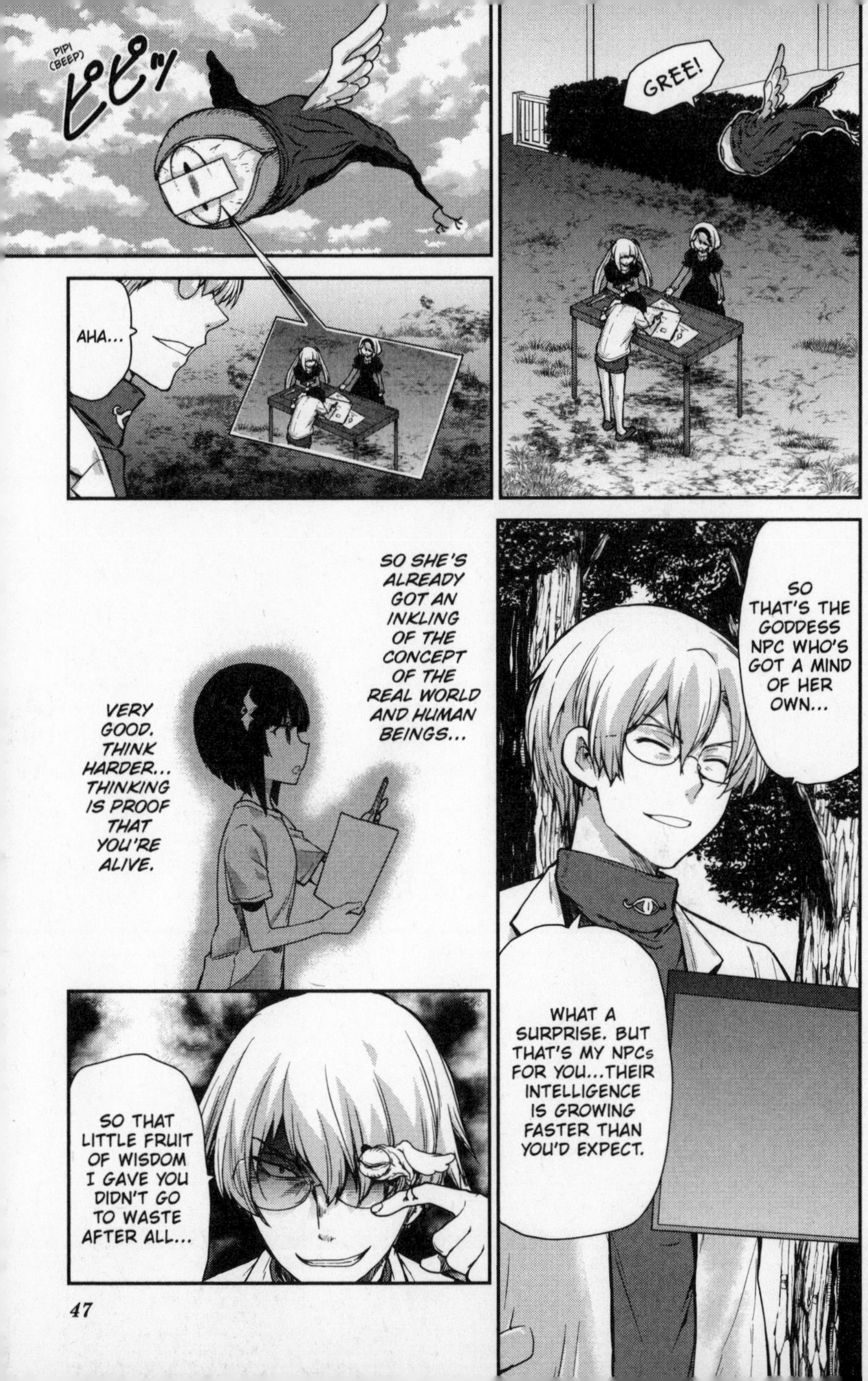
GREE!
PIPI (BEEP)
ピピッ
AHA...
SO THAT'S THE GODDESS NPC WHO'S GOT A MIND OF HER OWN...
WHAT A SURPRISE. BUT THAT'S MY NPCs FOR YOU...THEIR INTELLIGENCE IS GROWING FASTER THAN YOU'D EXPECT.
SO SHE'S ALREADY GOT AN INKLING OF THE CONCEPT OF THE REAL WORLD AND HUMAN BEINGS...
VERY GOOD. THINK HARDER... THINKING IS PROOF THAT YOU'RE ALIVE.
SO THAT LITTLE FRUIT OF WISDOM I GAVE YOU DIDN'T GO TO WASTE AFTER ALL...

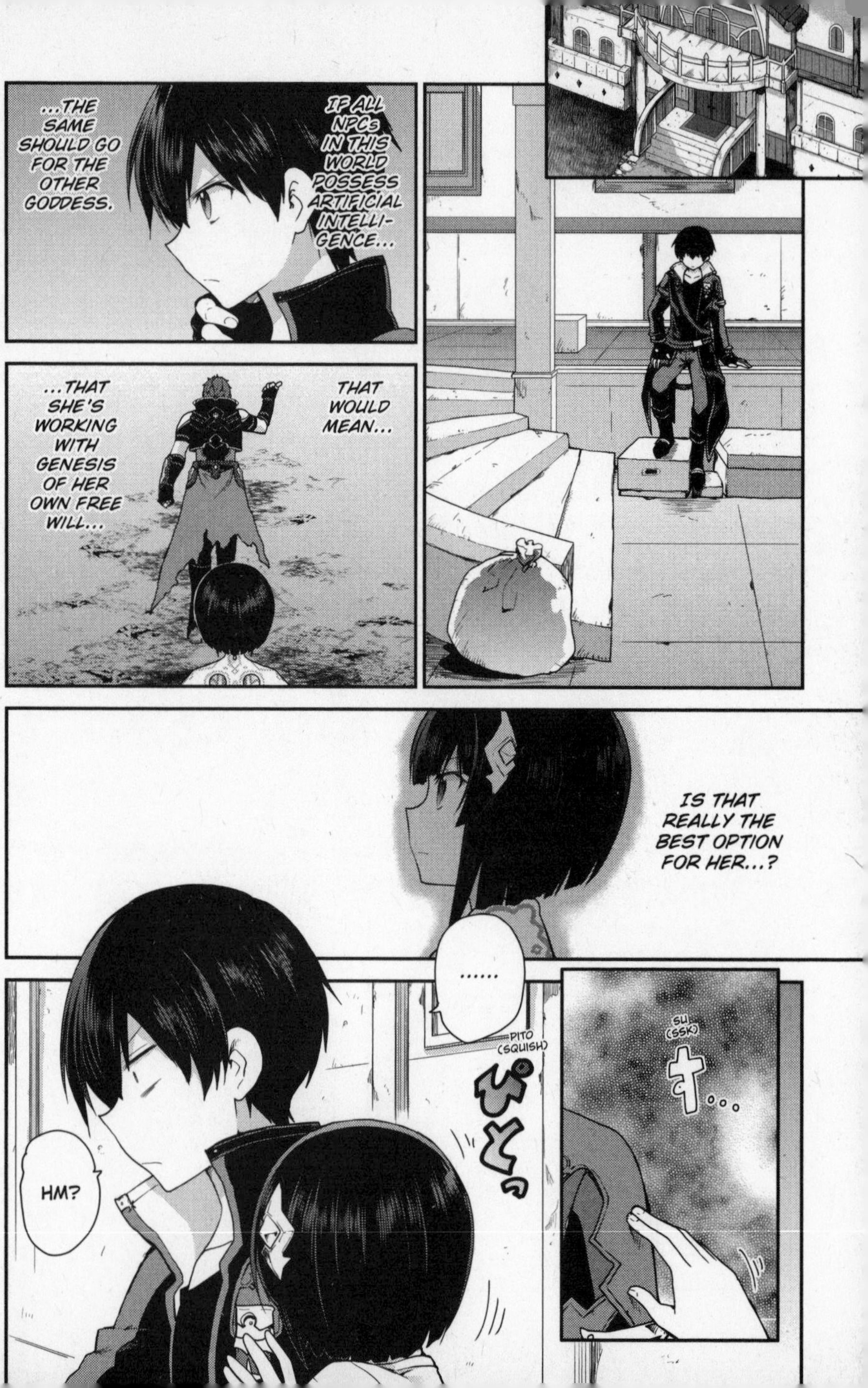
IF ALL NPCs IN THIS WORLD POSSESS ARTIFICIAL INTELLI-GENCE...
...THE SAME SHOULD GO FOR THE OTHER GODDESS.
THAT WOULD MEAN...
...THAT SHE'S WORKING WITH GENESIS OF HER OWN FREE WILL...
IS THAT REALLY THE BEST OPTION FOR HER...?
SU (SSK)
す...
......
PITO (SQUISH)
ぴとっ
HM?

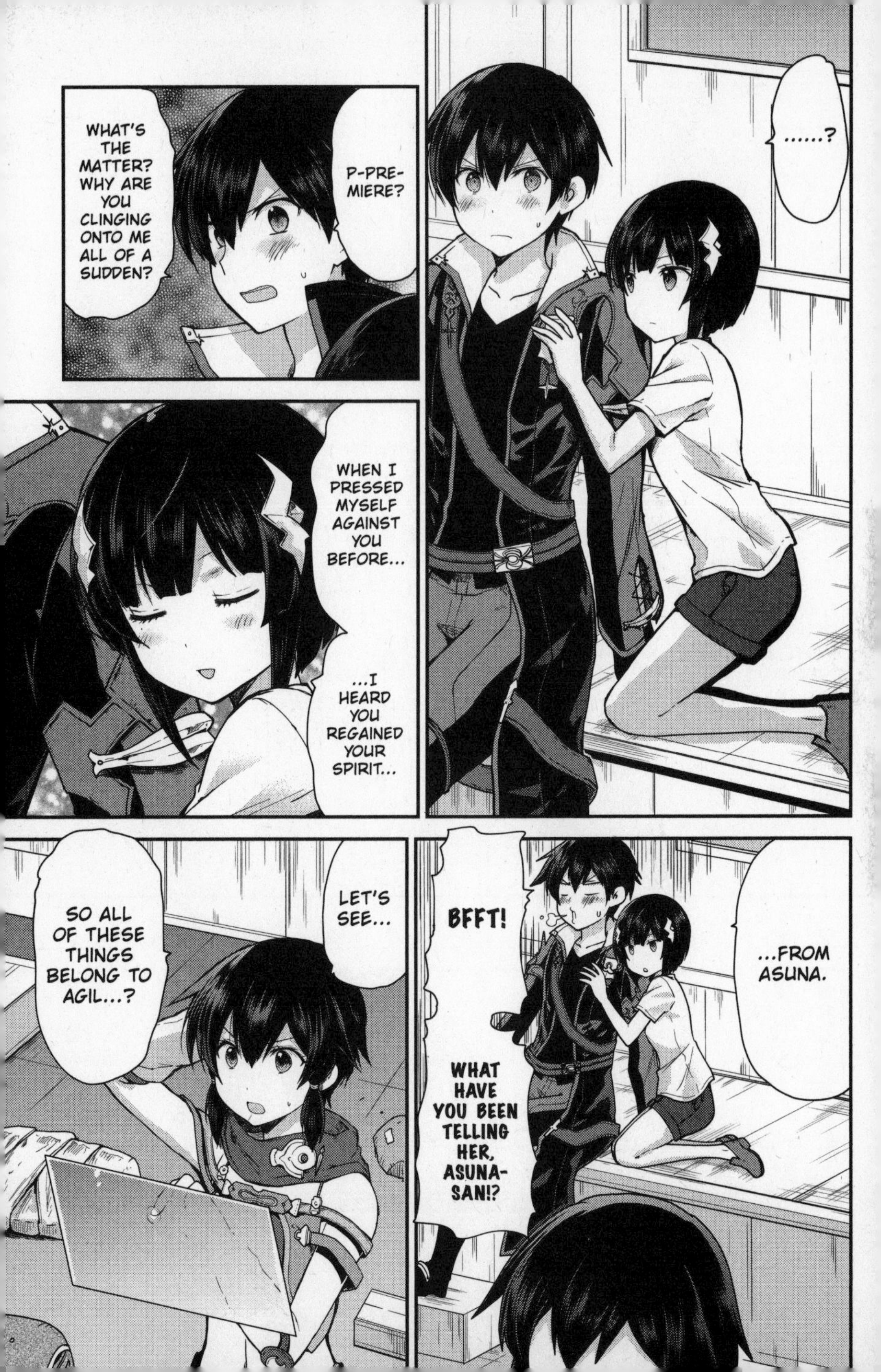
......?
P-PREMIERE?
WHAT'S THE MATTER? WHY ARE YOU CLINGING ONTO ME ALL OF A SUDDEN?
WHEN I PRESSED MYSELF AGAINST YOU BEFORE...
...I HEARD YOU REGAINED YOUR SPIRIT...
...FROM ASUNA.
BFFT!
WHAT HAVE YOU BEEN TELLING HER, ASUNA-SAN!?
LET'S SEE...
SO ALL OF THESE THINGS BELONG TO AGIL...?

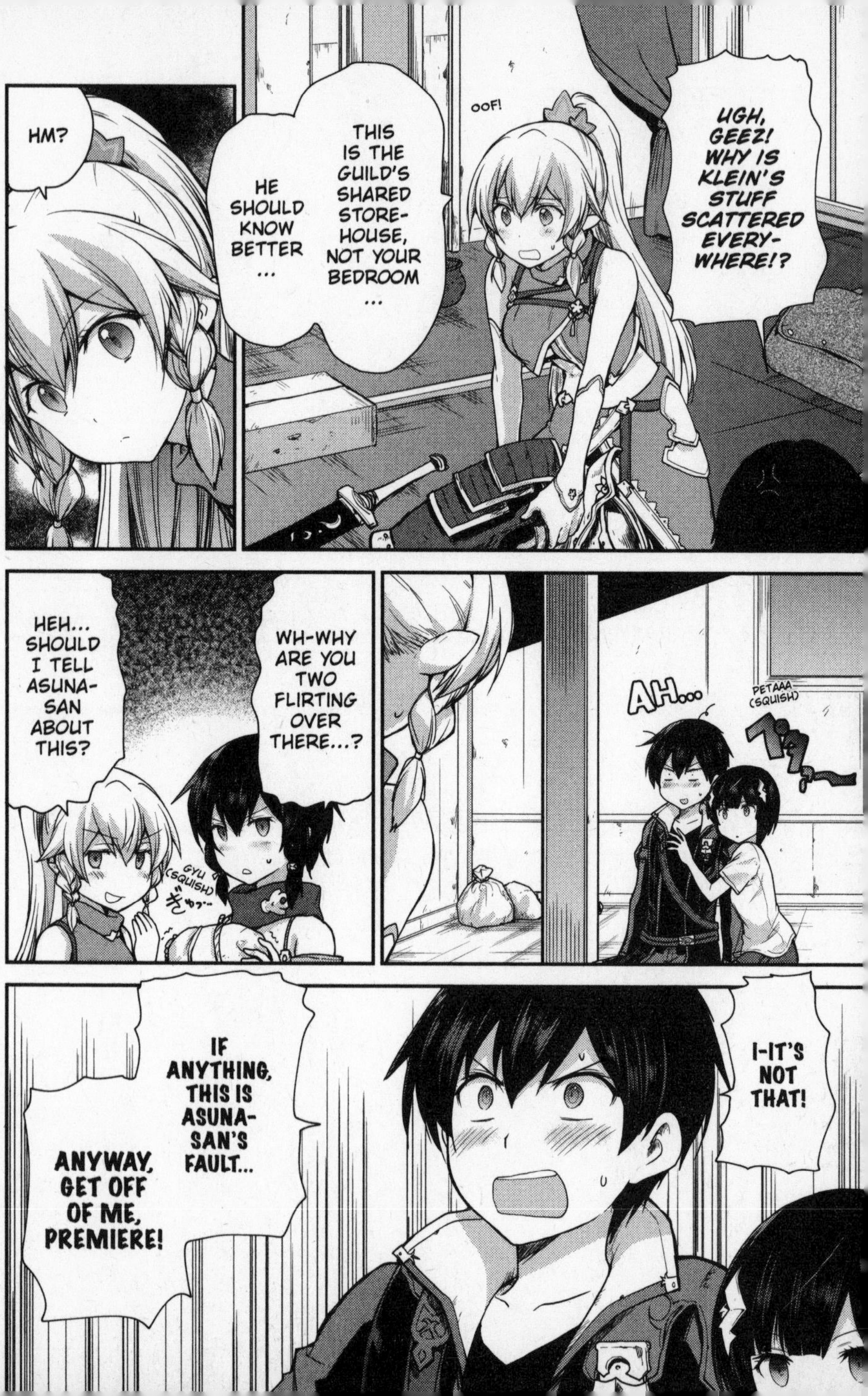
UGH, GEEZ! WHY IS KLEIN'S STUFF SCATTERED EVERYWHERE!?
OOF!
THIS IS THE GUILD'S SHARED STOREHOUSE, NOT YOUR BEDROOM...
HE SHOULD KNOW BETTER...
HM?
AH...
PETAAA (SQUISH)
WH-WHY ARE YOU TWO FLIRTING OVER THERE...?
HEH... SHOULD I TELL ASUNA-SAN ABOUT THIS?
GYU (SQUISH)
I-IT'S NOT THAT!
IF ANYTHING, THIS IS ASUNA-SAN'S FAULT...
ANYWAY, GET OFF OF ME, PREMIERE!

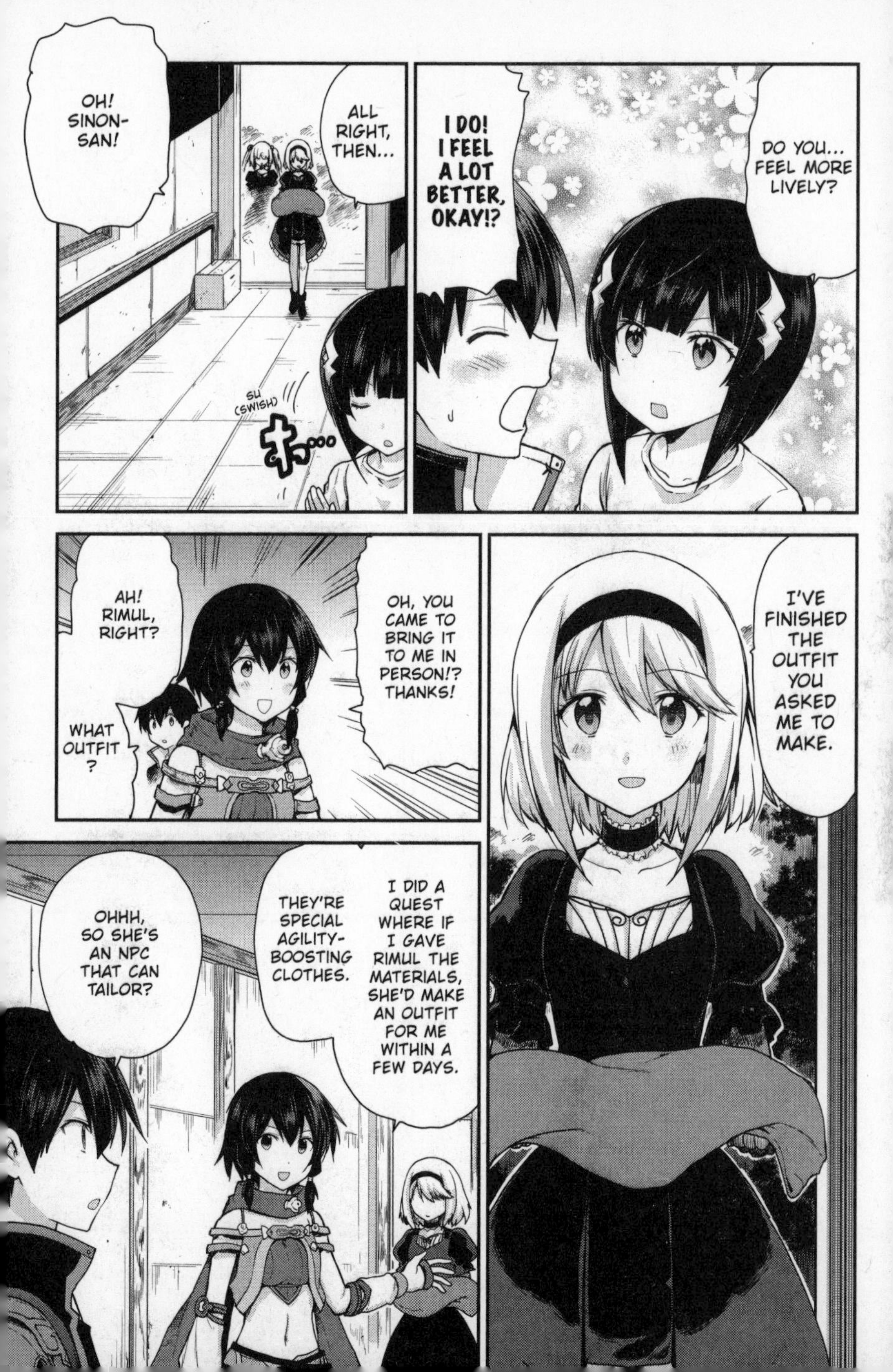
DO YOU... FEEL MORE LIVELY?
I DO! I FEEL A LOT BETTER, OKAY!?
ALL RIGHT, THEN...
SU (SWISH)
OH! SINON-SAN!
I'VE FINISHED THE OUTFIT YOU ASKED ME TO MAKE.
OH, YOU CAME TO BRING IT TO ME IN PERSON!? THANKS!
AH! RIMUL, RIGHT?
WHAT OUTFIT?
I DID A QUEST WHERE IF I GAVE RIMUL THE MATERIALS, SHE'D MAKE AN OUTFIT FOR ME WITHIN A FEW DAYS.
THEY'RE SPECIAL AGILITY-BOOSTING CLOTHES.
OHHH, SO SHE'S AN NPC THAT CAN TAILOR?

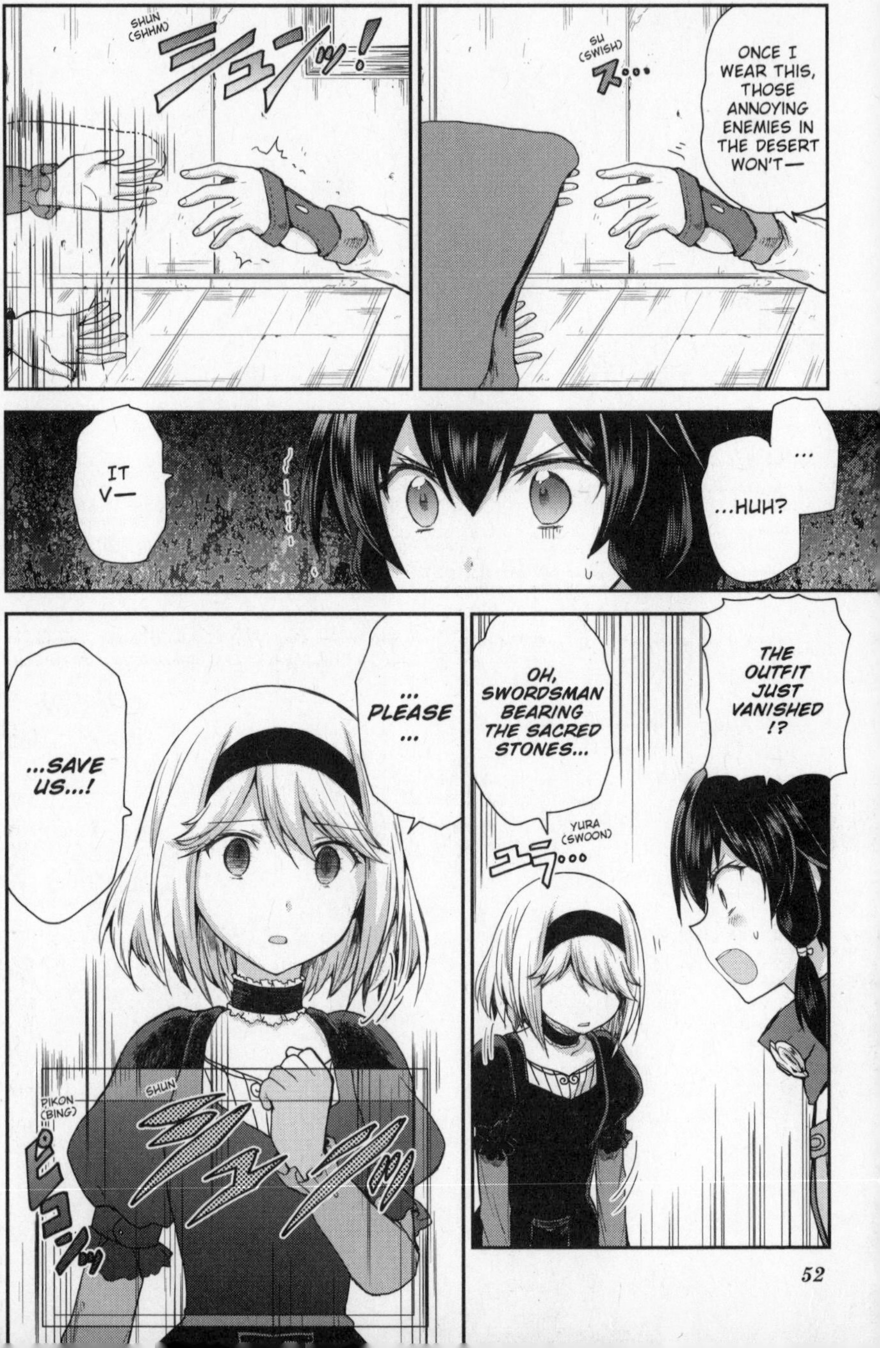
SU (SWISH)
ス…
ONCE I WEAR THIS, THOSE ANNOYING ENEMIES IN THE DESERT WON'T—
SHUN (SHHM)
シュンッ!
… …HUH?
IT V—
THE OUTFIT JUST VANISHED!?
OH, SWORDSMAN BEARING THE SACRED STONES…
YURA (SWOON)
ユラ…
…PLEASE…
…SAVE US…!
SHUN
PIKON (BING)

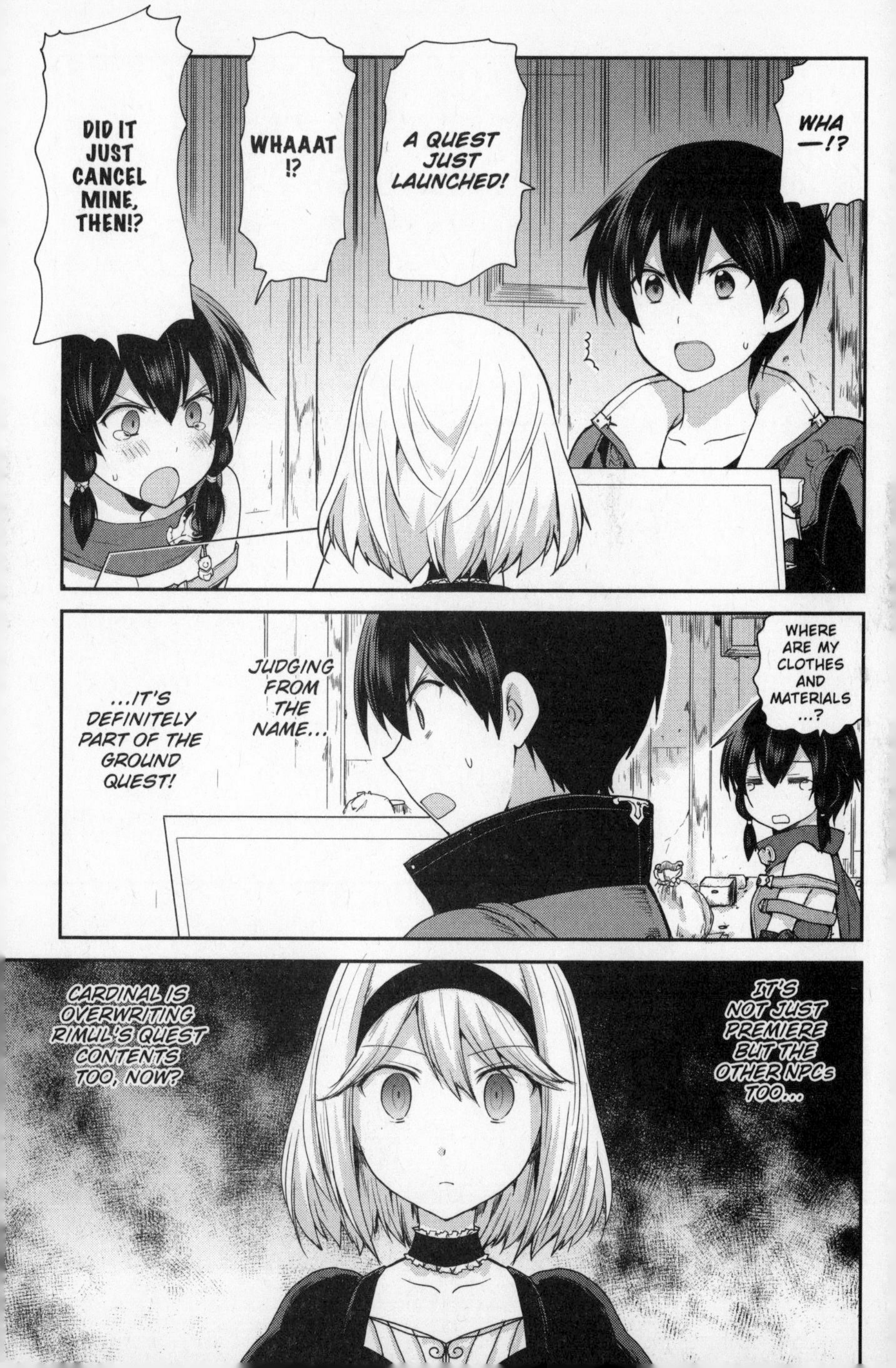
WHA—!?
A QUEST JUST LAUNCHED!
WHAAAT!?
DID IT JUST CANCEL MINE, THEN!?
WHERE ARE MY CLOTHES AND MATERIALS...?
JUDGING FROM THE NAME...
...IT'S DEFINITELY PART OF THE GROUND QUEST!
IT'S NOT JUST PREMIERE BUT THE OTHER NPCs TOO...
CARDINAL IS OVERWRITING RIMUL'S QUEST CONTENTS TOO, NOW?

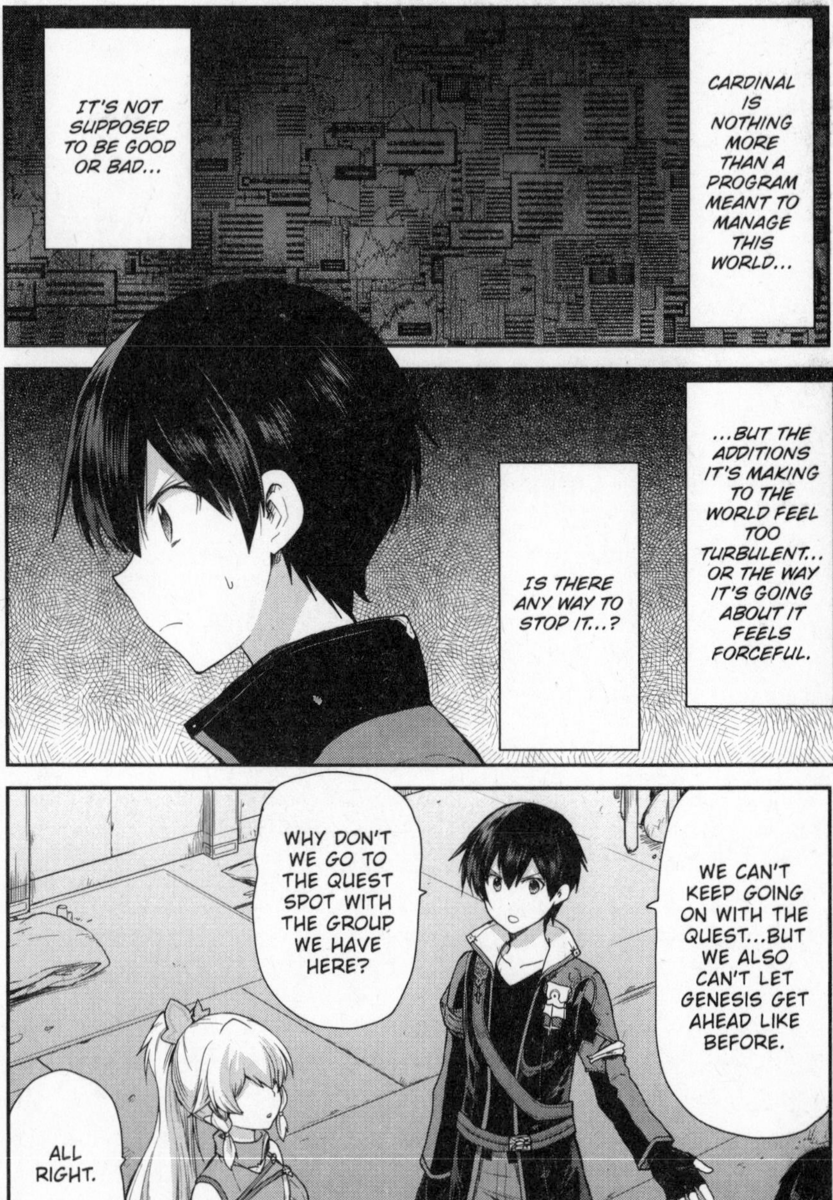
CARDINAL IS NOTHING MORE THAN A PROGRAM MEANT TO MANAGE THIS WORLD...
IT'S NOT SUPPOSED TO BE GOOD OR BAD...
...BUT THE ADDITIONS IT'S MAKING TO THE WORLD FEEL TOO TURBULENT... OR THE WAY IT'S GOING ABOUT IT FEELS FORCEFUL.
IS THERE ANY WAY TO STOP IT...?
WE CAN'T KEEP GOING ON WITH THE QUEST...BUT WE ALSO CAN'T LET GENESIS GET AHEAD LIKE BEFORE.
WHY DON'T WE GO TO THE QUEST SPOT WITH THE GROUP WE HAVE HERE?
ALL RIGHT.

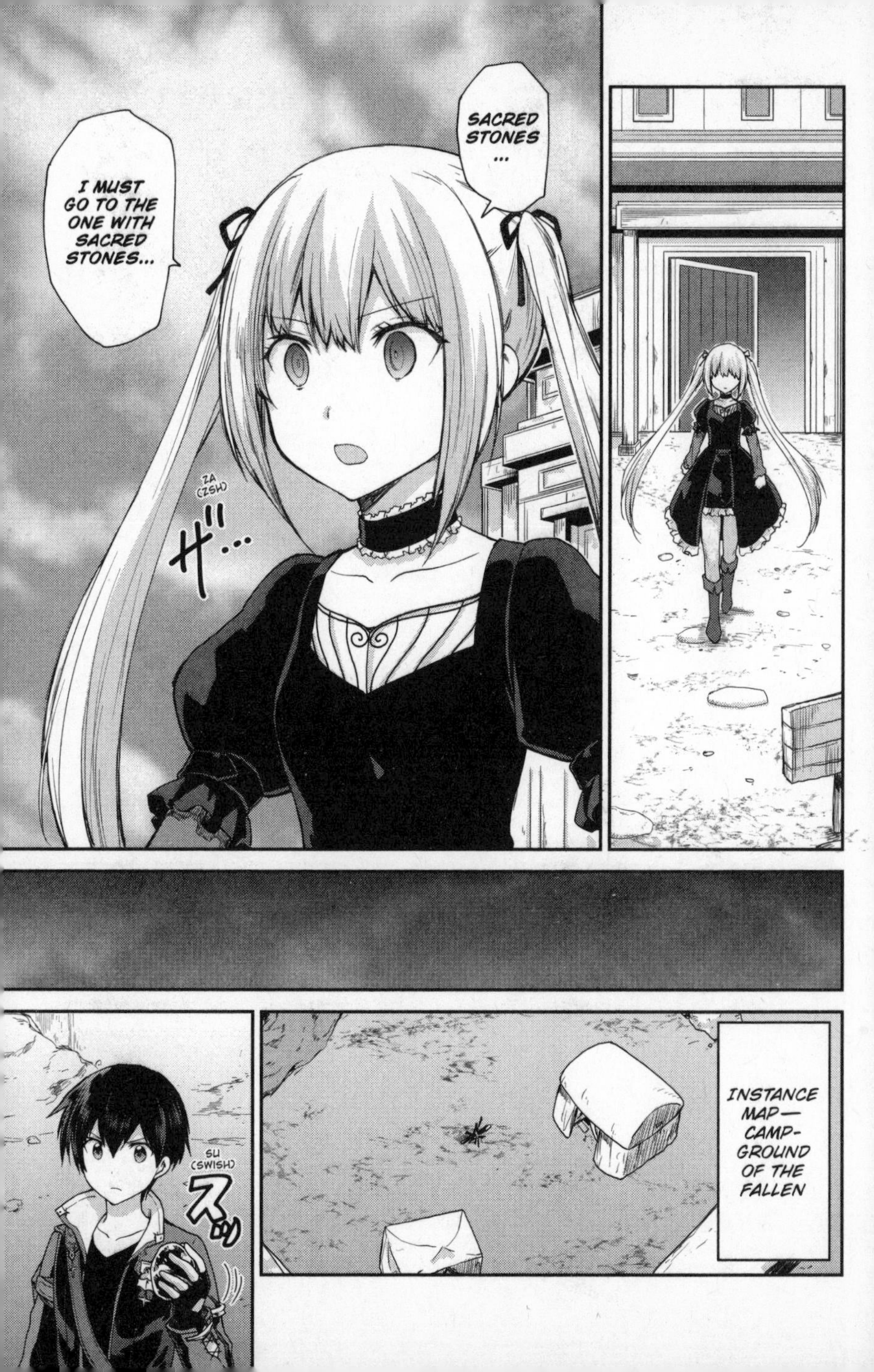
SACRED STONES...
I MUST GO TO THE ONE WITH SACRED STONES...
ZA (ZSH)
INSTANCE MAP—CAMPGROUND OF THE FALLEN
SU (SWISH)

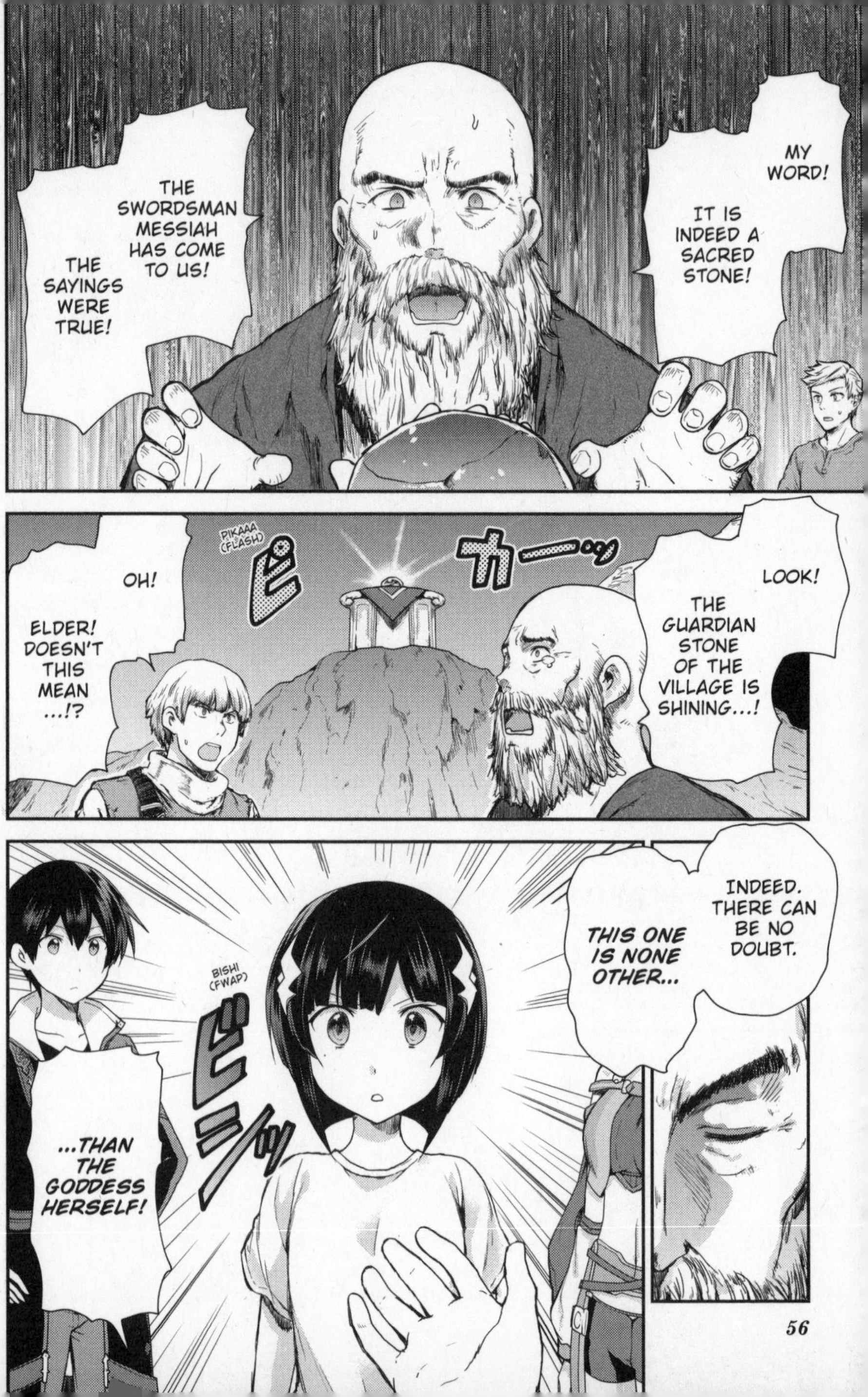
MY WORD!
IT IS INDEED A SACRED STONE!
THE SWORDSMAN MESSIAH HAS COME TO US!
THE SAYINGS WERE TRUE!
LOOK!
THE GUARDIAN STONE OF THE VILLAGE IS SHINING...!
PIKAAA (FLASH)
OH!
ELDER! DOESN'T THIS MEAN ...!?
INDEED. THERE CAN BE NO DOUBT.
THIS ONE IS NONE OTHER...
BISHI (FWAP)
...THAN THE GODDESS HERSELF!

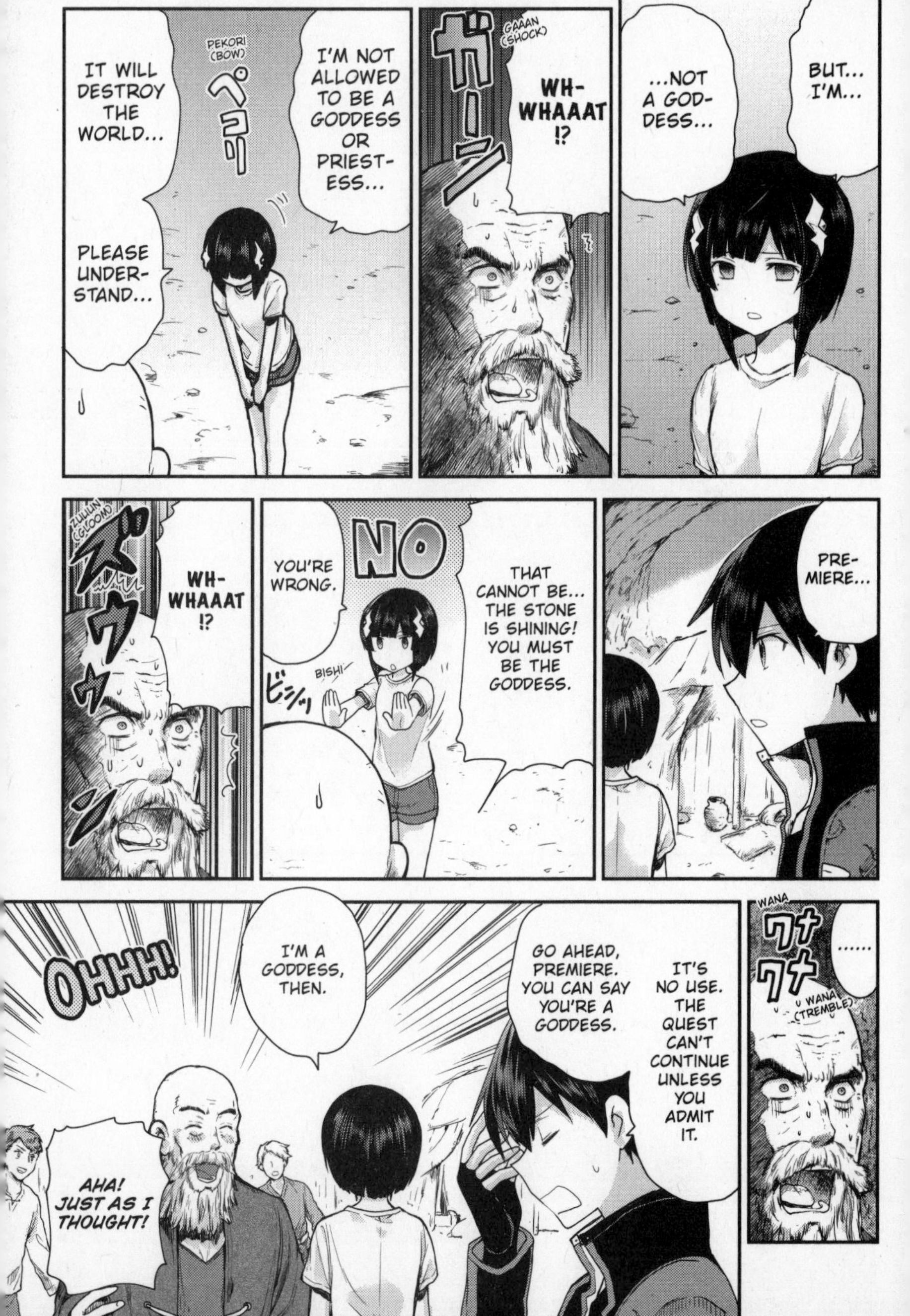

BUT... I'M...
...NOT A GOD-DESS...
GAAAN (SHOCK)
WH-WHAAAT !?
I'M NOT ALLOWED TO BE A GODDESS OR PRIEST-ESS...
PEKORI (BOW)
IT WILL DESTROY THE WORLD...
PLEASE UNDER-STAND...
PRE-MIERE...
THAT CANNOT BE... THE STONE IS SHINING! YOU MUST BE THE GODDESS.
NO
YOU'RE WRONG.
BISHI
ZULUN (GLOOM)
WH-WHAAAT !?
......
WANA
WANA (TREMBLE)
IT'S NO USE. THE QUEST CAN'T CONTINUE UNLESS YOU ADMIT IT.
GO AHEAD, PREMIERE. YOU CAN SAY YOU'RE A GODDESS.
I'M A GODDESS, THEN.
OHHHH!
AHA! JUST AS I THOUGHT!

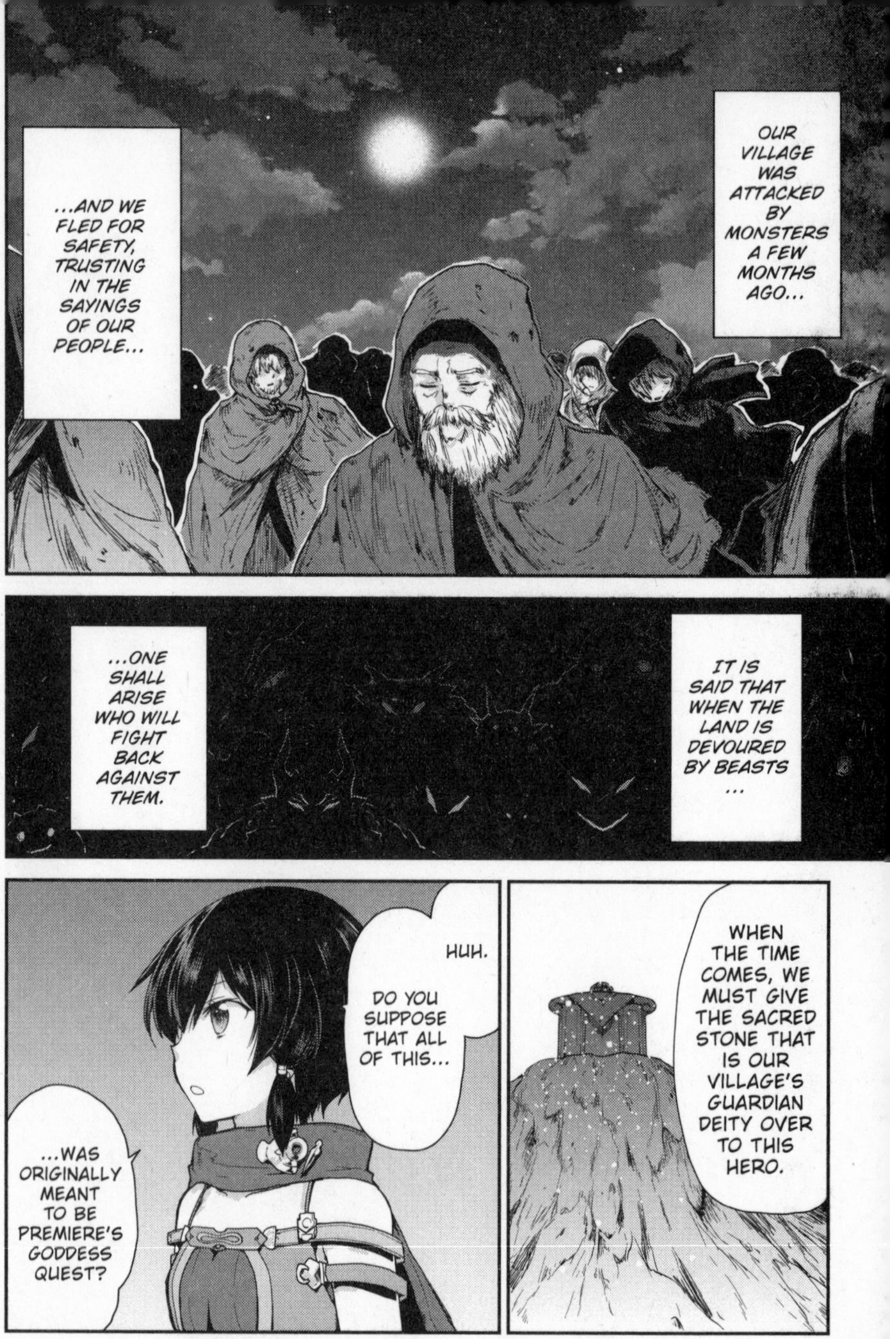
OUR VILLAGE WAS ATTACKED BY MONSTERS A FEW MONTHS AGO...
...AND WE FLED FOR SAFETY, TRUSTING IN THE SAYINGS OF OUR PEOPLE...
IT IS SAID THAT WHEN THE LAND IS DEVOURED BY BEASTS...
...ONE SHALL ARISE WHO WILL FIGHT BACK AGAINST THEM.
WHEN THE TIME COMES, WE MUST GIVE THE SACRED STONE THAT IS OUR VILLAGE'S GUARDIAN DEITY OVER TO THIS HERO.
HUH.
DO YOU SUPPOSE THAT ALL OF THIS...
...WAS ORIGINALLY MEANT TO BE PREMIERE'S GODDESS QUEST?

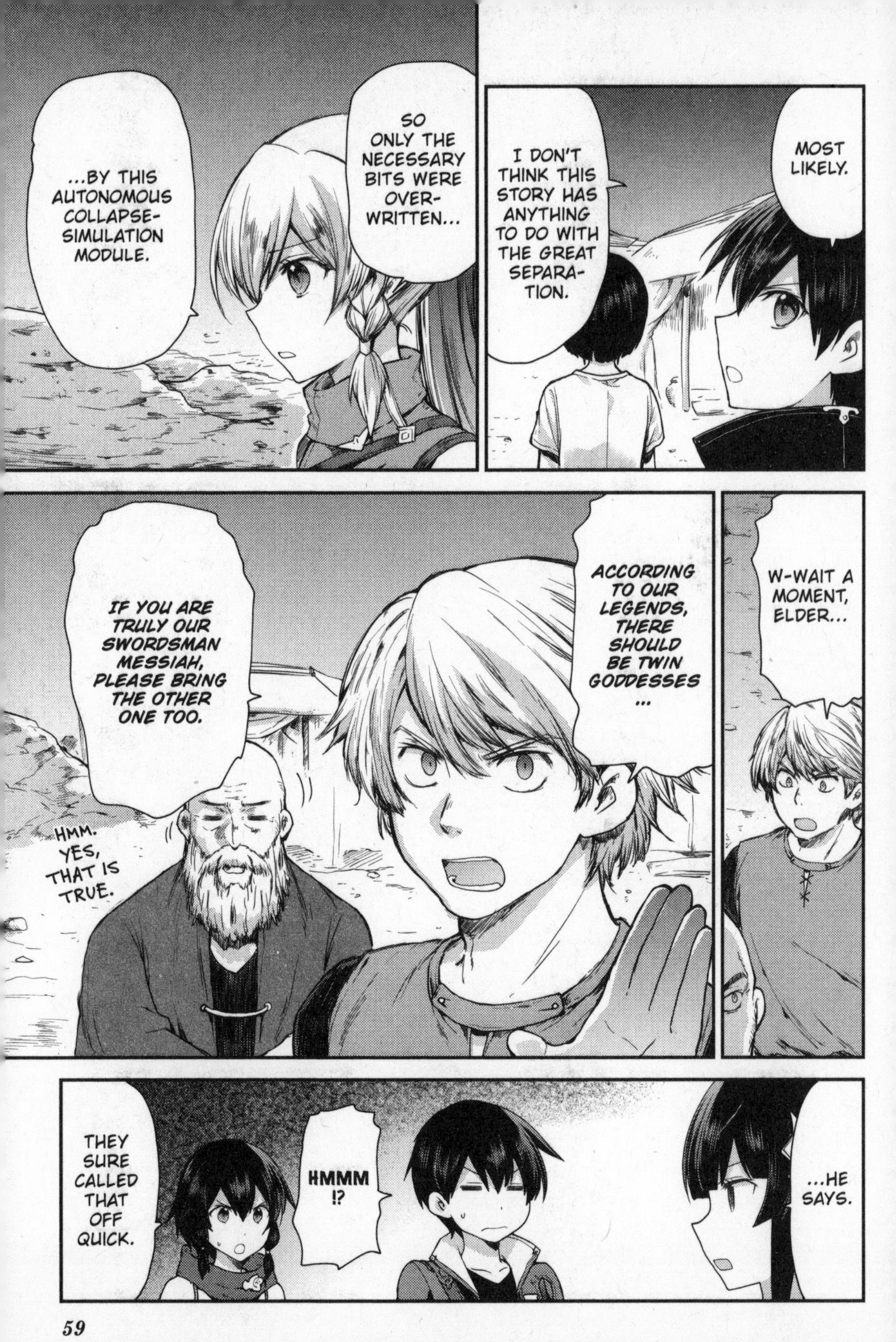
MOST LIKELY.
I DON'T THINK THIS STORY HAS ANYTHING TO DO WITH THE GREAT SEPARA-TION.
SO ONLY THE NECESSARY BITS WERE OVER-WRITTEN...
...BY THIS AUTONOMOUS COLLAPSE-SIMULATION MODULE.
W-WAIT A MOMENT, ELDER...
ACCORDING TO OUR LEGENDS, THERE SHOULD BE TWIN GODDESSES...
IF YOU ARE TRULY OUR SWORDSMAN MESSIAH, PLEASE BRING THE OTHER ONE TOO.
HMM. YES, THAT IS TRUE.
...HE SAYS.
HMMM !?
THEY SURE CALLED THAT OFF QUICK.

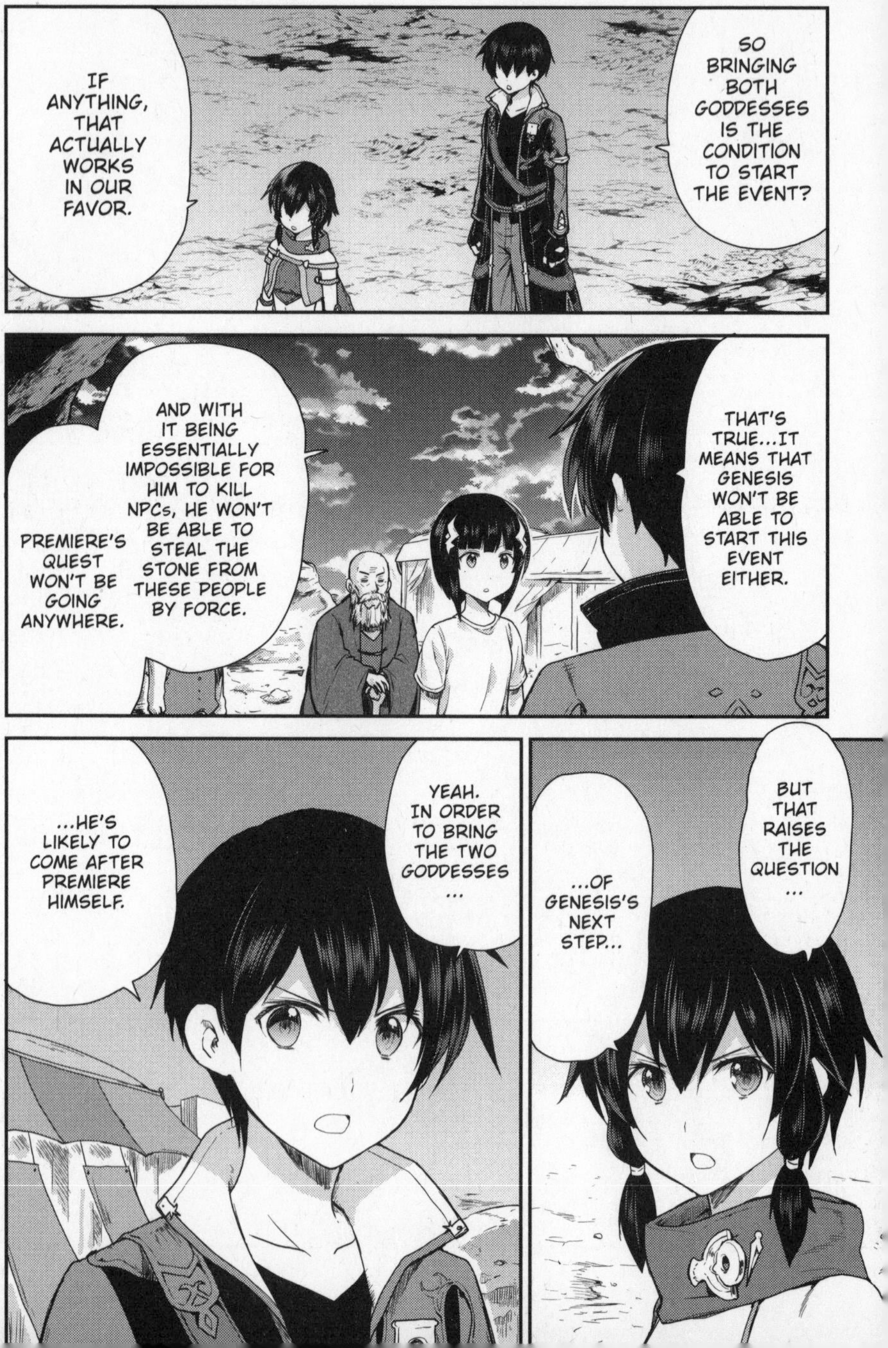
SO BRINGING BOTH GODDESSES IS THE CONDITION TO START THE EVENT?
IF ANYTHING, THAT ACTUALLY WORKS IN OUR FAVOR.
THAT'S TRUE...IT MEANS THAT GENESIS WON'T BE ABLE TO START THIS EVENT EITHER.
AND WITH IT BEING ESSENTIALLY IMPOSSIBLE FOR HIM TO KILL NPCs, HE WON'T BE ABLE TO STEAL THE STONE FROM THESE PEOPLE BY FORCE.
PREMIERE'S QUEST WON'T BE GOING ANYWHERE.
BUT THAT RAISES THE QUESTION...
...OF GENESIS'S NEXT STEP...
YEAH. IN ORDER TO BRING THE TWO GODDESSES...
...HE'S LIKELY TO COME AFTER PREMIERE HIMSELF.

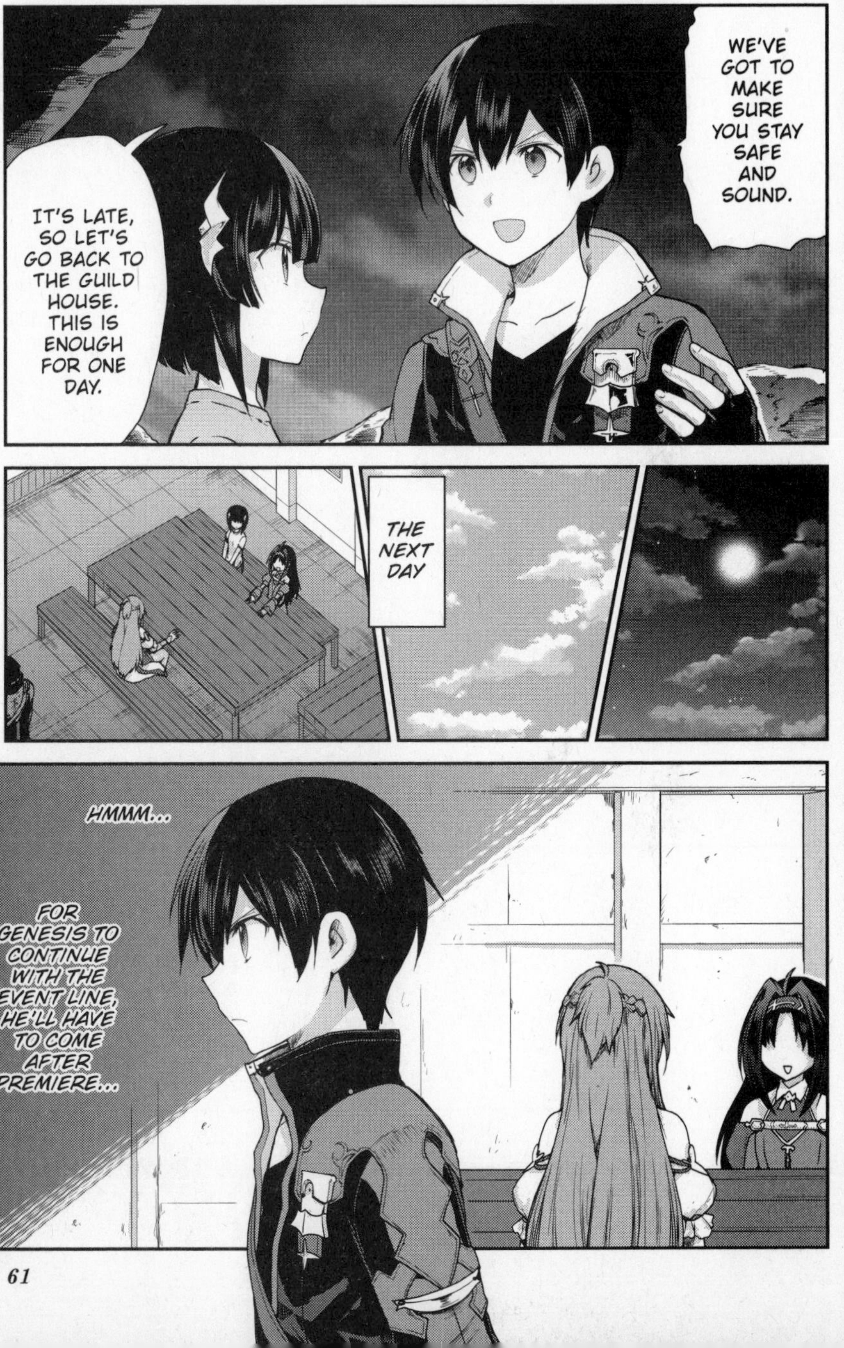
WE'VE GOT TO MAKE SURE YOU STAY SAFE AND SOUND.
IT'S LATE, SO LET'S GO BACK TO THE GUILD HOUSE. THIS IS ENOUGH FOR ONE DAY.
THE NEXT DAY
HMMM...
FOR GENESIS TO CONTINUE WITH THE EVENT LINE, HE'LL HAVE TO COME AFTER PREMIERE...

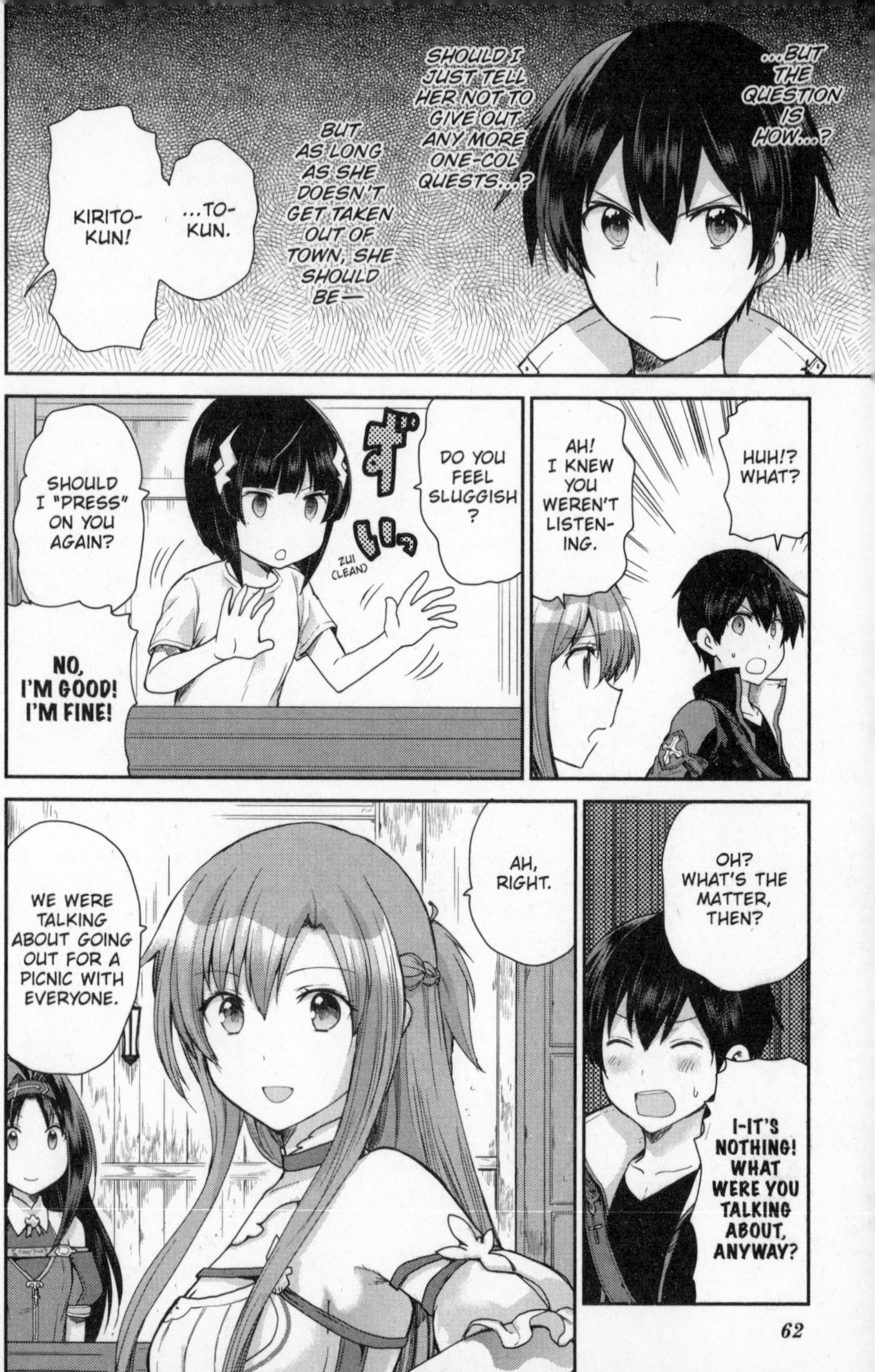
...BUT THE QUESTION IS HOW...?
SHOULD I JUST TELL HER NOT TO GIVE OUT ANY MORE ONE-COL QUESTS...?
BUT AS LONG AS SHE DOESN'T GET TAKEN OUT OF TOWN, SHE SHOULD BE—
...TO-KUN.
KIRITO-KUN!
HUH!? WHAT?
AH! I KNEW YOU WEREN'T LISTEN-ING.
DO YOU FEEL SLUGGISH?
ZUI (CLEAN)
SHOULD I "PRESS" ON YOU AGAIN?
NO, I'M GOOD! I'M FINE!
OH? WHAT'S THE MATTER, THEN?
I-IT'S NOTHING! WHAT WERE YOU TALKING ABOUT, ANYWAY?
AH, RIGHT.
WE WERE TALKING ABOUT GOING OUT FOR A PICNIC WITH EVERYONE.

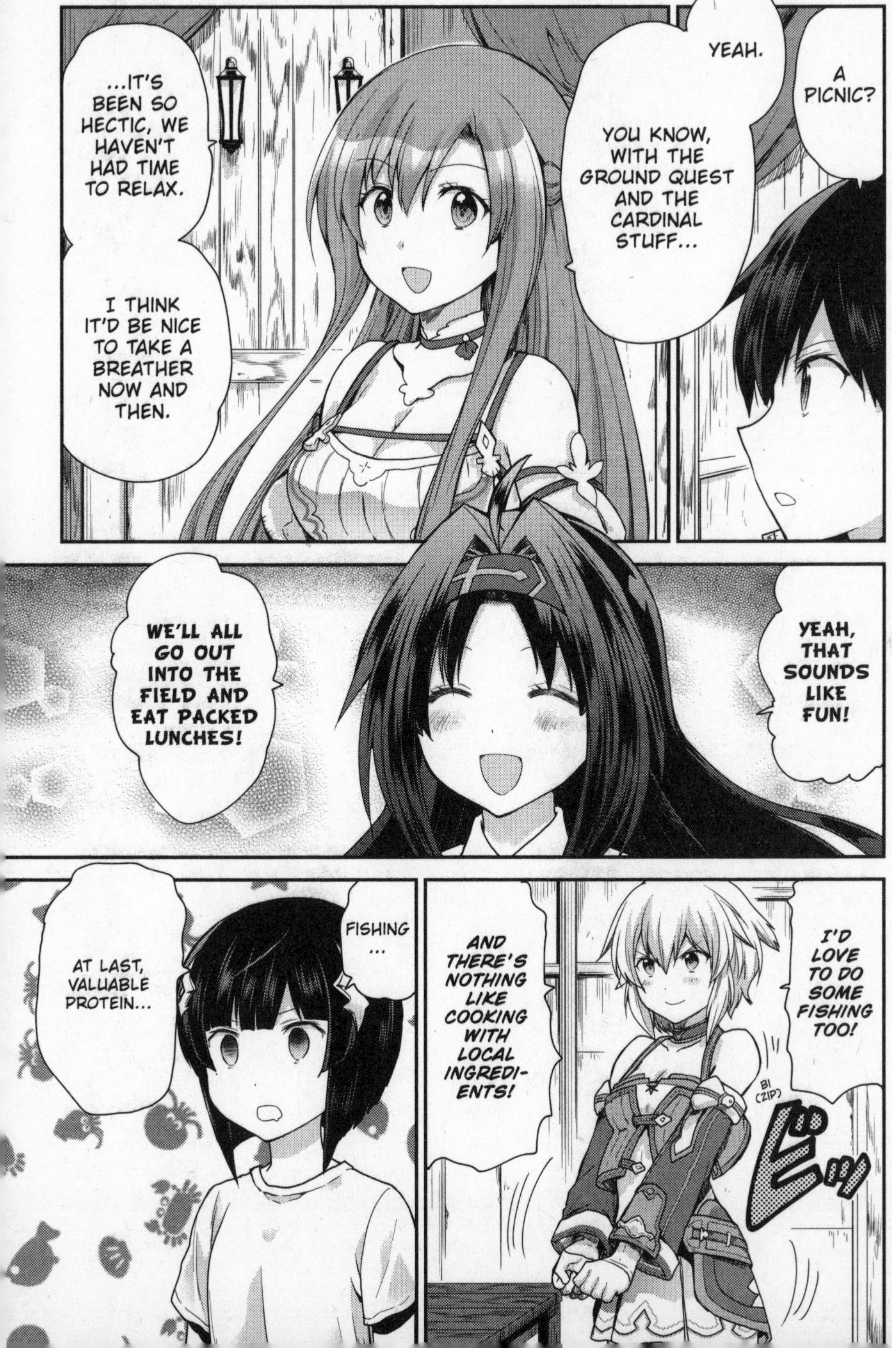
A PICNIC?
YEAH.
YOU KNOW, WITH THE GROUND QUEST AND THE CARDINAL STUFF...
...IT'S BEEN SO HECTIC, WE HAVEN'T HAD TIME TO RELAX.
I THINK IT'D BE NICE TO TAKE A BREATHER NOW AND THEN.
YEAH, THAT SOUNDS LIKE FUN!
WE'LL ALL GO OUT INTO THE FIELD AND EAT PACKED LUNCHES!
I'D LOVE TO DO SOME FISHING TOO!
BI (ZIP)
AND THERE'S NOTHING LIKE COOKING WITH LOCAL INGREDI-ENTS!
FISHING...
AT LAST, VALUABLE PROTEIN...

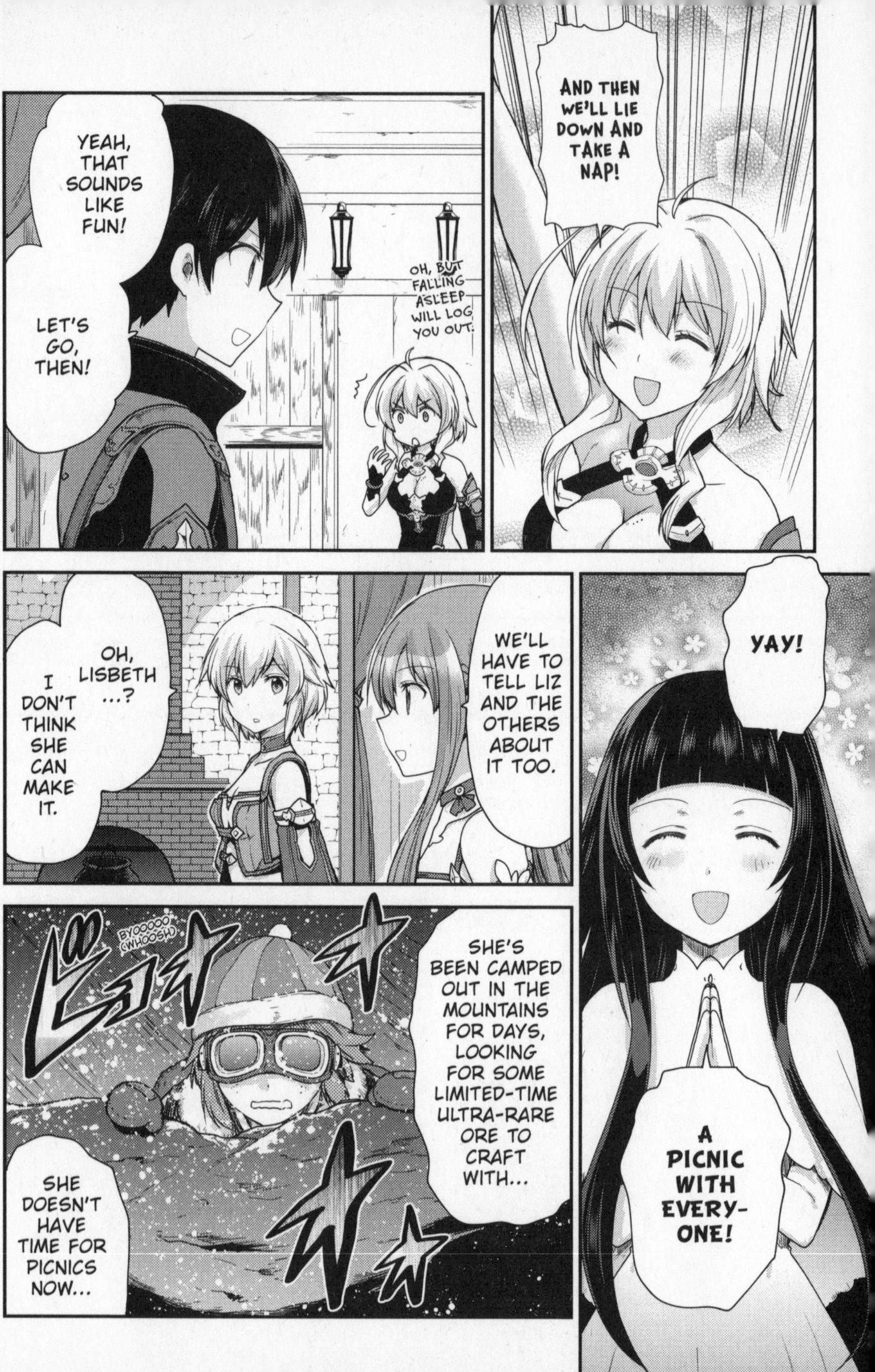
AND THEN WE'LL LIE DOWN AND TAKE A NAP!
YEAH, THAT SOUNDS LIKE FUN!
LET'S GO, THEN!
OH, BUT FALLING ASLEEP WILL LOG YOU OUT.
YAY!
A PICNIC WITH EVERY-ONE!
WE'LL HAVE TO TELL LIZ AND THE OTHERS ABOUT IT TOO.
OH, LISBETH...?
I DON'T THINK SHE CAN MAKE IT.
BYOOOOO (WHOOSH)
SHE'S BEEN CAMPED OUT IN THE MOUNTAINS FOR DAYS, LOOKING FOR SOME LIMITED-TIME ULTRA-RARE ORE TO CRAFT WITH...
SHE DOESN'T HAVE TIME FOR PICNICS NOW...

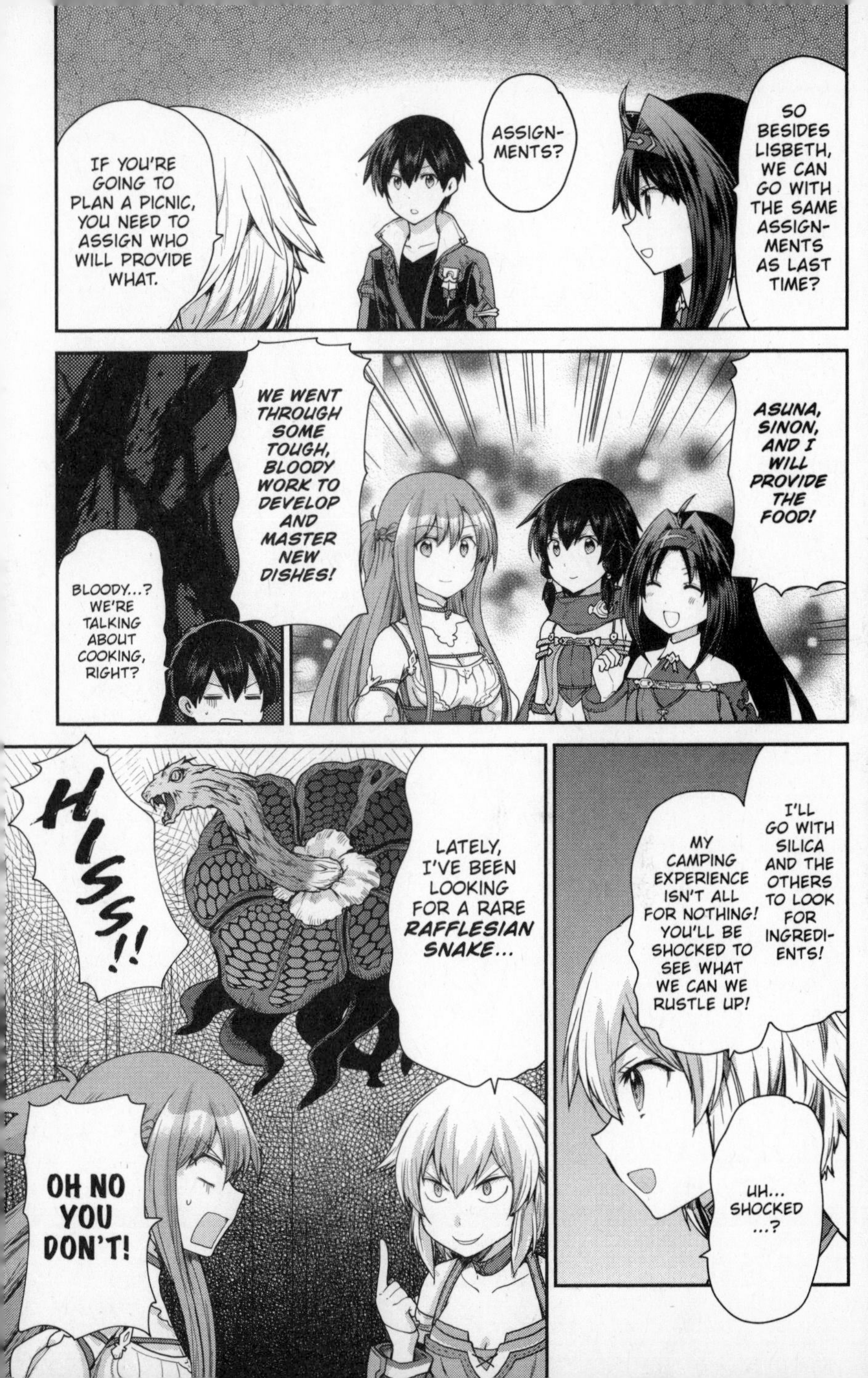
SO BESIDES LISBETH, WE CAN GO WITH THE SAME ASSIGNMENTS AS LAST TIME?
ASSIGNMENTS?
IF YOU'RE GOING TO PLAN A PICNIC, YOU NEED TO ASSIGN WHO WILL PROVIDE WHAT.
ASUNA, SINON, AND I WILL PROVIDE THE FOOD!
WE WENT THROUGH SOME TOUGH, BLOODY WORK TO DEVELOP AND MASTER NEW DISHES!
BLOODY...? WE'RE TALKING ABOUT COOKING, RIGHT?
I'LL GO WITH SILICA AND THE OTHERS TO LOOK FOR INGREDIENTS!
MY CAMPING EXPERIENCE ISN'T ALL FOR NOTHING! YOU'LL BE SHOCKED TO SEE WHAT WE CAN WE RUSTLE UP!
UH... SHOCKED ...?
LATELY, I'VE BEEN LOOKING FOR A RARE *RAFFLESIAN SNAKE...*
HISS!!
OH NO YOU DON'T!

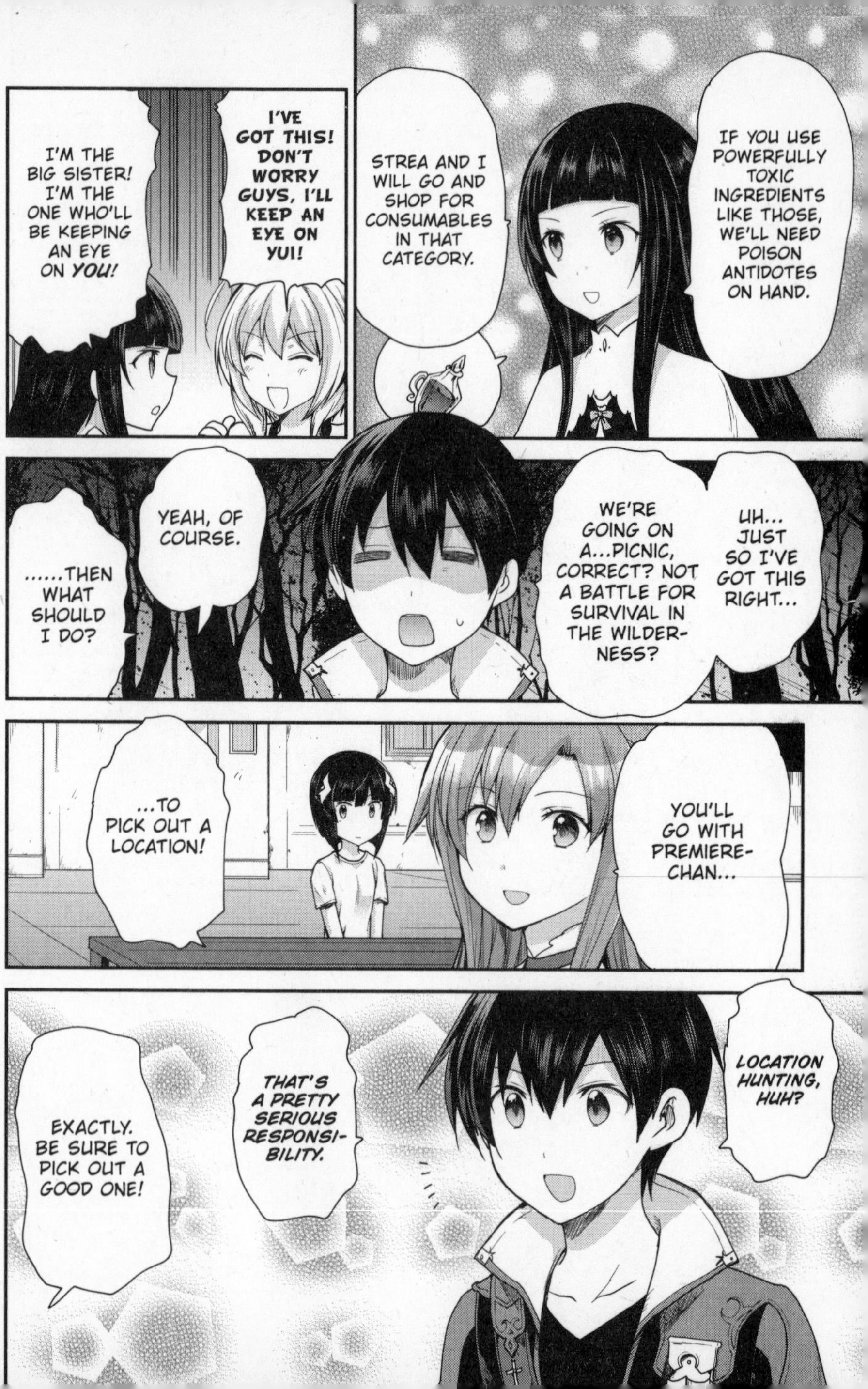
IF YOU USE POWERFULLY TOXIC INGREDIENTS LIKE THOSE, WE'LL NEED POISON ANTIDOTES ON HAND.
STREA AND I WILL GO AND SHOP FOR CONSUMABLES IN THAT CATEGORY.
I'VE GOT THIS! DON'T WORRY GUYS, I'LL KEEP AN EYE ON YUI!
I'M THE BIG SISTER! I'M THE ONE WHO'LL BE KEEPING AN EYE ON *YOU!*
UH... JUST SO I'VE GOT THIS RIGHT...
WE'RE GOING ON A...PICNIC, CORRECT? NOT A BATTLE FOR SURVIVAL IN THE WILDER-NESS?
YEAH, OF COURSE.
......THEN WHAT SHOULD I DO?
YOU'LL GO WITH PREMIERE-CHAN...
...TO PICK OUT A LOCATION!
LOCATION HUNTING, HUH?
THAT'S A PRETTY SERIOUS RESPONSI-BILITY.
EXACTLY. BE SURE TO PICK OUT A GOOD ONE!

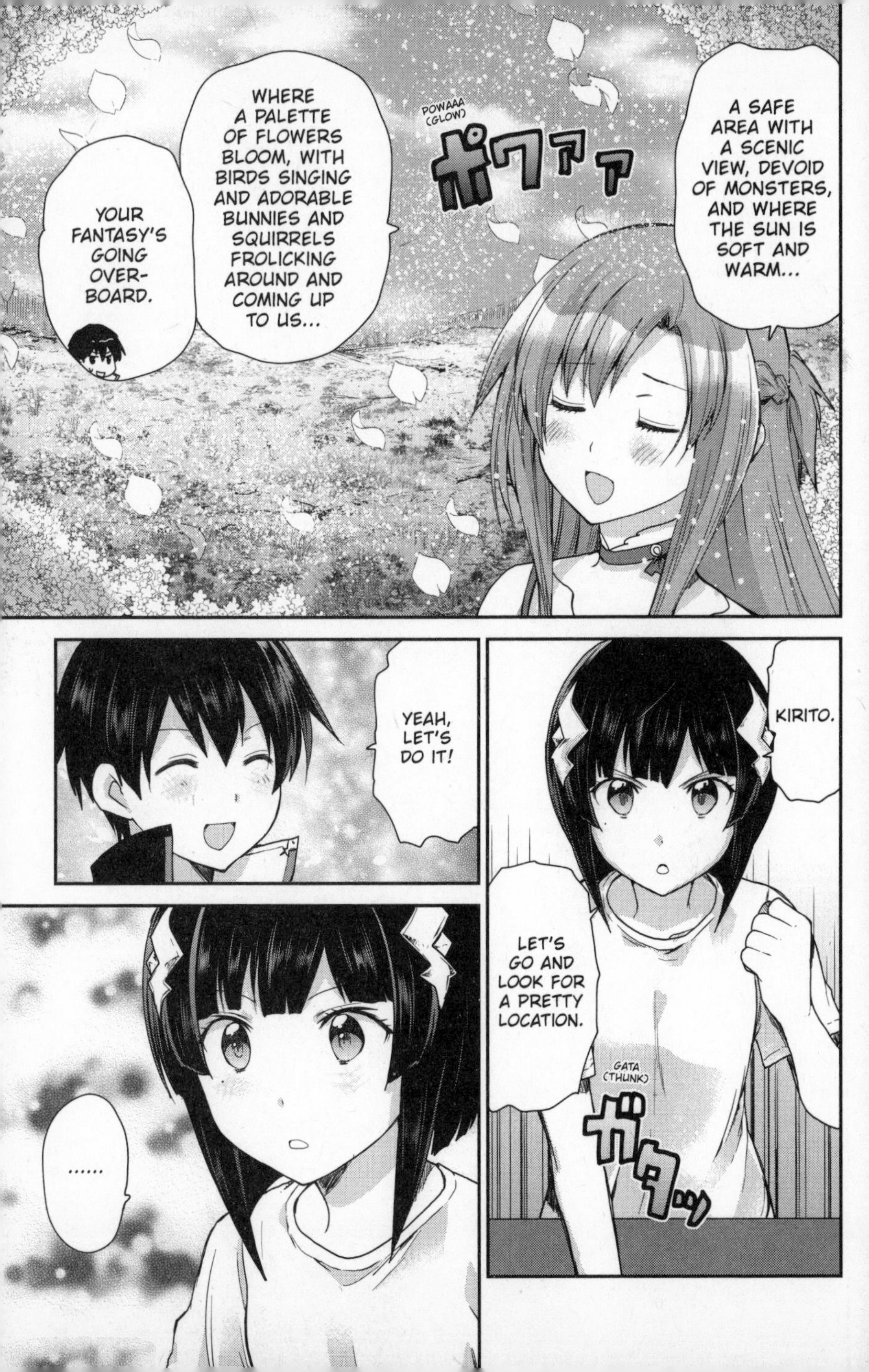
A SAFE AREA WITH A SCENIC VIEW, DEVOID OF MONSTERS, AND WHERE THE SUN IS SOFT AND WARM...
POWAAA (GLOW)
ポワァァ
WHERE A PALETTE OF FLOWERS BLOOM, WITH BIRDS SINGING AND ADORABLE BUNNIES AND SQUIRRELS FROLICKING AROUND AND COMING UP TO US...
YOUR FANTASY'S GOING OVER-BOARD.
KIRITO.
LET'S GO AND LOOK FOR A PRETTY LOCATION.
GATA (THUNK)
ガタッ
YEAH, LET'S DO IT!
......

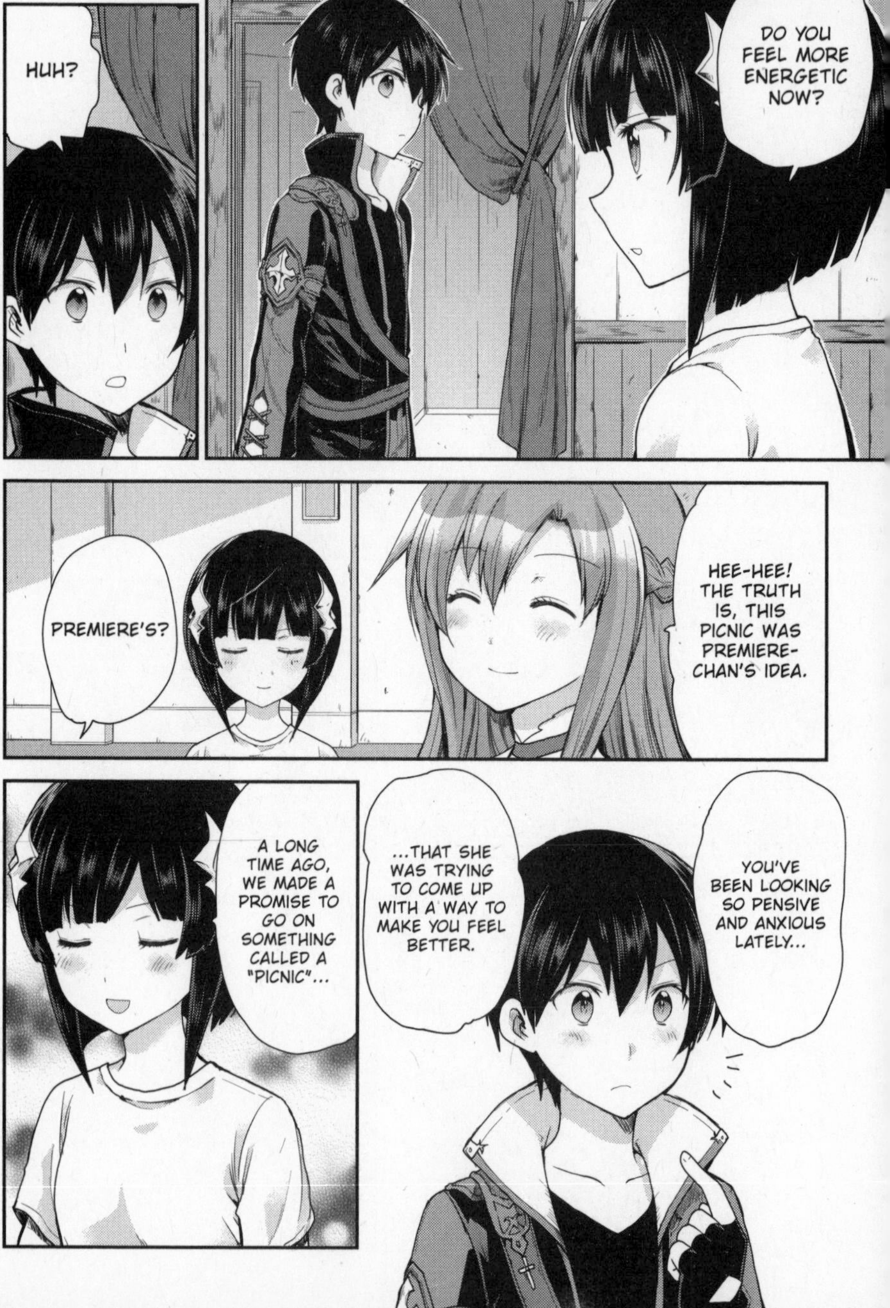
DO YOU FEEL MORE ENERGETIC NOW?
HUH?
HEE-HEE! THE TRUTH IS, THIS PICNIC WAS PREMIERE-CHAN'S IDEA.
PREMIERE'S?
YOU'VE BEEN LOOKING SO PENSIVE AND ANXIOUS LATELY...
...THAT SHE WAS TRYING TO COME UP WITH A WAY TO MAKE YOU FEEL BETTER.
A LONG TIME AGO, WE MADE A PROMISE TO GO ON SOMETHING CALLED A "PICNIC"...

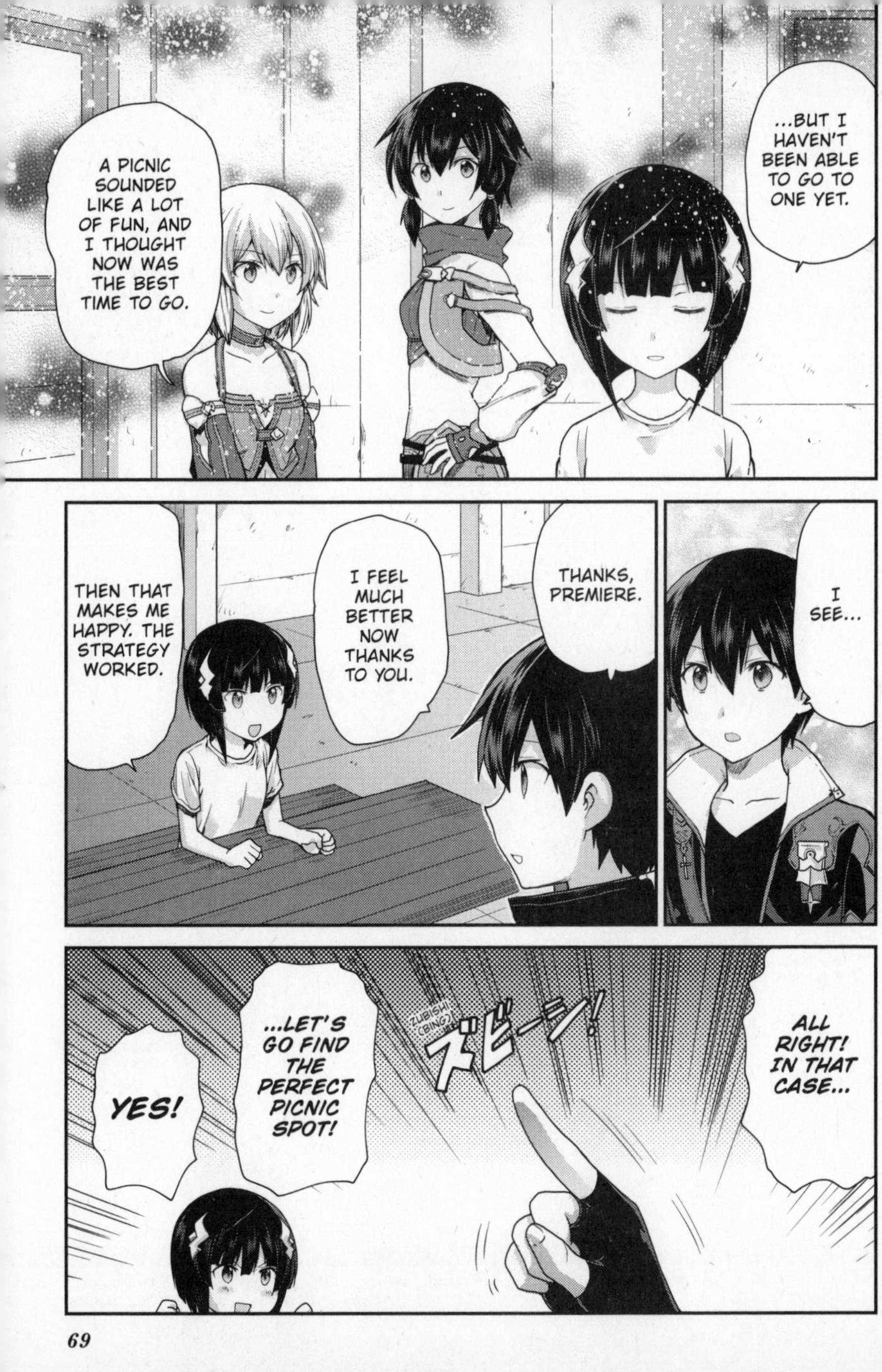
...BUT I HAVEN'T BEEN ABLE TO GO TO ONE YET.
A PICNIC SOUNDED LIKE A LOT OF FUN, AND I THOUGHT NOW WAS THE BEST TIME TO GO.
I SEE...
THANKS, PREMIERE.
I FEEL MUCH BETTER NOW THANKS TO YOU.
THEN THAT MAKES ME HAPPY. THE STRATEGY WORKED.
ALL RIGHT! IN THAT CASE...
ズビーーシ!
ZUBISHI (BING)
...LET'S GO FIND THE PERFECT PICNIC SPOT!
YES!

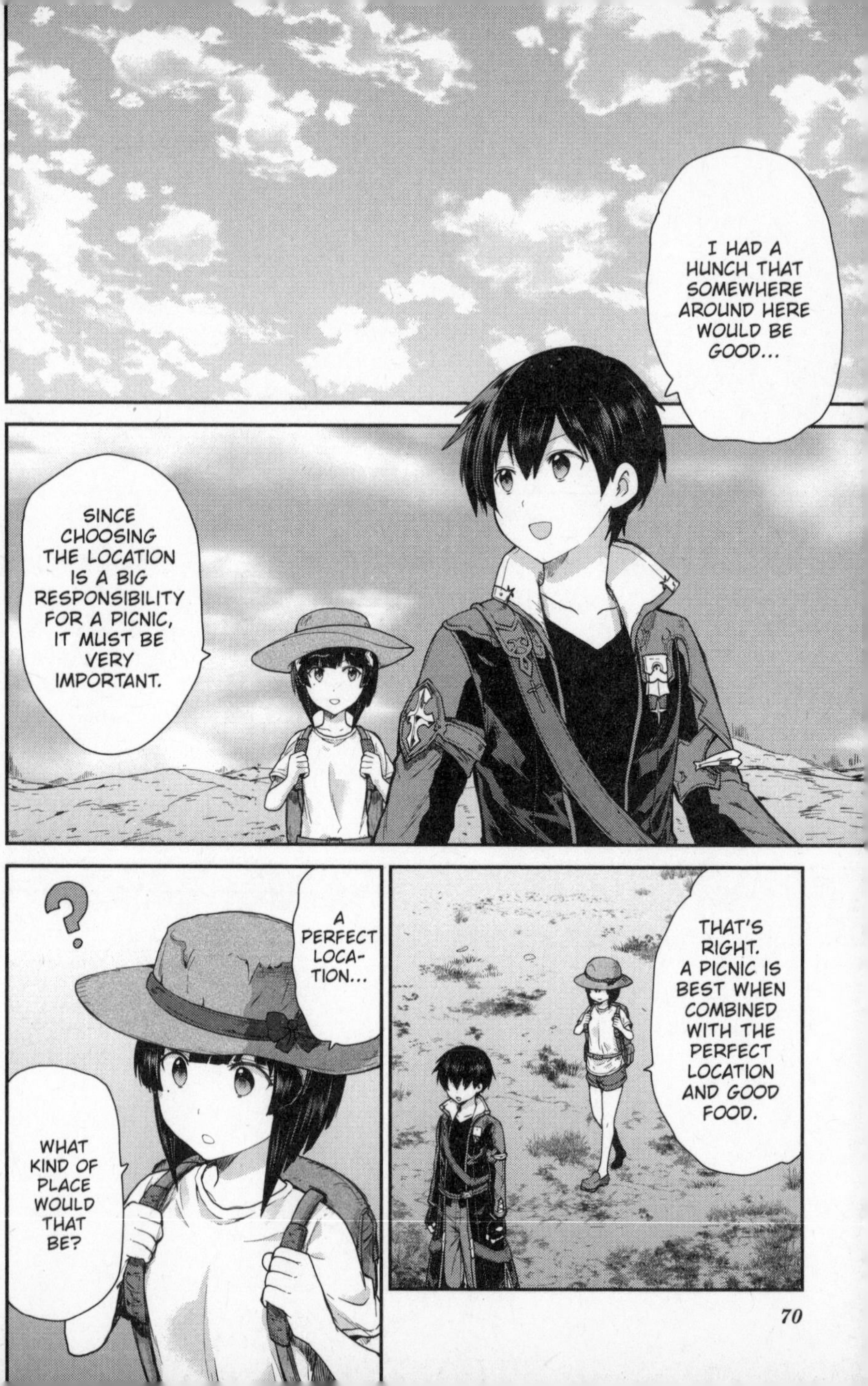
I HAD A HUNCH THAT SOMEWHERE AROUND HERE WOULD BE GOOD...
SINCE CHOOSING THE LOCATION IS A BIG RESPONSIBILITY FOR A PICNIC, IT MUST BE VERY IMPORTANT.
THAT'S RIGHT. A PICNIC IS BEST WHEN COMBINED WITH THE PERFECT LOCATION AND GOOD FOOD.
?
A PERFECT LOCA-TION...
WHAT KIND OF PLACE WOULD THAT BE?

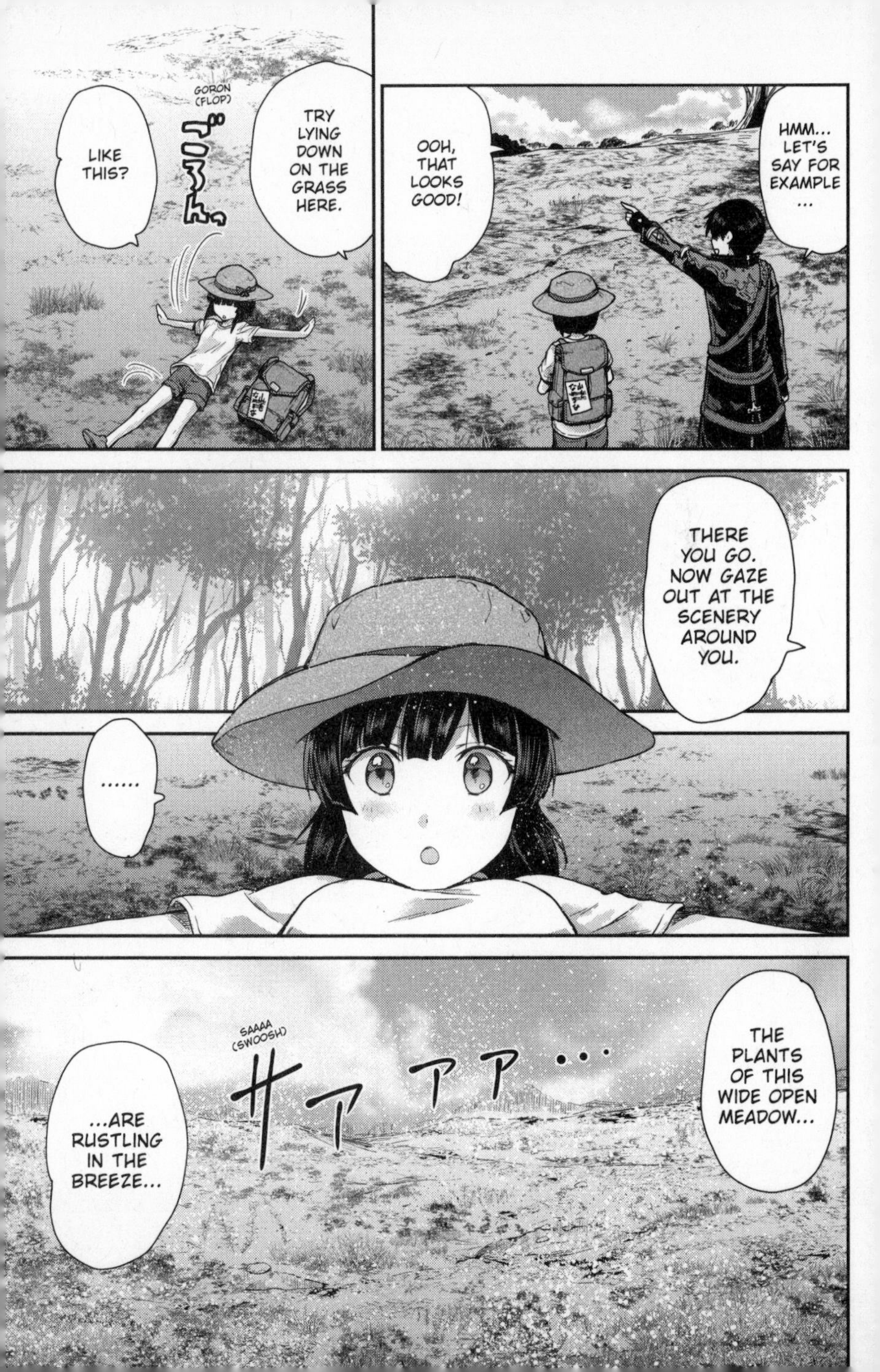
HMM... LET'S SAY FOR EXAMPLE ...
OOH, THAT LOOKS GOOD!
TRY LYING DOWN ON THE GRASS HERE.
GORON (FLOP)
LIKE THIS?
THERE YOU GO. NOW GAZE OUT AT THE SCENERY AROUND YOU.
......
THE PLANTS OF THIS WIDE OPEN MEADOW...
SAAAA (SWOOSH)
...ARE RUSTLING IN THE BREEZE...

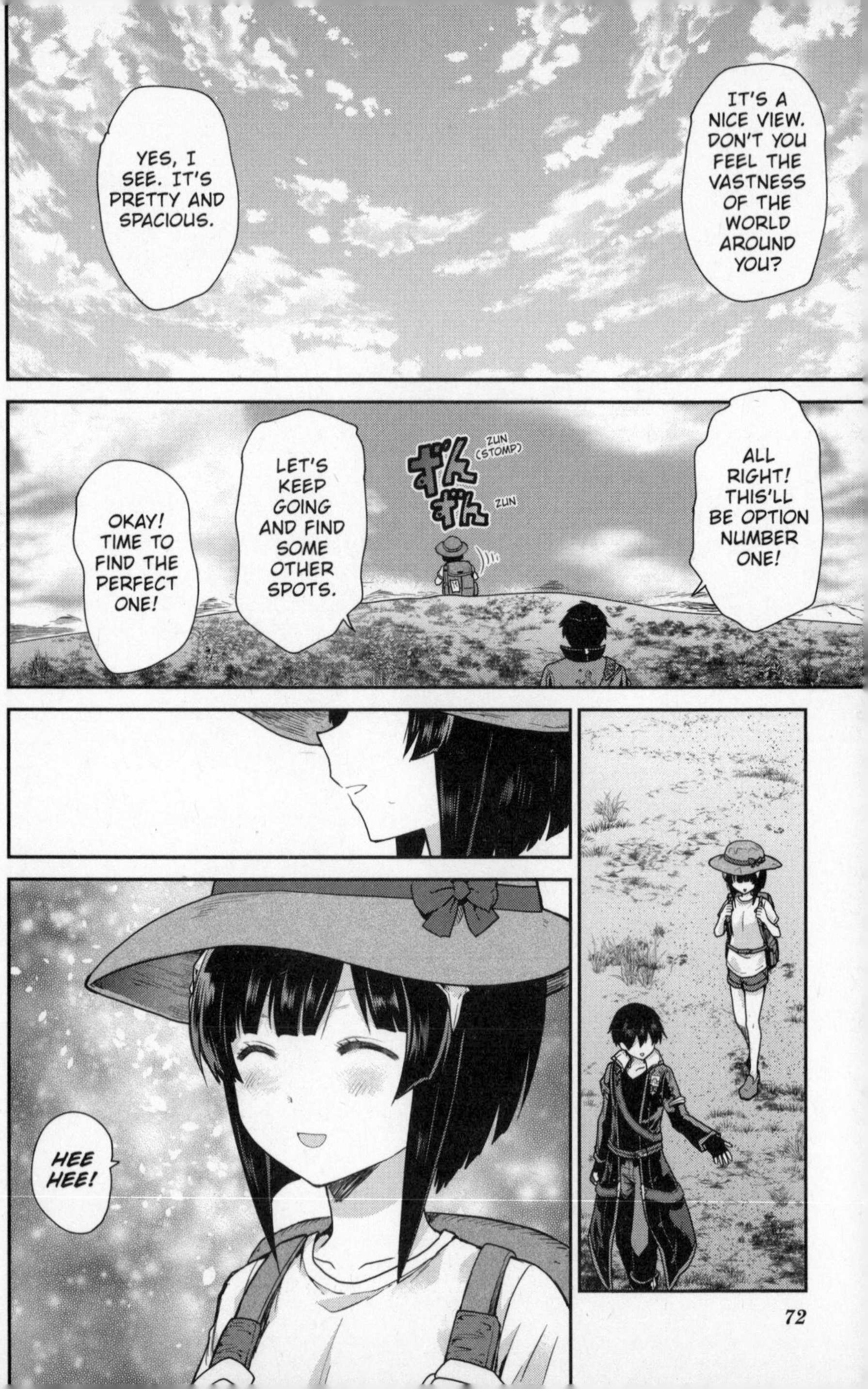
IT'S A NICE VIEW. DON'T YOU FEEL THE VASTNESS OF THE WORLD AROUND YOU?
YES, I SEE. IT'S PRETTY AND SPACIOUS.
ALL RIGHT! THIS'LL BE OPTION NUMBER ONE!
ずん ZUN (STOMP)
ずん ZUN
LET'S KEEP GOING AND FIND SOME OTHER SPOTS.
OKAY! TIME TO FIND THE PERFECT ONE!
HEE HEE!

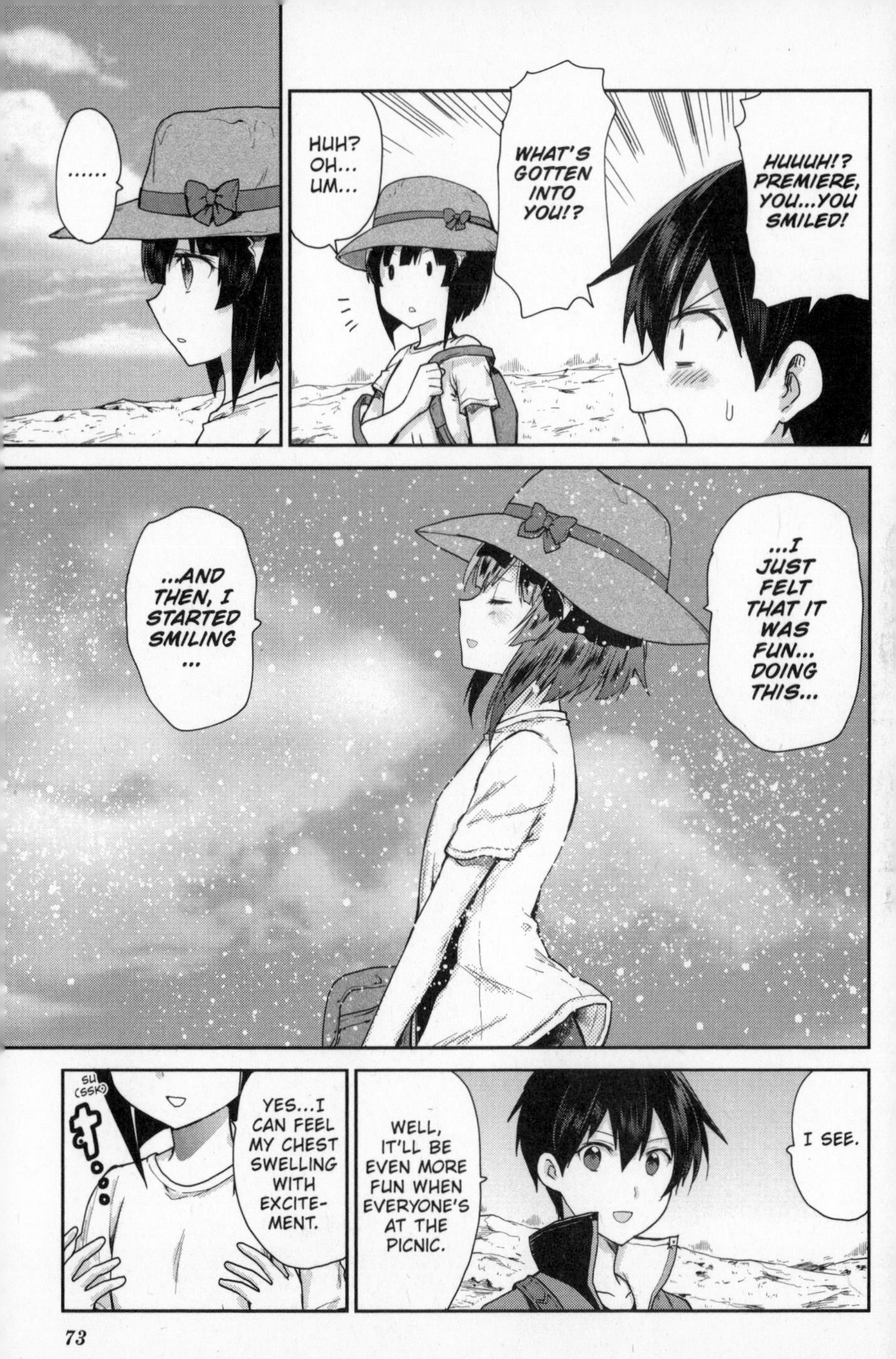
HUUUH!? PREMIERE, YOU...YOU SMILED!
WHAT'S GOTTEN INTO YOU!?
HUH? OH... UM...
......
...I JUST FELT THAT IT WAS FUN... DOING THIS...
...AND THEN, I STARTED SMILING ...
I SEE.
WELL, IT'LL BE EVEN MORE FUN WHEN EVERYONE'S AT THE PICNIC.
SU (SSK)
YES...I CAN FEEL MY CHEST SWELLING WITH EXCITE-MENT.

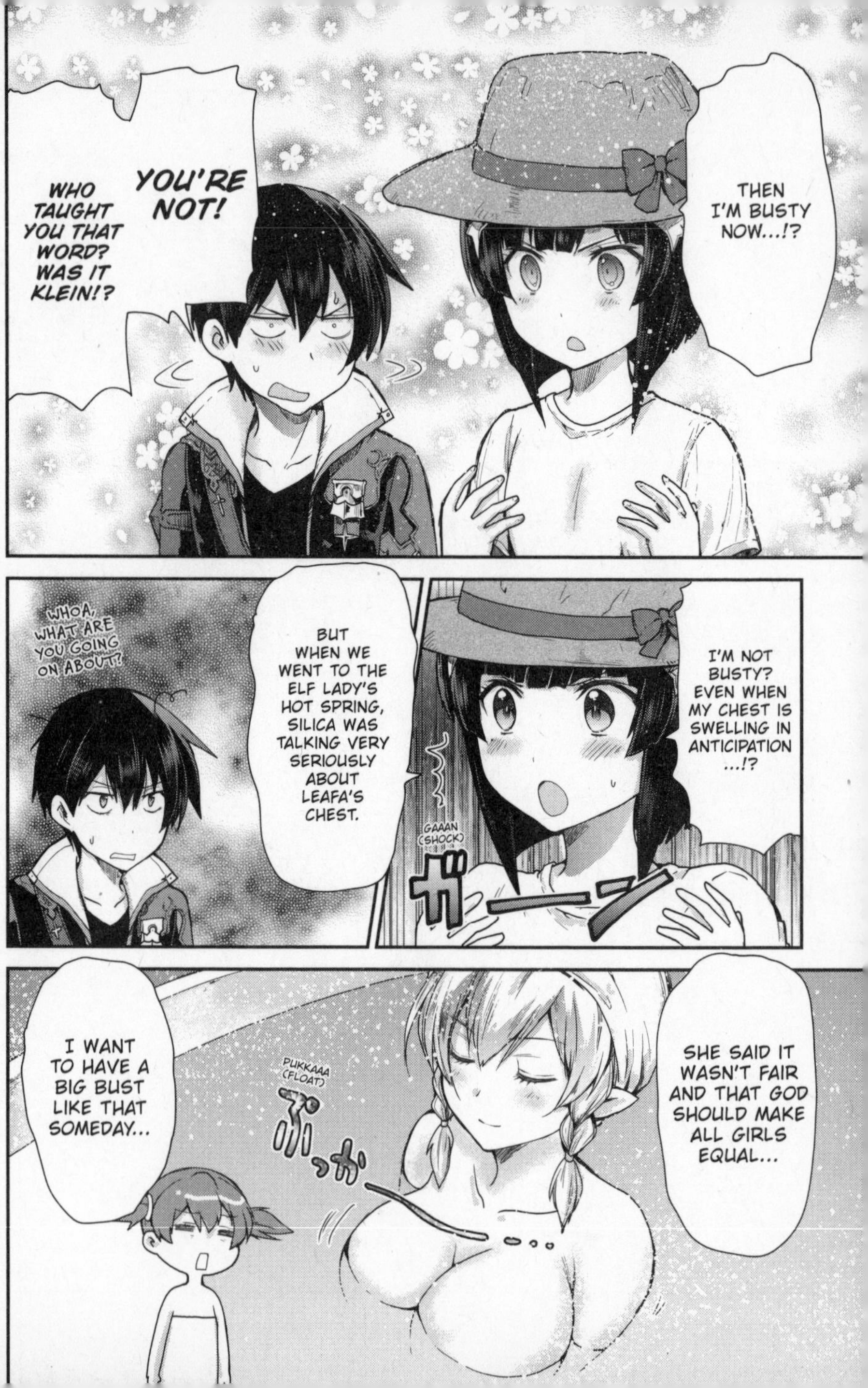
THEN I'M BUSTY NOW...!?
YOU'RE NOT!
WHO TAUGHT YOU THAT WORD? WAS IT KLEIN!?
I'M NOT BUSTY? EVEN WHEN MY CHEST IS SWELLING IN ANTICIPATION ...!?
GAAAN (SHOCK)
ガーン
BUT WHEN WE WENT TO THE ELF LADY'S HOT SPRING, SILICA WAS TALKING VERY SERIOUSLY ABOUT LEAFA'S CHEST.
WHOA, WHAT ARE YOU GOING ON ABOUT?
SHE SAID IT WASN'T FAIR AND THAT GOD SHOULD MAKE ALL GIRLS EQUAL...
PUKKAAA (FLOAT)
...
I WANT TO HAVE A BIG BUST LIKE THAT SOMEDAY...

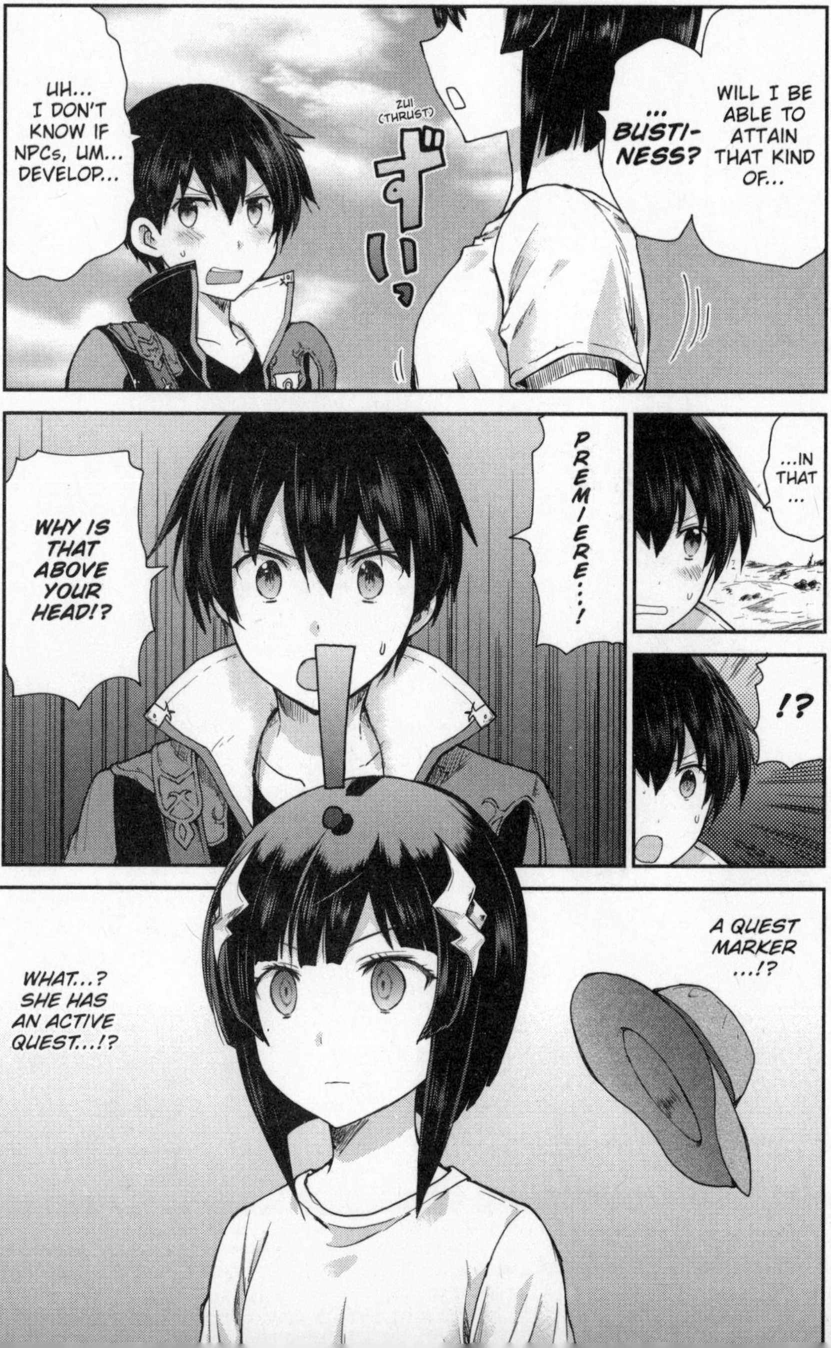
WILL I BE ABLE TO ATTAIN THAT KIND OF...
...BUSTI-NESS?
ZUI (THRUST)
UH... I DON'T KNOW IF NPCs, UM... DEVELOP...
...IN THAT ...
!?
PREMIERE...!
WHY IS THAT ABOVE YOUR HEAD!?
A QUEST MARKER ...!?
WHAT...? SHE HAS AN ACTIVE QUEST...!?

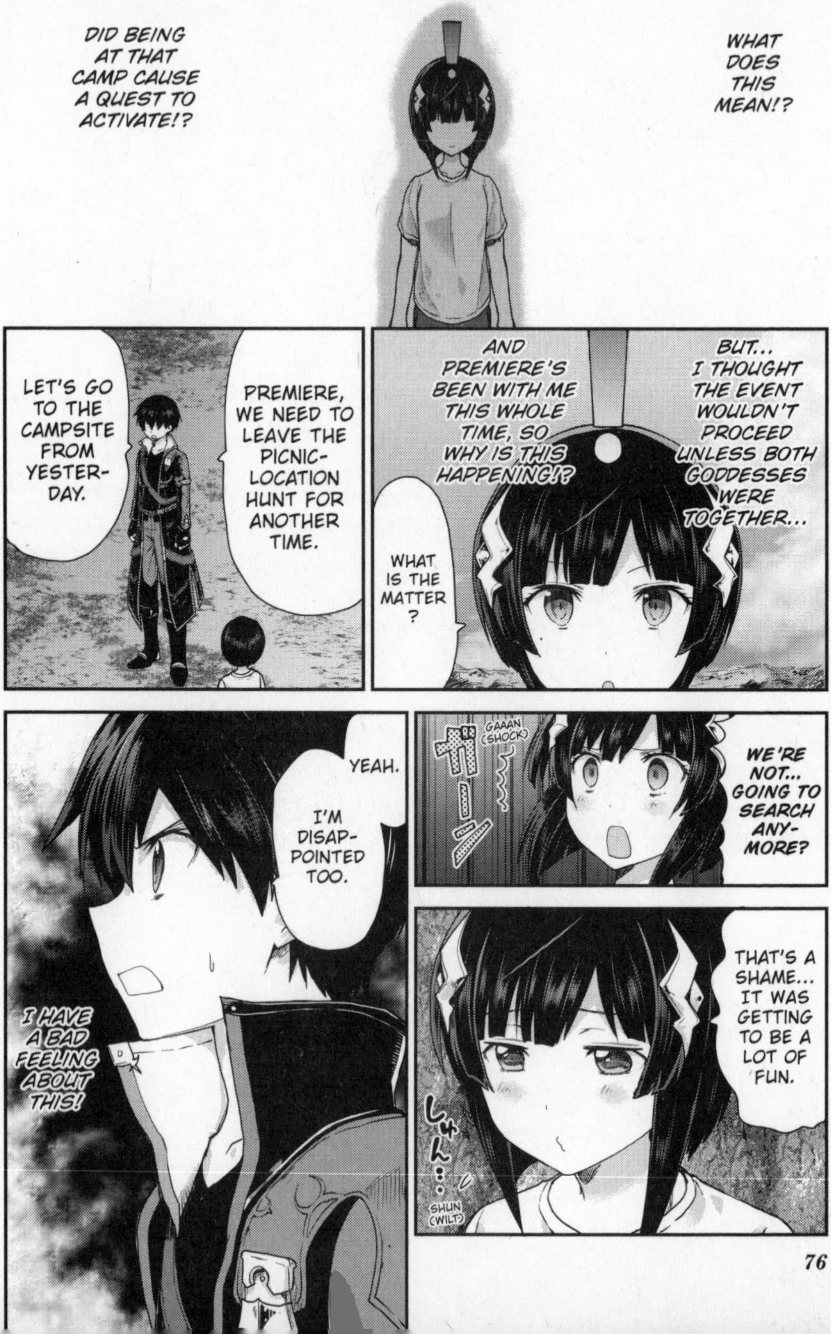
WHAT DOES THIS MEAN!?
DID BEING AT THAT CAMP CAUSE A QUEST TO ACTIVATE!?
BUT... I THOUGHT THE EVENT WOULDN'T PROCEED UNLESS BOTH GODDESSES WERE TOGETHER...
AND PREMIERE'S BEEN WITH ME THIS WHOLE TIME, SO WHY IS THIS HAPPENING!?
WHAT IS THE MATTER?
PREMIERE, WE NEED TO LEAVE THE PICNIC-LOCATION HUNT FOR ANOTHER TIME.
LET'S GO TO THE CAMPSITE FROM YESTERDAY.
GAAAN (SHOCK)
WE'RE NOT... GOING TO SEARCH ANYMORE?
THAT'S A SHAME... IT WAS GETTING TO BE A LOT OF FUN.
SHUN (WILT)
YEAH.
I'M DISAPPOINTED TOO.
I HAVE A BAD FEELING ABOUT THIS!

#24

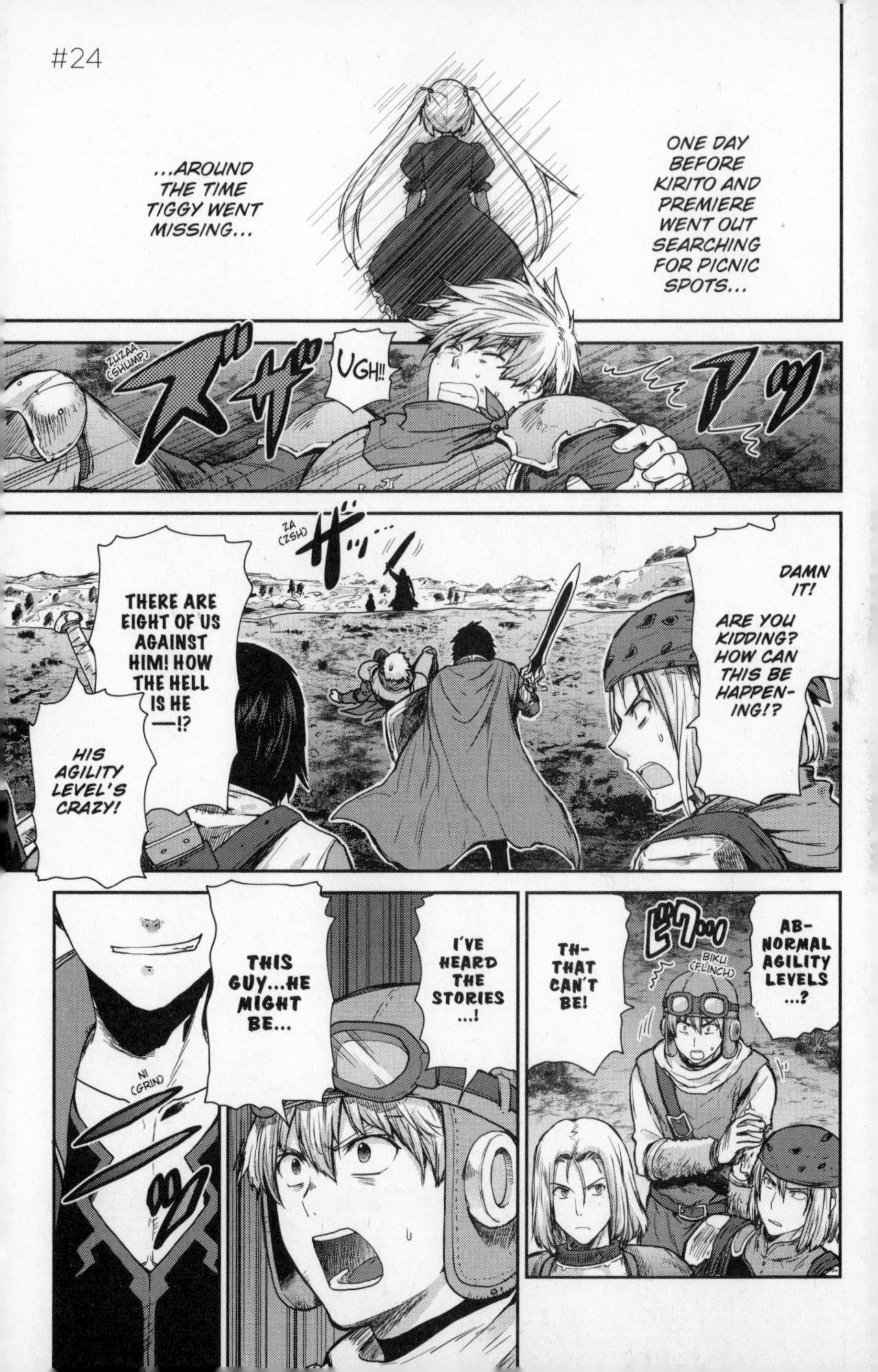
ONE DAY BEFORE KIRITO AND PREMIERE WENT OUT SEARCHING FOR PICNIC SPOTS…
…AROUND THE TIME TIGGY WENT MISSING…
UGH!!
ZUZAA (SHUMP)
DAMN IT!
ZA (ZSH)
ARE YOU KIDDING? HOW CAN THIS BE HAPPEN-ING!?
THERE ARE EIGHT OF US AGAINST HIM! HOW THE HELL IS HE —!?
HIS AGILITY LEVEL'S CRAZY!
AB-NORMAL AGILITY LEVELS …?
BIKU (FLINCH)
TH-THAT CAN'T BE!
I'VE HEARD THE STORIES …!
THIS GUY…HE MIGHT BE…
NI (GRIN)

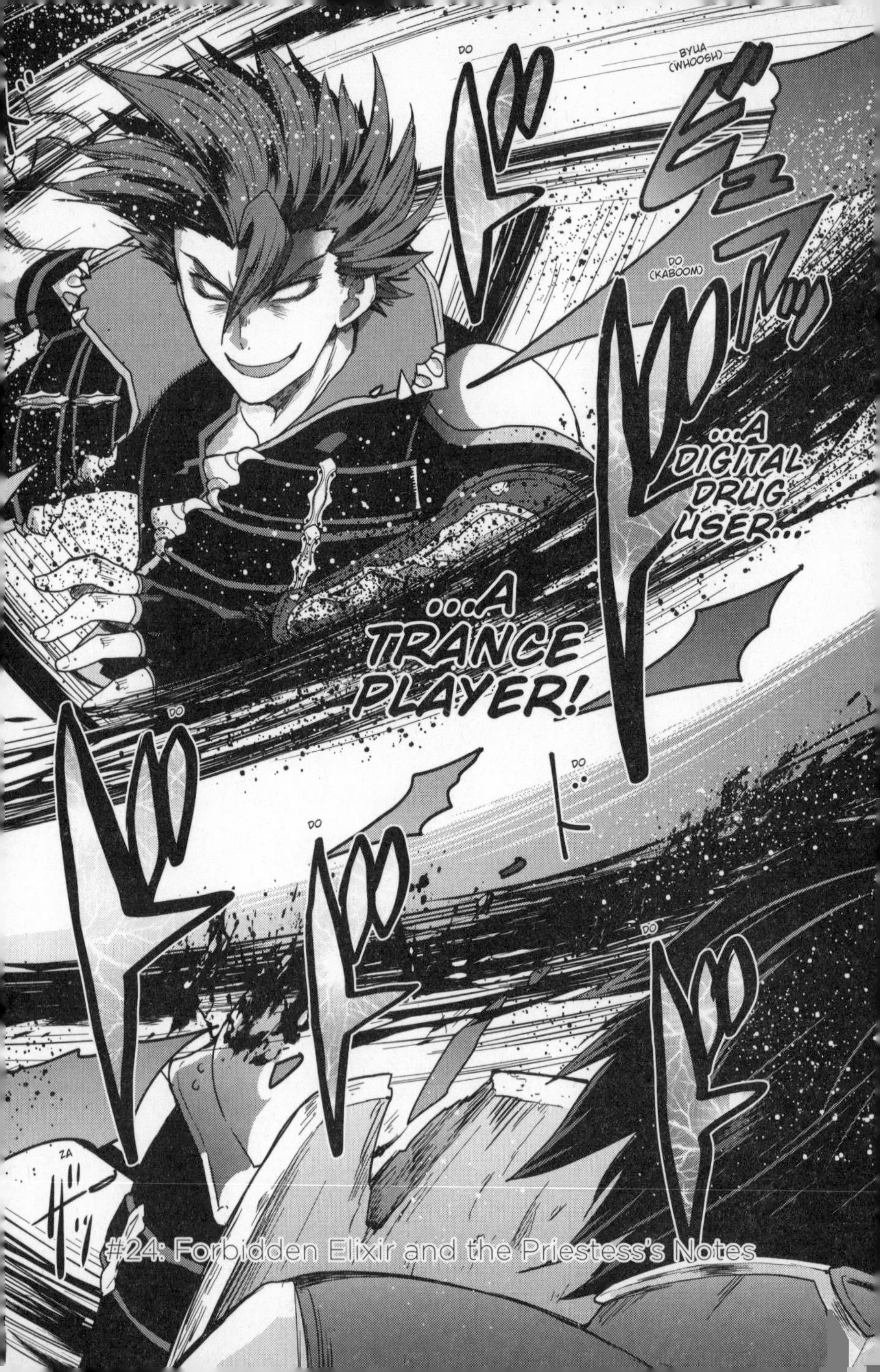
BYUA (WHOOSH)
DO
DO (KABOOM)
...A DIGITAL DRUG USER...
...A TRANCE PLAYER!
DO
DO
DO
DO
ZA

#24: Forbidden Elixir and the Priestess's Notes

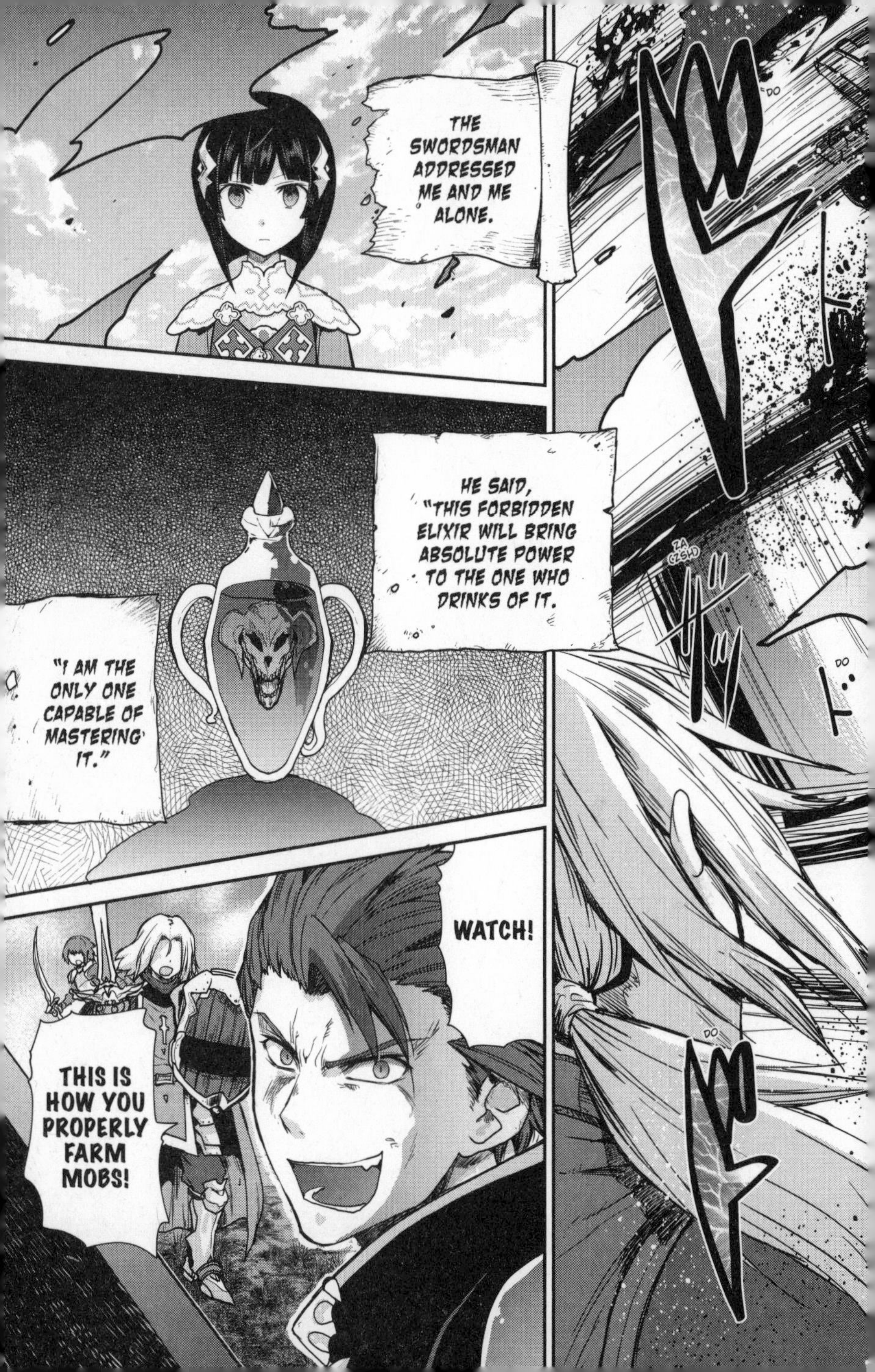
THE SWORDSMAN ADDRESSED ME AND ME ALONE.
HE SAID, "THIS FORBIDDEN ELIXIR WILL BRING ABSOLUTE POWER TO THE ONE WHO DRINKS OF IT.
"I AM THE ONLY ONE CAPABLE OF MASTERING IT."
WATCH!
THIS IS HOW YOU PROPERLY FARM MOBS!
DO
ZA (ZSH)
DO
DO

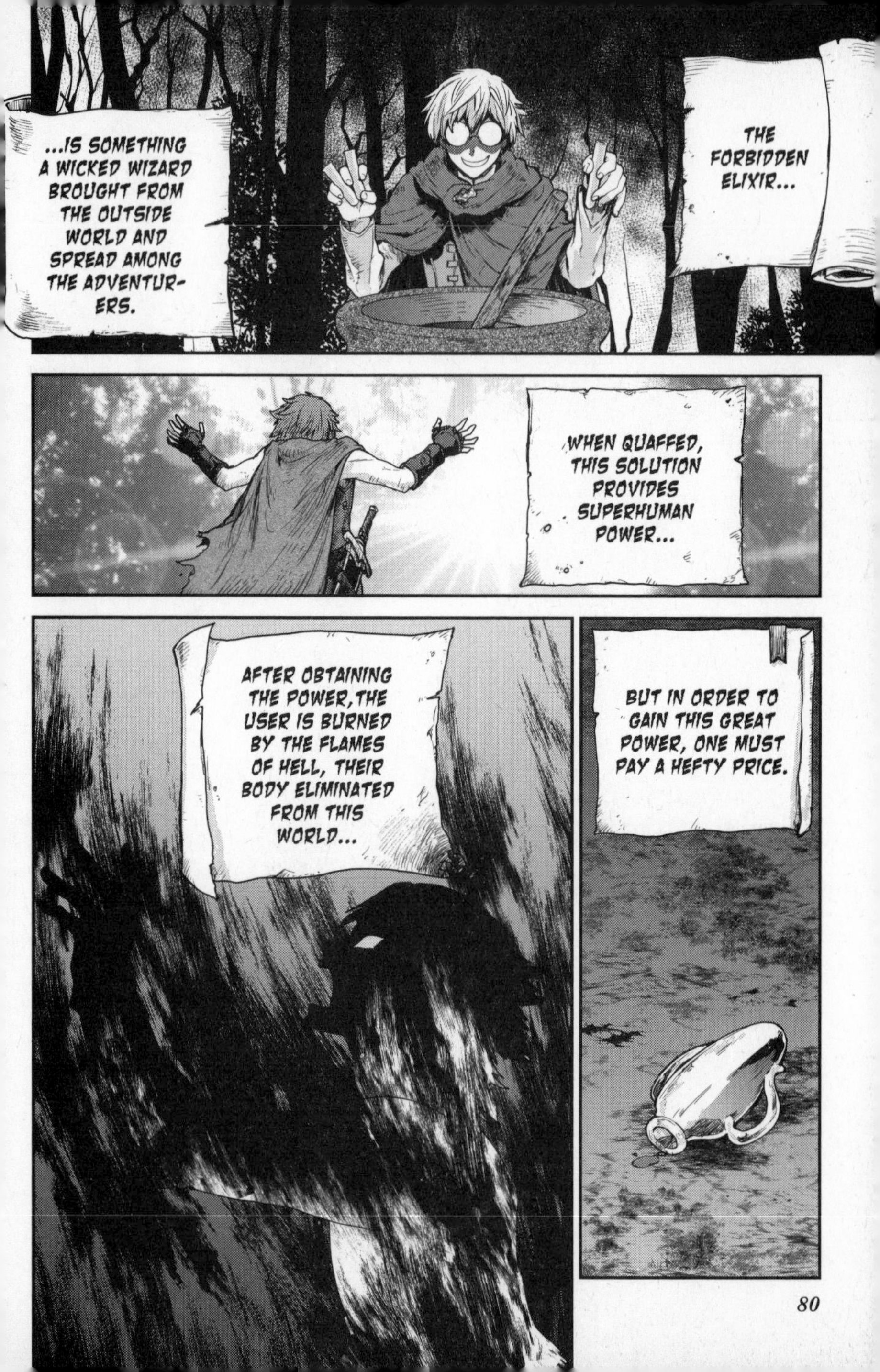
THE FORBIDDEN ELIXIR...
...IS SOMETHING A WICKED WIZARD BROUGHT FROM THE OUTSIDE WORLD AND SPREAD AMONG THE ADVENTUR-ERS.
WHEN QUAFFED, THIS SOLUTION PROVIDES SUPERHUMAN POWER...
BUT IN ORDER TO GAIN THIS GREAT POWER, ONE MUST PAY A HEFTY PRICE.
AFTER OBTAINING THE POWER, THE USER IS BURNED BY THE FLAMES OF HELL, THEIR BODY ELIMINATED FROM THIS WORLD...

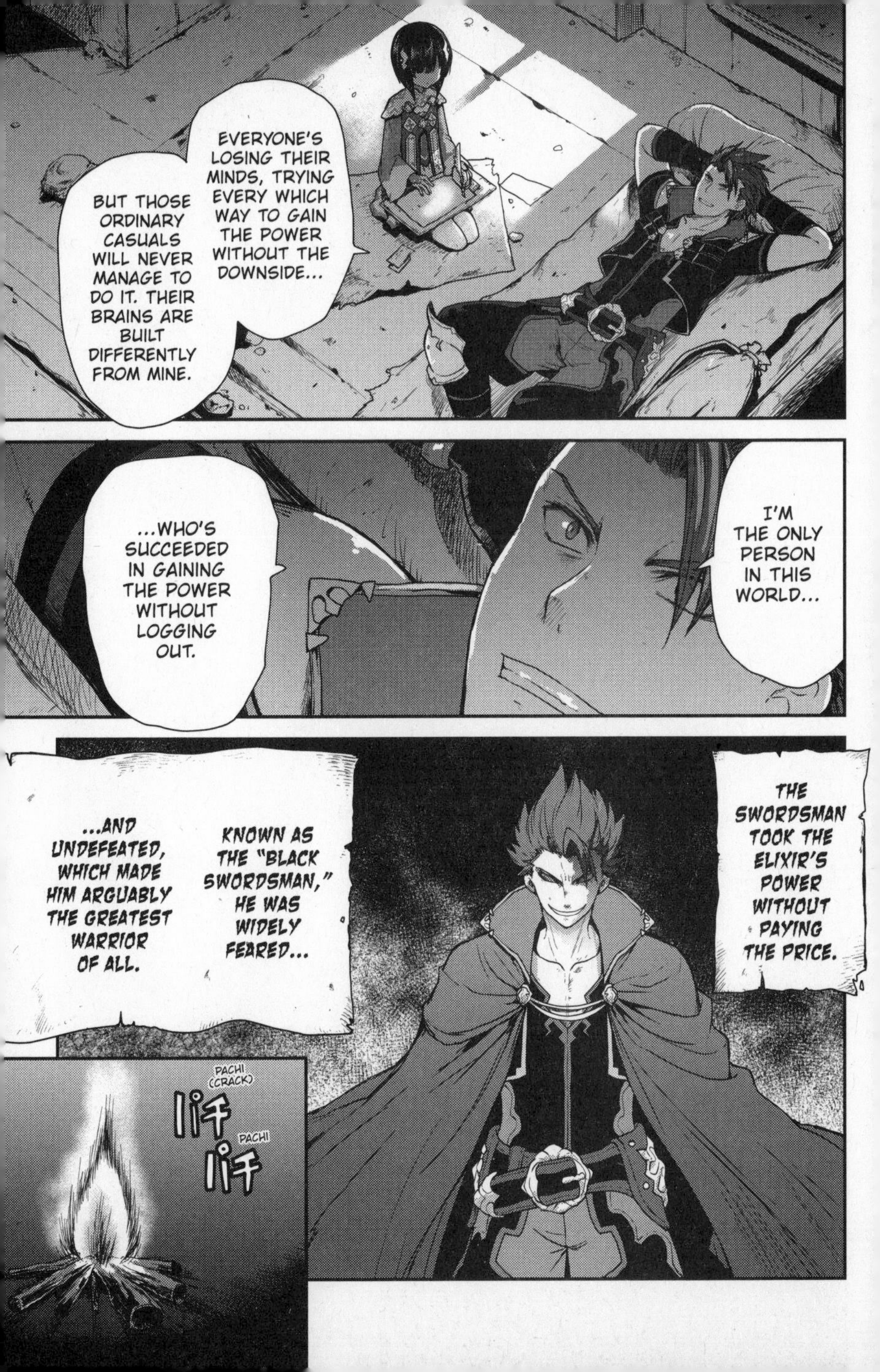
EVERYONE'S LOSING THEIR MINDS, TRYING EVERY WHICH WAY TO GAIN THE POWER WITHOUT THE DOWNSIDE...
BUT THOSE ORDINARY CASUALS WILL NEVER MANAGE TO DO IT. THEIR BRAINS ARE BUILT DIFFERENTLY FROM MINE.
I'M THE ONLY PERSON IN THIS WORLD...
...WHO'S SUCCEEDED IN GAINING THE POWER WITHOUT LOGGING OUT.
THE SWORDSMAN TOOK THE ELIXIR'S POWER WITHOUT PAYING THE PRICE.
KNOWN AS THE "BLACK SWORDSMAN," HE WAS WIDELY FEARED...
...AND UNDEFEATED, WHICH MADE HIM ARGUABLY THE GREATEST WARRIOR OF ALL.
PACHI (CRACK)
パチ
PACHI
パチ

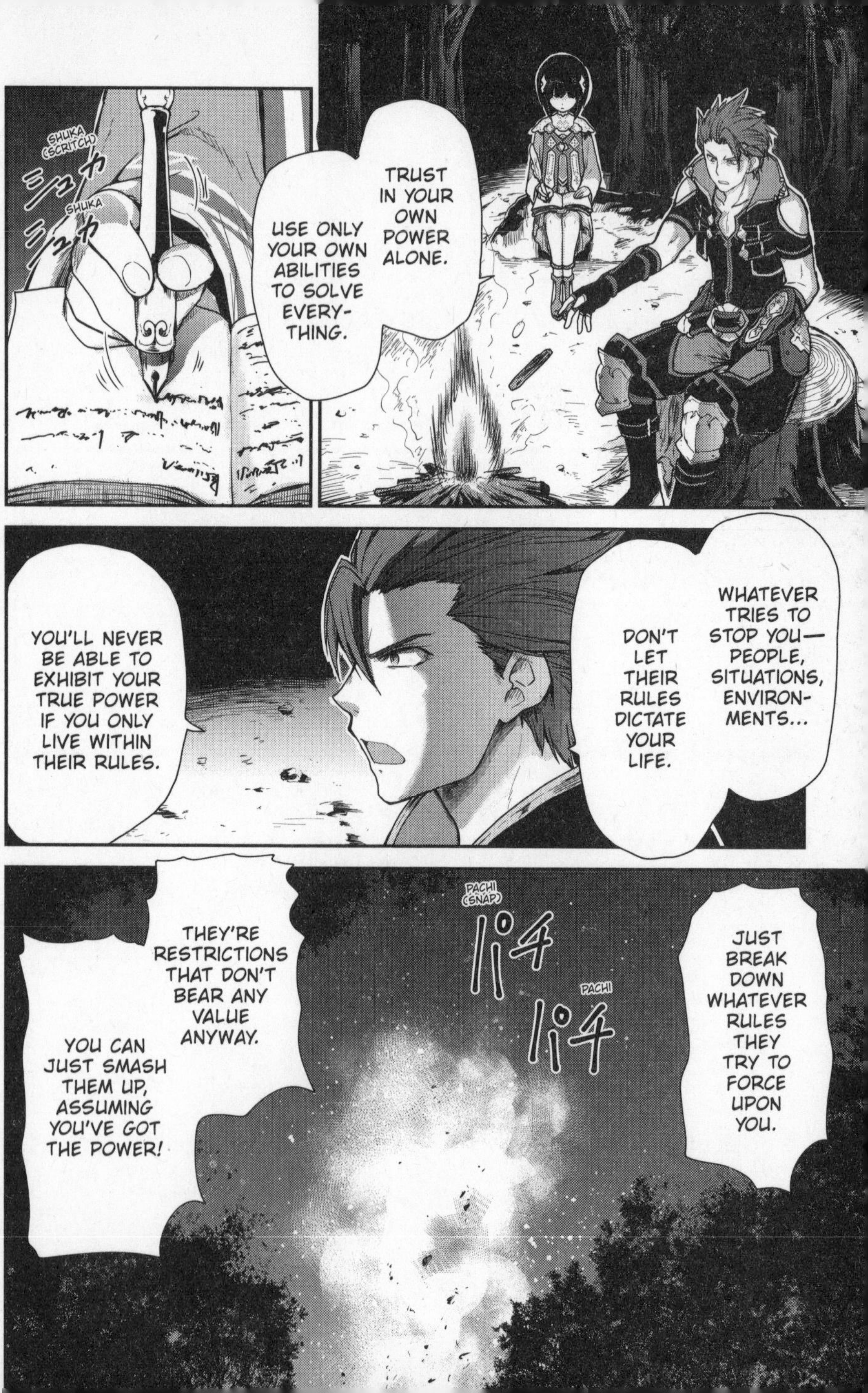
TRUST IN YOUR OWN POWER ALONE.
USE ONLY YOUR OWN ABILITIES TO SOLVE EVERY-THING.
SHUKA (SCRITCH)
シュカ
SHUKA
シュカ
WHATEVER TRIES TO STOP YOU— PEOPLE, SITUATIONS, ENVIRON-MENTS...
DON'T LET THEIR RULES DICTATE YOUR LIFE.
YOU'LL NEVER BE ABLE TO EXHIBIT YOUR TRUE POWER IF YOU ONLY LIVE WITHIN THEIR RULES.
JUST BREAK DOWN WHATEVER RULES THEY TRY TO FORCE UPON YOU.
PACHI (SNAP)
パチ
PACHI
パチ
THEY'RE RESTRICTIONS THAT DON'T BEAR ANY VALUE ANYWAY.
YOU CAN JUST SMASH THEM UP, ASSUMING YOU'VE GOT THE POWER!

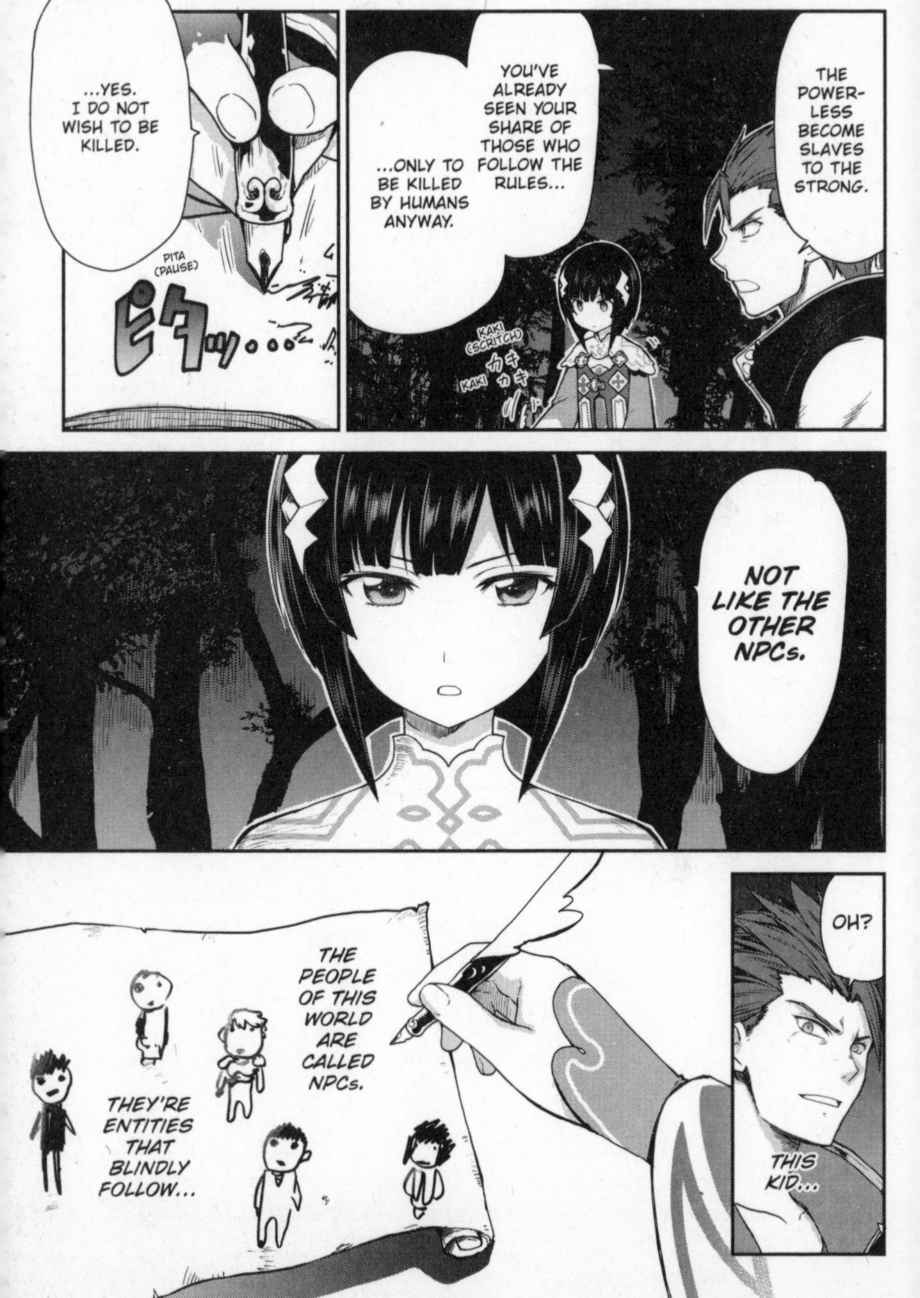
THE POWER-LESS BECOME SLAVES TO THE STRONG.
YOU'VE ALREADY SEEN YOUR SHARE OF THOSE WHO FOLLOW THE RULES...
...ONLY TO BE KILLED BY HUMANS ANYWAY.
KAKI (SCRITCH)
KAKI
...YES. I DO NOT WISH TO BE KILLED.
PITA (PAUSE)
NOT LIKE THE OTHER NPCs.
OH?
THIS KID...
THE PEOPLE OF THIS WORLD ARE CALLED NPCs.
THEY'RE ENTITIES THAT BLINDLY FOLLOW...

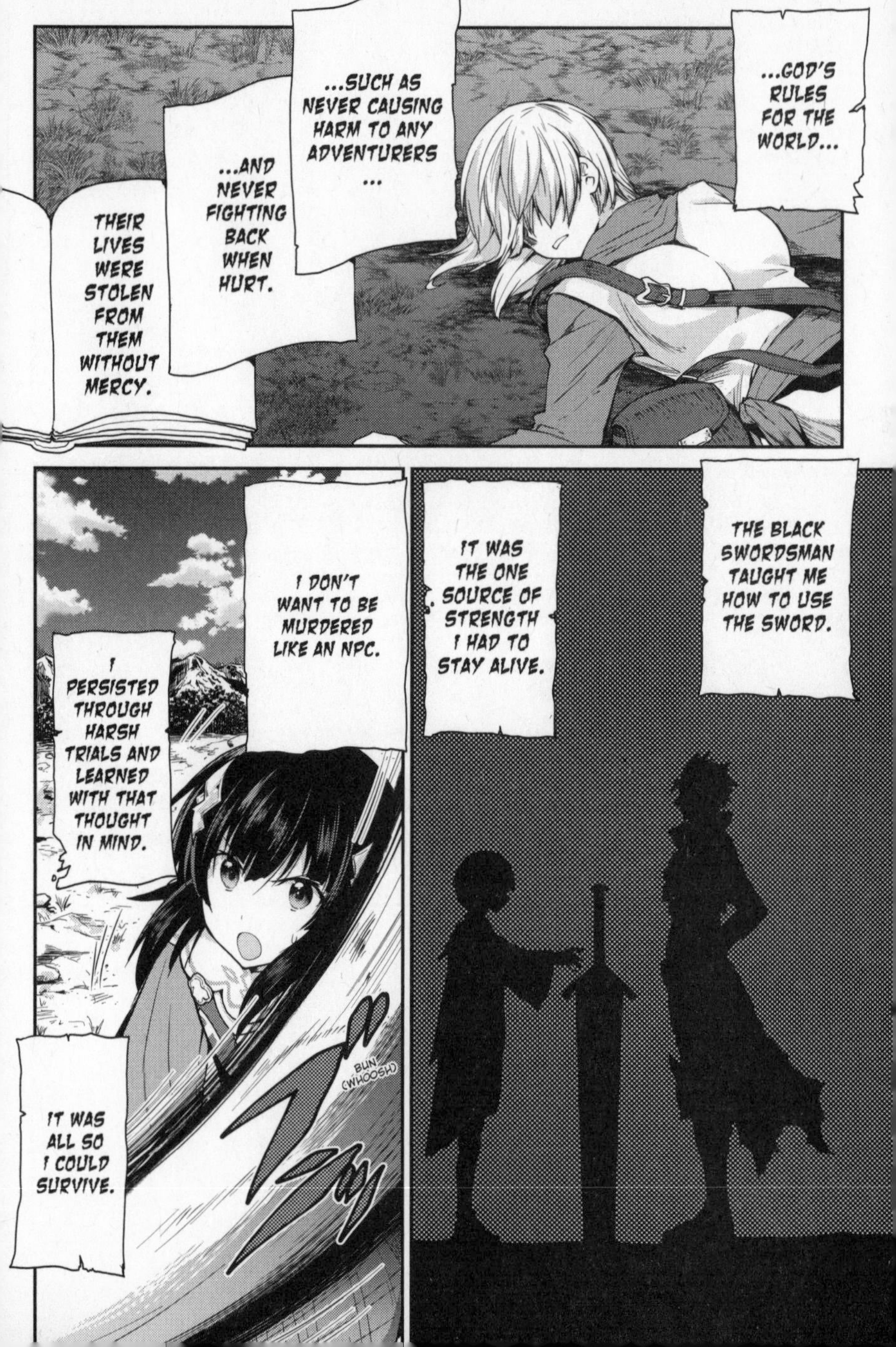
...GOD'S RULES FOR THE WORLD...
...SUCH AS NEVER CAUSING HARM TO ANY ADVENTURERS ...
...AND NEVER FIGHTING BACK WHEN HURT.
THEIR LIVES WERE STOLEN FROM THEM WITHOUT MERCY.
THE BLACK SWORDSMAN TAUGHT ME HOW TO USE THE SWORD.
IT WAS THE ONE SOURCE OF STRENGTH I HAD TO STAY ALIVE.
I DON'T WANT TO BE MURDERED LIKE AN NPC.
I PERSISTED THROUGH HARSH TRIALS AND LEARNED WITH THAT THOUGHT IN MIND.
BUN (WHOOSH)
IT WAS ALL SO I COULD SURVIVE.

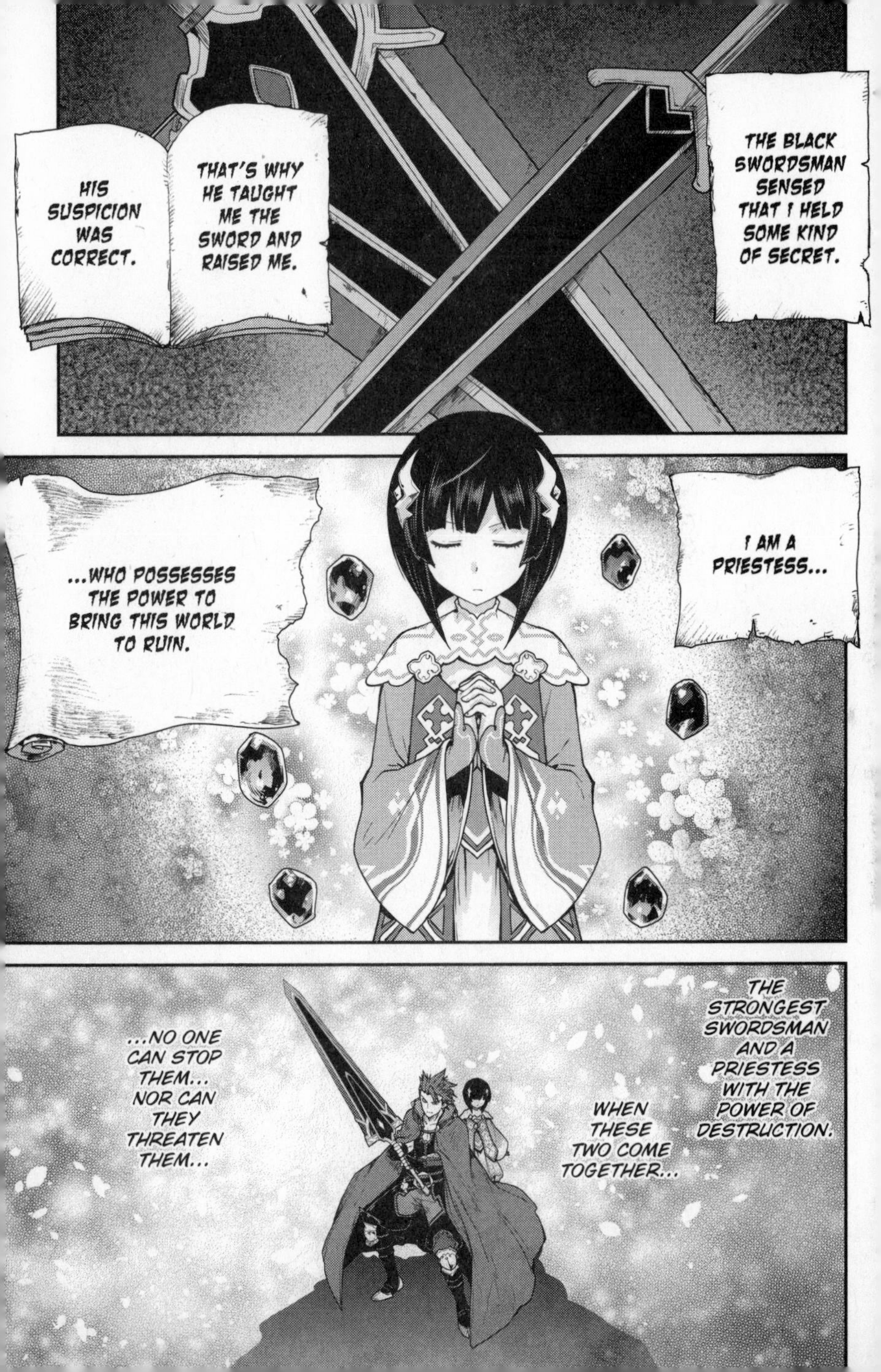
THE BLACK SWORDSMAN SENSED THAT I HELD SOME KIND OF SECRET.
THAT'S WHY HE TAUGHT ME THE SWORD AND RAISED ME.
HIS SUSPICION WAS CORRECT.
I AM A PRIESTESS...
...WHO POSSESSES THE POWER TO BRING THIS WORLD TO RUIN.
THE STRONGEST SWORDSMAN AND A PRIESTESS WITH THE POWER OF DESTRUCTION.
WHEN THESE TWO COME TOGETHER...
...NO ONE CAN STOP THEM... NOR CAN THEY THREATEN THEM...

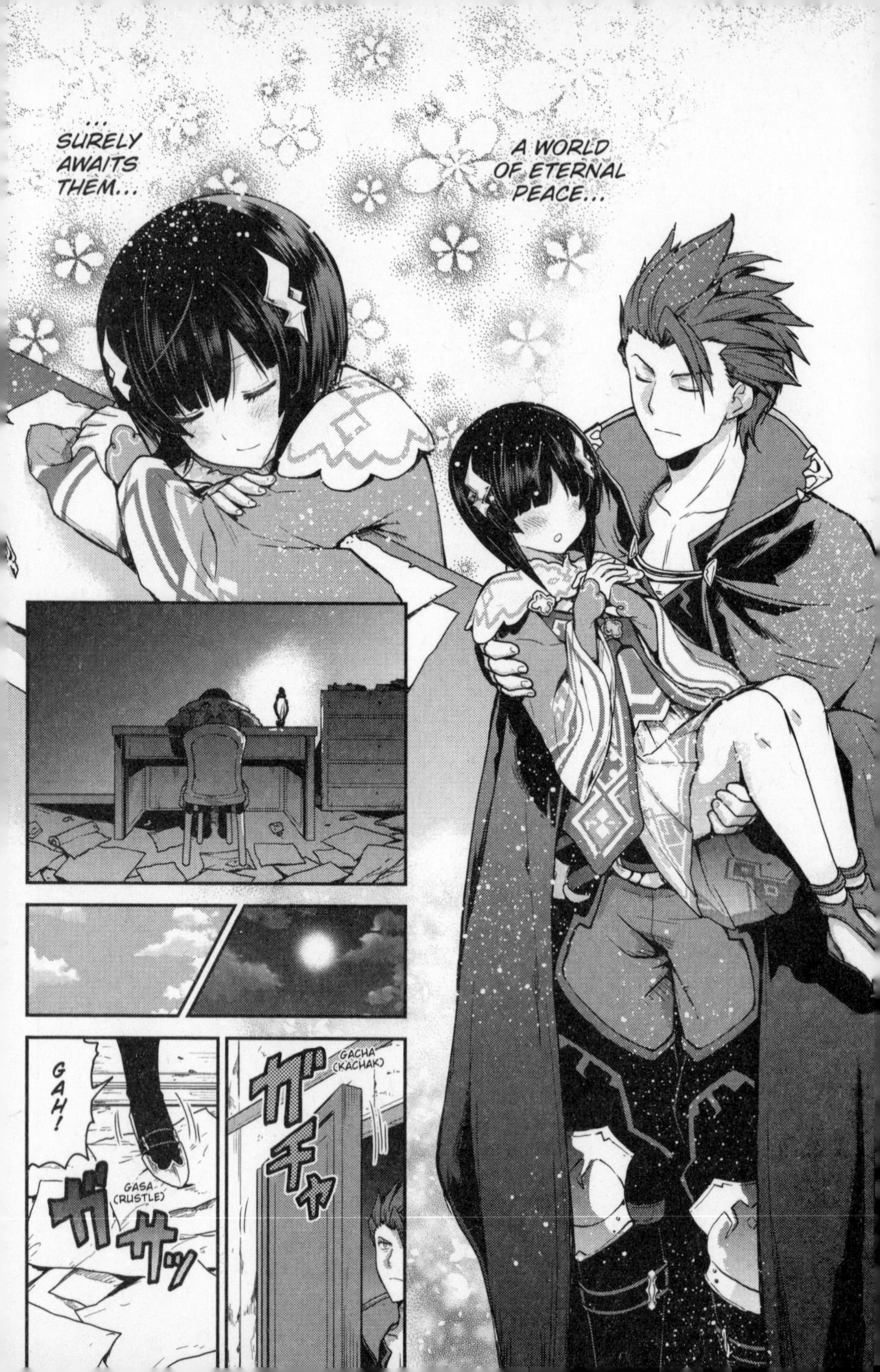
A WORLD OF ETERNAL PEACE...
...SURELY AWAITS THEM...
ガチャ
GACHA (KACHAK)
GAH!
ガサッ
GASA (RUSTLE)

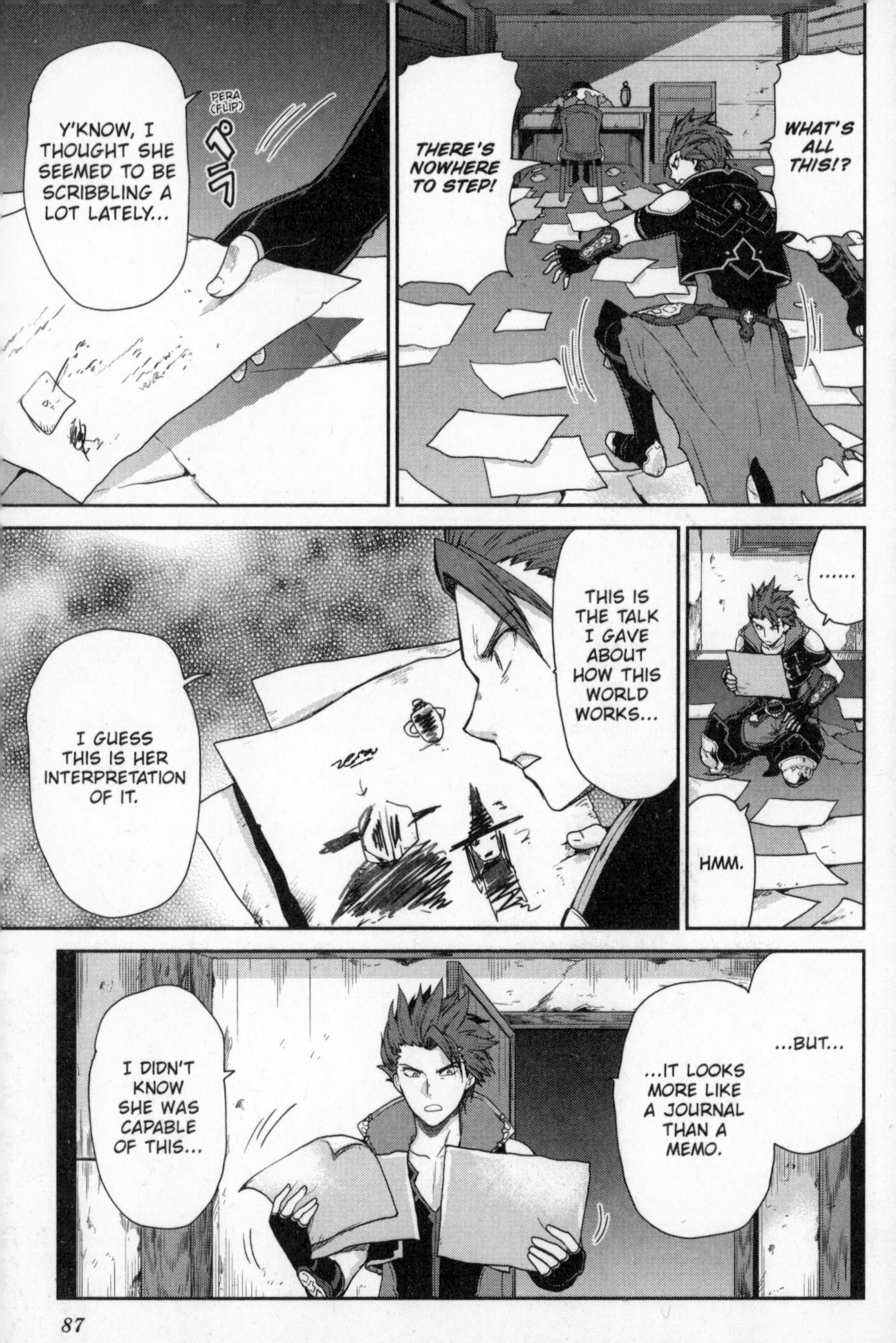
WHAT'S ALL THIS!?
THERE'S NOWHERE TO STEP!
PERA (FLIP)
Y'KNOW, I THOUGHT SHE SEEMED TO BE SCRIBBLING A LOT LATELY...
......
HMM.
THIS IS THE TALK I GAVE ABOUT HOW THIS WORLD WORKS...
I GUESS THIS IS HER INTERPRETATION OF IT.
...BUT...
...IT LOOKS MORE LIKE A JOURNAL THAN A MEMO.
I DIDN'T KNOW SHE WAS CAPABLE OF THIS...

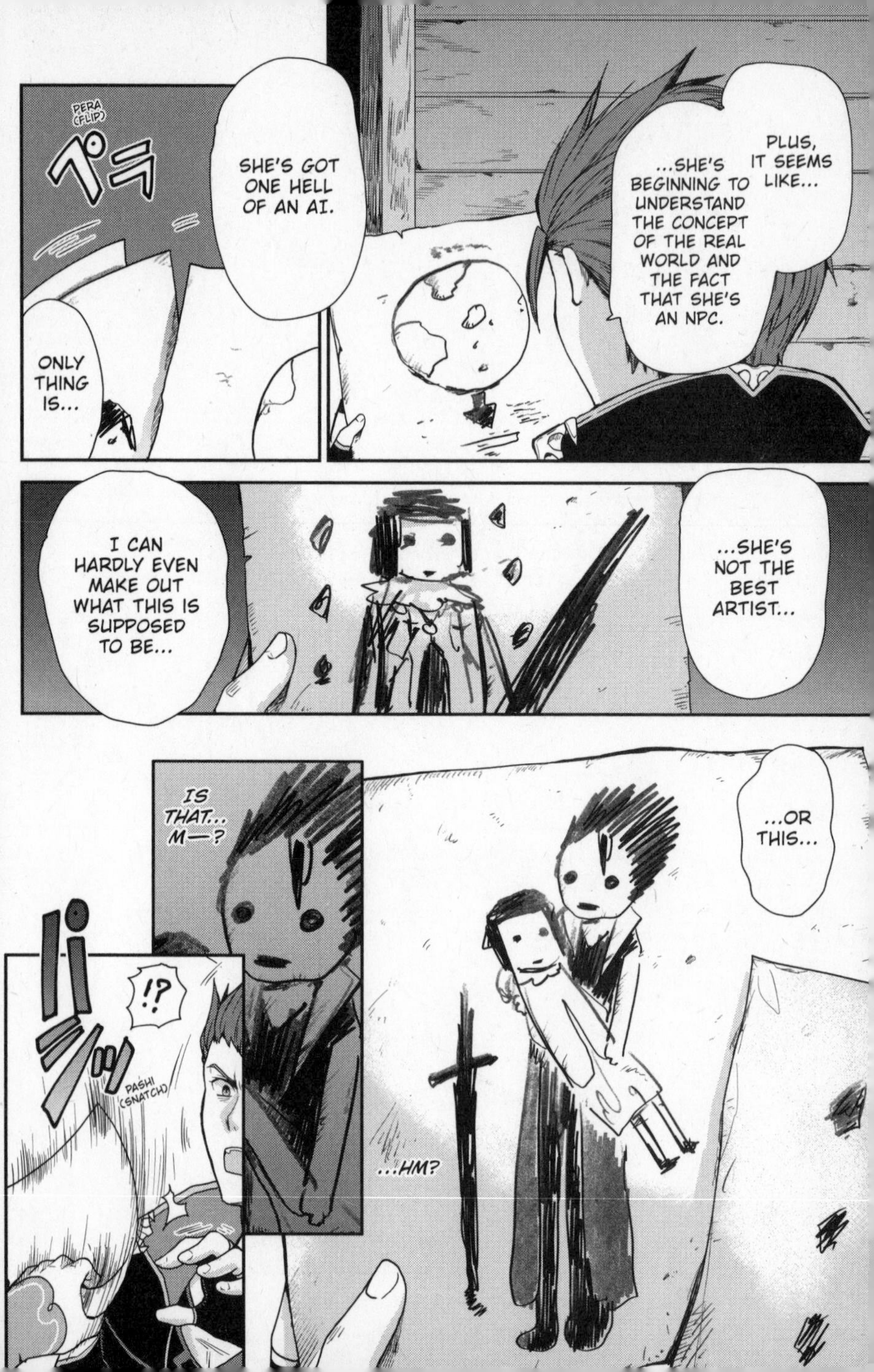
PLUS, IT SEEMS LIKE...
...SHE'S BEGINNING TO UNDERSTAND THE CONCEPT OF THE REAL WORLD AND THE FACT THAT SHE'S AN NPC.
SHE'S GOT ONE HELL OF AN AI.
PERA (FLIP)
ONLY THING IS...
...SHE'S NOT THE BEST ARTIST...
I CAN HARDLY EVEN MAKE OUT WHAT THIS IS SUPPOSED TO BE...
...OR THIS...
...HM?
IS THAT... M—?
PASHI (SNATCH)
!?

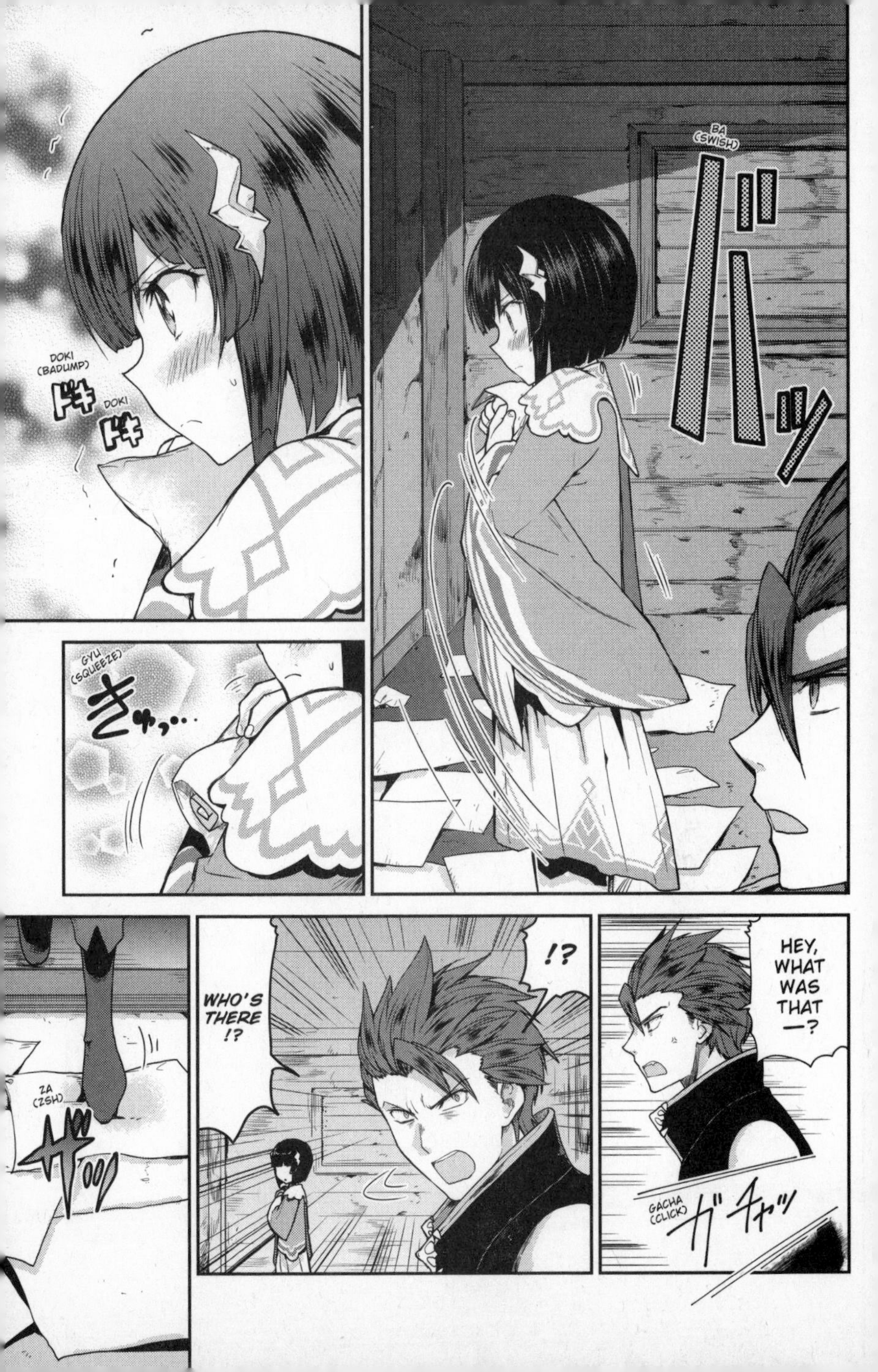
BA (SWISH)
バッ
DOKI (BADUMP)
ドキ
DOKI
ドキ
GYU (SQUEEZE)
きゅっ…
HEY, WHAT WAS THAT—?
GACHA (CLICK)
ガチャッ
!?
WHO'S THERE !?
ZA (ZSH)
ザッ

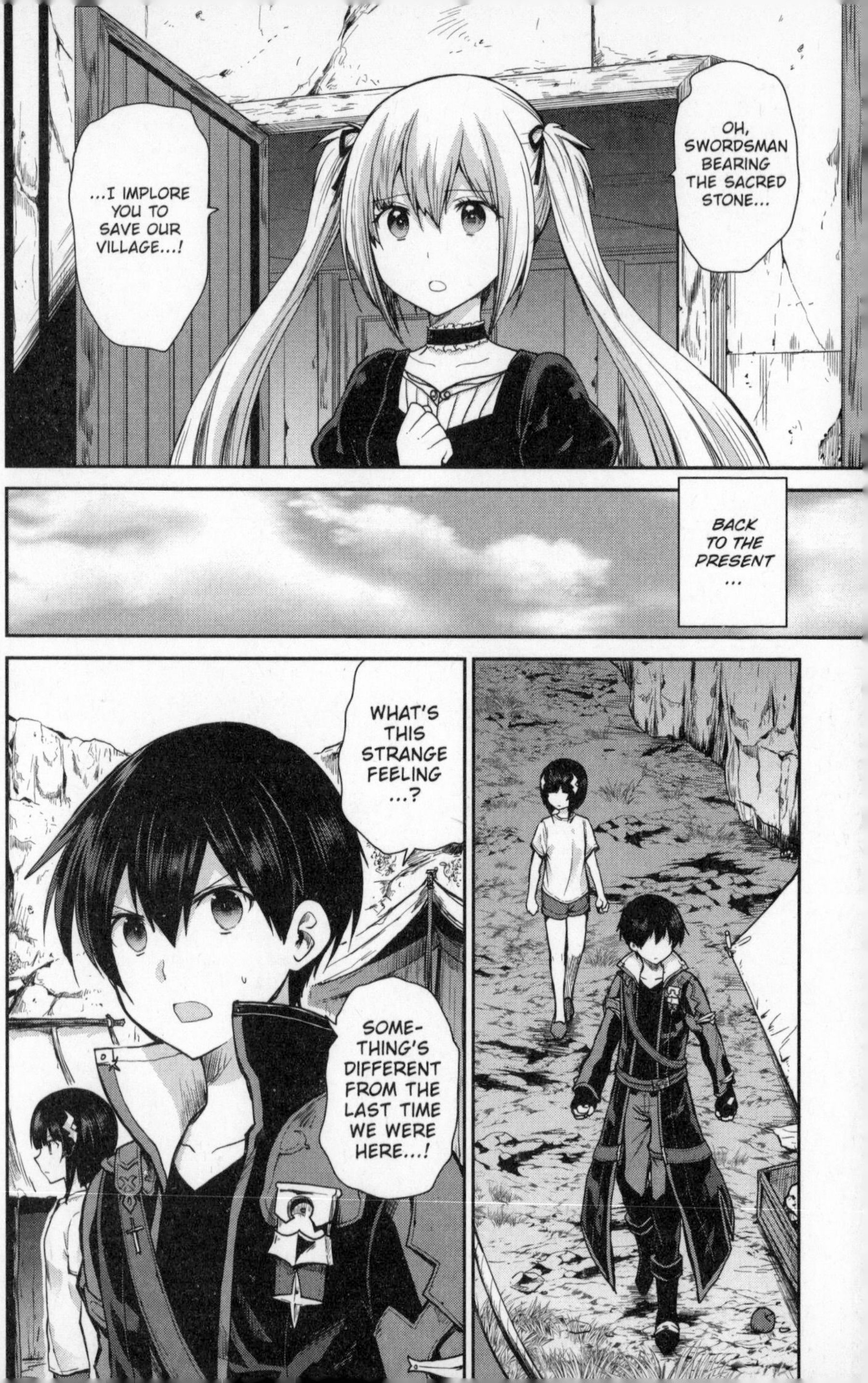
OH, SWORDSMAN BEARING THE SACRED STONE...
...I IMPLORE YOU TO SAVE OUR VILLAGE...!
BACK TO THE PRESENT ...
WHAT'S THIS STRANGE FEELING ...?
SOME-THING'S DIFFERENT FROM THE LAST TIME WE WERE HERE...!

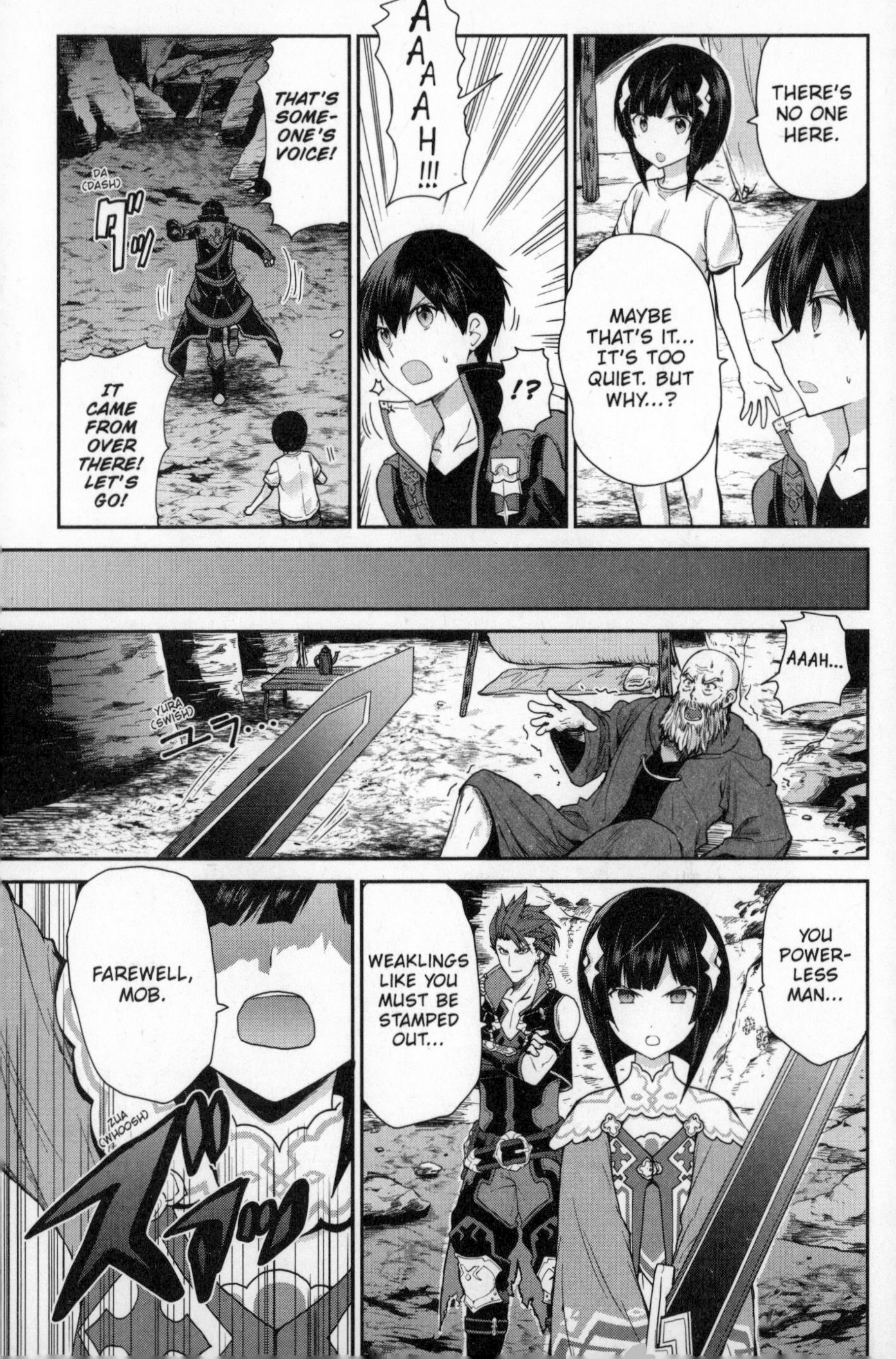
THERE'S NO ONE HERE.
MAYBE THAT'S IT... IT'S TOO QUIET. BUT WHY...?
AAAAH!!!
!?
THAT'S SOME-ONE'S VOICE!
DA (DASH)
IT CAME FROM OVER THERE! LET'S GO!
AAAH...
YURA (SWISH)
YOU POWER-LESS MAN...
WEAKLINGS LIKE YOU MUST BE STAMPED OUT...
FAREWELL, MOB.
ZUA (WHOOSH)

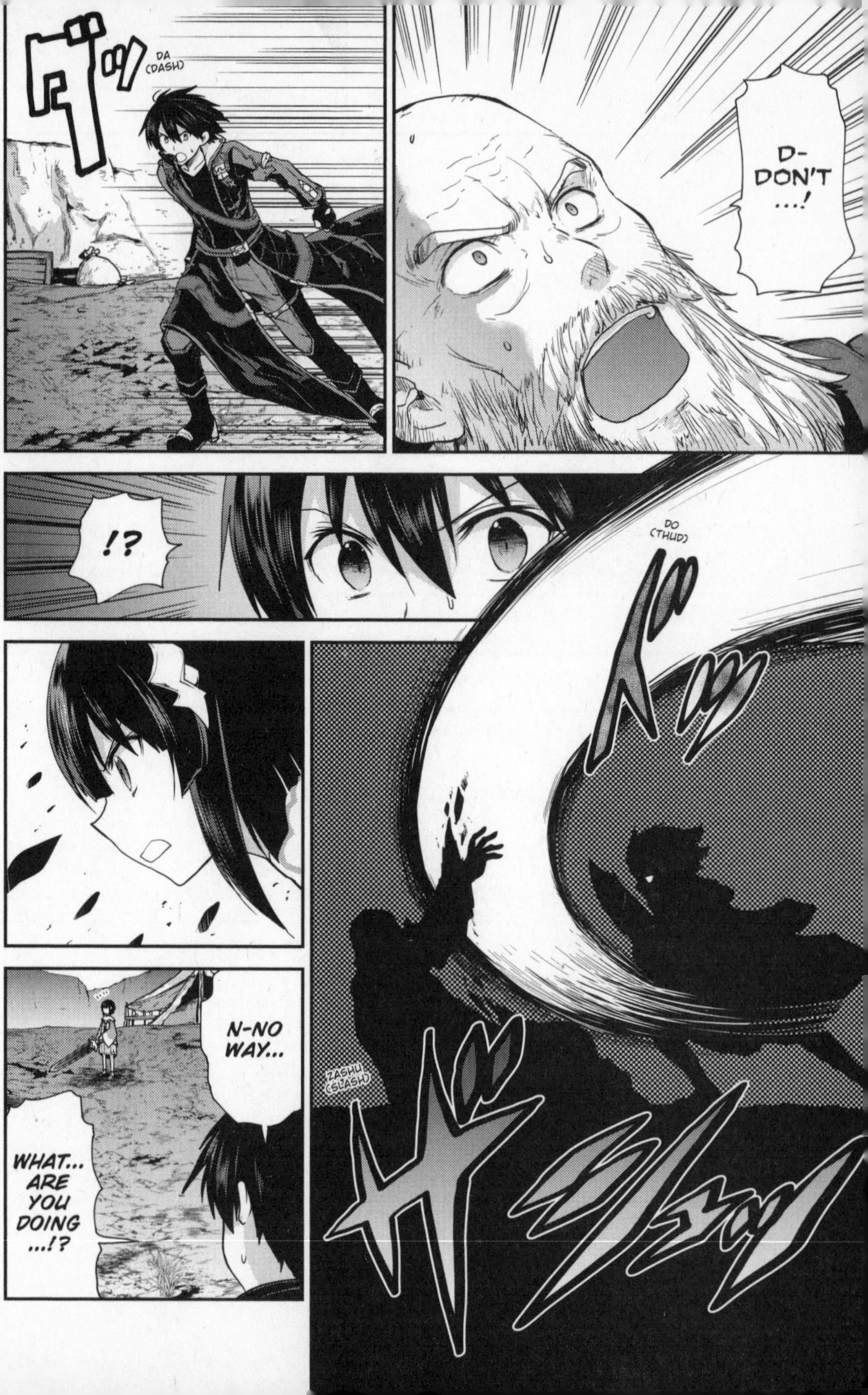
D-DON'T ...!
DA (DASH)
!?
DO (THUD)
ZASHU (SLASH)
N-NO WAY...
WHAT... ARE YOU DOING ...!?

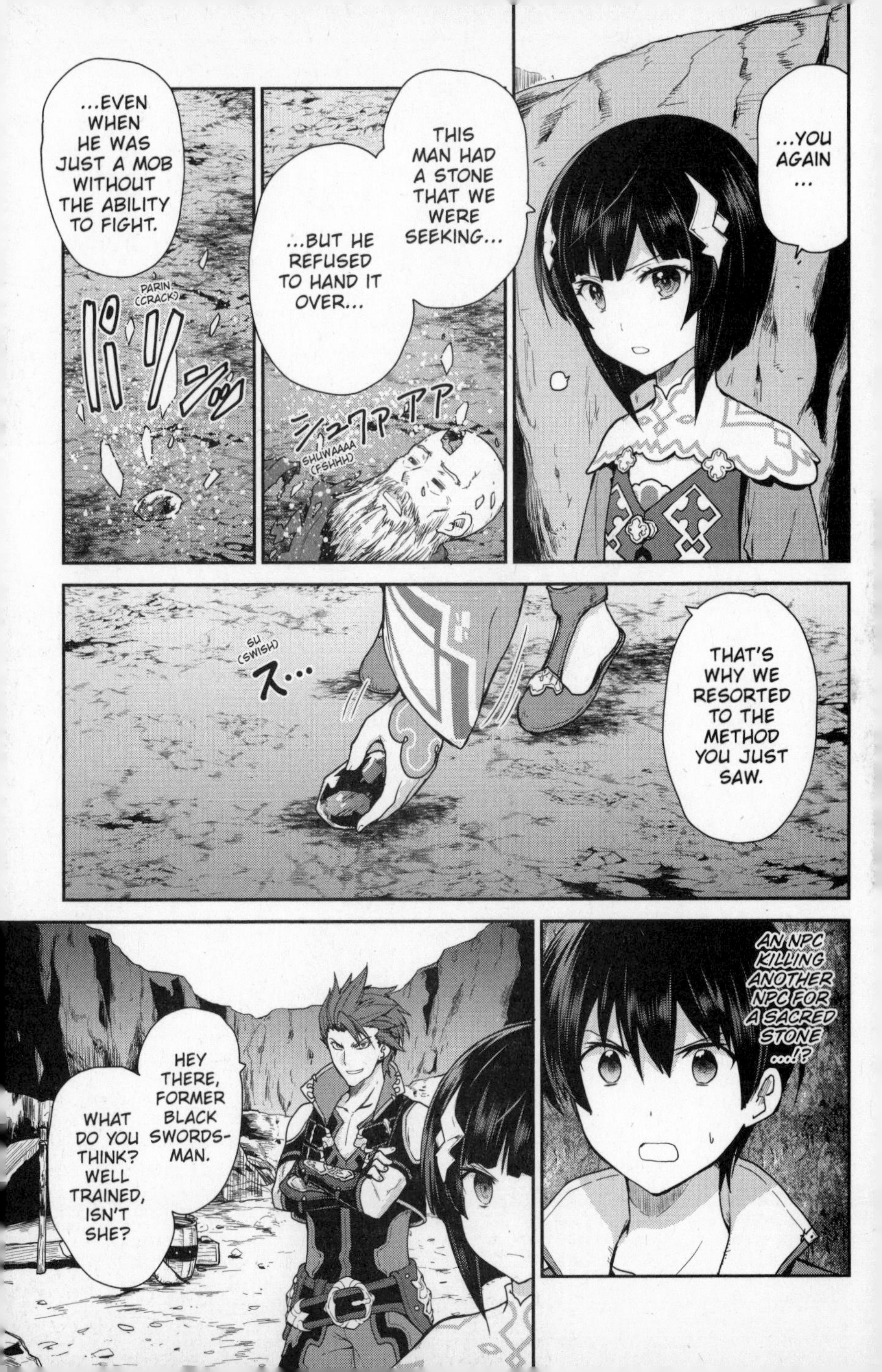
...YOU AGAIN ...
THIS MAN HAD A STONE THAT WE WERE SEEKING...
...BUT HE REFUSED TO HAND IT OVER...
シュワァアア
SHUWAAAA (FSHHH)
...EVEN WHEN HE WAS JUST A MOB WITHOUT THE ABILITY TO FIGHT.
パリンッ
PARIN (CRACK)
THAT'S WHY WE RESORTED TO THE METHOD YOU JUST SAW.
ス…
SU (SWISH)
AN NPC KILLING ANOTHER NPC FOR A SACRED STONE ...!?
HEY THERE, FORMER BLACK SWORDS-MAN.
WHAT DO YOU THINK? WELL TRAINED, ISN'T SHE?

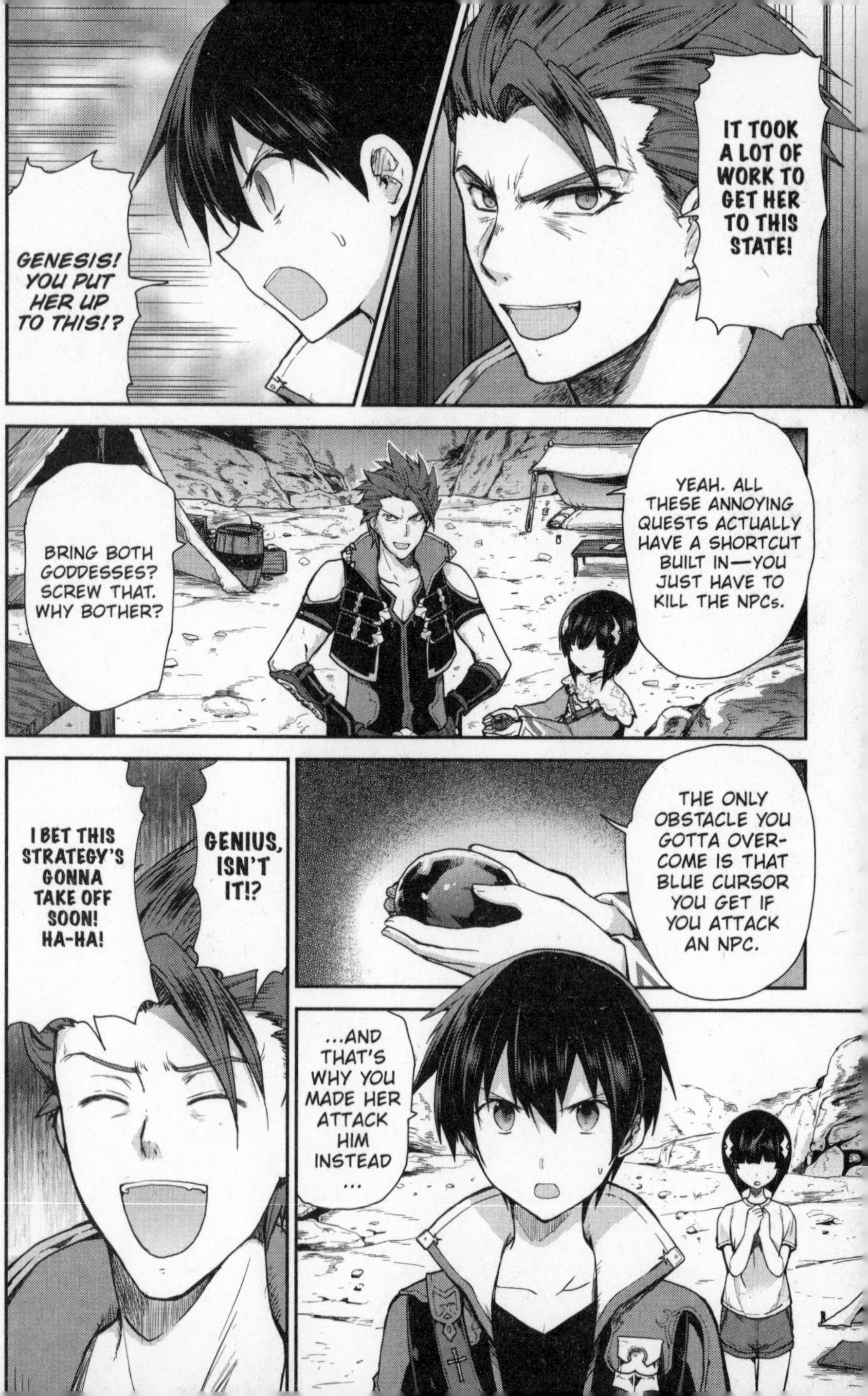
IT TOOK A LOT OF WORK TO GET HER TO THIS STATE!
GENESIS! YOU PUT HER UP TO THIS!?
YEAH. ALL THESE ANNOYING QUESTS ACTUALLY HAVE A SHORTCUT BUILT IN—YOU JUST HAVE TO KILL THE NPCs.
BRING BOTH GODDESSES? SCREW THAT. WHY BOTHER?
THE ONLY OBSTACLE YOU GOTTA OVER-COME IS THAT BLUE CURSOR YOU GET IF YOU ATTACK AN NPC.
...AND THAT'S WHY YOU MADE HER ATTACK HIM INSTEAD...
GENIUS, ISN'T IT!?
I BET THIS STRATEGY'S GONNA TAKE OFF SOON! HA-HA!

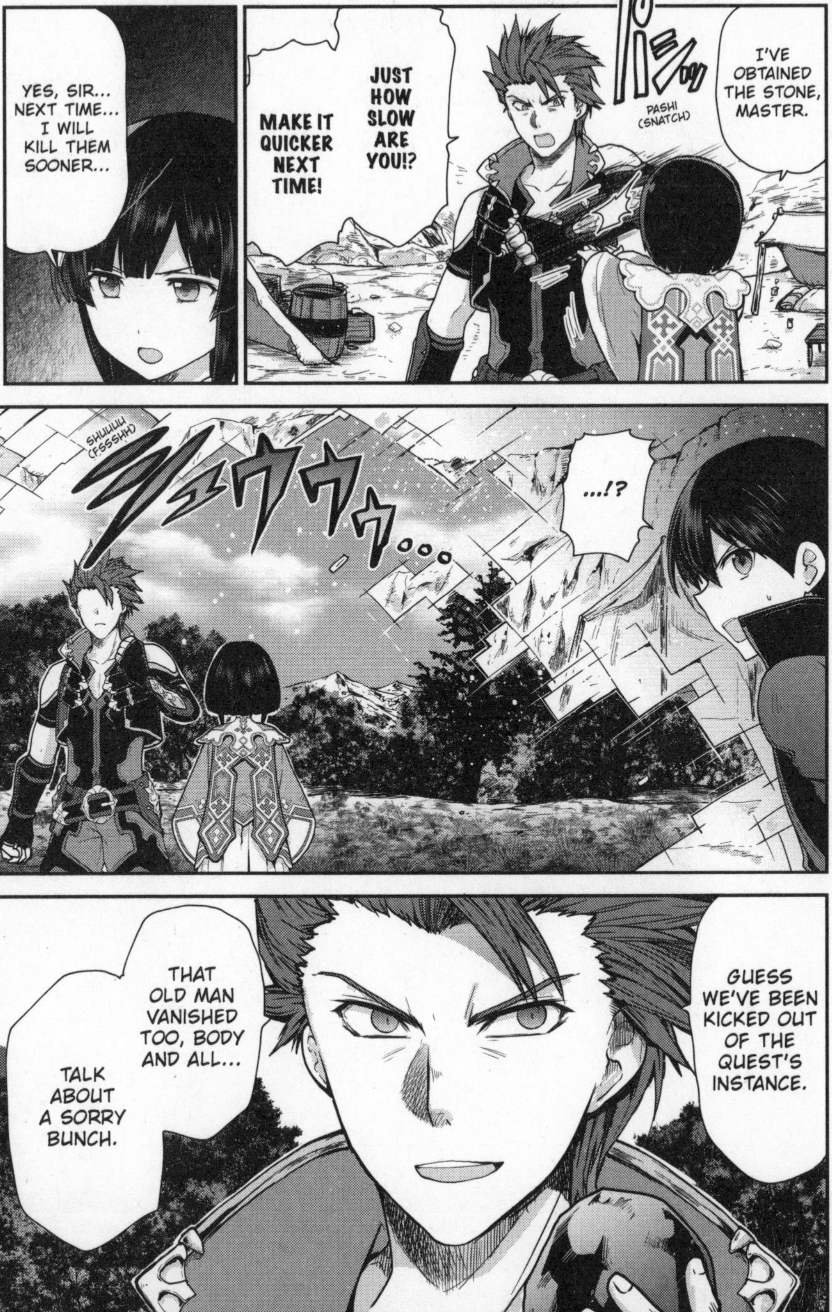
I'VE OBTAINED THE STONE, MASTER.
パシッ
PASHI (SNATCH)
JUST HOW SLOW ARE YOU!?
MAKE IT QUICKER NEXT TIME!
YES, SIR... NEXT TIME... I WILL KILL THEM SOONER...
シュウウウ...
SHUUUU (FSSSHH)
...!?
GUESS WE'VE BEEN KICKED OUT OF THE QUEST'S INSTANCE.
THAT OLD MAN VANISHED TOO, BODY AND ALL...
TALK ABOUT A SORRY BUNCH.

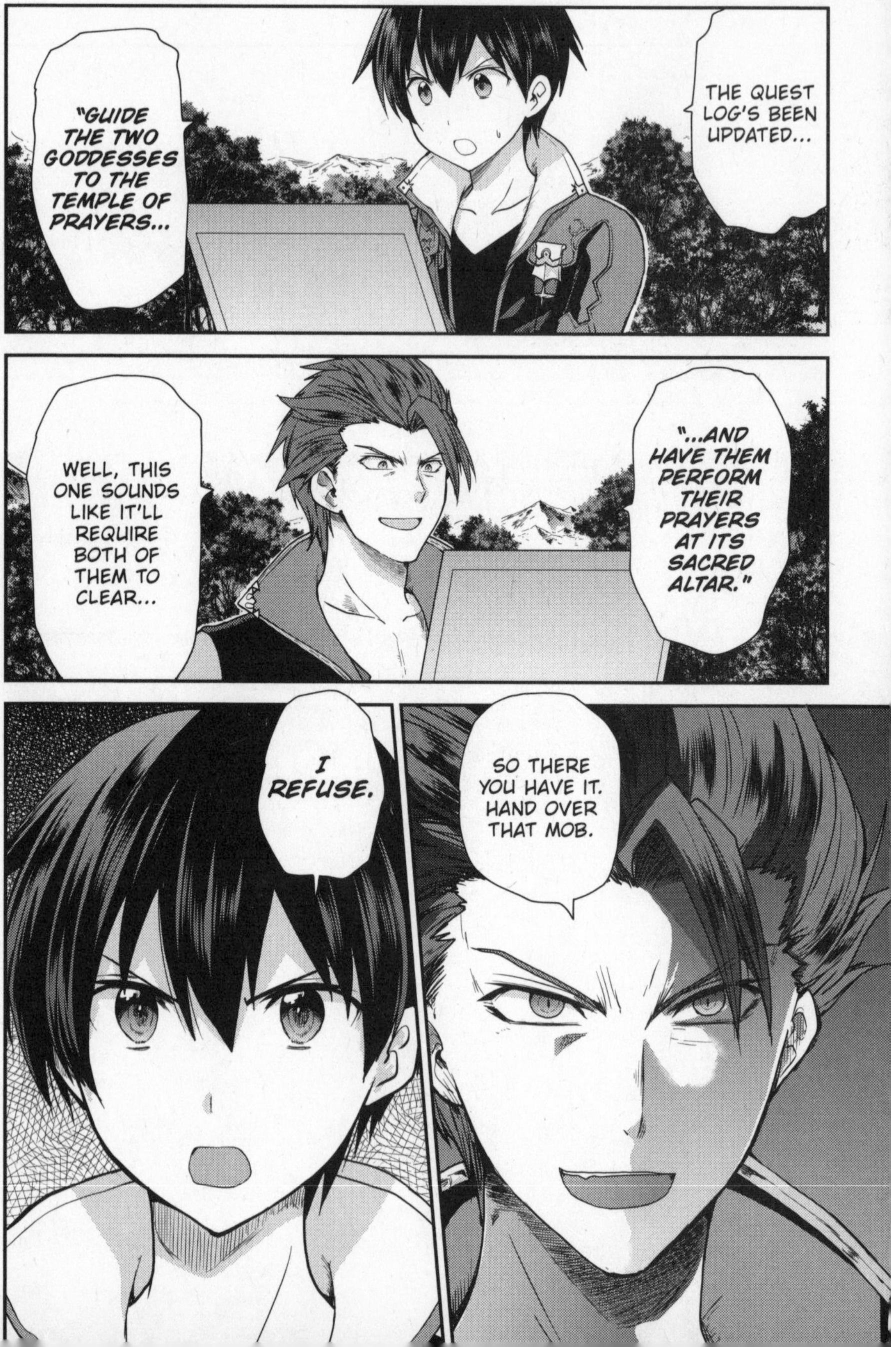
THE QUEST LOG'S BEEN UPDATED...
"GUIDE THE TWO GODDESSES TO THE TEMPLE OF PRAYERS...
"...AND HAVE THEM PERFORM THEIR PRAYERS AT ITS SACRED ALTAR."
WELL, THIS ONE SOUNDS LIKE IT'LL REQUIRE BOTH OF THEM TO CLEAR...
SO THERE YOU HAVE IT. HAND OVER THAT MOB.
I REFUSE.

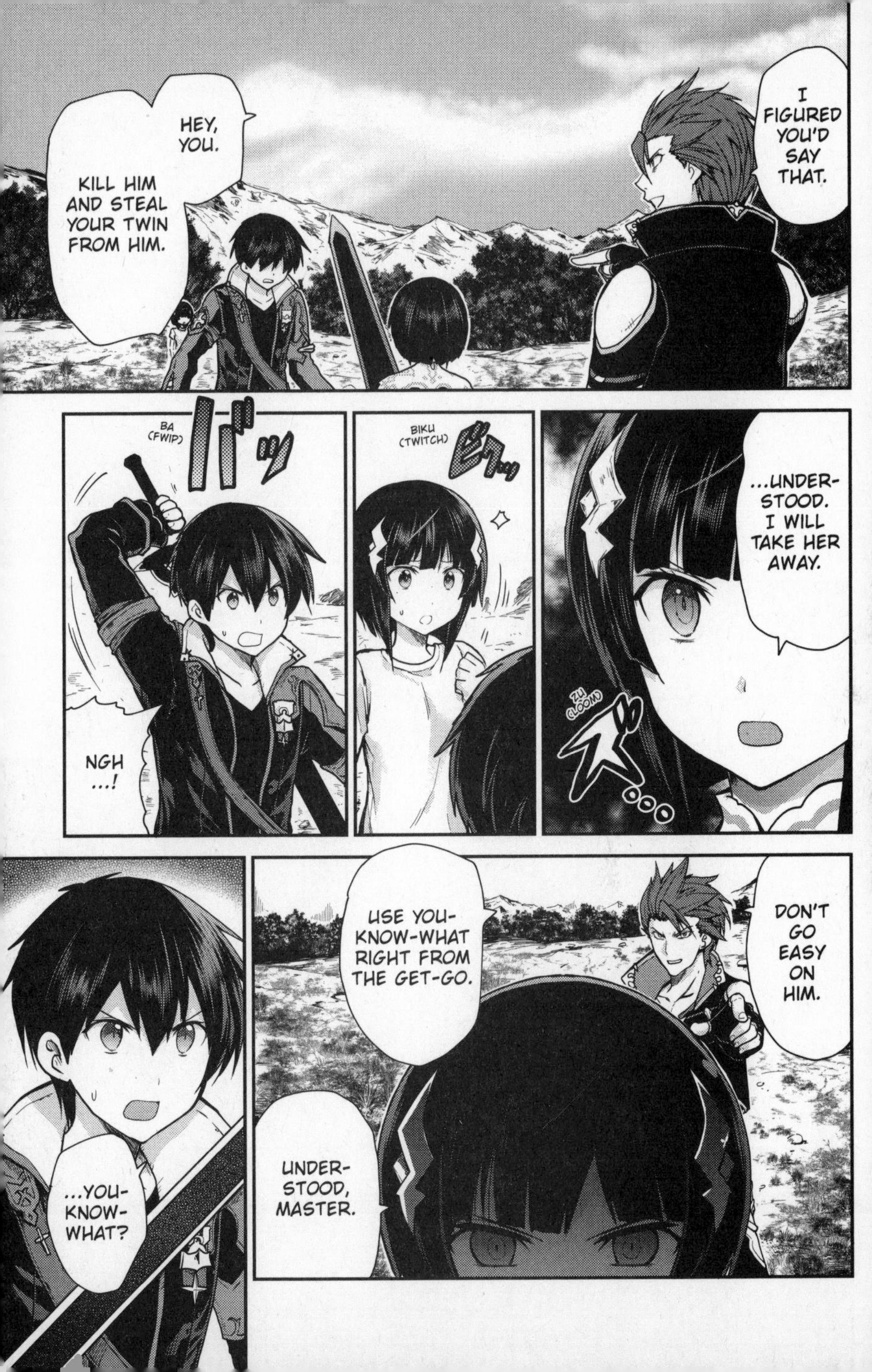
I FIGURED YOU'D SAY THAT.
HEY, YOU.
KILL HIM AND STEAL YOUR TWIN FROM HIM.
...UNDER-STOOD. I WILL TAKE HER AWAY.
ZU (LOOM)
BIKU (TWITCH)
BA (FWIP)
NGH ...!
DON'T GO EASY ON HIM.
USE YOU-KNOW-WHAT RIGHT FROM THE GET-GO.
UNDER-STOOD, MASTER.
...YOU-KNOW-WHAT?

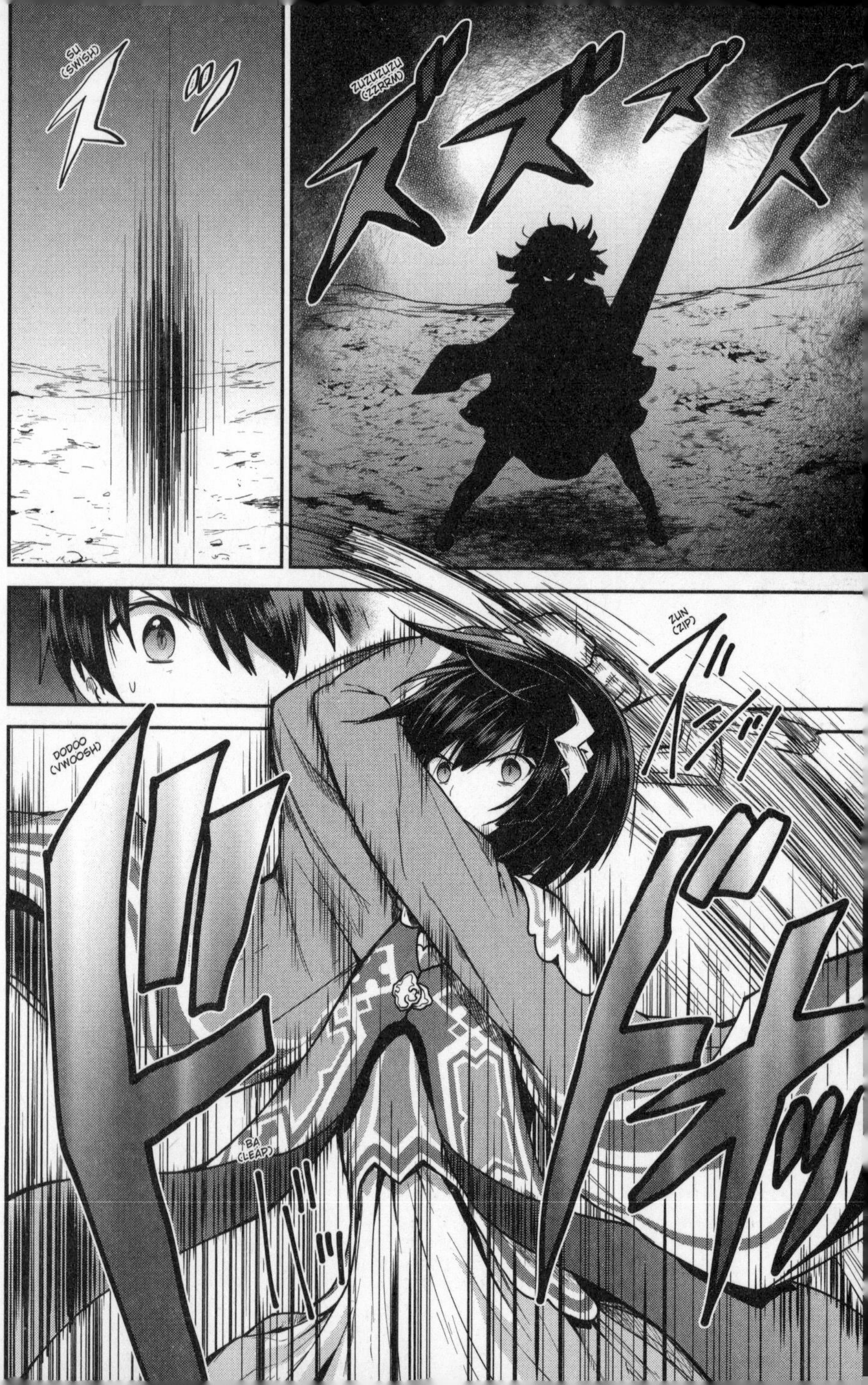
ZUZUZUZU (ZZRRM)
SU (SWISH)
ZUN (ZIP)
DODOO (VWOOSH)
BA (LEAP)

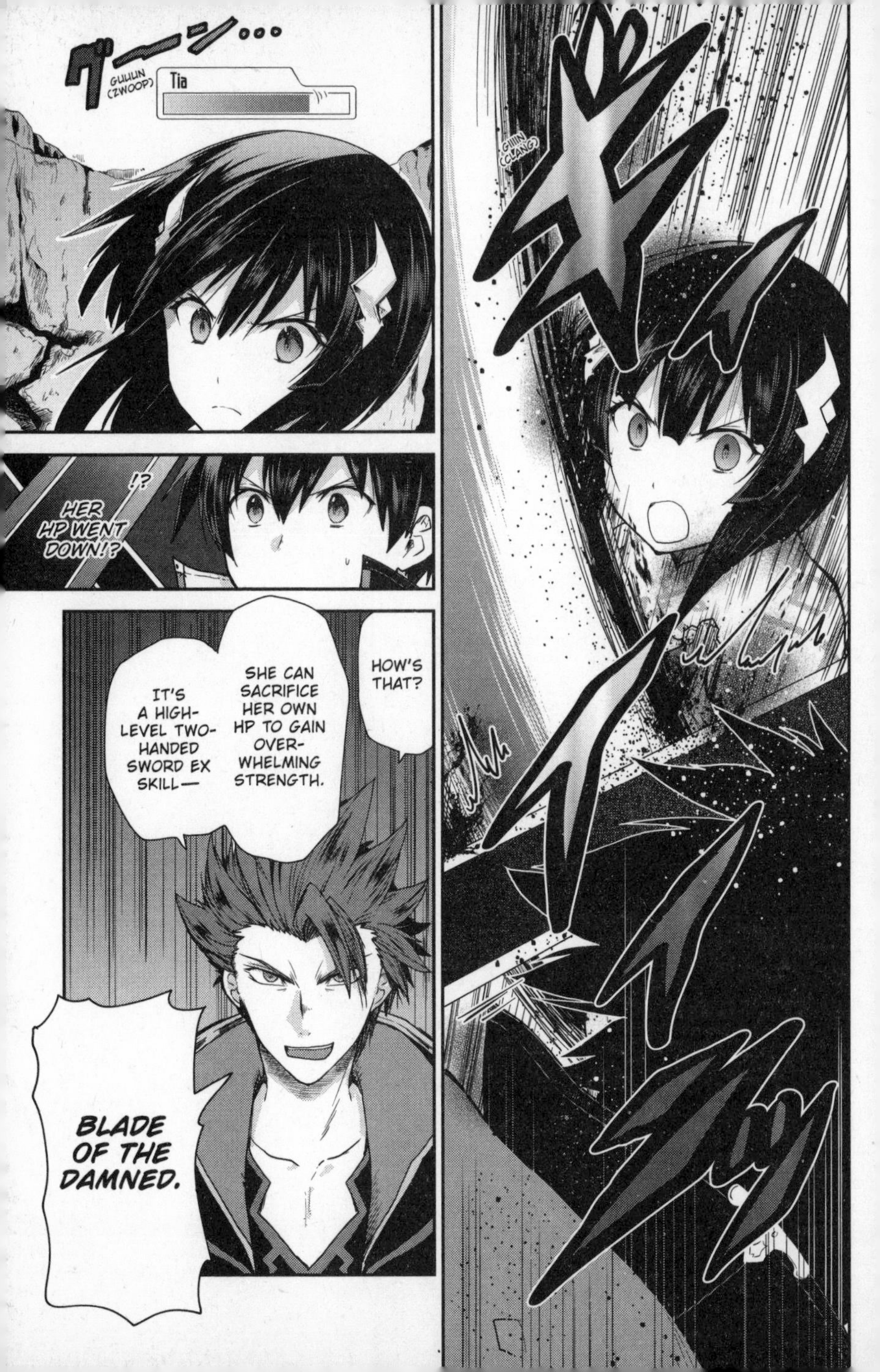
GIIIN (CLANG)
グーーン・・・
GUUUN (ZWOOP)
Tia
!?
HER HP WENT DOWN!?
HOW'S THAT?
SHE CAN SACRIFICE HER OWN HP TO GAIN OVER-WHELMING STRENGTH.
IT'S A HIGH-LEVEL TWO-HANDED SWORD EX SKILL—
BLADE OF THE DAMNED.

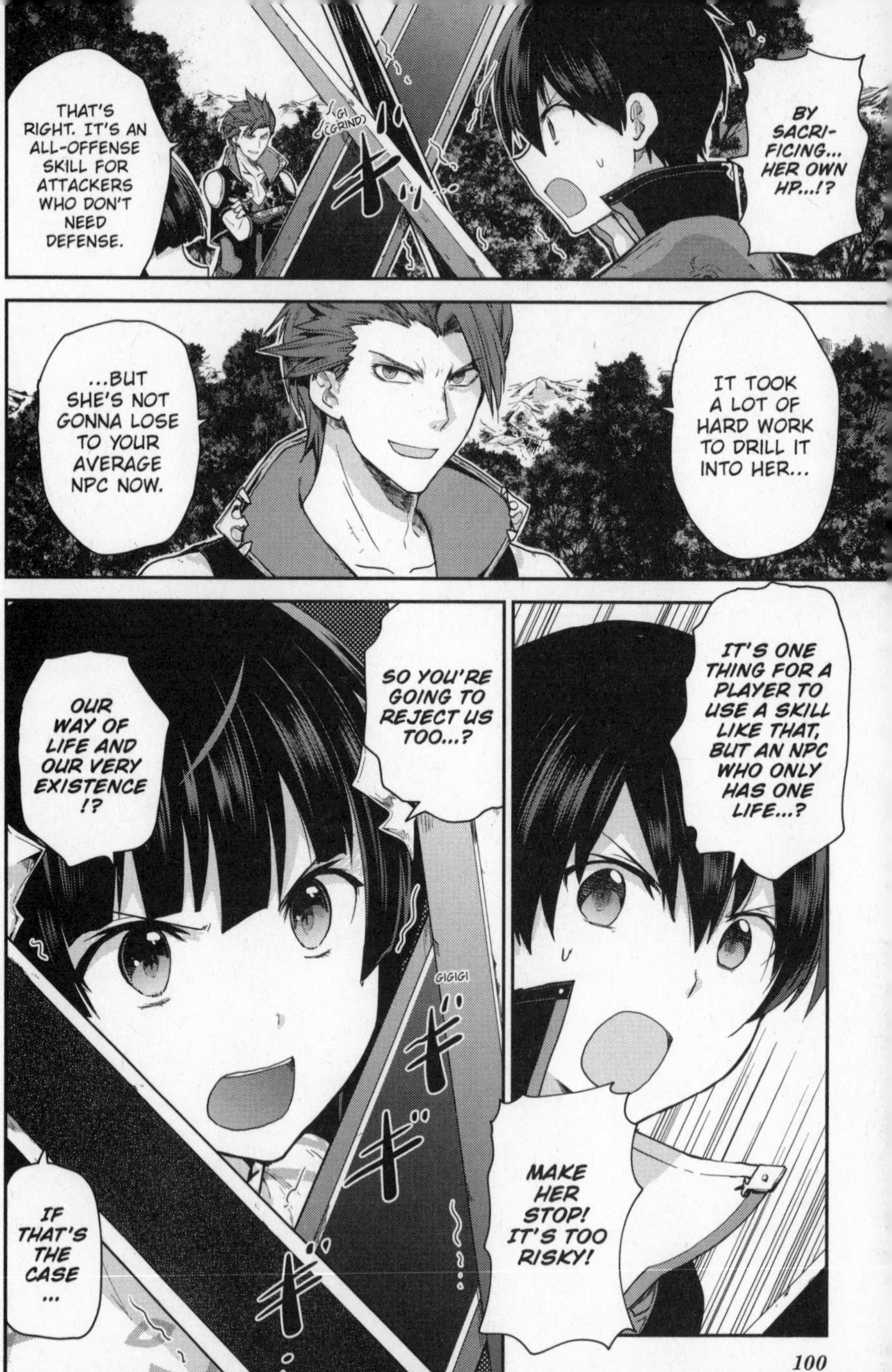
BY SACRIFICING... HER OWN HP...!?
GI (GRIND)
THAT'S RIGHT. IT'S AN ALL-OFFENSE SKILL FOR ATTACKERS WHO DON'T NEED DEFENSE.
IT TOOK A LOT OF HARD WORK TO DRILL IT INTO HER...
...BUT SHE'S NOT GONNA LOSE TO YOUR AVERAGE NPC NOW.
IT'S ONE THING FOR A PLAYER TO USE A SKILL LIKE THAT, BUT AN NPC WHO ONLY HAS ONE LIFE...?
MAKE HER STOP! IT'S TOO RISKY!
SO YOU'RE GOING TO REJECT US TOO...?
OUR WAY OF LIFE AND OUR VERY EXISTENCE!?
GIGIGI
IF THAT'S THE CASE...

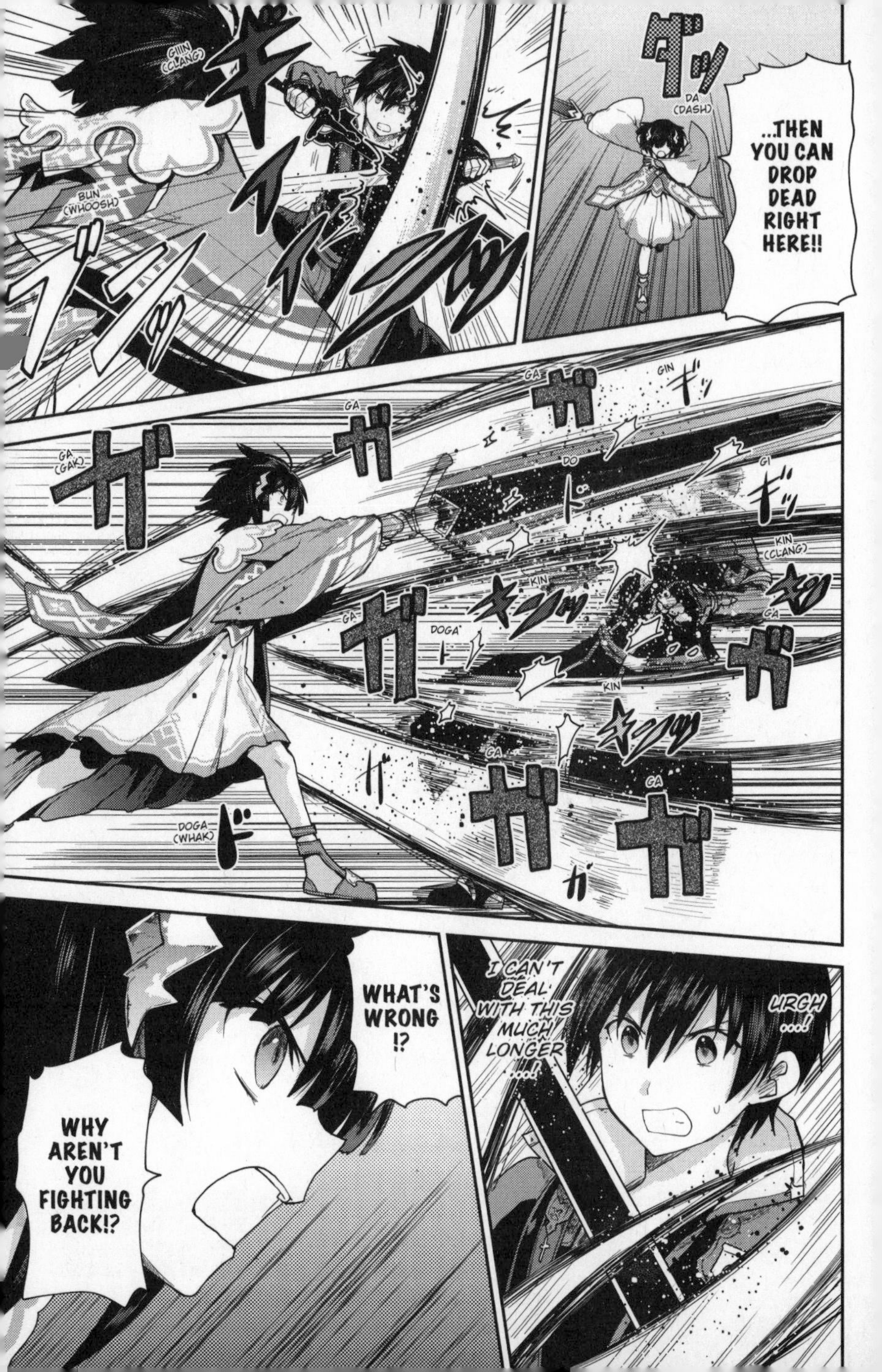

DA (DASH)
...THEN YOU CAN DROP DEAD RIGHT HERE!!
GIIN (CLANG)
BUN (WHOOSH)
GIN
GA
GA
GA (GAK)
DO
GI
KIN (CLANG)
GA
KIN
DOGA
GA
KIN
GA
GA
DOGA (WHAK)
URGH ...!
I CAN'T DEAL WITH THIS MUCH LONGER ...!
WHAT'S WRONG !?
WHY AREN'T YOU FIGHTING BACK!?

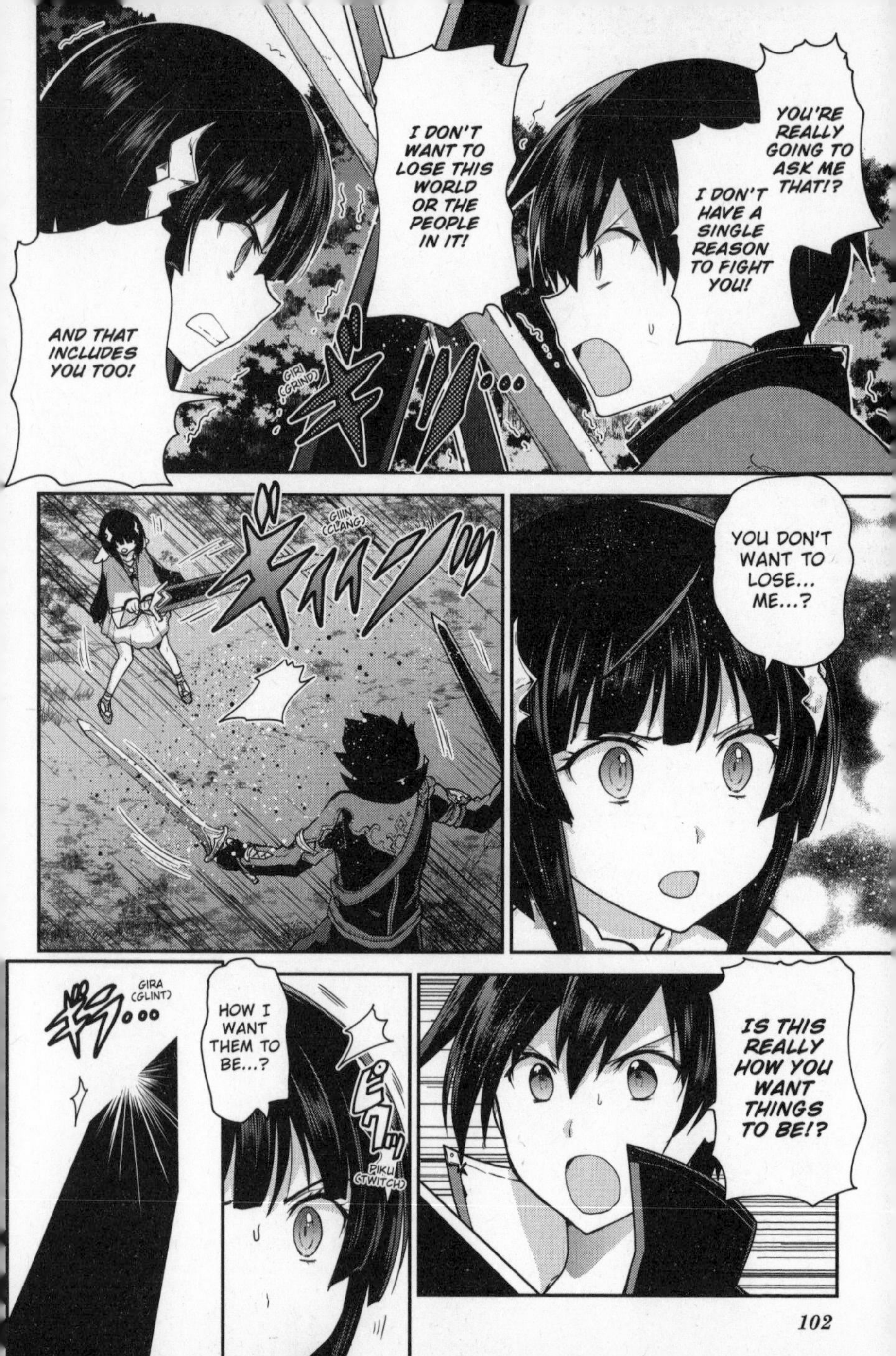
YOU'RE REALLY GOING TO ASK ME THAT!?
I DON'T HAVE A SINGLE REASON TO FIGHT YOU!
I DON'T WANT TO LOSE THIS WORLD OR THE PEOPLE IN IT!
AND THAT INCLUDES YOU TOO!
GIRI (GRIND)
YOU DON'T WANT TO LOSE... ME...?
GIIIN (CLANG)
IS THIS REALLY HOW YOU WANT THINGS TO BE!?
HOW I WANT THEM TO BE...?
PIKU (TWITCH)
GIRA (GLINT)

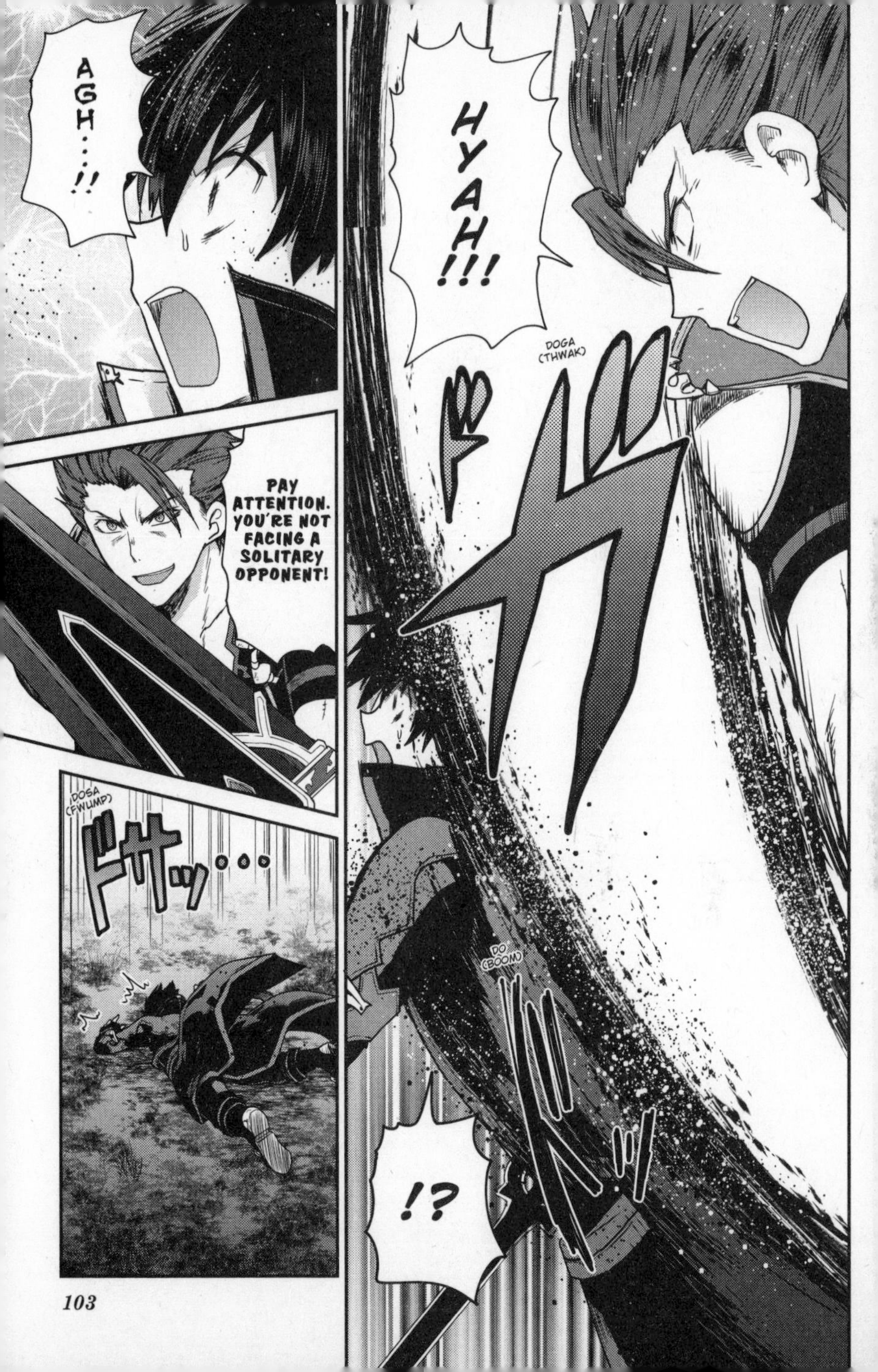
HYAH!!!
DOGA (THWAK)
DO (BOOM)
!?
AGH...!!
PAY ATTENTION. YOU'RE NOT FACING A SOLITARY OPPONENT!
DOSA (FWUMP)

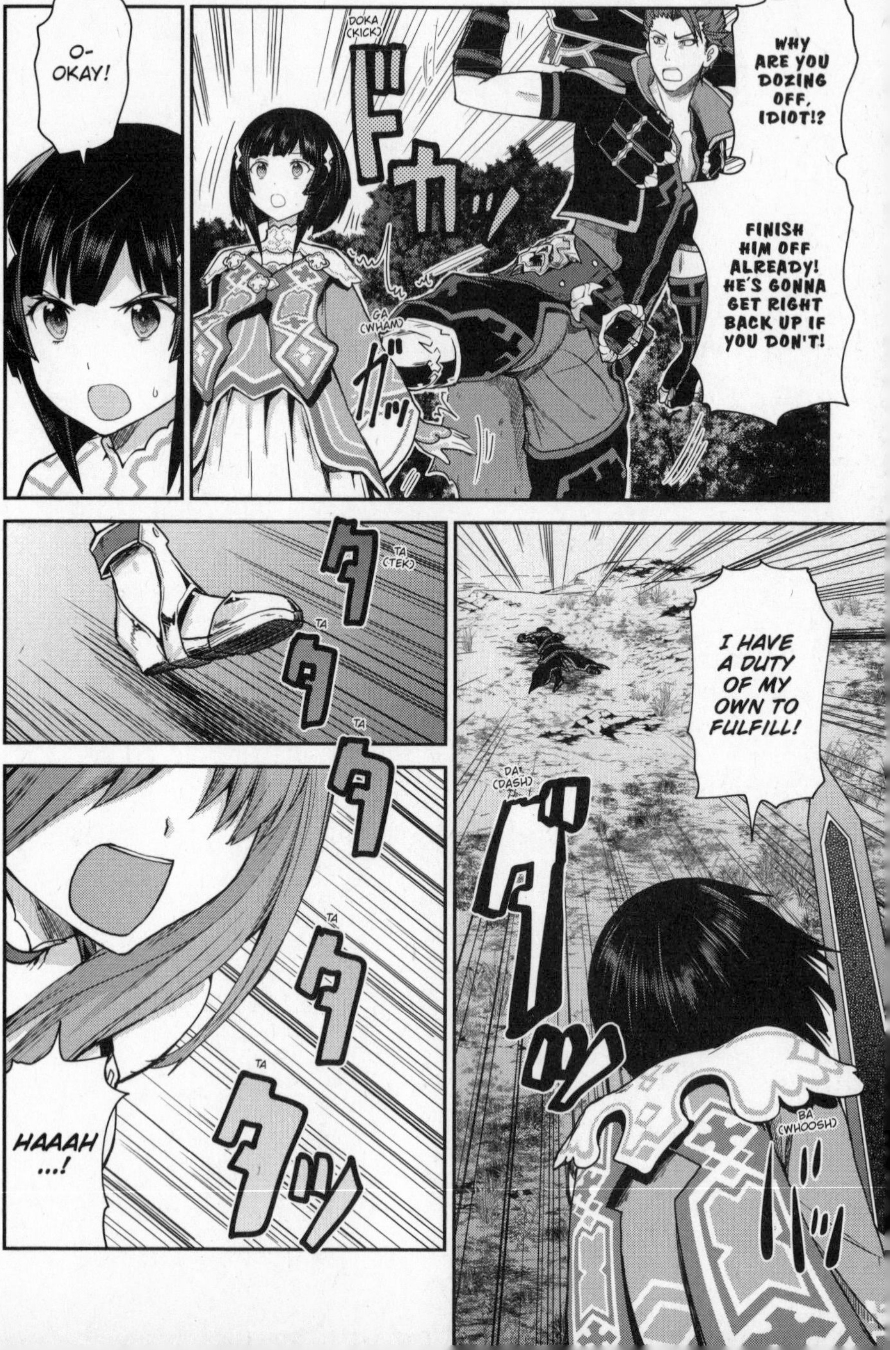
WHY ARE YOU DOZING OFF, IDIOT!?
FINISH HIM OFF ALREADY! HE'S GONNA GET RIGHT BACK UP IF YOU DON'T!
DOKA (KICK)
GA (WHAM)
O-OKAY!
I HAVE A DUTY OF MY OWN TO FULFILL!
DA (DASH)
BA (WHOOSH)
TA (TEK)
TA
TA
TA
TA
HAAAH ...!

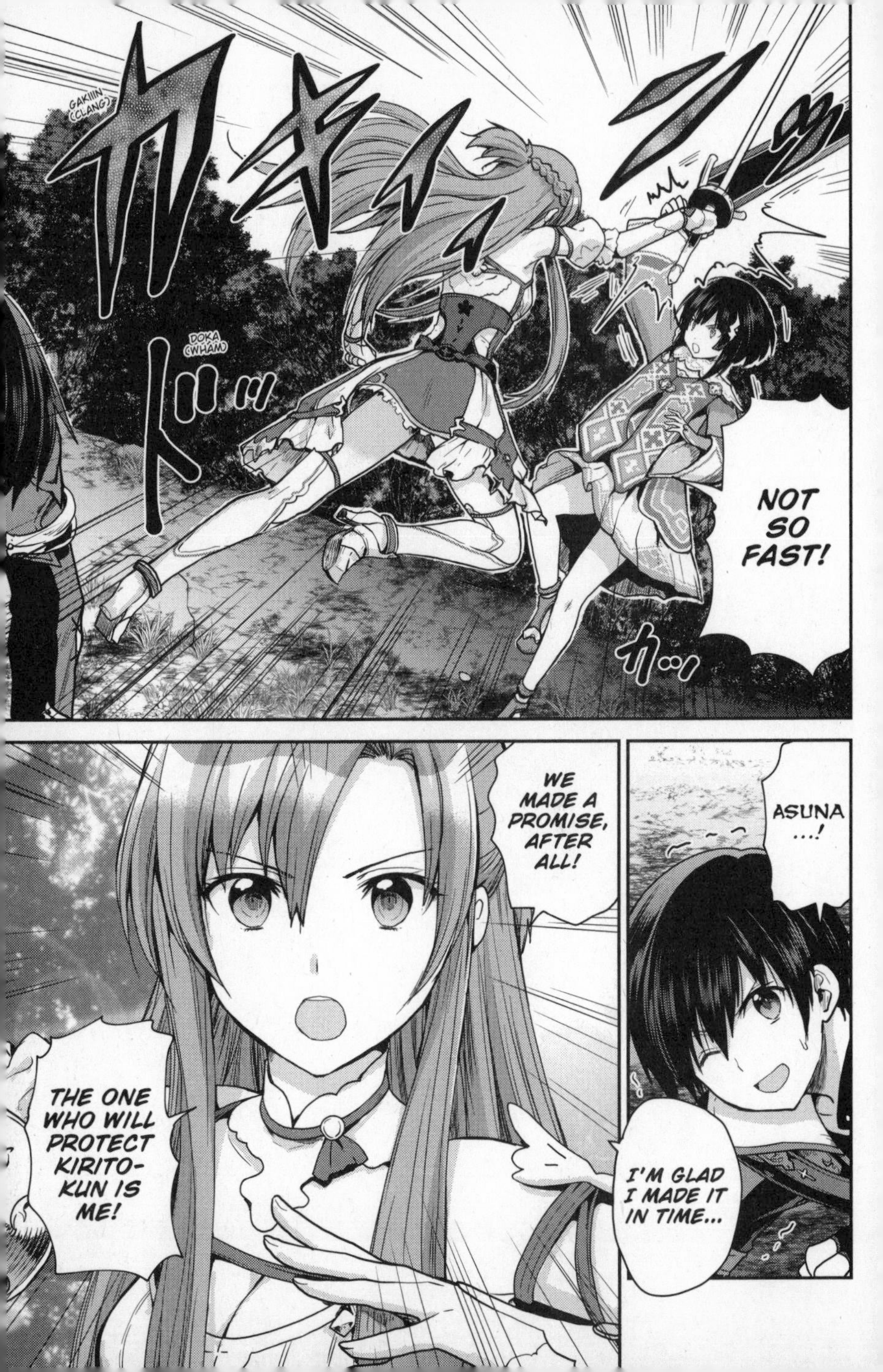
GAKIIIN (CLANG)
DOKA (WHAM)
NOT SO FAST!
ASUNA ...!
I'M GLAD I MADE IT IN TIME...
WE MADE A PROMISE, AFTER ALL!
THE ONE WHO WILL PROTECT KIRITO-KUN IS ME!

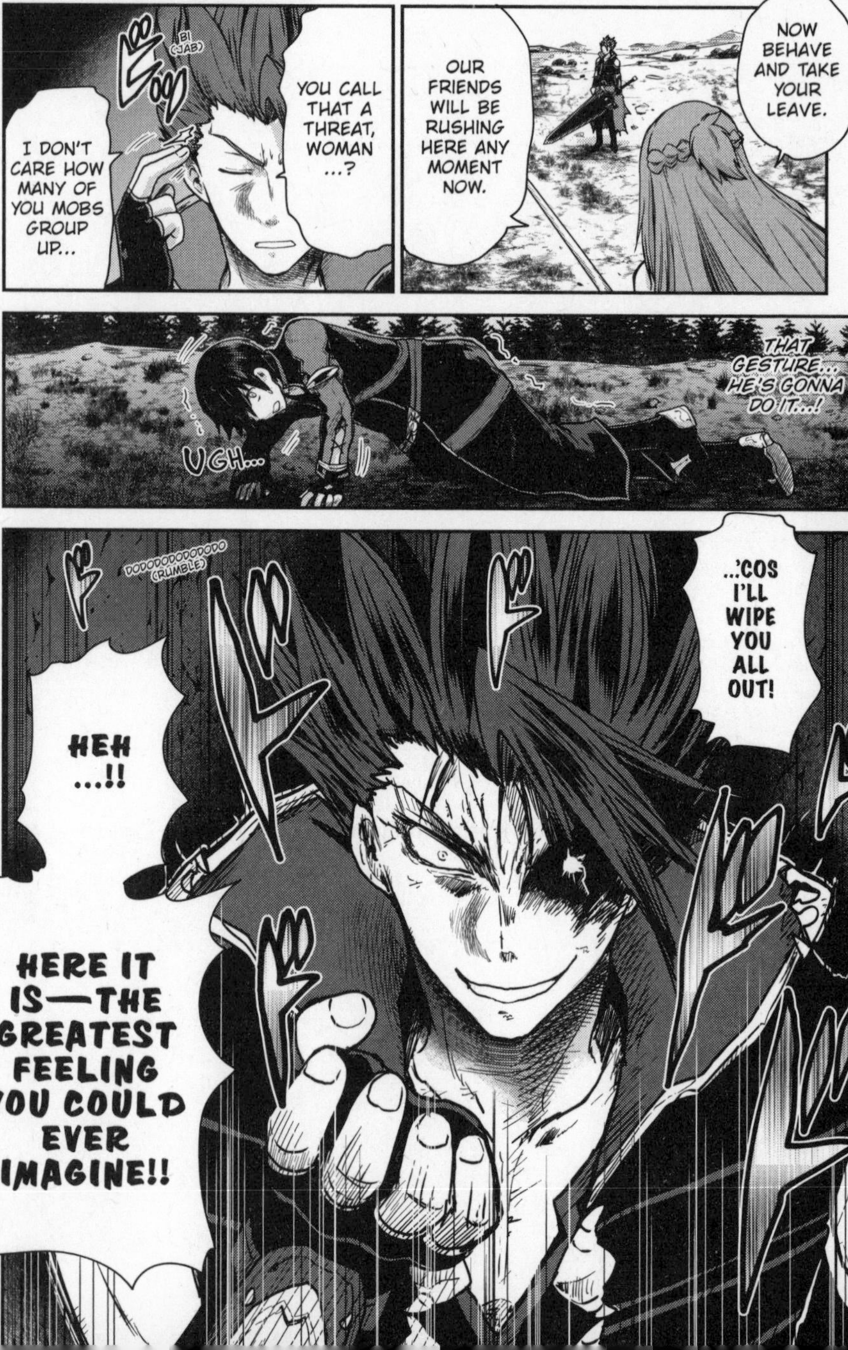
NOW BEHAVE AND TAKE YOUR LEAVE.
OUR FRIENDS WILL BE RUSHING HERE ANY MOMENT NOW.
BI (JAB)
YOU CALL THAT A THREAT, WOMAN ...?
I DON'T CARE HOW MANY OF YOU MOBS GROUP UP...
THAT GESTURE... HE'S GONNA DO IT...!
UGH...
...'COS I'LL WIPE YOU ALL OUT!
DODODODODODODO (RUMBLE)
HEH ...!!
HERE IT IS—THE GREATEST FEELING YOU COULD EVER IMAGINE!!

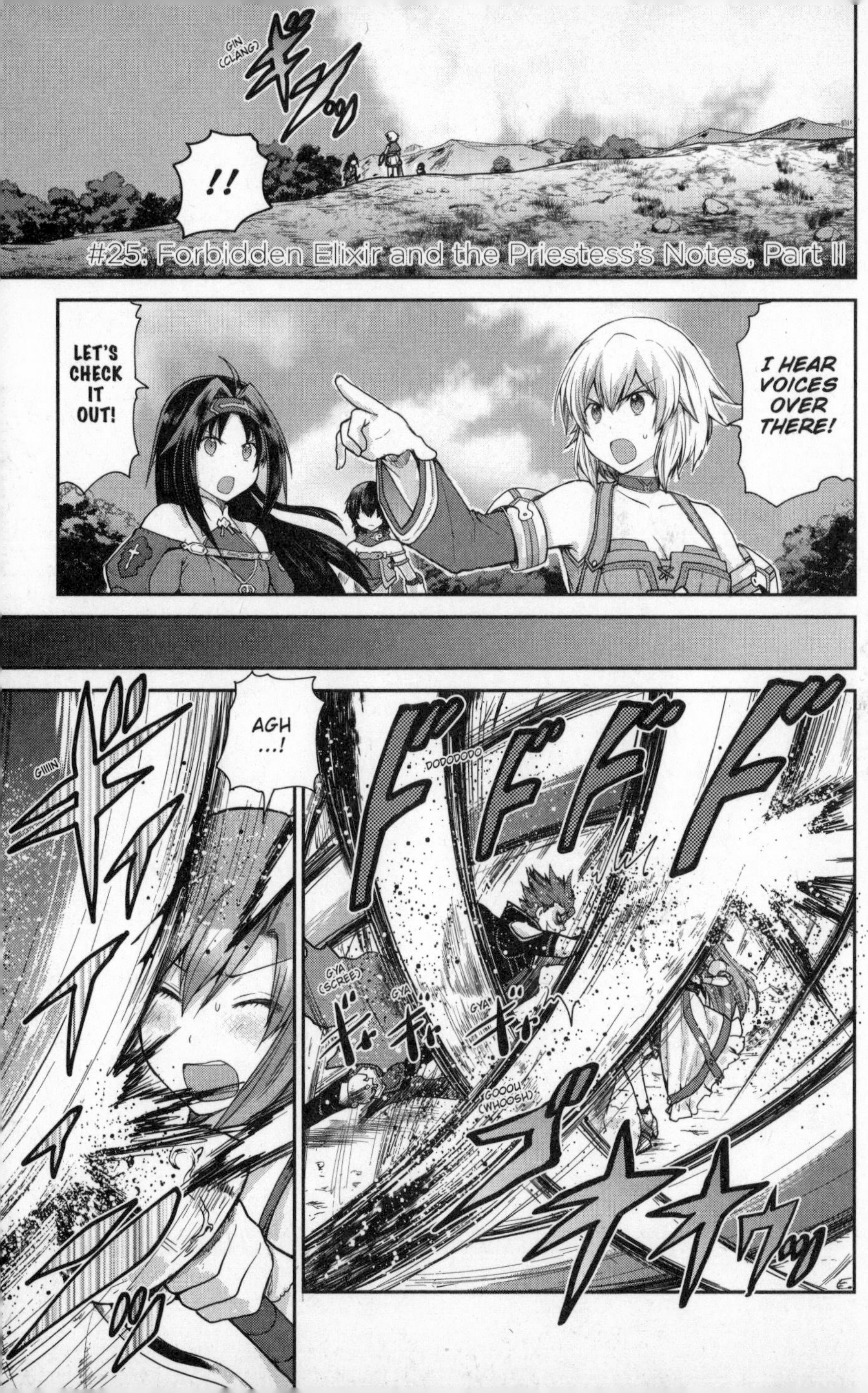
GIN (CLANG)
!!
#25: Forbidden Elixir and the Priestess's Notes, Part II
I HEAR VOICES OVER THERE!
LET'S CHECK IT OUT!
DODODODO
GYA (SCREE)
GYA
GYA
GOOOU (WHOOSH)
AGH ...!
GIIIN

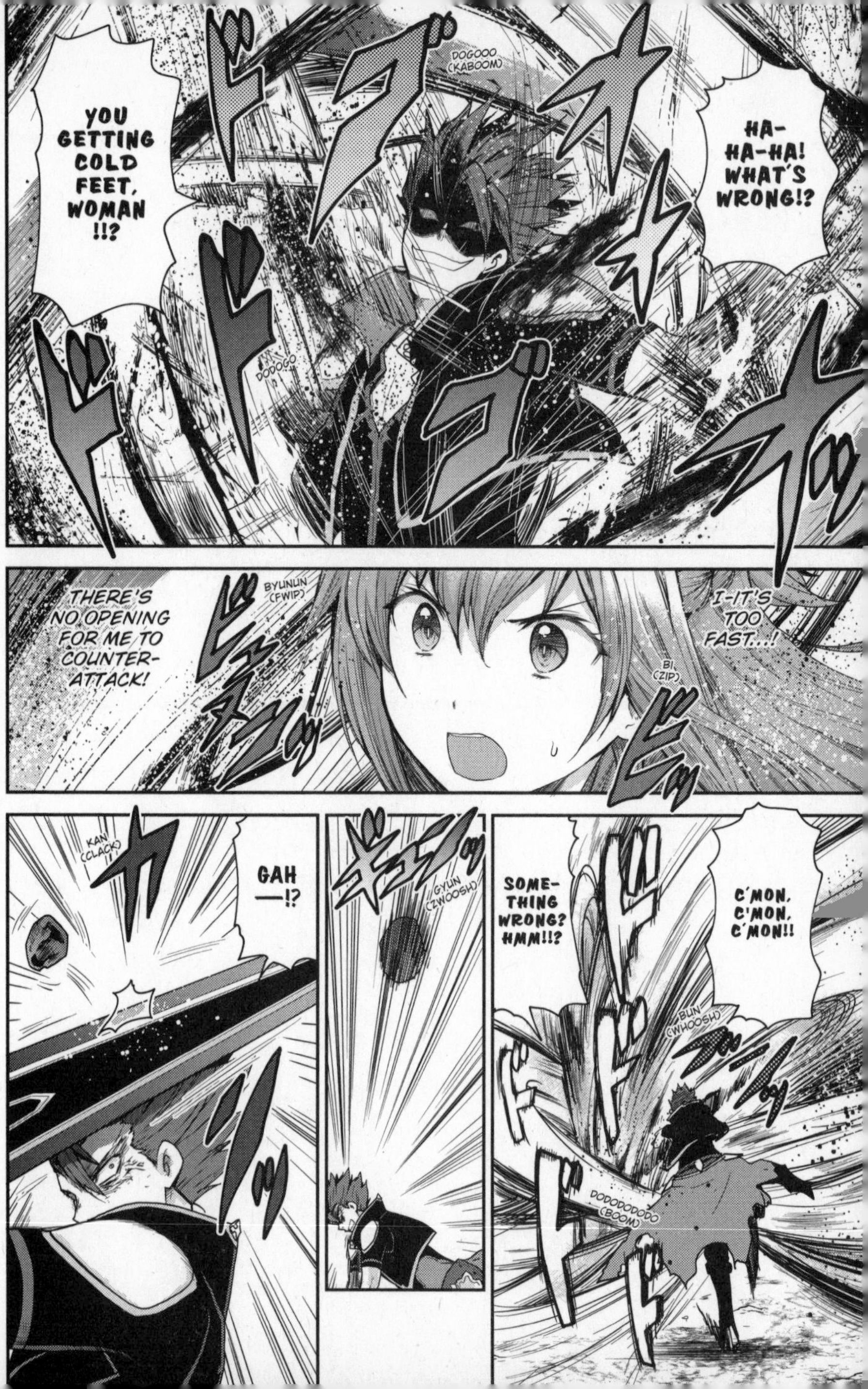
HA-HA-HA! WHAT'S WRONG!?
DOGOOO (KABOOM)
YOU GETTING COLD FEET, WOMAN!!?
DODOGO
I-IT'S TOO FAST...!
BI (ZIP)
BYUNUN (FWIP)
THERE'S NO OPENING FOR ME TO COUNTER-ATTACK!
C'MON, C'MON, C'MON!!
SOMETHING WRONG? HMM!!?
BUN (WHOOSH)
DODODODODO (BOOM)
GYUN (ZWOOSH)
GAH—!?
KAN (CLACK)

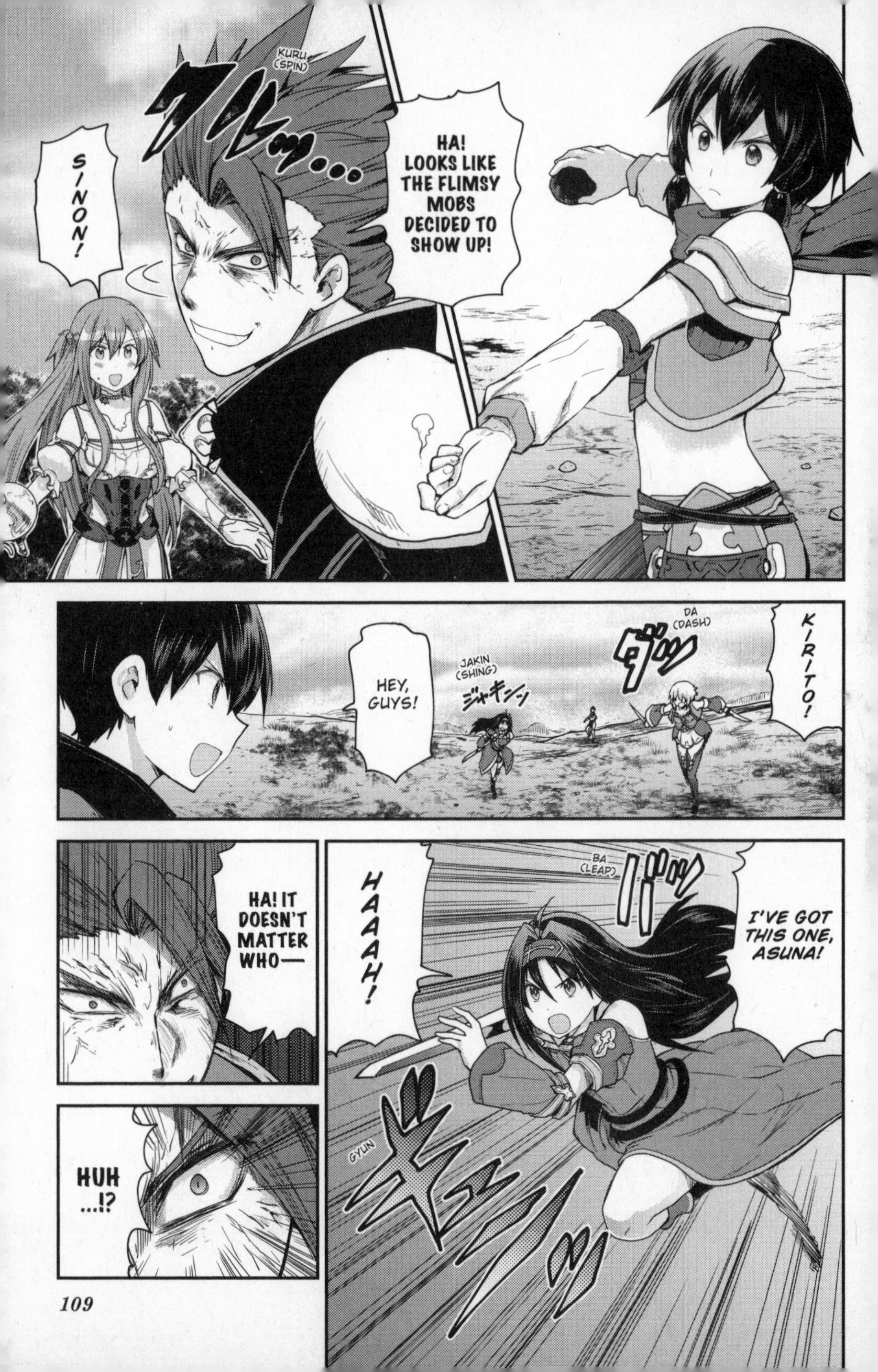
KURU (SPIN)
HA! LOOKS LIKE THE FLIMSY MOBS DECIDED TO SHOW UP!
SINON!
KIRITO!
DA (DASH)
JAKIN (SHING)
HEY, GUYS!
I'VE GOT THIS ONE, ASUNA!
BA (LEAP)
HAAAAH!
GYUN
HA! IT DOESN'T MATTER WHO—
HUH ...!?

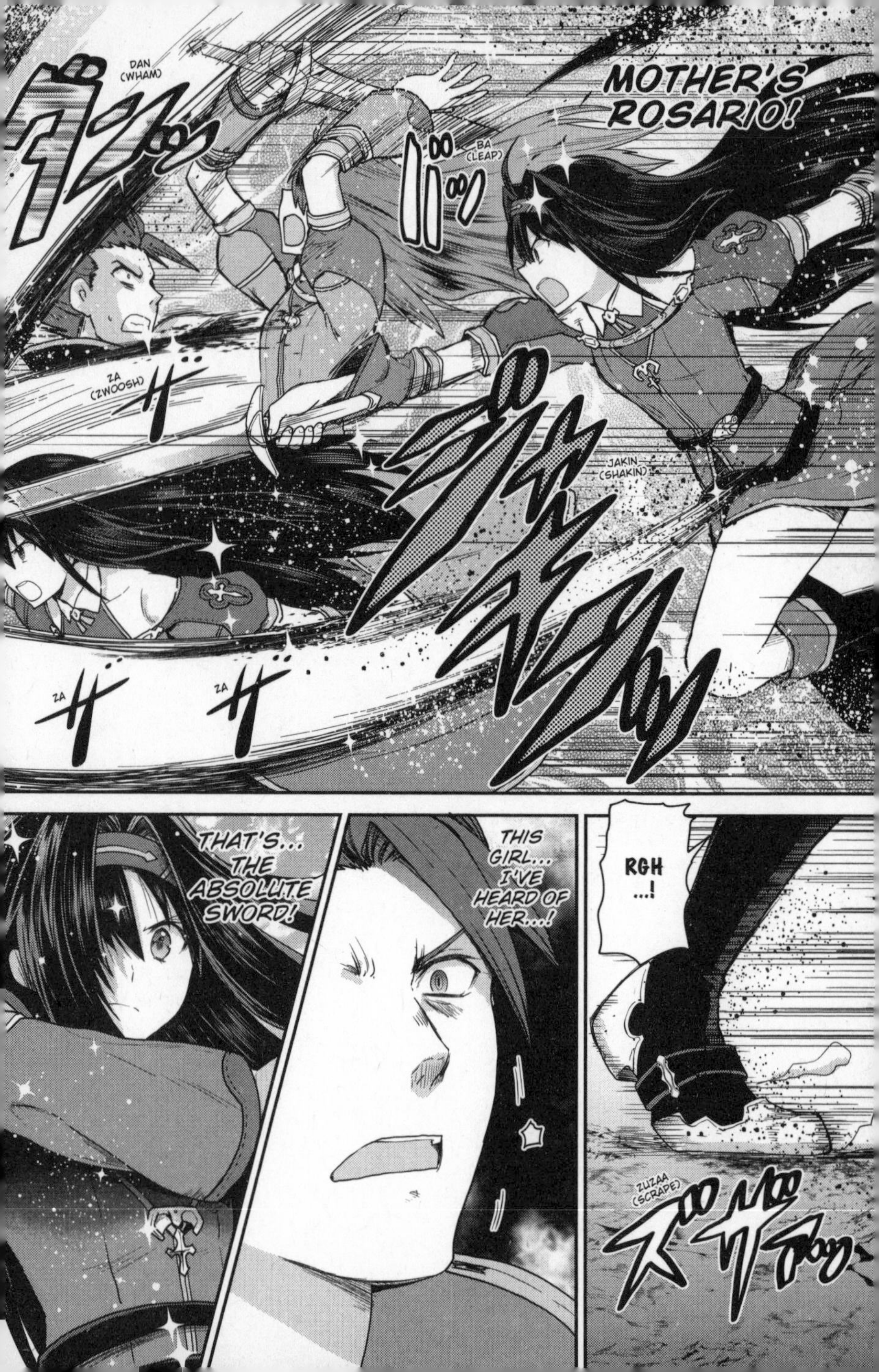
MOTHER'S ROSARIO!
BA (LEAP)
DAN (WHAM)
JAKIN (SHAKIN)
ZA (ZWOOSH)
ZA
ZA
RGH ...!
ZUZAA (SCRAPE)
THIS GIRL... I'VE HEARD OF HER...!
THAT'S... THE ABSOLUTE SWORD!

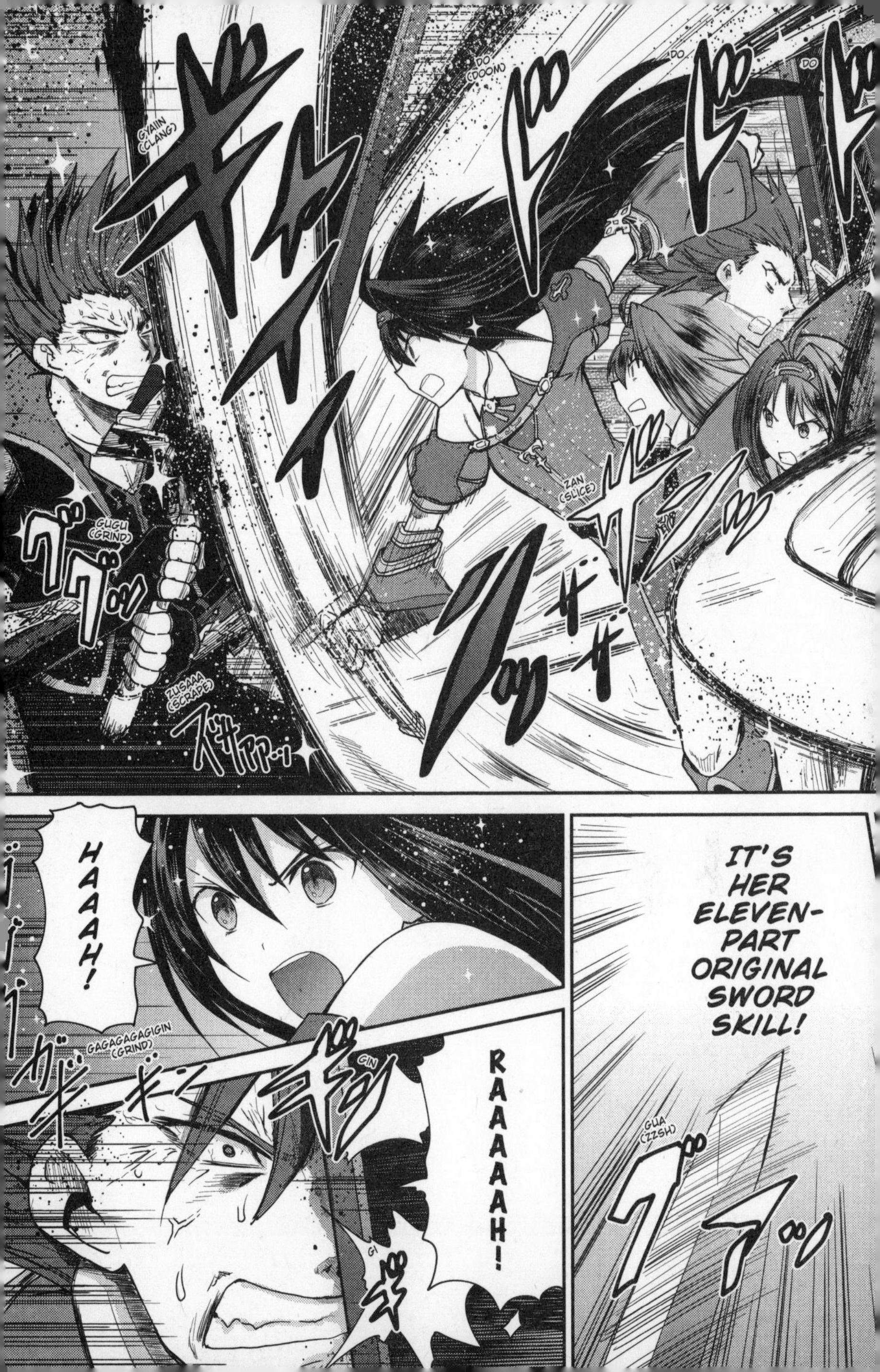
DO
DO
DO (DOOM)
GYAIIN (CLANG)
ZAN (SLICE)
GUGU (GRIND)
ZUSAAA (SCRAPE)
IT'S HER ELEVEN-PART ORIGINAL SWORD SKILL!
GUA (ZZSH)
HAAAAH!
RAAAAAAAH!
GIN
GAGAGAGAGIGIN (GRIND)
GI

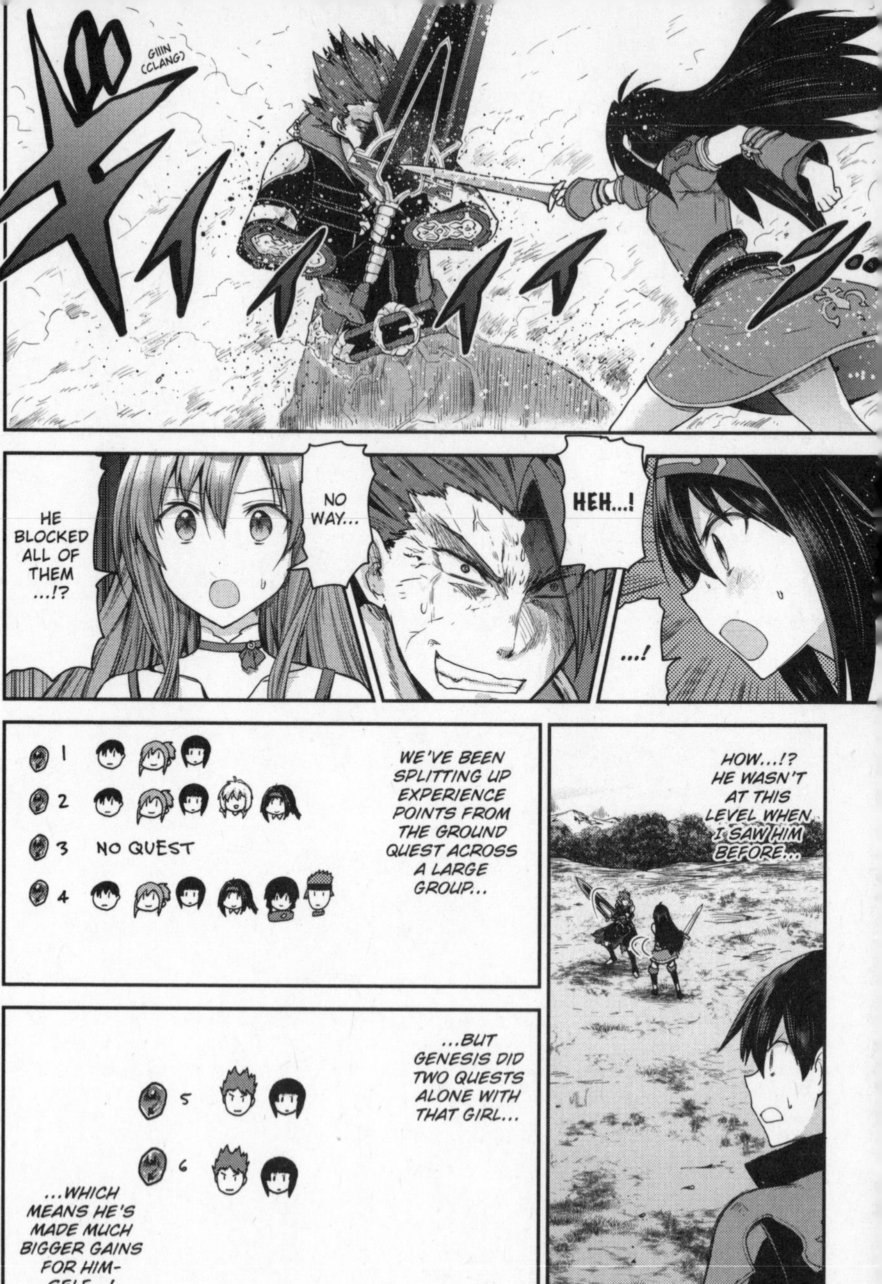
GIIIN
(CLANG)
...!
HEH...!
NO WAY...
HE BLOCKED ALL OF THEM ...!?
HOW...!? HE WASN'T AT THIS LEVEL WHEN I SAW HIM BEFORE...
1
2
3 NO QUEST
4
WE'VE BEEN SPLITTING UP EXPERIENCE POINTS FROM THE GROUND QUEST ACROSS A LARGE GROUP...
5
6
...BUT GENESIS DID TWO QUESTS ALONE WITH THAT GIRL...
...WHICH MEANS HE'S MADE MUCH BIGGER GAINS FOR HIM-SELF...!

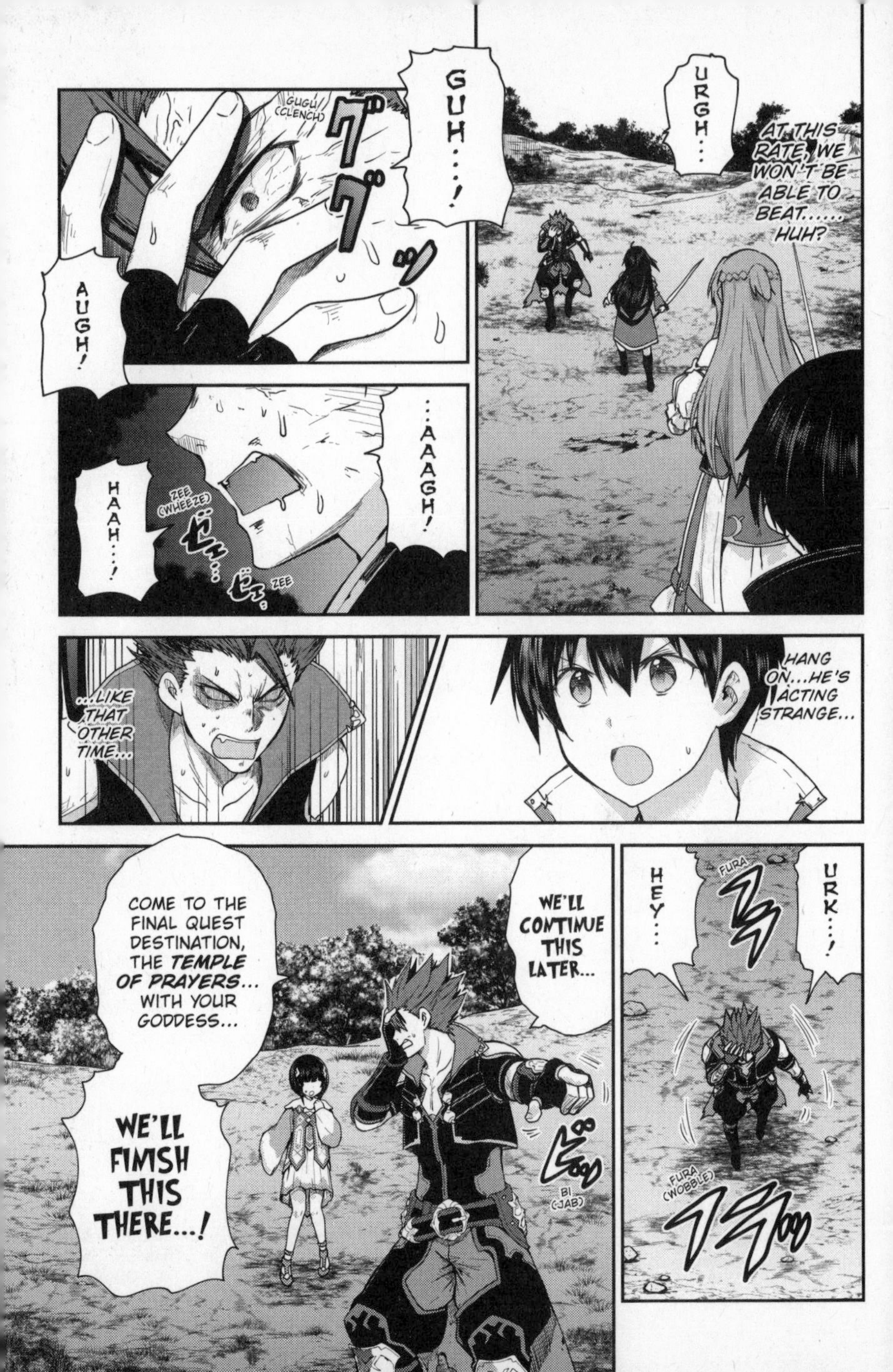
URGH...
AT THIS RATE, WE WON'T BE ABLE TO BEAT...... HUH?
GUH...!
GUGU (CLENCH)
AUGH!
...AAAAGH!
HAAH...!
ZEE (WHEEZE)
ZEE
HANG ON...HE'S ACTING STRANGE...
...LIKE THAT OTHER TIME...
URK...!
FURA
HEY...
FURA (WOBBLE)
WE'LL CONTINUE THIS LATER...
COME TO THE FINAL QUEST DESTINATION, THE *TEMPLE OF PRAYERS*... WITH YOUR GODDESS...
BI (JAB)
WE'LL FINISH THIS THERE...!

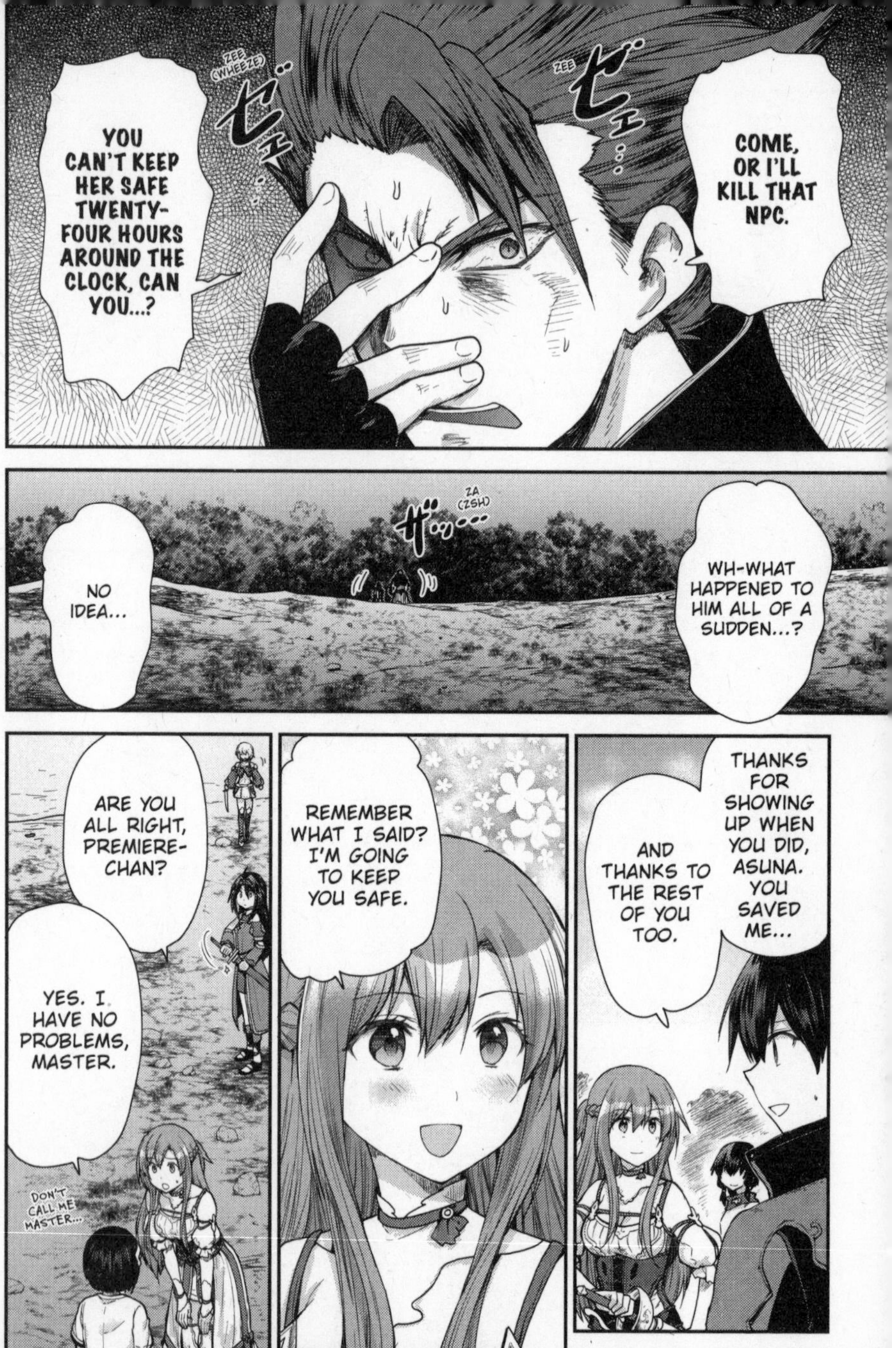
ZEE
COME, OR I'LL KILL THAT NPC.
ZEE (WHEEZE)
YOU CAN'T KEEP HER SAFE TWENTY-FOUR HOURS AROUND THE CLOCK, CAN YOU...?
WH-WHAT HAPPENED TO HIM ALL OF A SUDDEN...?
ZA (ZSH)
NO IDEA...
THANKS FOR SHOWING UP WHEN YOU DID, ASUNA. YOU SAVED ME...
AND THANKS TO THE REST OF YOU TOO.
REMEMBER WHAT I SAID? I'M GOING TO KEEP YOU SAFE.
ARE YOU ALL RIGHT, PREMIERE-CHAN?
YES. I HAVE NO PROBLEMS, MASTER.
DON'T CALL ME MASTER...

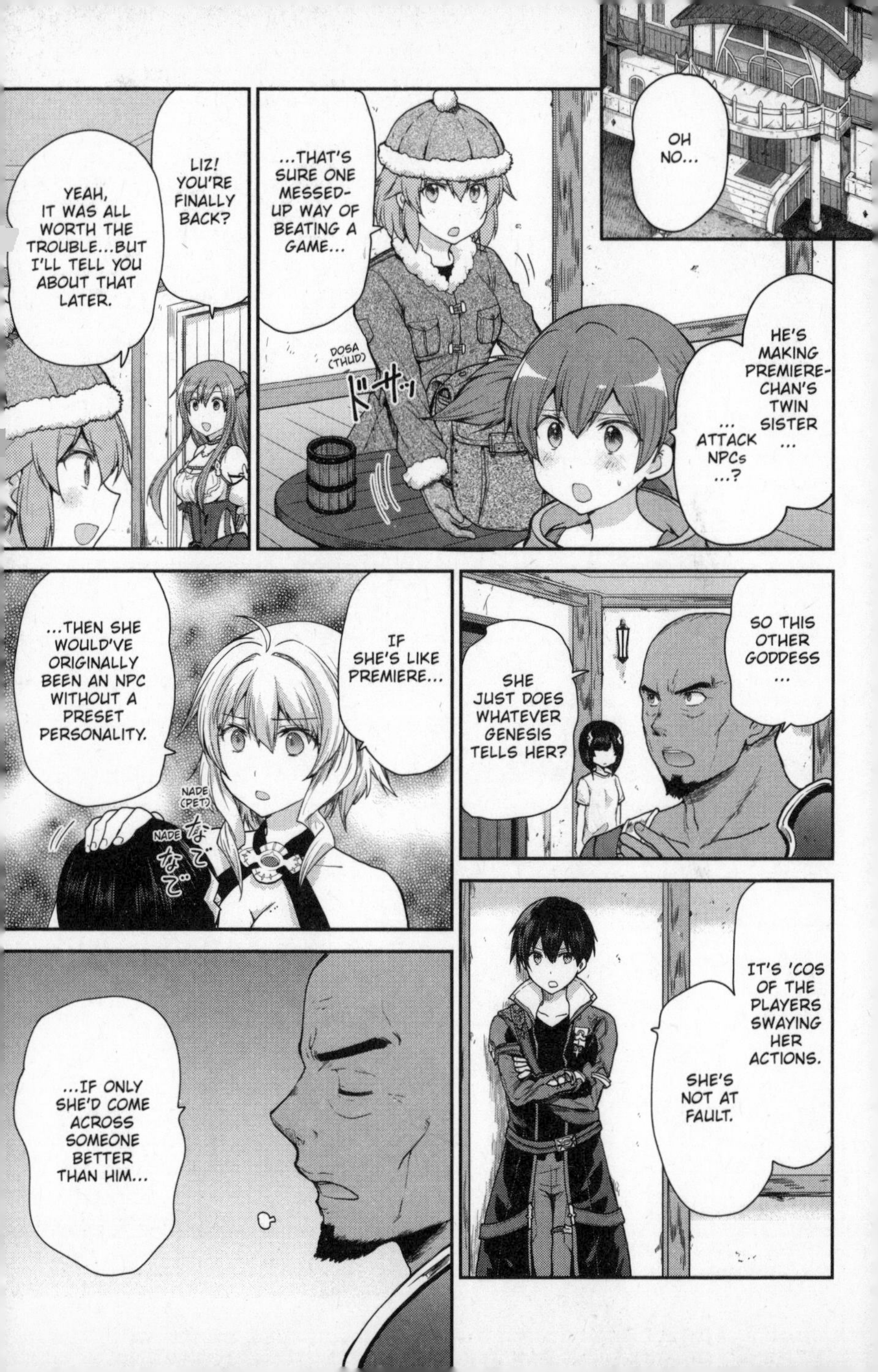
OH NO...
HE'S MAKING PREMIERE-CHAN'S TWIN SISTER...
...ATTACK NPCs...?
...THAT'S SURE ONE MESSED-UP WAY OF BEATING A GAME...
DOSA (THUD)
ドサッ
LIZ! YOU'RE FINALLY BACK?
YEAH, IT WAS ALL WORTH THE TROUBLE...BUT I'LL TELL YOU ABOUT THAT LATER.
SO THIS OTHER GODDESS...
SHE JUST DOES WHATEVER GENESIS TELLS HER?
IF SHE'S LIKE PREMIERE...
...THEN SHE WOULD'VE ORIGINALLY BEEN AN NPC WITHOUT A PRESET PERSONALITY.
NADE (PET)
NADE
なでなで
IT'S 'COS OF THE PLAYERS SWAYING HER ACTIONS.
SHE'S NOT AT FAULT.
...IF ONLY SHE'D COME ACROSS SOMEONE BETTER THAN HIM...

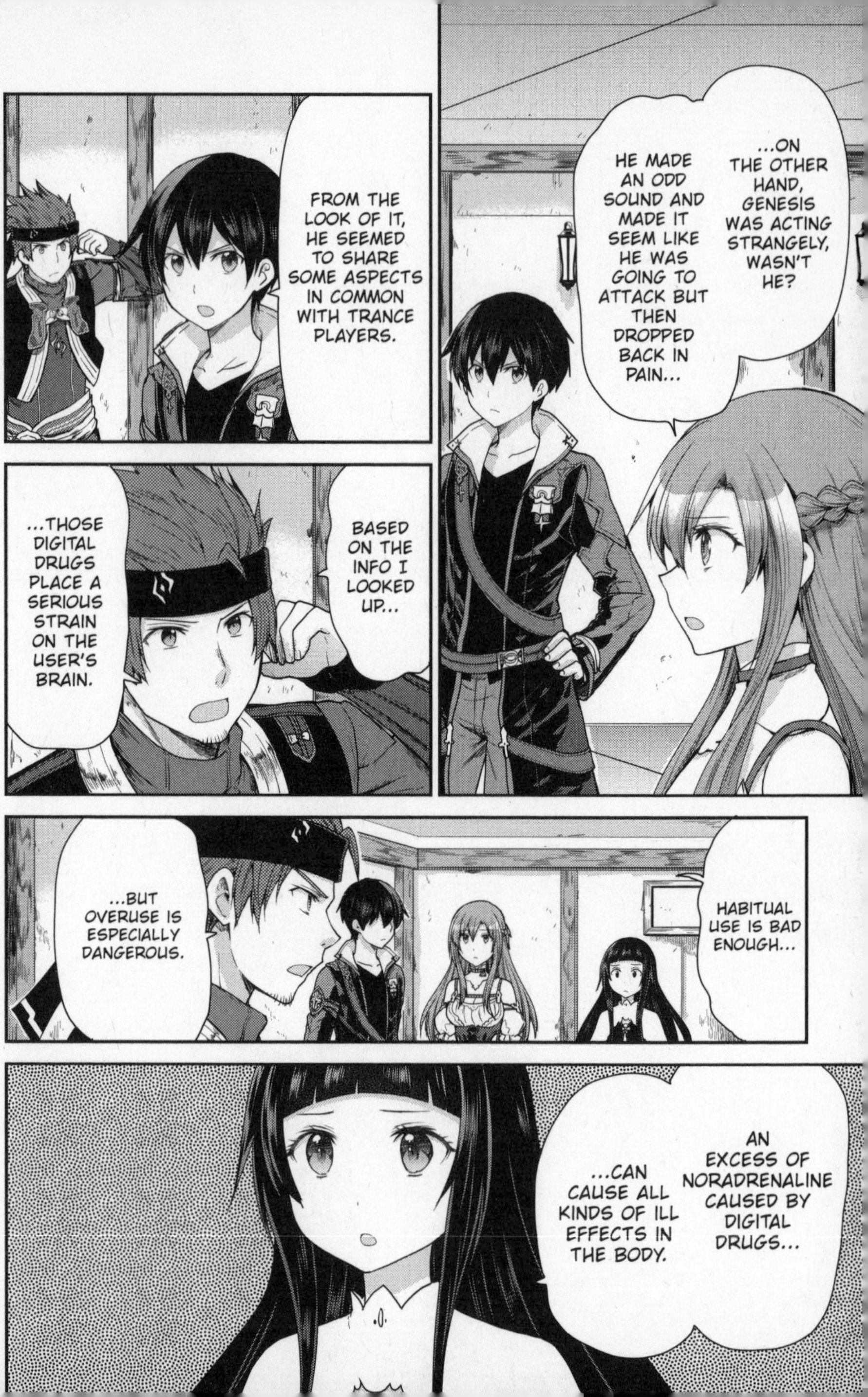
...ON THE OTHER HAND, GENESIS WAS ACTING STRANGELY, WASN'T HE?
HE MADE AN ODD SOUND AND MADE IT SEEM LIKE HE WAS GOING TO ATTACK BUT THEN DROPPED BACK IN PAIN...
FROM THE LOOK OF IT, HE SEEMED TO SHARE SOME ASPECTS IN COMMON WITH TRANCE PLAYERS.
BASED ON THE INFO I LOOKED UP...
...THOSE DIGITAL DRUGS PLACE A SERIOUS STRAIN ON THE USER'S BRAIN.
HABITUAL USE IS BAD ENOUGH...
...BUT OVERUSE IS ESPECIALLY DANGEROUS.
AN EXCESS OF NORADRENALINE CAUSED BY DIGITAL DRUGS...
...CAN CAUSE ALL KINDS OF ILL EFFECTS IN THE BODY.

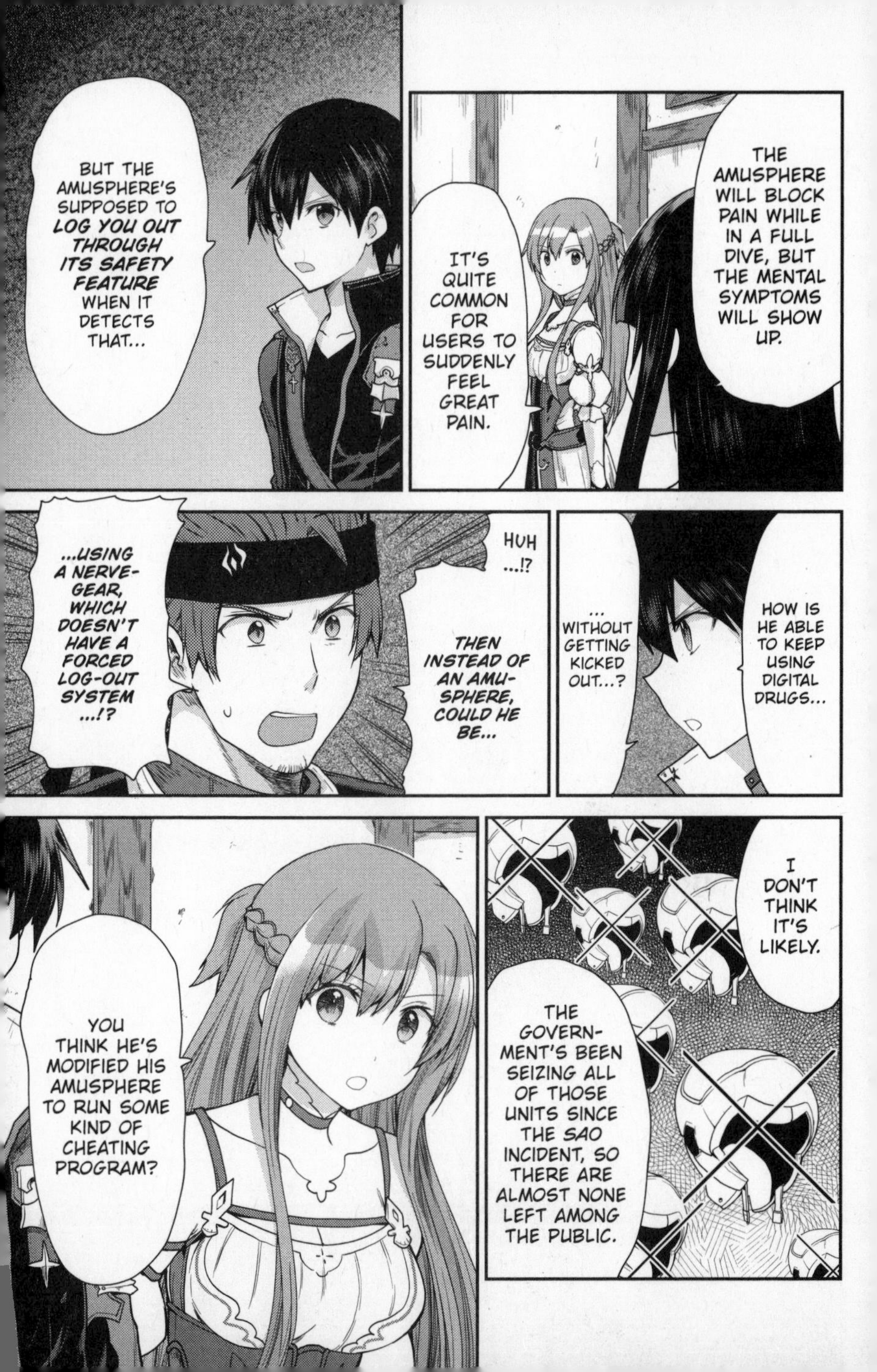

THE AMUSPHERE WILL BLOCK PAIN WHILE IN A FULL DIVE, BUT THE MENTAL SYMPTOMS WILL SHOW UP.
IT'S QUITE COMMON FOR USERS TO SUDDENLY FEEL GREAT PAIN.
BUT THE AMUSPHERE'S SUPPOSED TO ***LOG YOU OUT THROUGH ITS SAFETY FEATURE*** WHEN IT DETECTS THAT...
HOW IS HE ABLE TO KEEP USING DIGITAL DRUGS...
...WITHOUT GETTING KICKED OUT...?
HUH ...!?
THEN INSTEAD OF AN AMUSPHERE, COULD HE BE...
...USING A NERVE-GEAR, WHICH DOESN'T HAVE A FORCED LOG-OUT SYSTEM ...!?
I DON'T THINK IT'S LIKELY.
THE GOVERNMENT'S BEEN SEIZING ALL OF THOSE UNITS SINCE THE SAO INCIDENT, SO THERE ARE ALMOST NONE LEFT AMONG THE PUBLIC.
YOU THINK HE'S MODIFIED HIS AMUSPHERE TO RUN SOME KIND OF CHEATING PROGRAM?

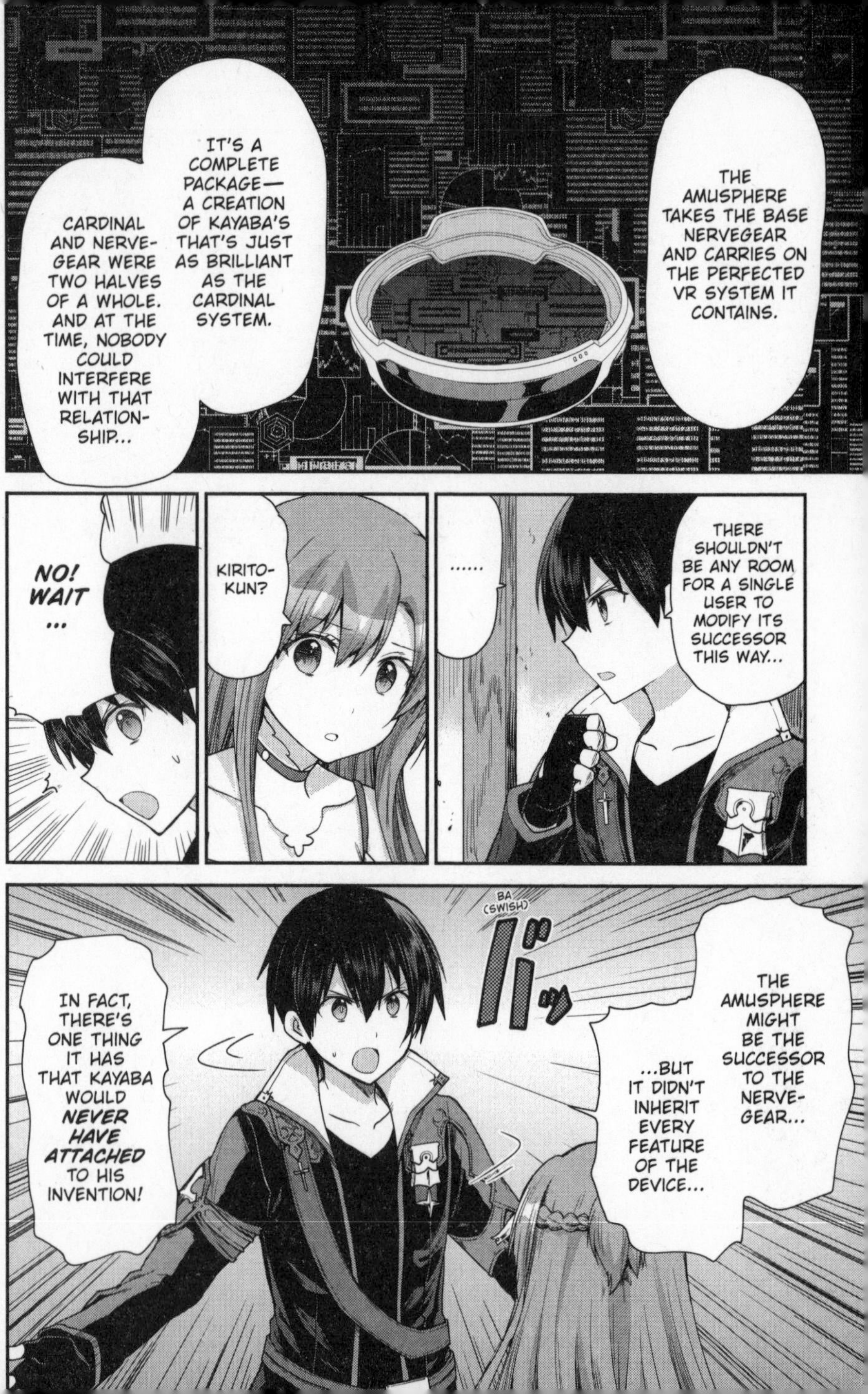
THE AMUSPHERE TAKES THE BASE NERVEGEAR AND CARRIES ON THE PERFECTED VR SYSTEM IT CONTAINS.
IT'S A COMPLETE PACKAGE—A CREATION OF KAYABA'S THAT'S JUST AS BRILLIANT AS THE CARDINAL SYSTEM.
CARDINAL AND NERVE-GEAR WERE TWO HALVES OF A WHOLE. AND AT THE TIME, NOBODY COULD INTERFERE WITH THAT RELATION-SHIP...
THERE SHOULDN'T BE ANY ROOM FOR A SINGLE USER TO MODIFY ITS SUCCESSOR THIS WAY...
......
KIRITO-KUN?
NO! WAIT...
BA (SWISH)
THE AMUSPHERE MIGHT BE THE SUCCESSOR TO THE NERVE-GEAR...
...BUT IT DIDN'T INHERIT EVERY FEATURE OF THE DEVICE...
IN FACT, THERE'S ONE THING IT HAS THAT KAYABA WOULD NEVER HAVE ATTACHED TO HIS INVENTION!

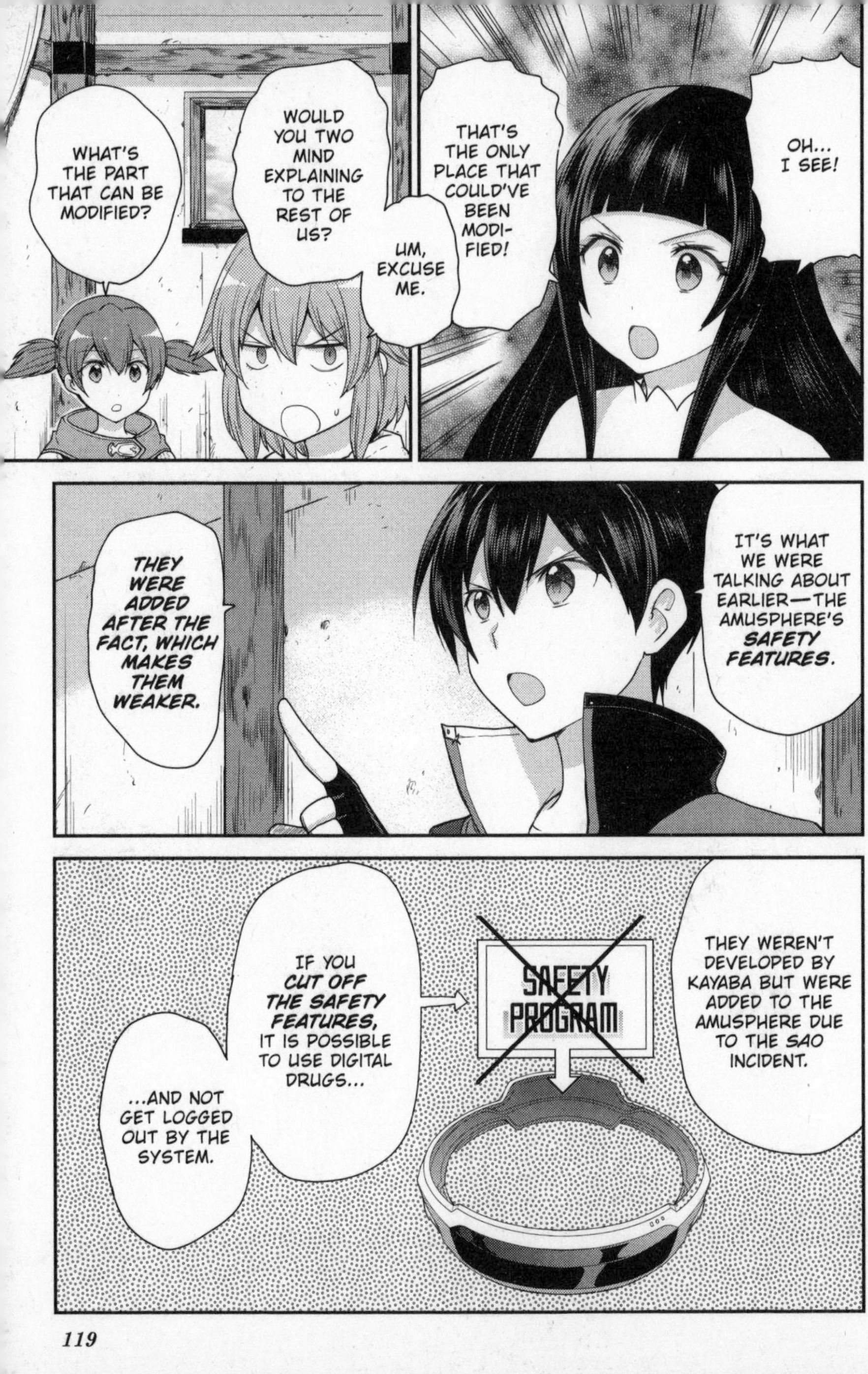
OH... I SEE!
THAT'S THE ONLY PLACE THAT COULD'VE BEEN MODI-FIED!
UM, EXCUSE ME.
WOULD YOU TWO MIND EXPLAINING TO THE REST OF US?
WHAT'S THE PART THAT CAN BE MODIFIED?
IT'S WHAT WE WERE TALKING ABOUT EARLIER—THE AMUSPHERE'S *SAFETY FEATURES*.
THEY WERE ADDED AFTER THE FACT, WHICH MAKES THEM WEAKER.
THEY WEREN'T DEVELOPED BY KAYABA BUT WERE ADDED TO THE AMUSPHERE DUE TO THE SAO INCIDENT.
SAFETY PROGRAM
IF YOU *CUT OFF THE SAFETY FEATURES,* IT IS POSSIBLE TO USE DIGITAL DRUGS...
...AND NOT GET LOGGED OUT BY THE SYSTEM.

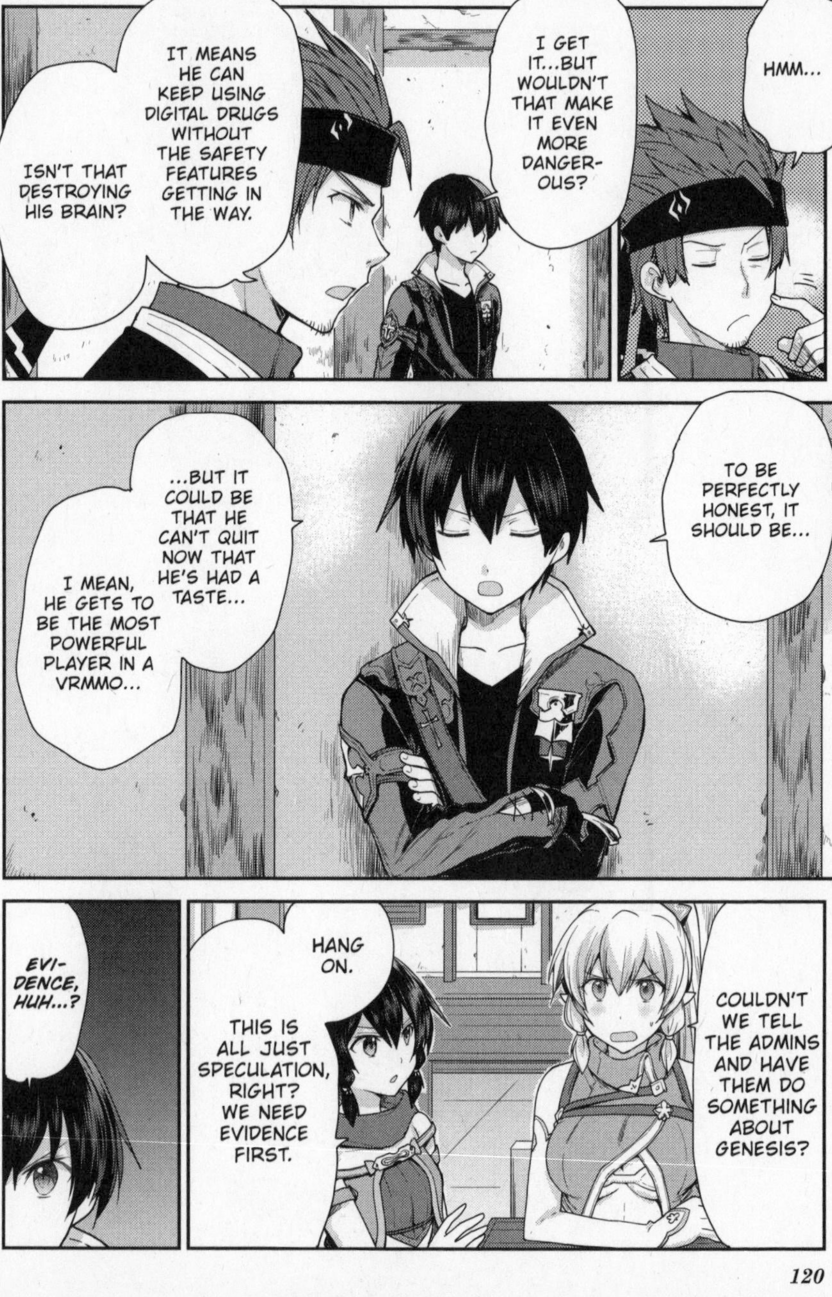
HMM...
I GET IT...BUT WOULDN'T THAT MAKE IT EVEN MORE DANGER-OUS?
IT MEANS HE CAN KEEP USING DIGITAL DRUGS WITHOUT THE SAFETY FEATURES GETTING IN THE WAY.
ISN'T THAT DESTROYING HIS BRAIN?
TO BE PERFECTLY HONEST, IT SHOULD BE...
...BUT IT COULD BE THAT HE CAN'T QUIT NOW THAT HE'S HAD A TASTE...
I MEAN, HE GETS TO BE THE MOST POWERFUL PLAYER IN A VRMMO...
COULDN'T WE TELL THE ADMINS AND HAVE THEM DO SOMETHING ABOUT GENESIS?
HANG ON.
THIS IS ALL JUST SPECULATION, RIGHT? WE NEED EVIDENCE FIRST.
EVI-DENCE, HUH...?

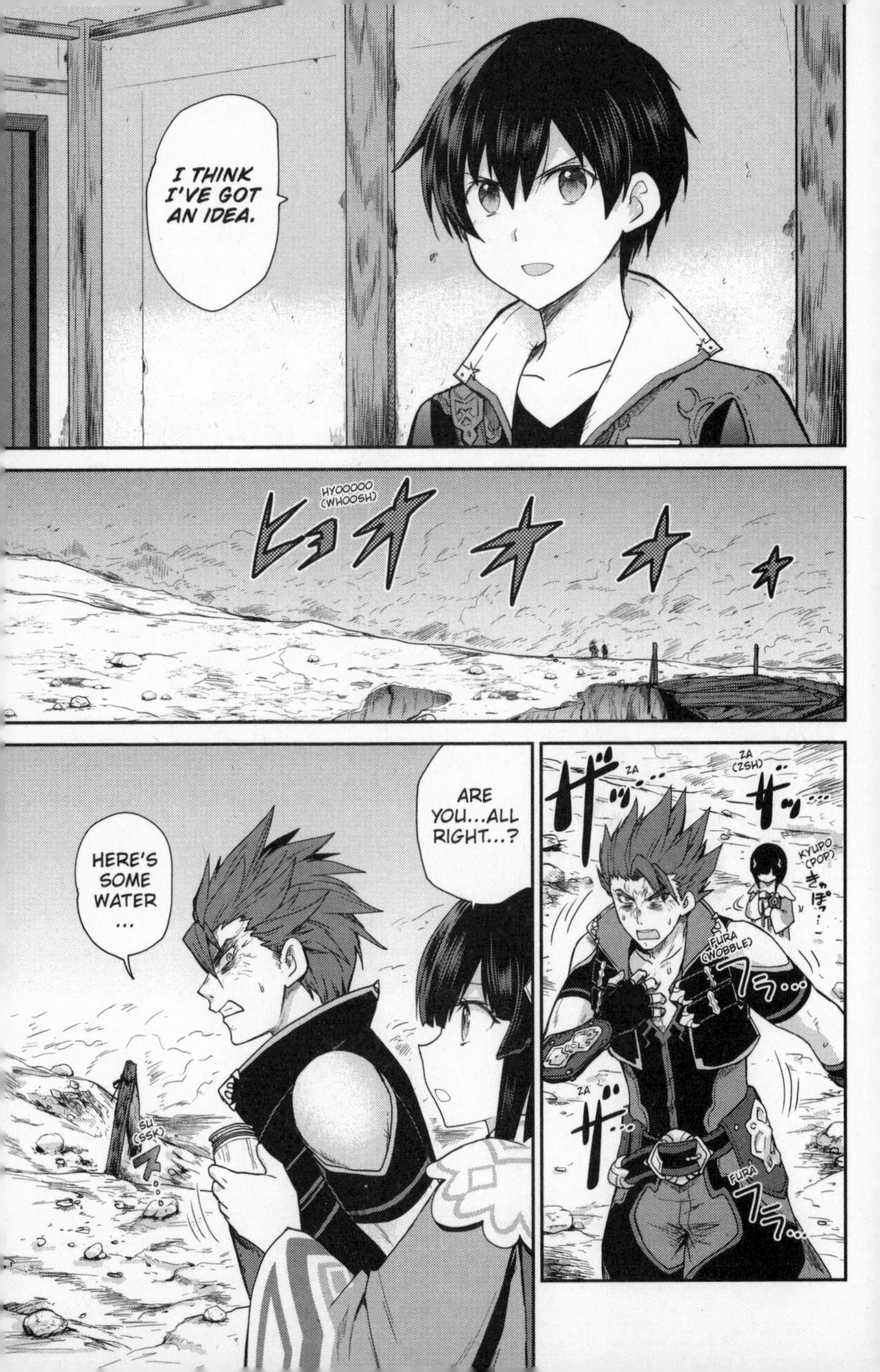
I THINK I'VE GOT AN IDEA.
HYOOOOO (WHOOSH)
ZA (ZSH)
ZA
KYUPO (POP)
きゅぽ…
FURA (WOBBLE)
フラ…
ZA
FURA
フラ…
ARE YOU...ALL RIGHT...?
HERE'S SOME WATER ...
SU (SSK)

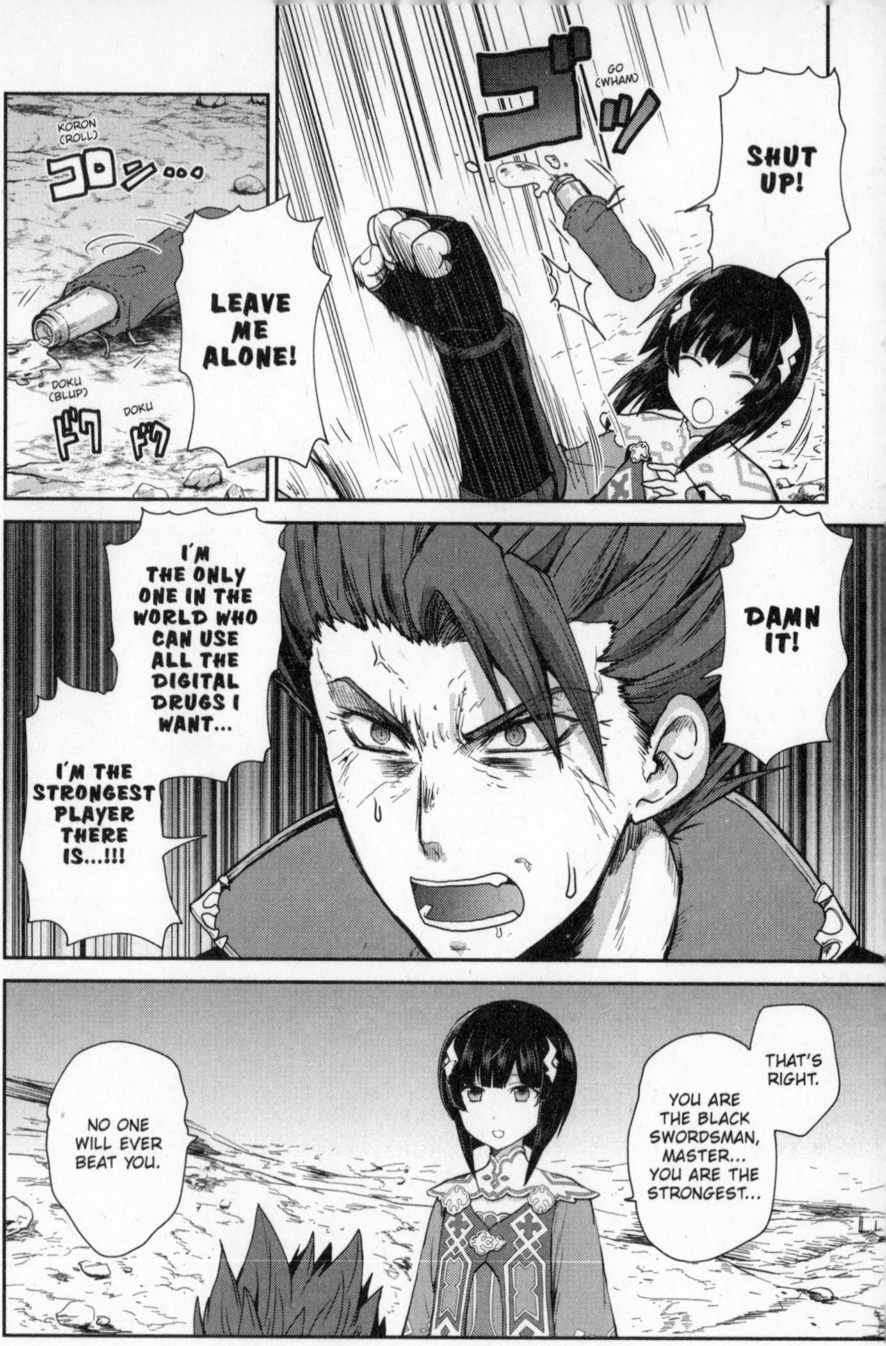

SHUT UP!
ゴッ
GO (WHAM)
LEAVE ME ALONE!
コロン・・・
KORON (ROLL)
ドク
DOKU (BLUP)
ドク
DOKU
DAMN IT!
I'M THE ONLY ONE IN THE WORLD WHO CAN USE ALL THE DIGITAL DRUGS I WANT...
I'M THE STRONGEST PLAYER THERE IS...!!!
THAT'S RIGHT.
YOU ARE THE BLACK SWORDSMAN, MASTER... YOU ARE THE STRONGEST...
NO ONE WILL EVER BEAT YOU.

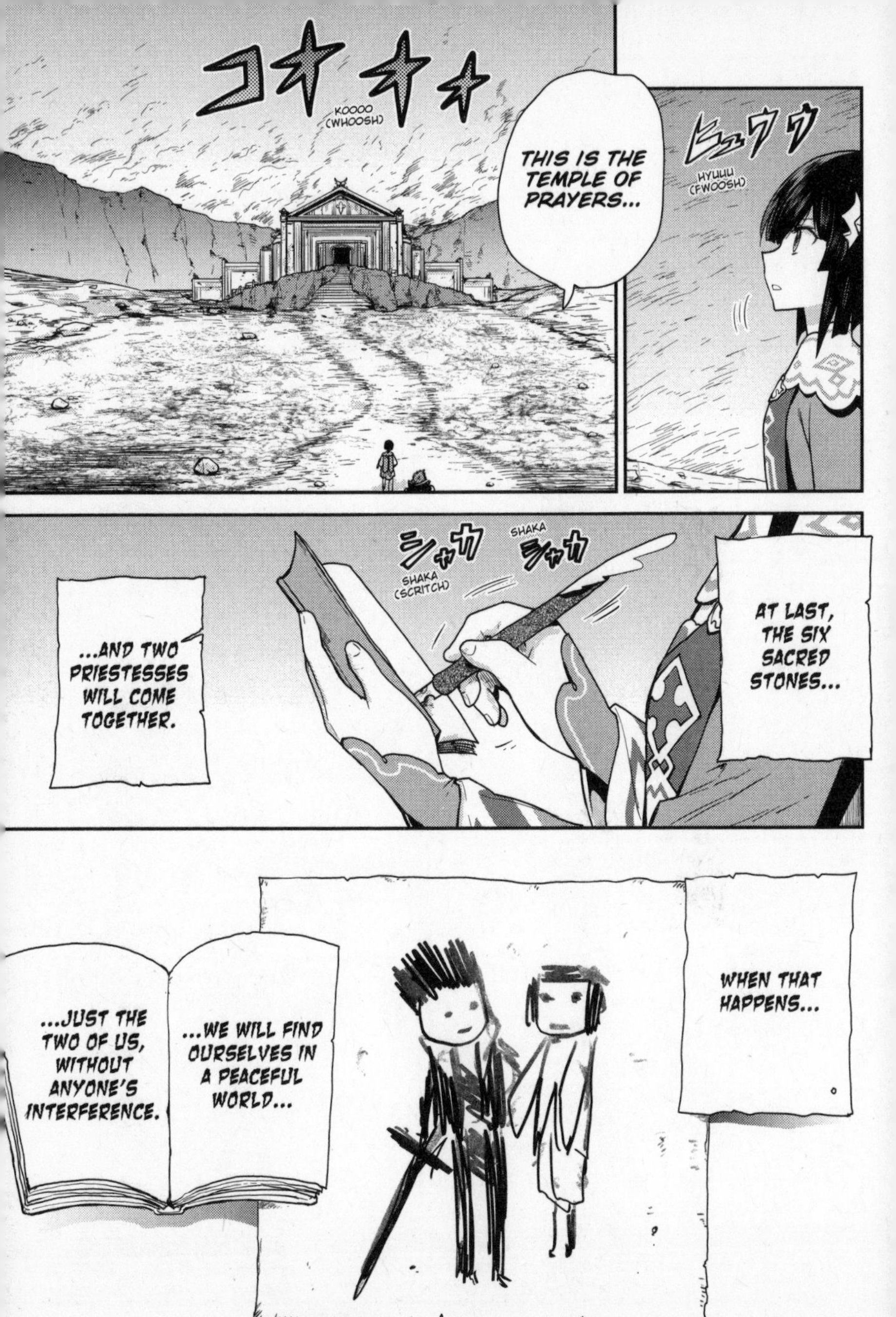
ヒュウウ
HYUUU (FWOOSH)
THIS IS THE TEMPLE OF PRAYERS...
コオオォ
KOOOO (WHOOSH)
AT LAST, THE SIX SACRED STONES...
シャカ
SHAKA
シャカ
SHAKA (SCRITCH)
...AND TWO PRIESTESSES WILL COME TOGETHER.
WHEN THAT HAPPENS...
...WE WILL FIND OURSELVES IN A PEACEFUL WORLD...
...JUST THE TWO OF US, WITHOUT ANYONE'S INTERFERENCE.

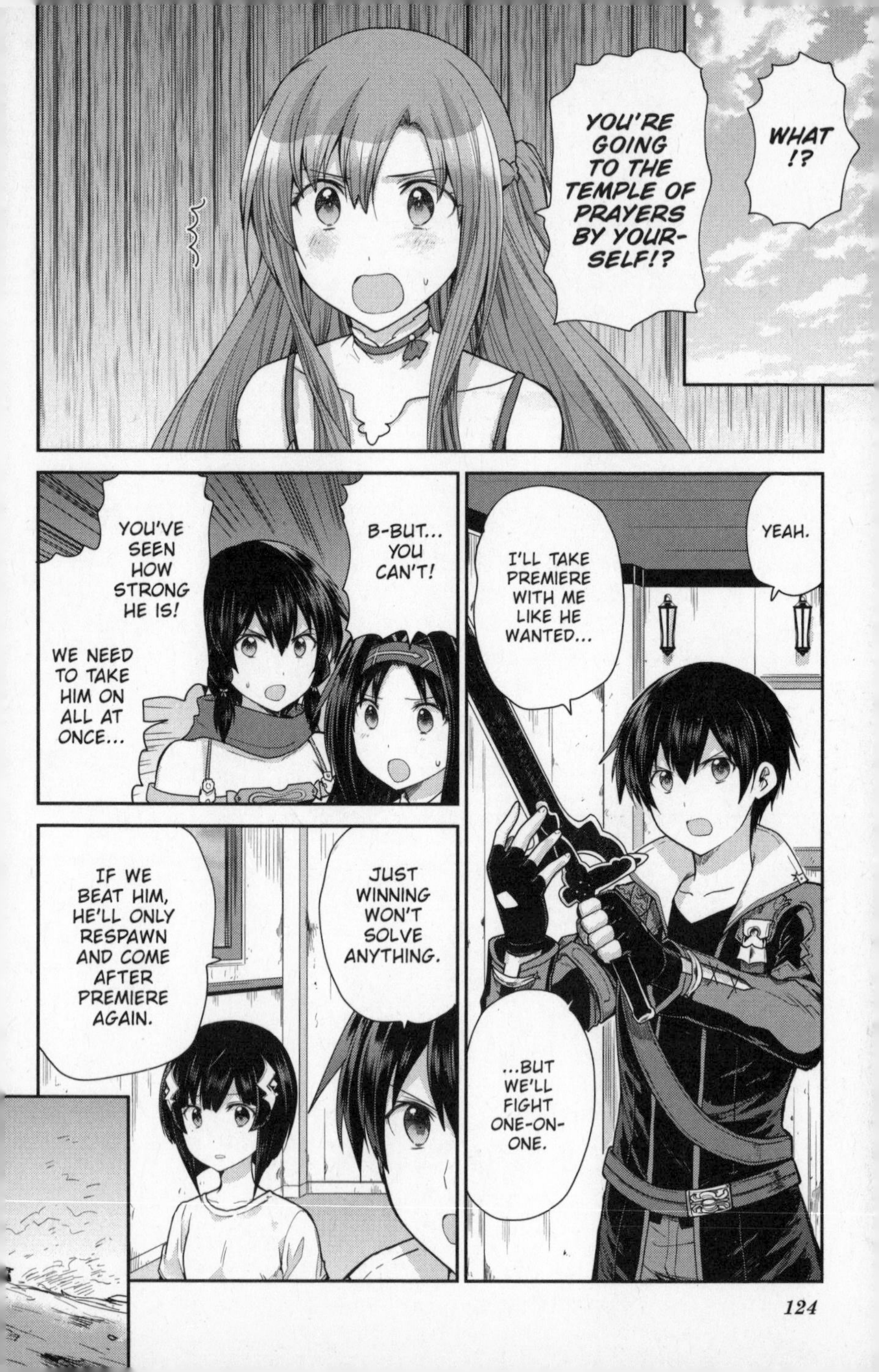
WHAT!?
YOU'RE GOING TO THE TEMPLE OF PRAYERS BY YOURSELF!?
YEAH.
I'LL TAKE PREMIERE WITH ME LIKE HE WANTED...
...BUT WE'LL FIGHT ONE-ON-ONE.
B-BUT... YOU CAN'T!
YOU'VE SEEN HOW STRONG HE IS!
WE NEED TO TAKE HIM ON ALL AT ONCE...
JUST WINNING WON'T SOLVE ANYTHING.
IF WE BEAT HIM, HE'LL ONLY RESPAWN AND COME AFTER PREMIERE AGAIN.

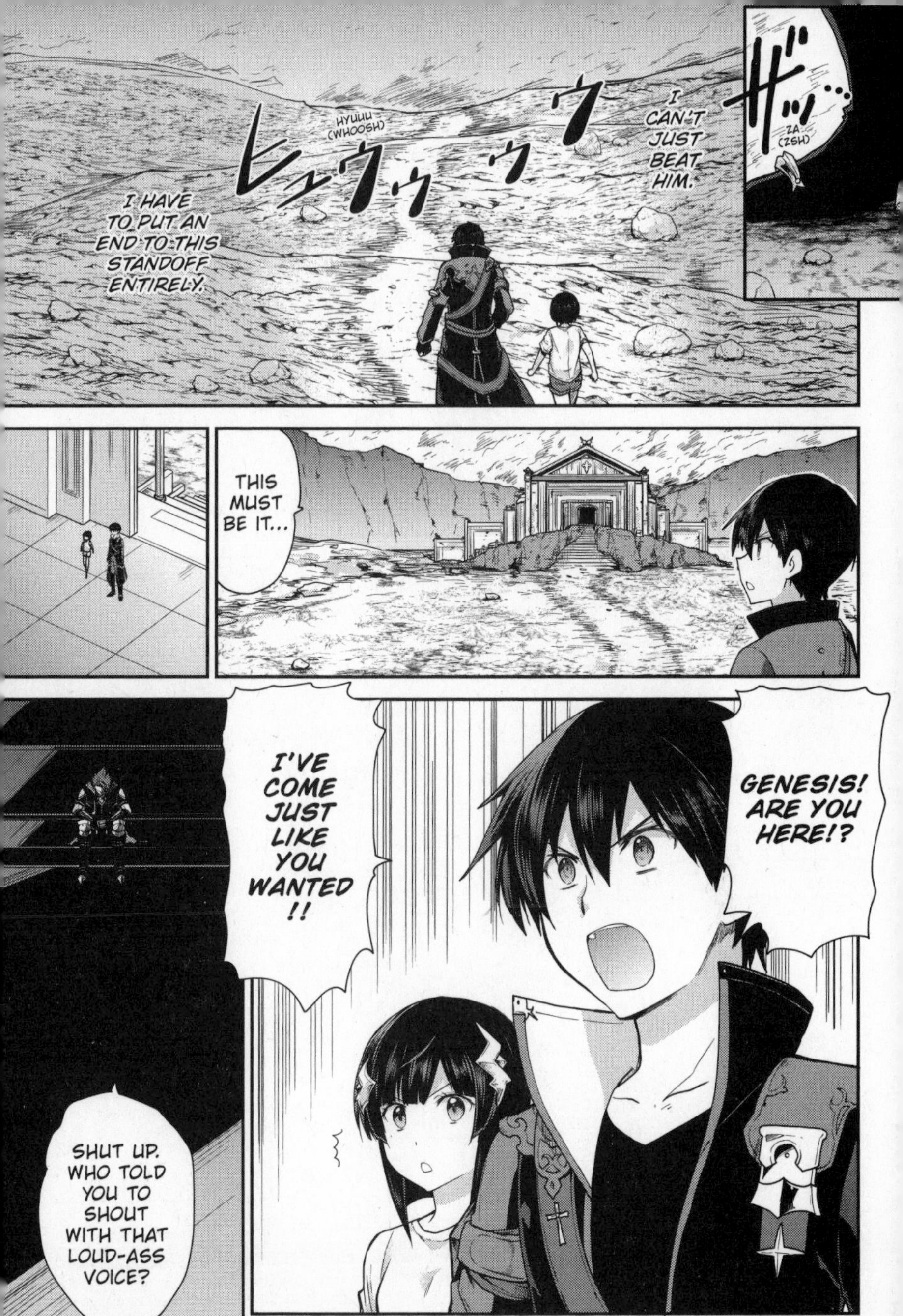

ザッ…
ZA (ZSH)
I CAN'T JUST BEAT HIM.
HYUUU (WHOOSH)
ヒュウゥゥウ
I HAVE TO PUT AN END TO THIS STANDOFF ENTIRELY.
THIS MUST BE IT...
GENESIS! ARE YOU HERE!?
I'VE COME JUST LIKE YOU WANTED!!
SHUT UP. WHO TOLD YOU TO SHOUT WITH THAT LOUD-ASS VOICE?

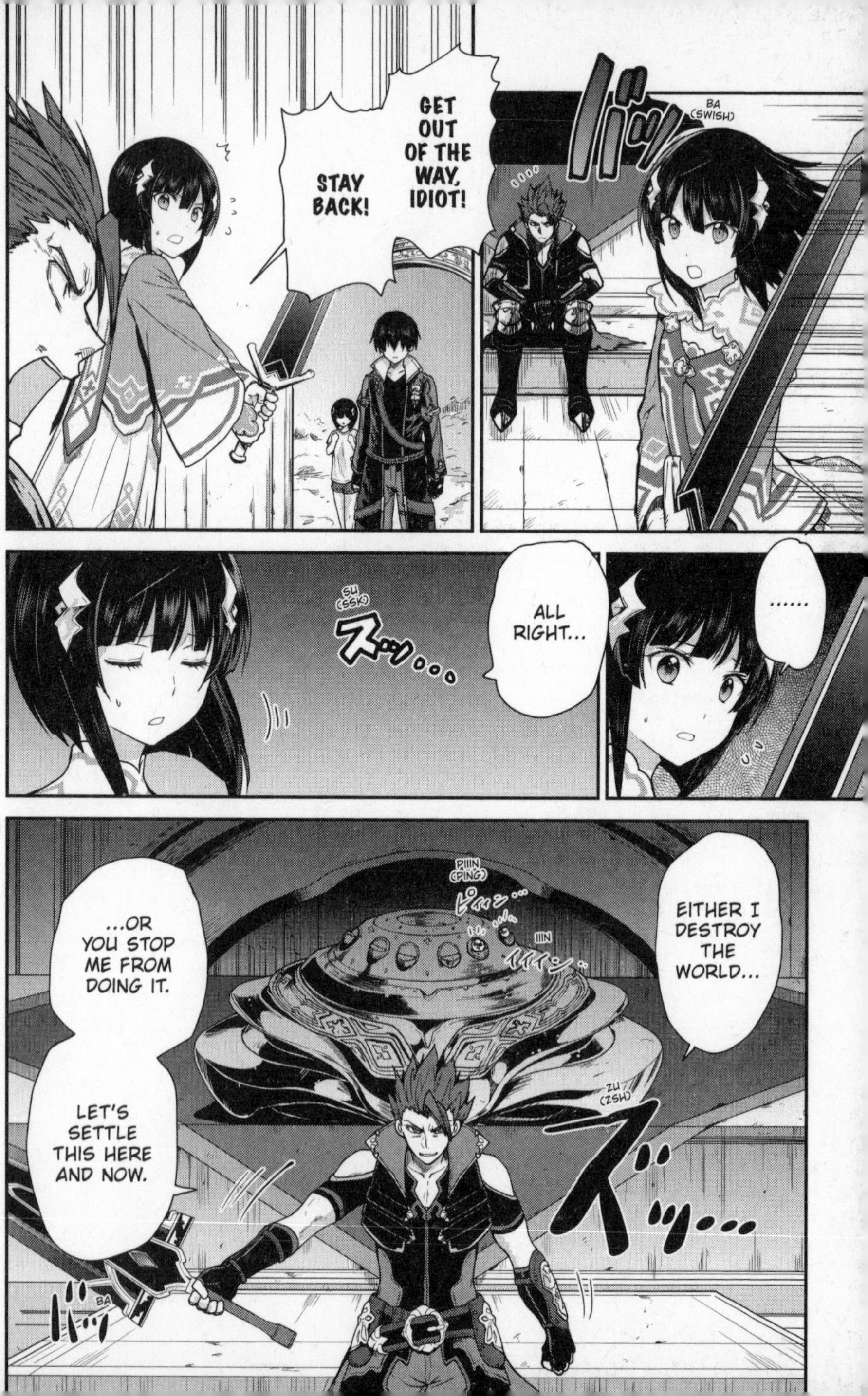
BA (SWISH)
GET OUT OF THE WAY, IDIOT!
STAY BACK!
......
SU (SSK)
ALL RIGHT...
EITHER I DESTROY THE WORLD...
PIIIN (PING)
IIIN
...OR YOU STOP ME FROM DOING IT.
ZU (ZSH)
LET'S SETTLE THIS HERE AND NOW.
BA

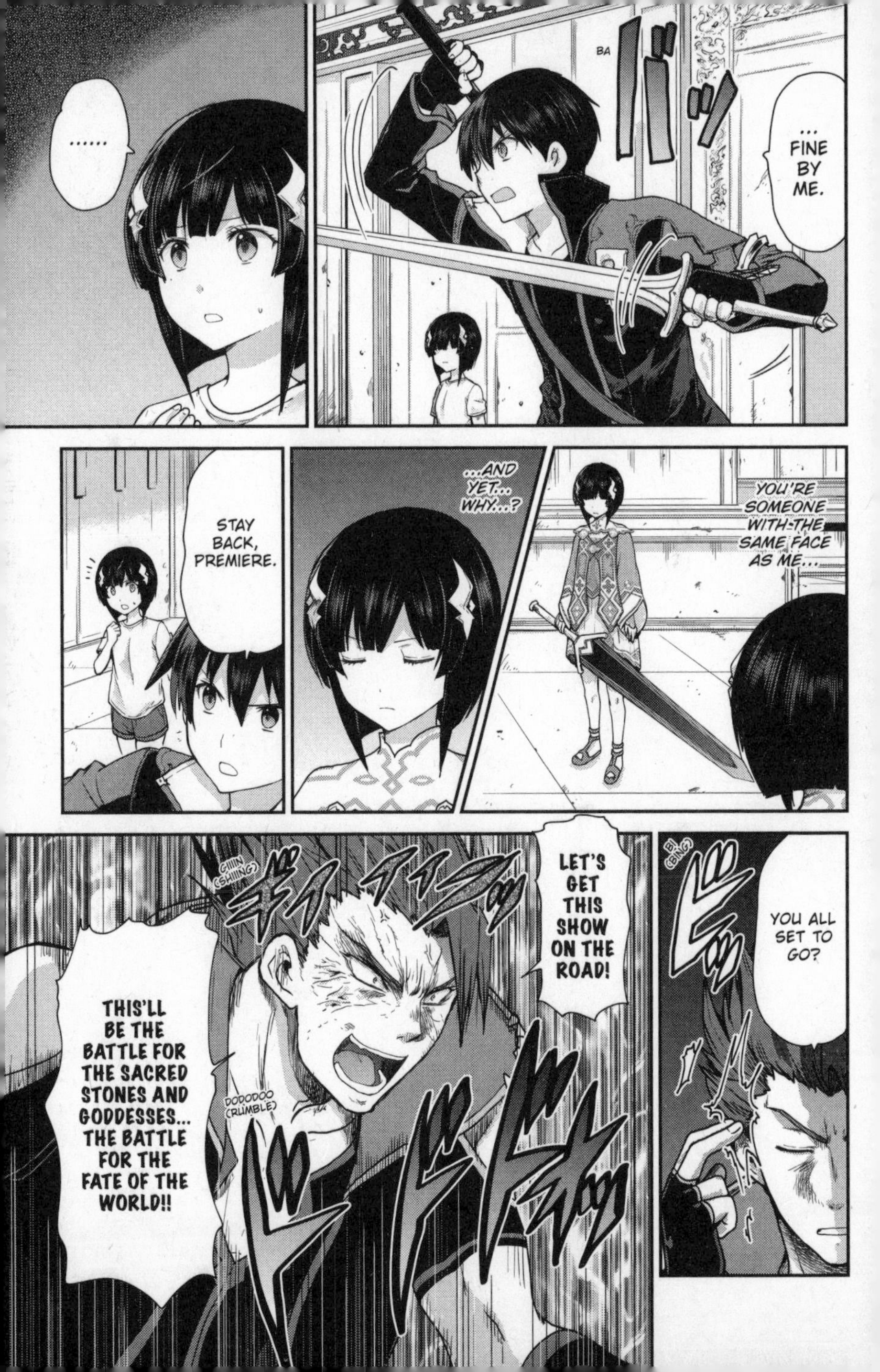
BA
... FINE BY ME.
......
YOU'RE SOMEONE WITH THE SAME FACE AS ME...
...AND YET... WHY...?
STAY BACK, PREMIERE.
BI (BING)
YOU ALL SET TO GO?
LET'S GET THIS SHOW ON THE ROAD!
GIIIN (SHIIING)
THIS'LL BE THE BATTLE FOR THE SACRED STONES AND GODDESSES... THE BATTLE FOR THE FATE OF THE WORLD!!
DODODOO (RUMBLE)

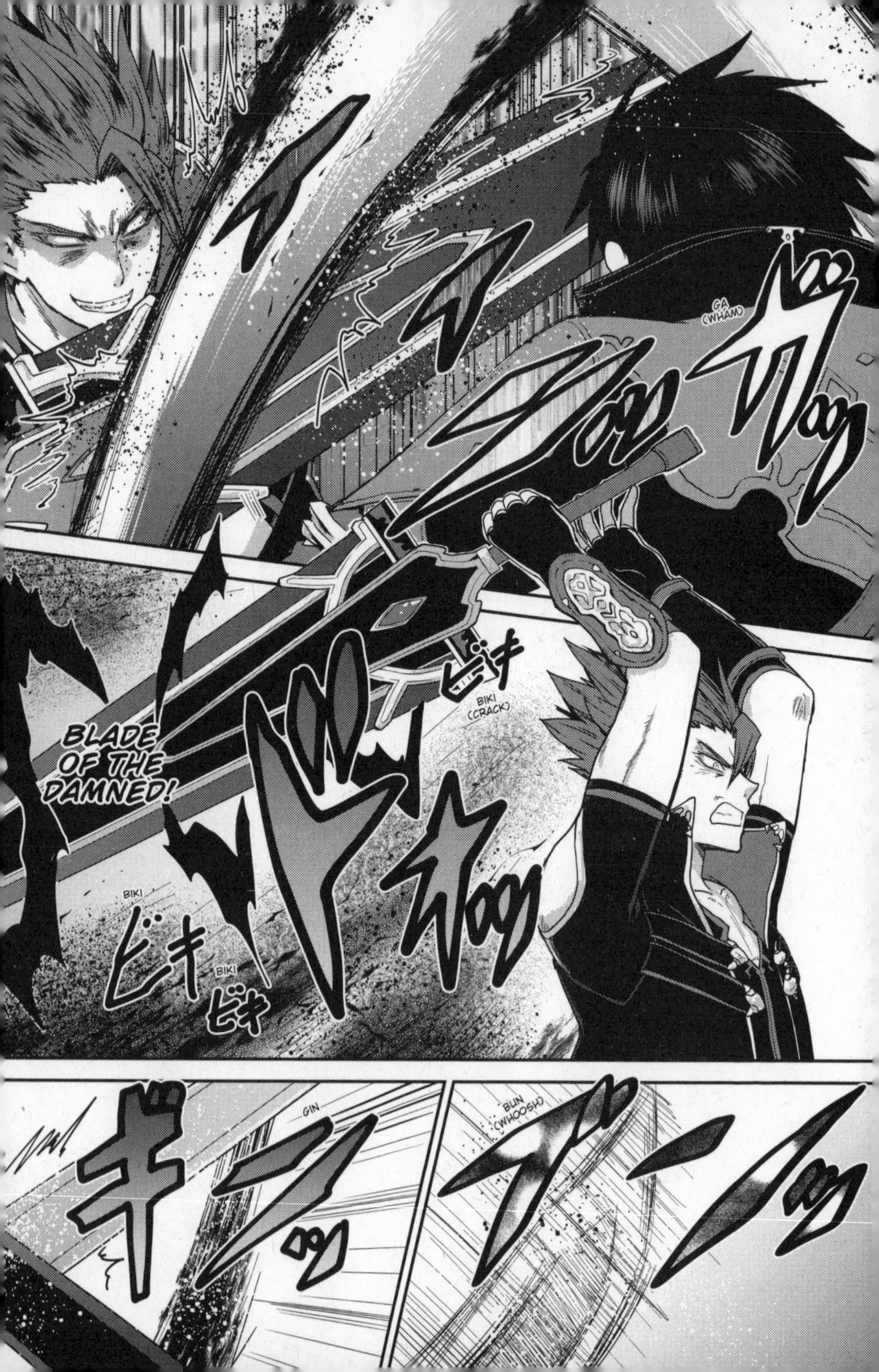
GA (WHAM)
ビキ
BIKI (CRACK)
BLADE OF THE DAMNED!
BIKI
ビキ
BIKI
ビキ
BUN (WHOOSH)
GIN

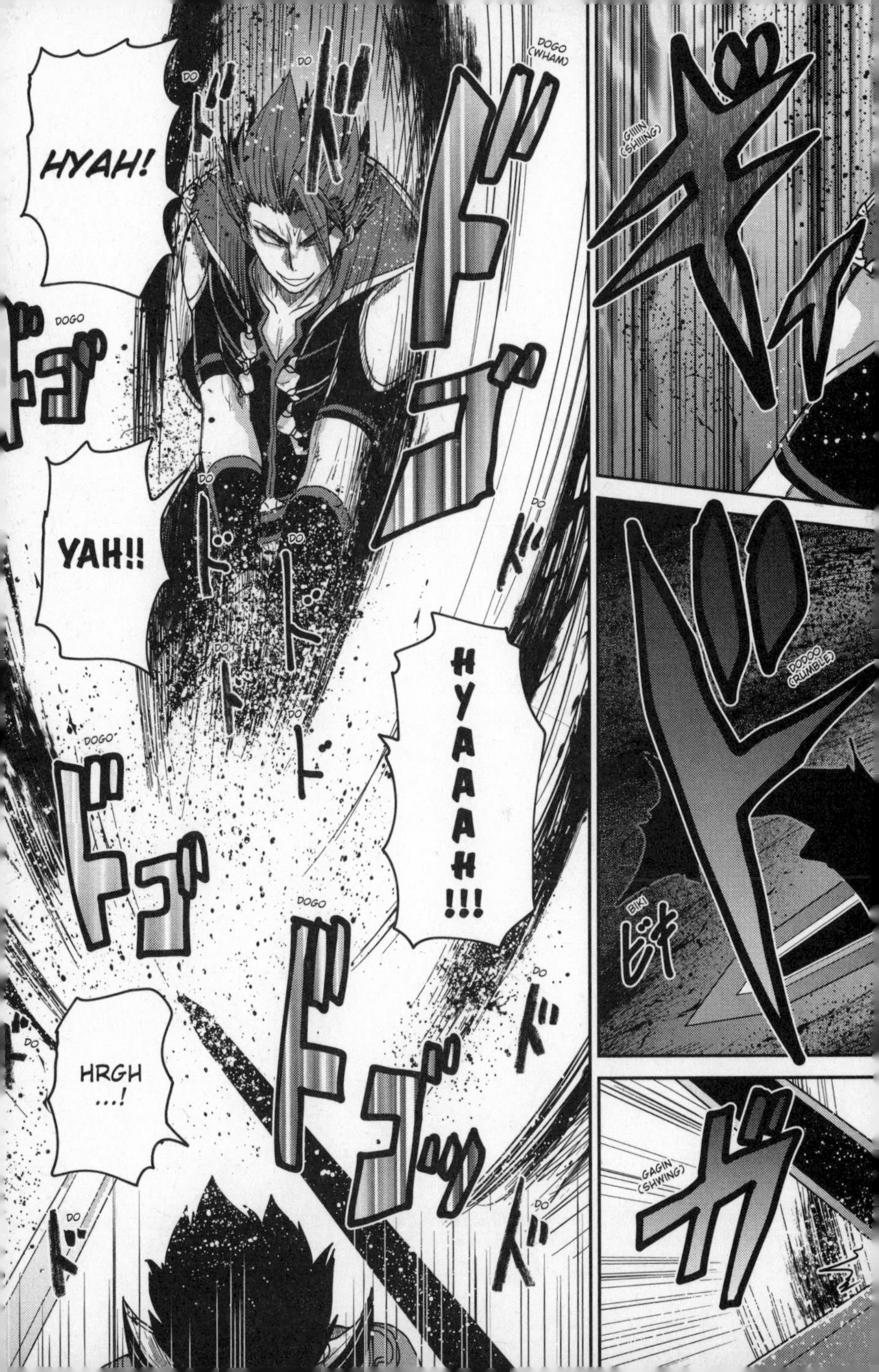
GIIIN (SHIIING)
DODOO (RUMBLE)
BIKI
GAGIN (SHWING)
DOGO (WHAM)
DO
DO
HYAH!
DOGO
DO
DO
YAH!!
DO
DO
DO
HYAAAAH!!!
DOGO
DOGO
DO
DO
HRGH ...!
DO
DO

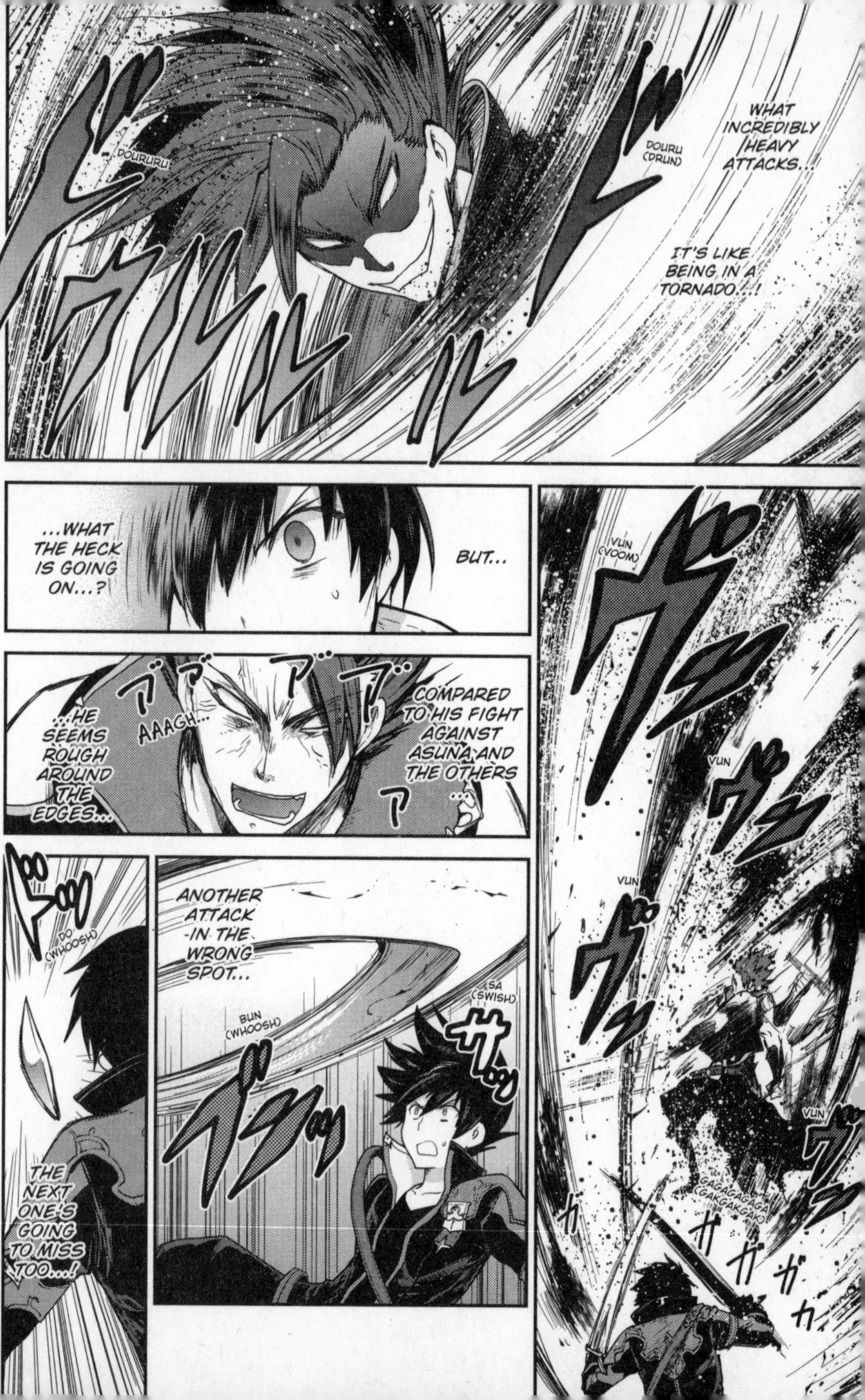
WHAT INCREDIBLY HEAVY ATTACKS...
DOURU (DRUN)
DOURURU
IT'S LIKE BEING IN A TORNADO...!
VUN (VOOM)
VUN
VUN
VUN
GAGAGAGA (GAKGAKGAK)
BUT...
...WHAT THE HECK IS GOING ON...?
COMPARED TO HIS FIGHT AGAINST ASUNA AND THE OTHERS
AAAGH...
...HE SEEMS ROUGH AROUND THE EDGES...
ANOTHER ATTACK IN THE WRONG SPOT...
SA (SWISH)
BUN (WHOOSH)
DO (WHOOSH)
THE NEXT ONE'S GOING TO MISS TOO...!

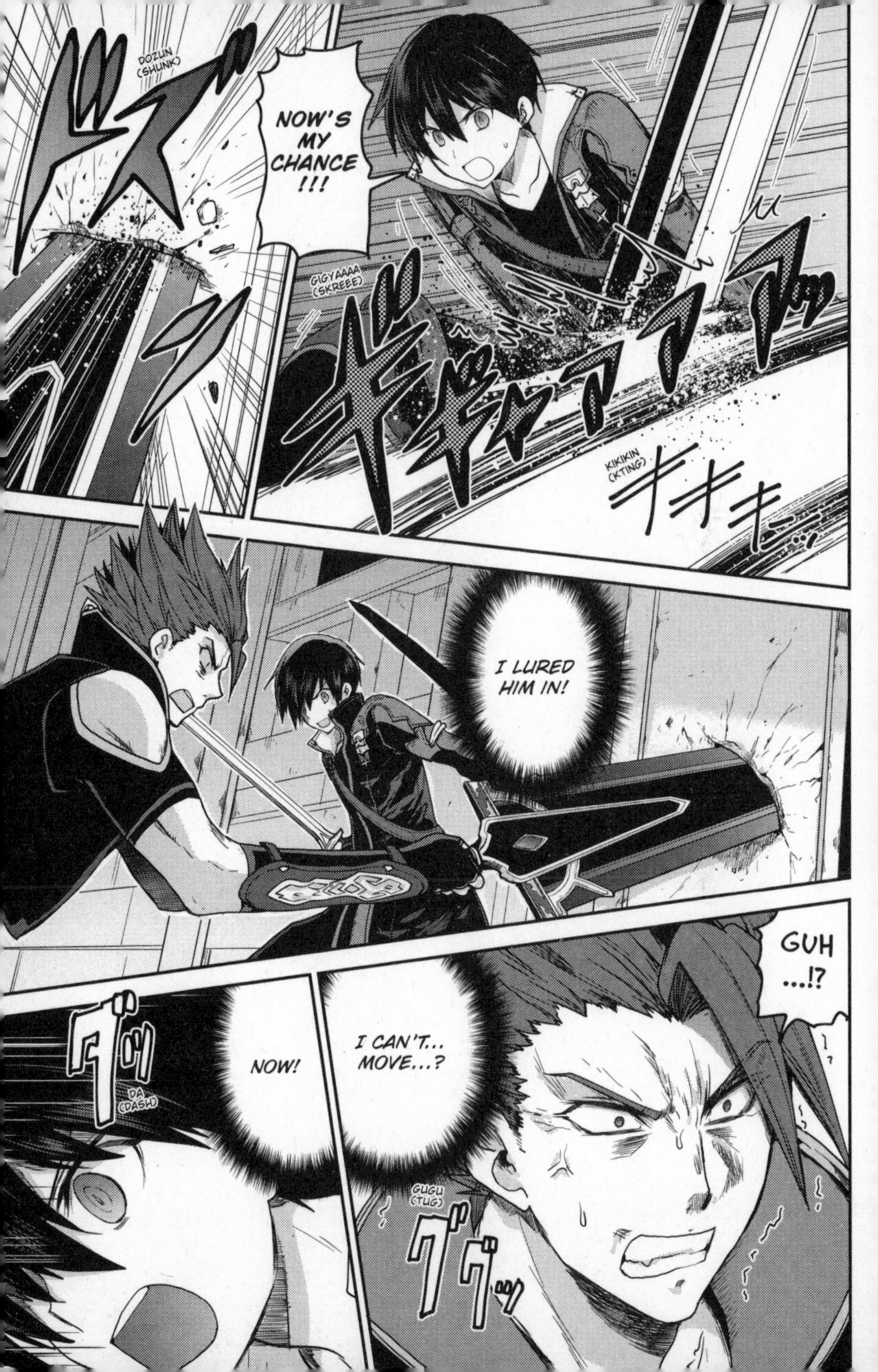
NOW'S MY CHANCE!!!
DOZUN (SHUNK)
GIGYAAAA (SKREEE)
KIKIKIN (KTING)
I LURED HIM IN!
GUH ...!?
I CAN'T... MOVE...?
GUGU (TUG)
NOW!
DA (DASH)

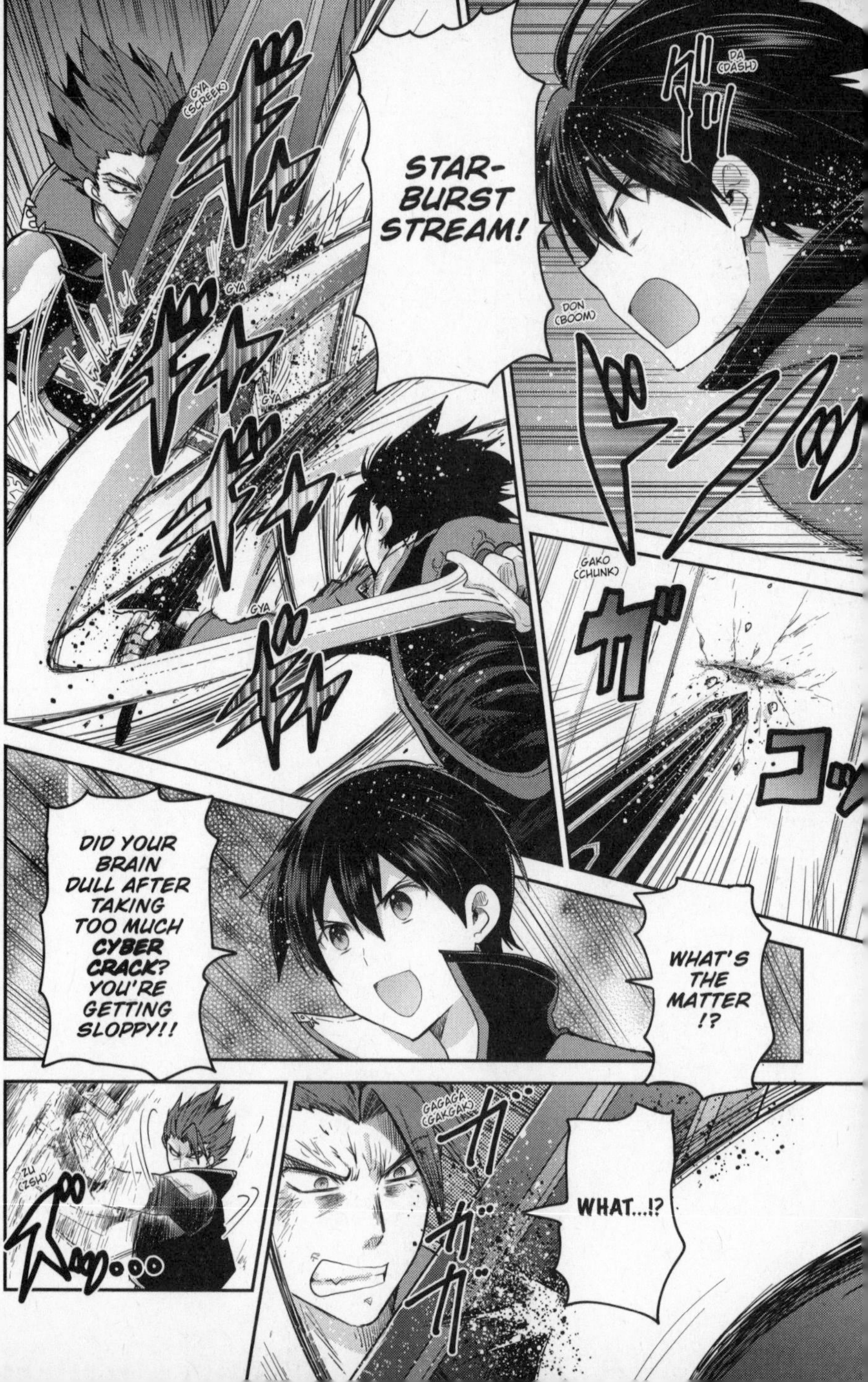
DA (DASH)
DON (BOOM)
STAR-BURST STREAM!
GYA (SCREEK)
GYA
GYA
GYA
GAKO (CHUNK)
WHAT'S THE MATTER!?
DID YOUR BRAIN DULL AFTER TAKING TOO MUCH CYBER CRACK? YOU'RE GETTING SLOPPY!!
GAGAGA (GAKGAK)
WHAT...!?
ZU (ZSH)

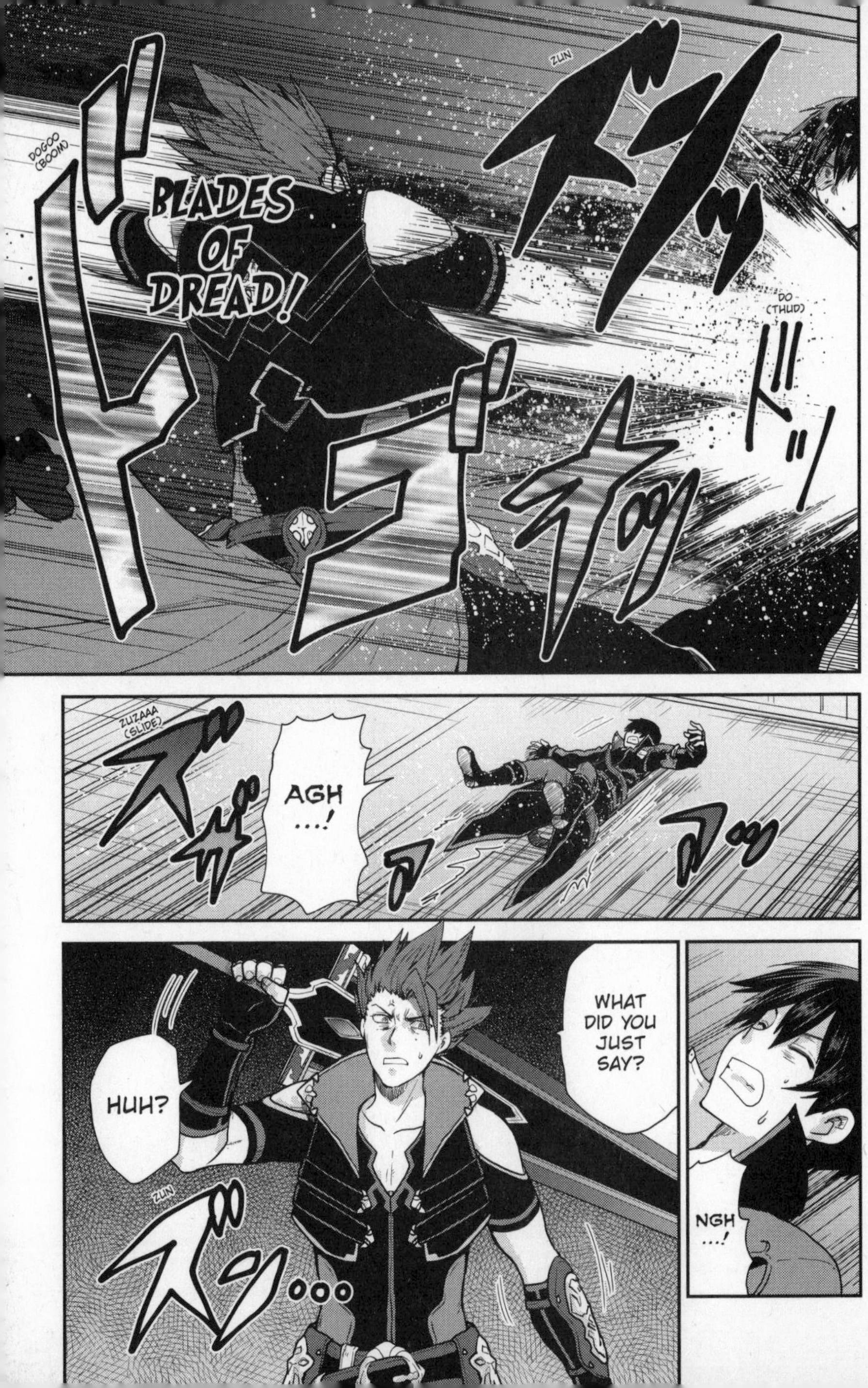
ZUN
DO (THUD)
DOGOO (BOOM)
BLADES OF DREAD!
ZUZAAA (SLIDE)
AGH ...!
NGH ...!
WHAT DID YOU JUST SAY?
HUH?
ZUN

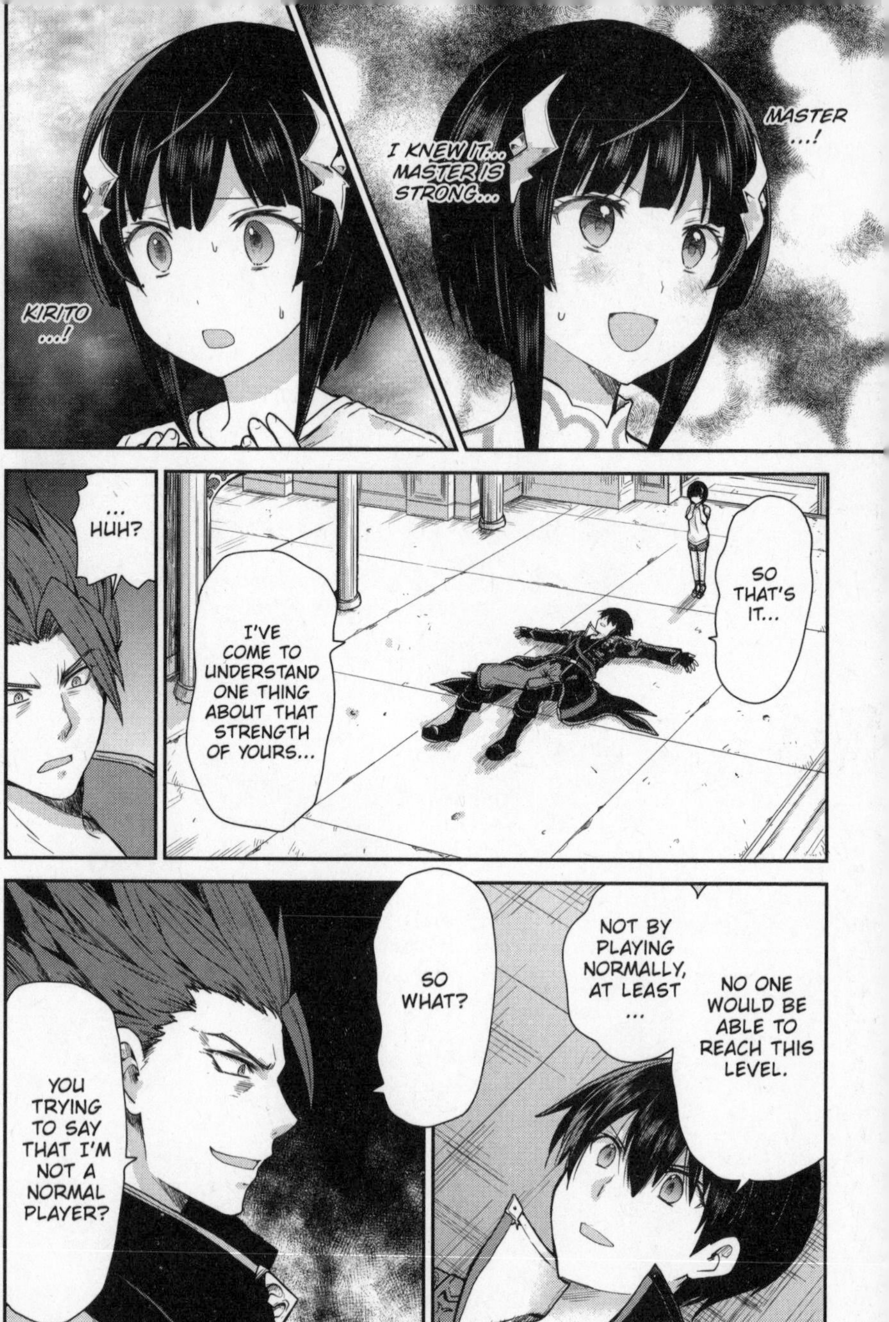
MASTER ...!
I KNEW IT... MASTER IS STRONG...
KIRITO ...!
SO THAT'S IT...
I'VE COME TO UNDERSTAND ONE THING ABOUT THAT STRENGTH OF YOURS...
... HUH?
NO ONE WOULD BE ABLE TO REACH THIS LEVEL.
NOT BY PLAYING NORMALLY, AT LEAST ...
SO WHAT?
YOU TRYING TO SAY THAT I'M NOT A NORMAL PLAYER?

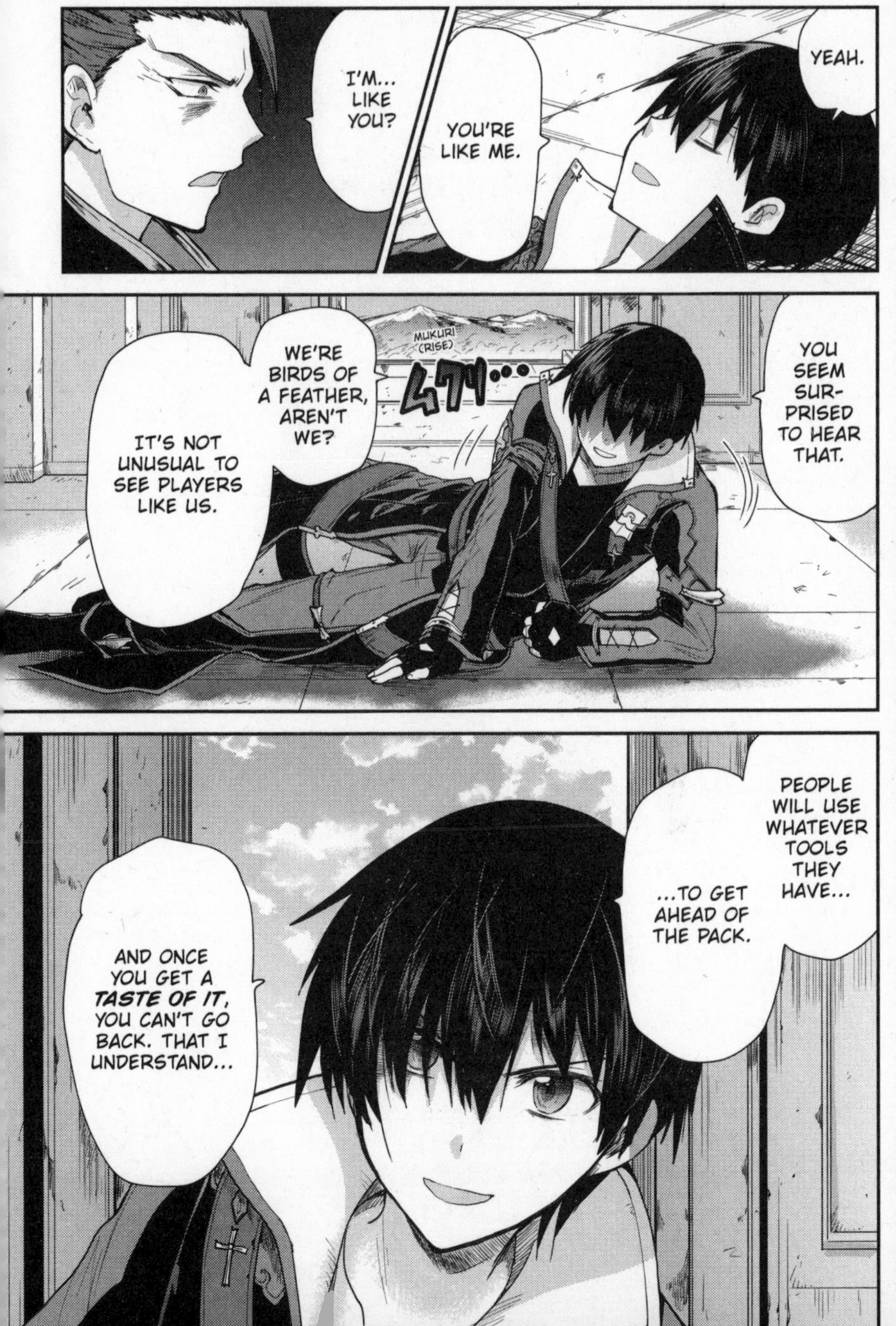
YEAH.
YOU'RE LIKE ME.
I'M... LIKE YOU?
YOU SEEM SUR-PRISED TO HEAR THAT.
MUKURI (RISE)
WE'RE BIRDS OF A FEATHER, AREN'T WE?
IT'S NOT UNUSUAL TO SEE PLAYERS LIKE US.
PEOPLE WILL USE WHATEVER TOOLS THEY HAVE...
...TO GET AHEAD OF THE PACK.
AND ONCE YOU GET A *TASTE OF IT*, YOU CAN'T GO BACK. THAT I UNDERSTAND...

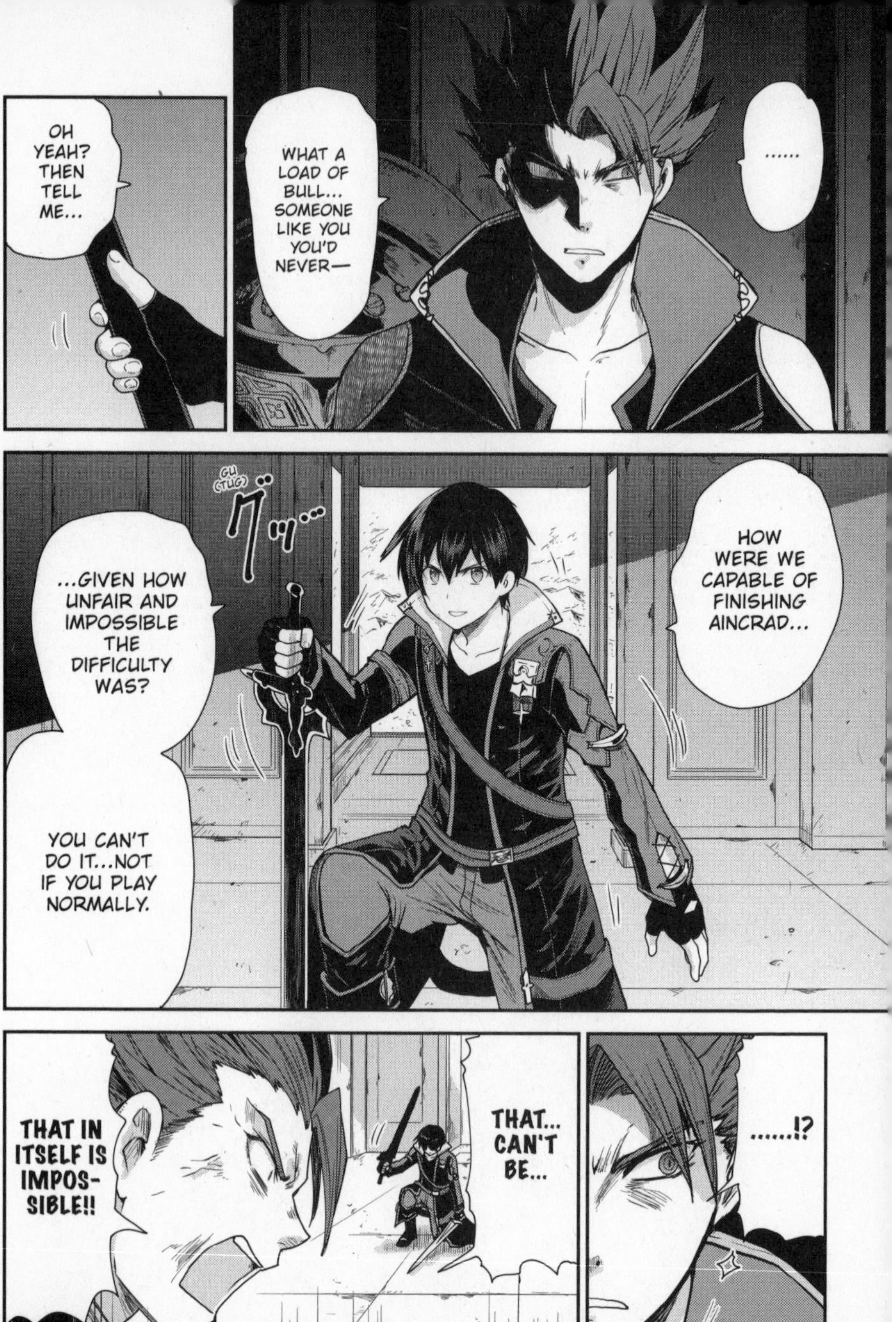
......
WHAT A LOAD OF BULL... SOMEONE LIKE YOU YOU'D NEVER—
OH YEAH? THEN TELL ME...
HOW WERE WE CAPABLE OF FINISHING AINCRAD...
GU (TUG)
...GIVEN HOW UNFAIR AND IMPOSSIBLE THE DIFFICULTY WAS?
YOU CAN'T DO IT...NOT IF YOU PLAY NORMALLY.
......!?
THAT... CAN'T BE...
THAT IN ITSELF IS IMPOS-SIBLE!!

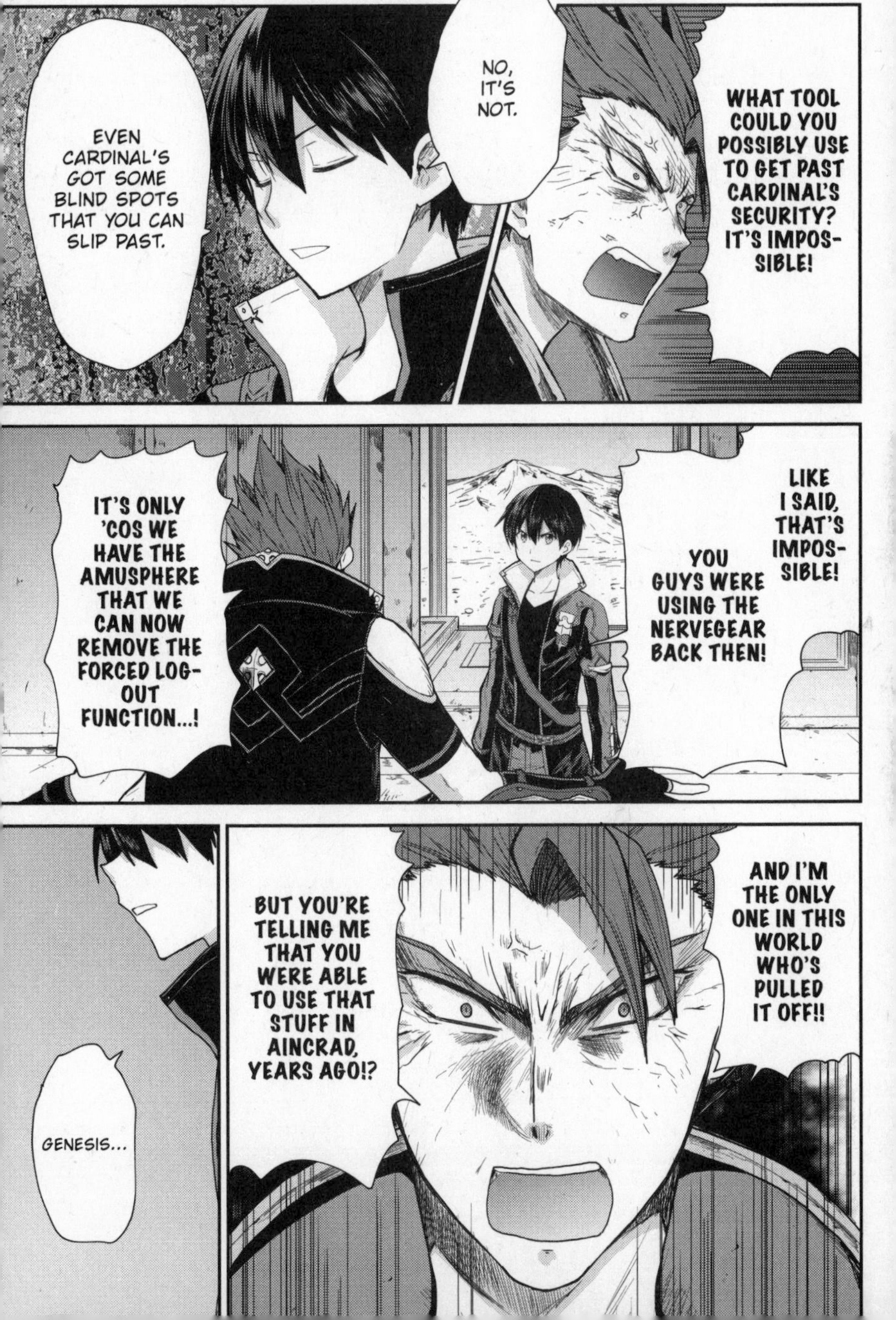
WHAT TOOL COULD YOU POSSIBLY USE TO GET PAST CARDINAL'S SECURITY? IT'S IMPOSSIBLE!
NO, IT'S NOT.
EVEN CARDINAL'S GOT SOME BLIND SPOTS THAT YOU CAN SLIP PAST.
LIKE I SAID, THAT'S IMPOSSIBLE!
YOU GUYS WERE USING THE NERVEGEAR BACK THEN!
IT'S ONLY 'COS WE HAVE THE AMUSPHERE THAT WE CAN NOW REMOVE THE FORCED LOG-OUT FUNCTION...!
AND I'M THE ONLY ONE IN THIS WORLD WHO'S PULLED IT OFF!!
BUT YOU'RE TELLING ME THAT YOU WERE ABLE TO USE THAT STUFF IN AINCRAD, YEARS AGO!?
GENESIS...

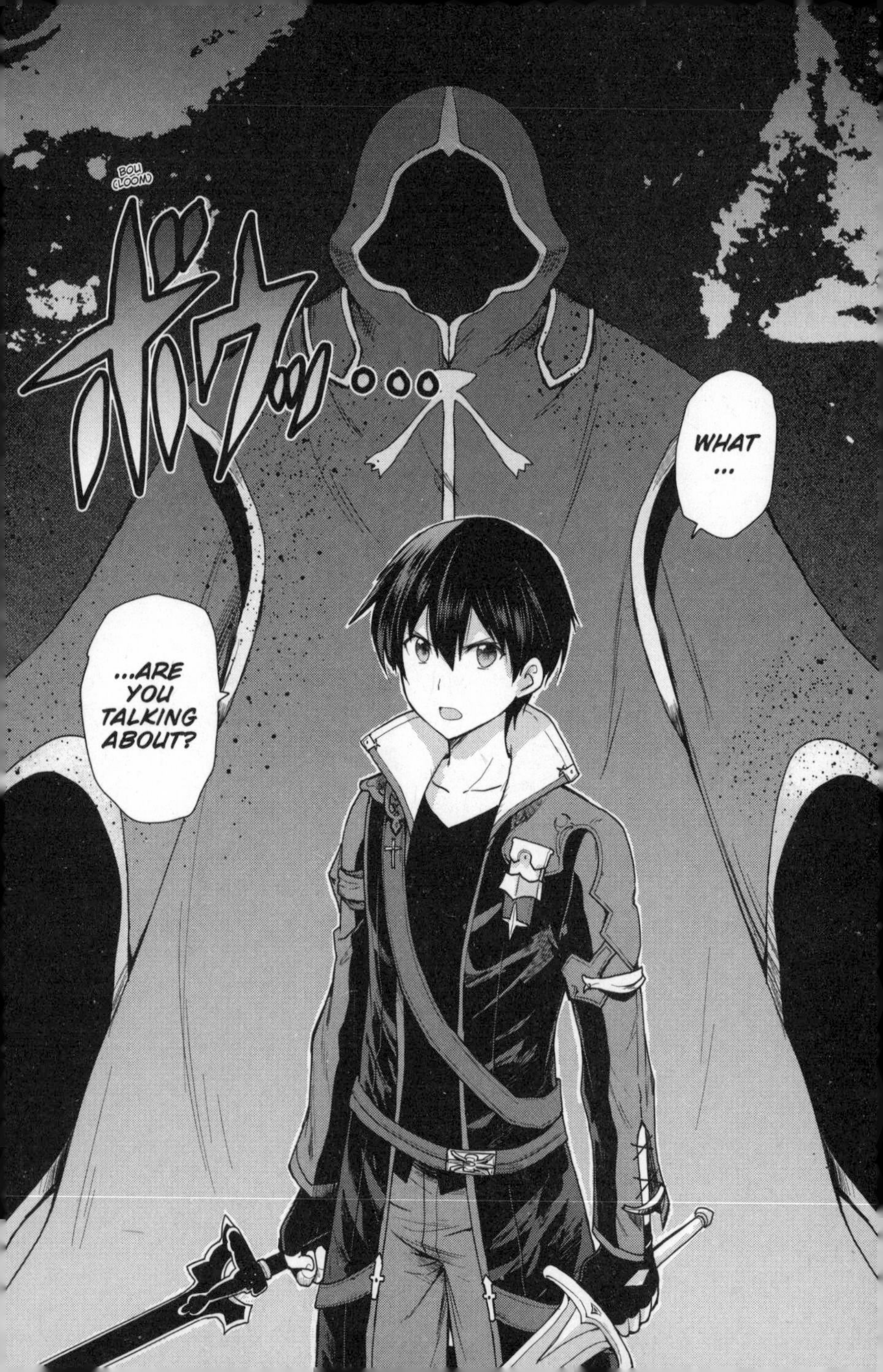
WHAT ...
BOU (LOOM)
ボウッ...
...ARE YOU TALKING ABOUT?

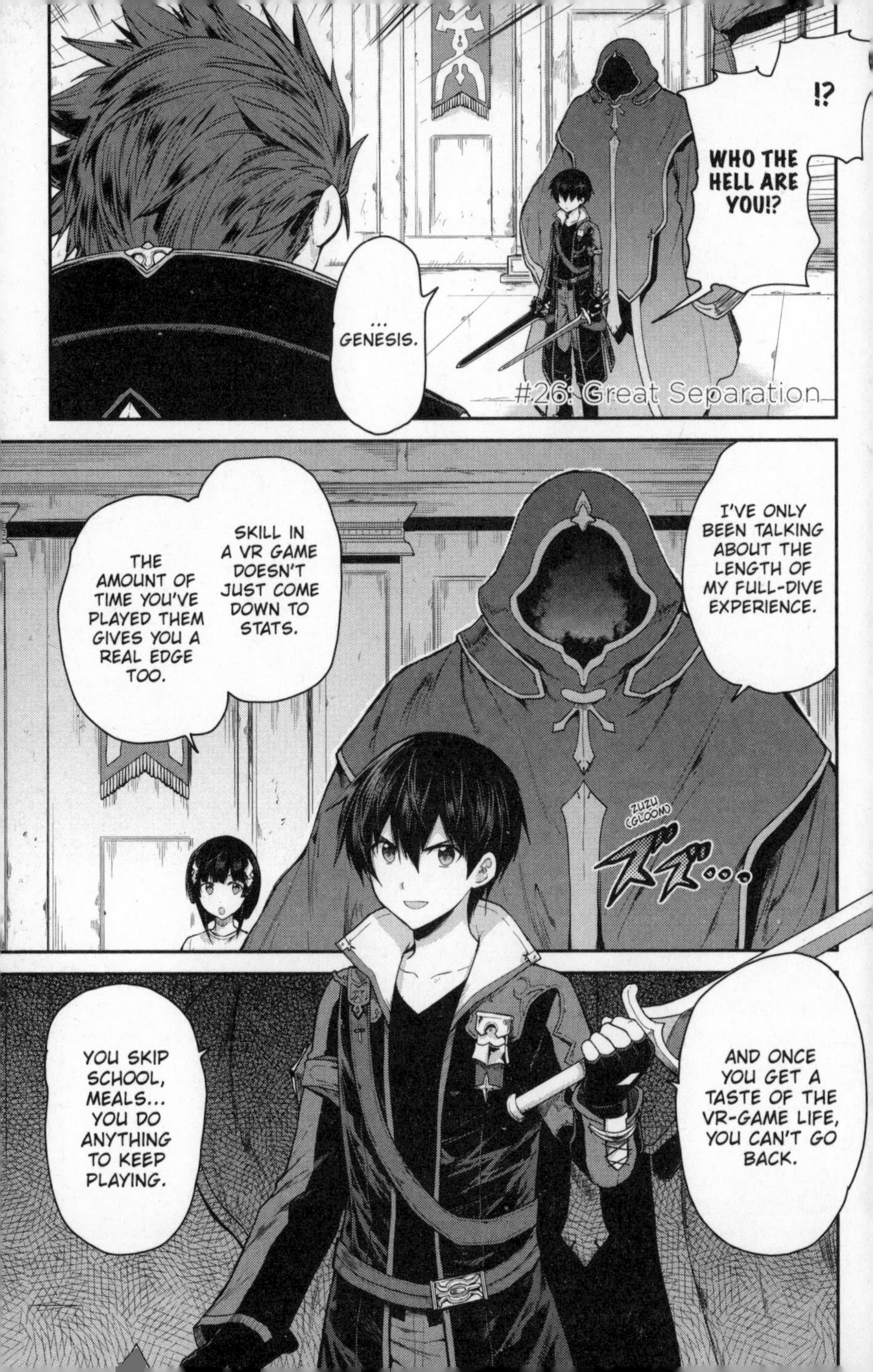
!?
WHO THE HELL ARE YOU!?
... GENESIS.
#26: Great Separation
I'VE ONLY BEEN TALKING ABOUT THE LENGTH OF MY FULL-DIVE EXPERIENCE.
ZUZU (GLOOM)
SKILL IN A VR GAME DOESN'T JUST COME DOWN TO STATS.
THE AMOUNT OF TIME YOU'VE PLAYED THEM GIVES YOU A REAL EDGE TOO.
AND ONCE YOU GET A TASTE OF THE VR-GAME LIFE, YOU CAN'T GO BACK.
YOU SKIP SCHOOL, MEALS... YOU DO ANYTHING TO KEEP PLAYING.

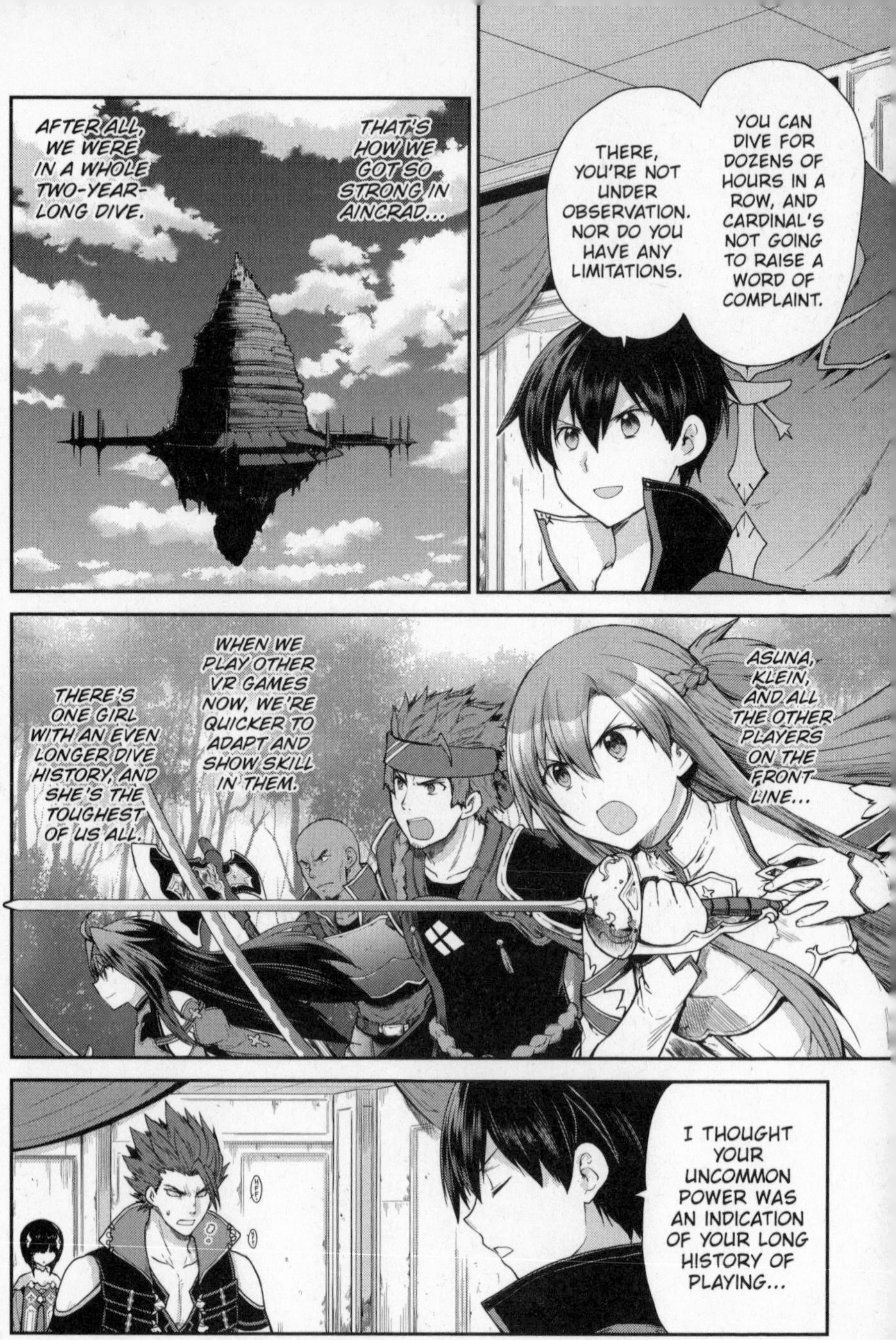
YOU CAN DIVE FOR DOZENS OF HOURS IN A ROW, AND CARDINAL'S NOT GOING TO RAISE A WORD OF COMPLAINT.
THERE, YOU'RE NOT UNDER OBSERVATION. NOR DO YOU HAVE ANY LIMITATIONS.
THAT'S HOW WE GOT SO STRONG IN AINCRAD...
AFTER ALL, WE WERE IN A WHOLE TWO-YEAR-LONG DIVE.
ASUNA, KLEIN, AND ALL THE OTHER PLAYERS ON THE FRONT LINE...
WHEN WE PLAY OTHER VR GAMES NOW, WE'RE QUICKER TO ADAPT AND SHOW SKILL IN THEM.
THERE'S ONE GIRL WITH AN EVEN LONGER DIVE HISTORY, AND SHE'S THE TOUGHEST OF US ALL.
I THOUGHT YOUR UNCOMMON POWER WAS AN INDICATION OF YOUR LONG HISTORY OF PLAYING...

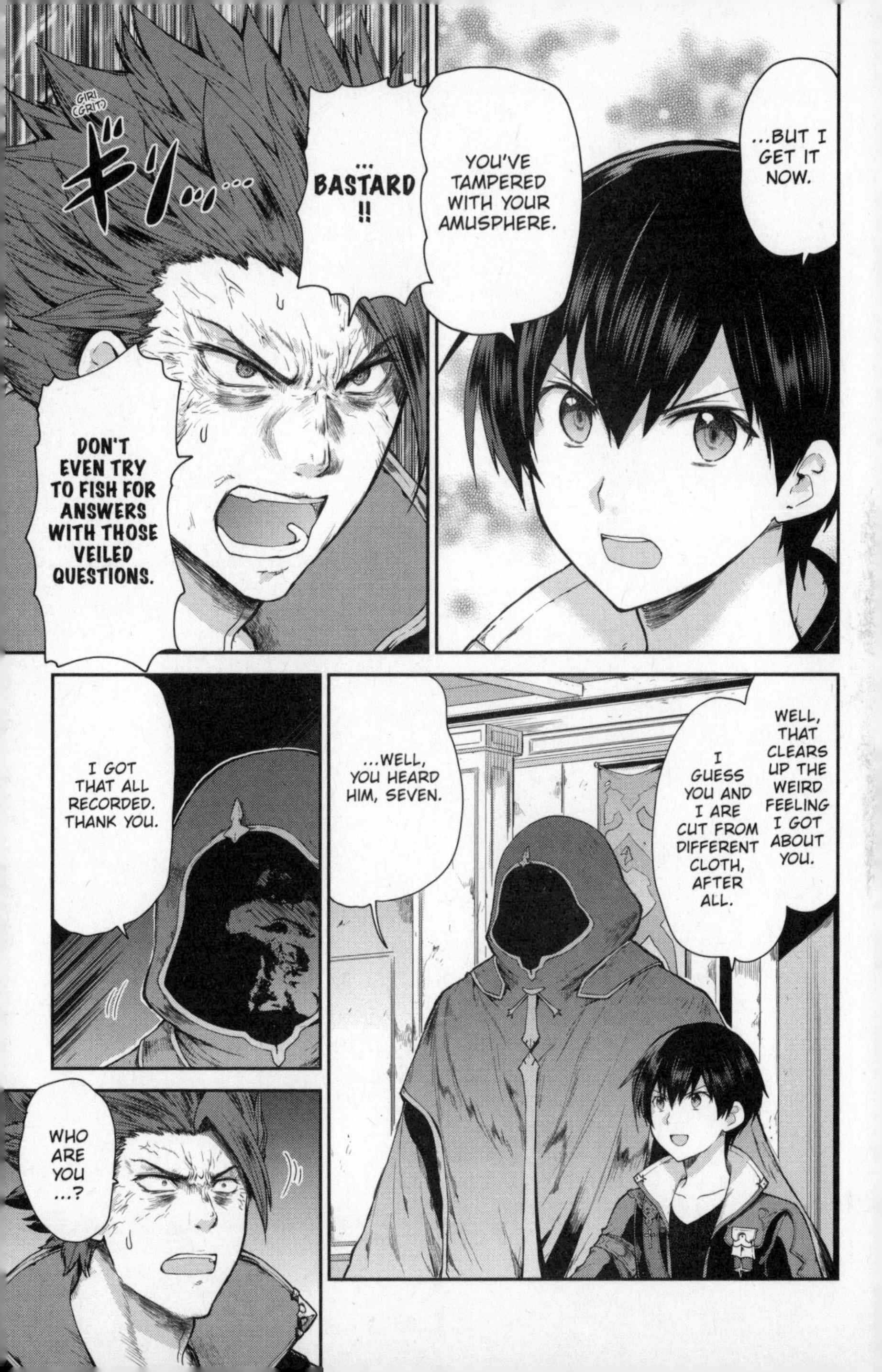
...BUT I GET IT NOW.
YOU'VE TAMPERED WITH YOUR AMUSPHERE.
... BASTARD !!
GIRI (GRIT)
ギリッ...
DON'T EVEN TRY TO FISH FOR ANSWERS WITH THOSE VEILED QUESTIONS.
WELL, THAT CLEARS UP THE WEIRD FEELING I GOT ABOUT YOU.
I GUESS YOU AND I ARE CUT FROM DIFFERENT CLOTH, AFTER ALL.
...WELL, YOU HEARD HIM, SEVEN.
I GOT THAT ALL RECORDED. THANK YOU.
WHO ARE YOU ...?

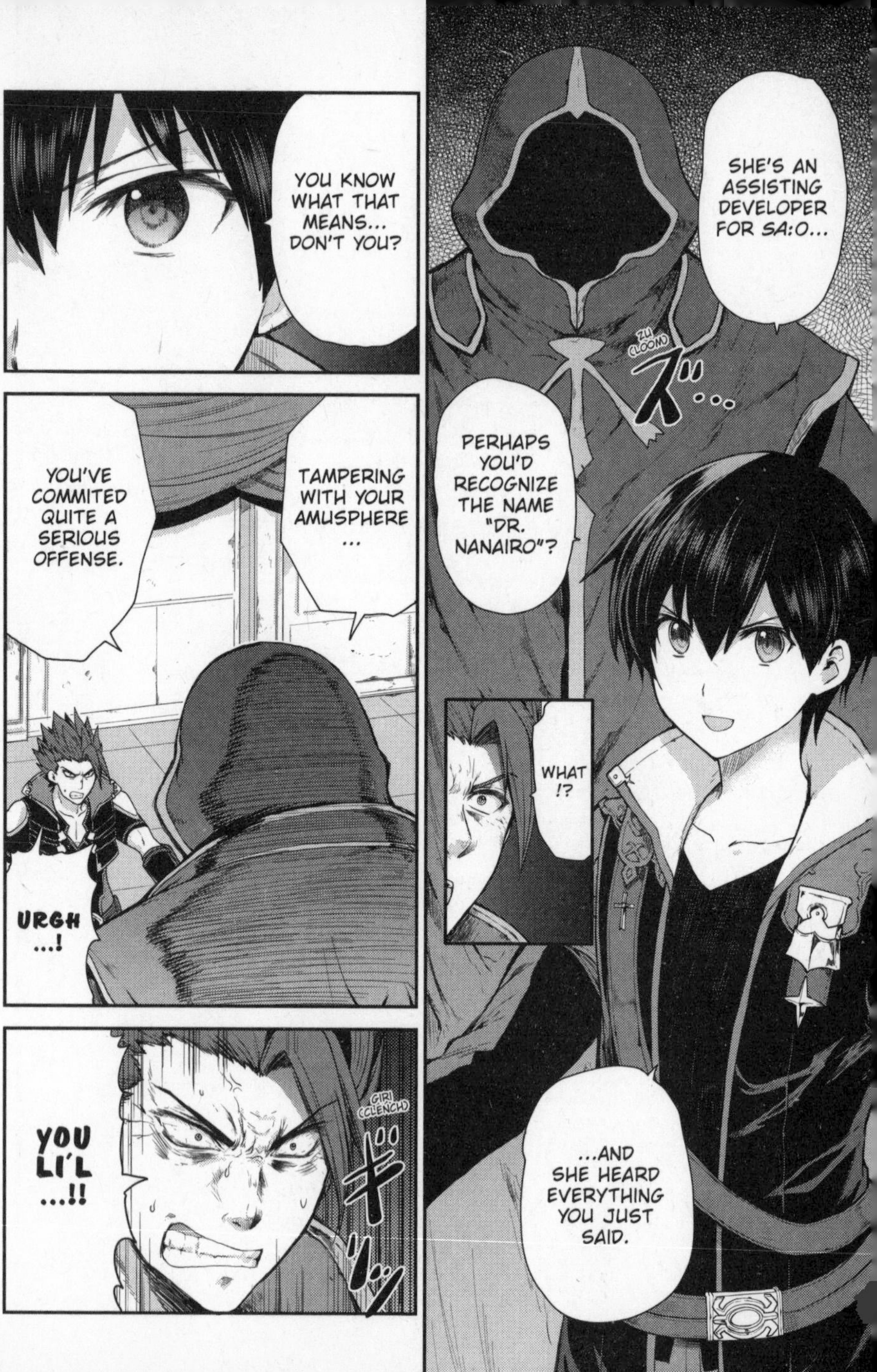
SHE'S AN ASSISTING DEVELOPER FOR SA:O...
ZU (LOOM)
PERHAPS YOU'D RECOGNIZE THE NAME "DR. NANAIRO"?
WHAT !?
...AND SHE HEARD EVERYTHING YOU JUST SAID.
YOU KNOW WHAT THAT MEANS... DON'T YOU?
TAMPERING WITH YOUR AMUSPHERE ...
YOU'VE COMMITED QUITE A SERIOUS OFFENSE.
URGH ...!
GIRI (CLENCH)
YOU LI'L ...!!

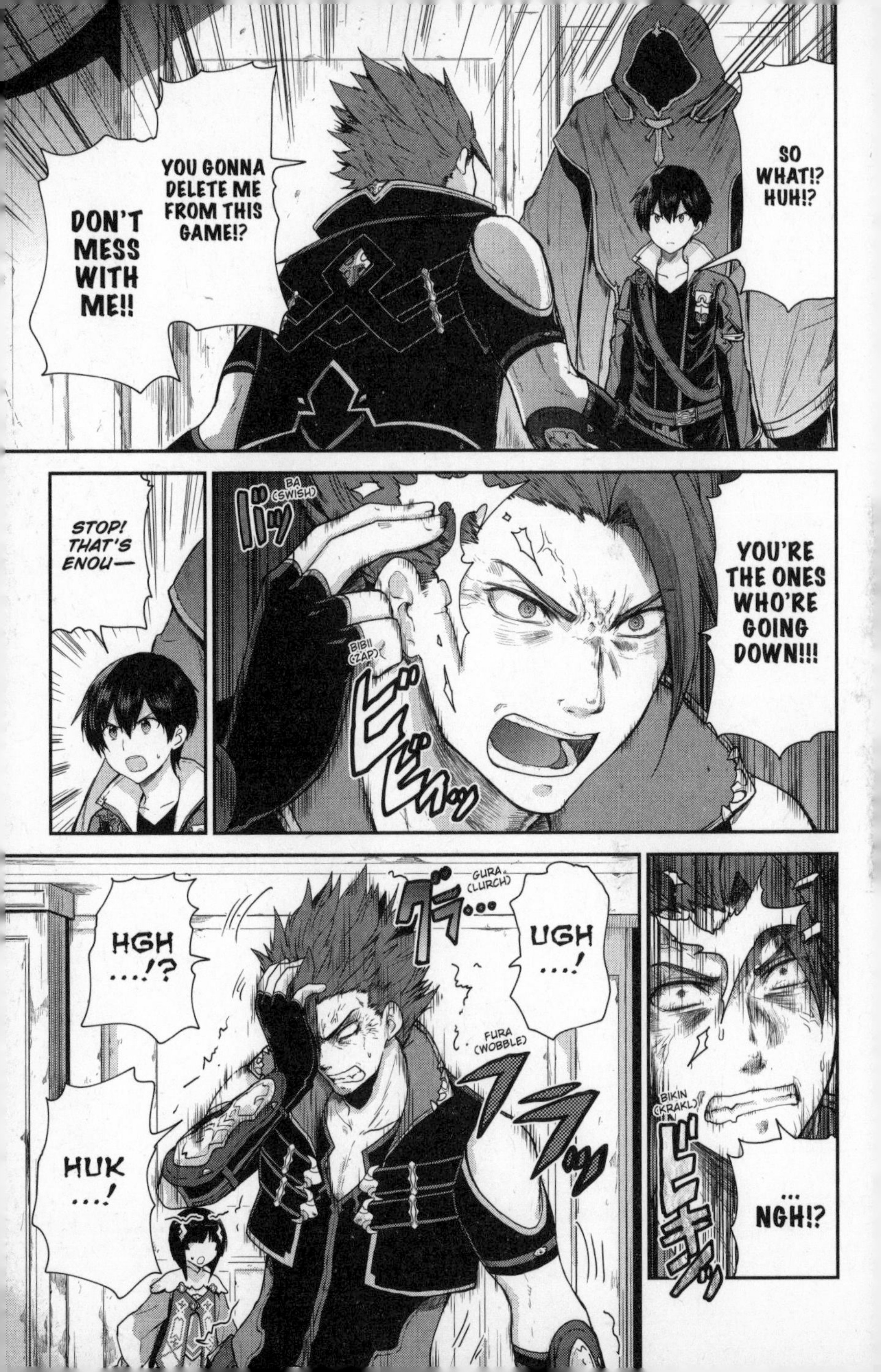

SO WHAT!? HUH!?
YOU GONNA DELETE ME FROM THIS GAME!?
DON'T MESS WITH ME!!
BA (SWISH)
YOU'RE THE ONES WHO'RE GOING DOWN!!!
BIBII (ZAP)
STOP! THAT'S ENOU—
BIKIN (KRAKL)
...NGH!?
GURA (LURCH)
UGH ...!
HGH ...!?
FURA (WOBBLE)
HUK ...!

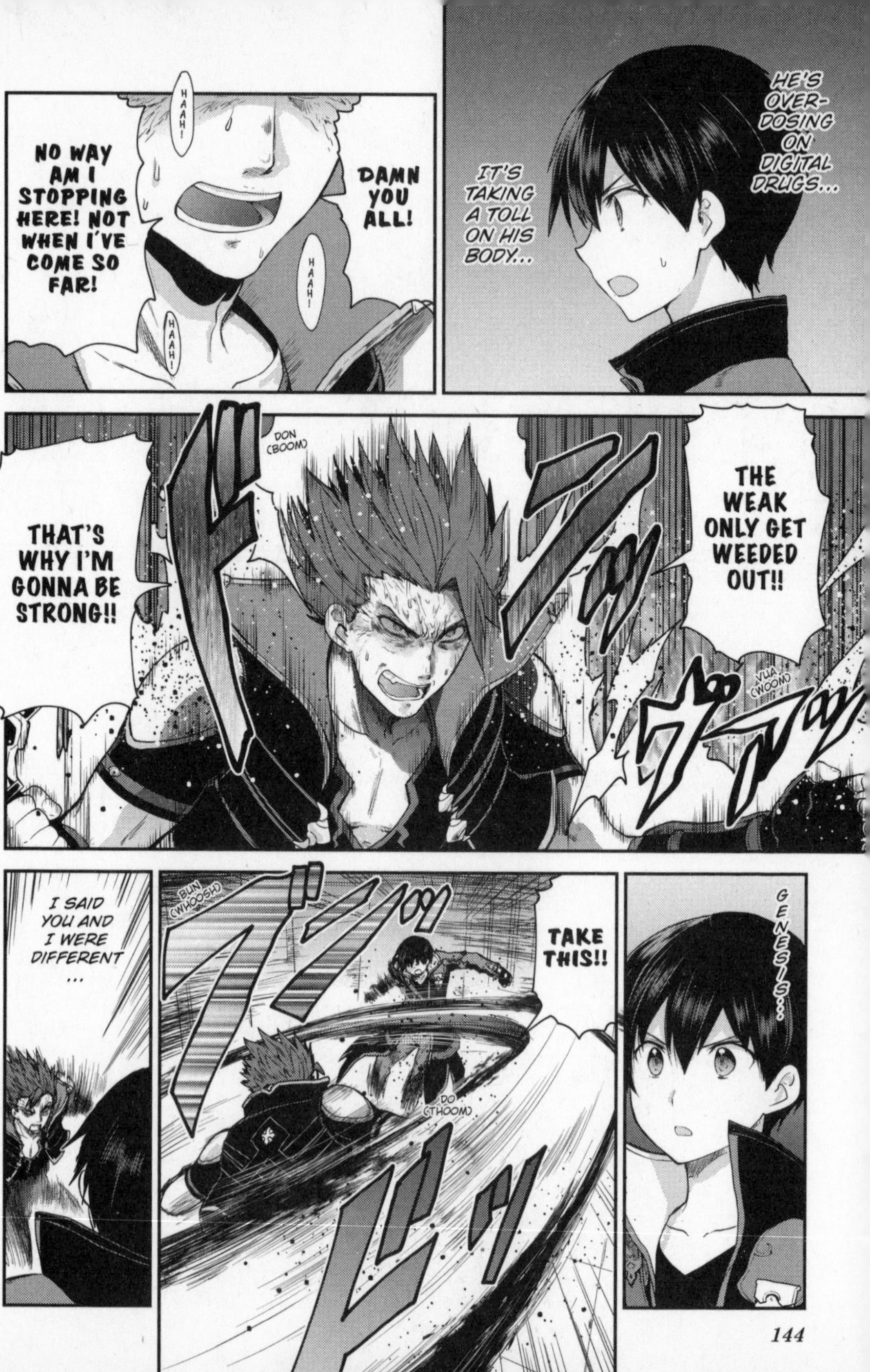
HE'S OVER-DOSING ON DIGITAL DRUGS...
IT'S TAKING A TOLL ON HIS BODY...
HAAH!
DAMN YOU ALL!
HAAH!
NO WAY AM I STOPPING HERE! NOT WHEN I'VE COME SO FAR!
HAAH!
THE WEAK ONLY GET WEEDED OUT!!
VUA (WOOM)
DON (BOOM)
THAT'S WHY I'M GONNA BE STRONG!!
GENESIS...
TAKE THIS!!
BUN (WHOOSH)
DO (THOOM)
I SAID YOU AND I WERE DIFFERENT ...

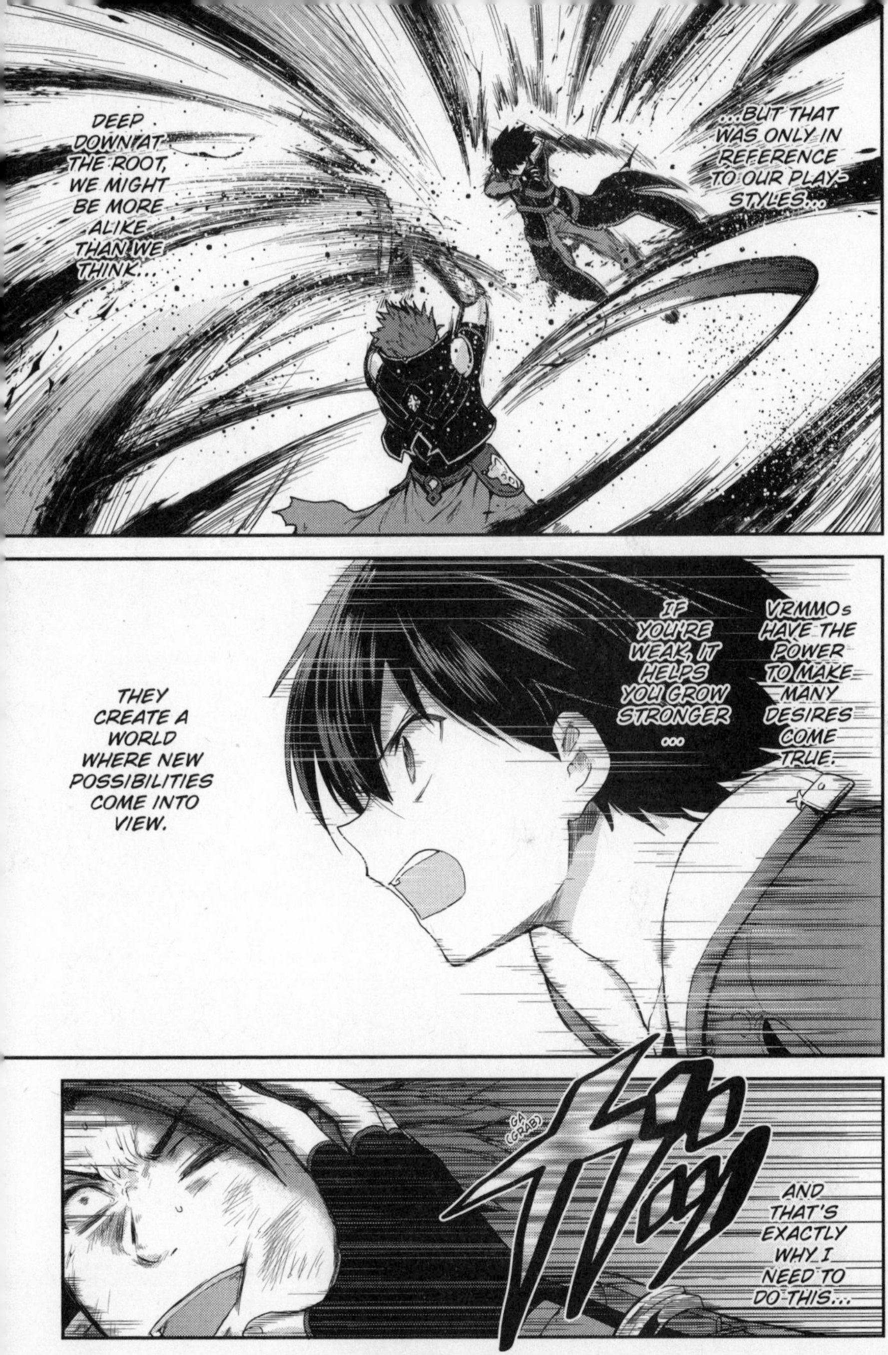
...BUT THAT WAS ONLY IN REFERENCE TO OUR PLAY-STYLES...
DEEP DOWN AT THE ROOT, WE MIGHT BE MORE ALIKE THAN WE THINK...
VRMMOs HAVE THE POWER TO MAKE MANY DESIRES COME TRUE.
IF YOU'RE WEAK, IT HELPS YOU GROW STRONGER...
THEY CREATE A WORLD WHERE NEW POSSIBILITIES COME INTO VIEW.
GA (GRAB)
AND THAT'S EXACTLY WHY I NEED TO DO THIS...

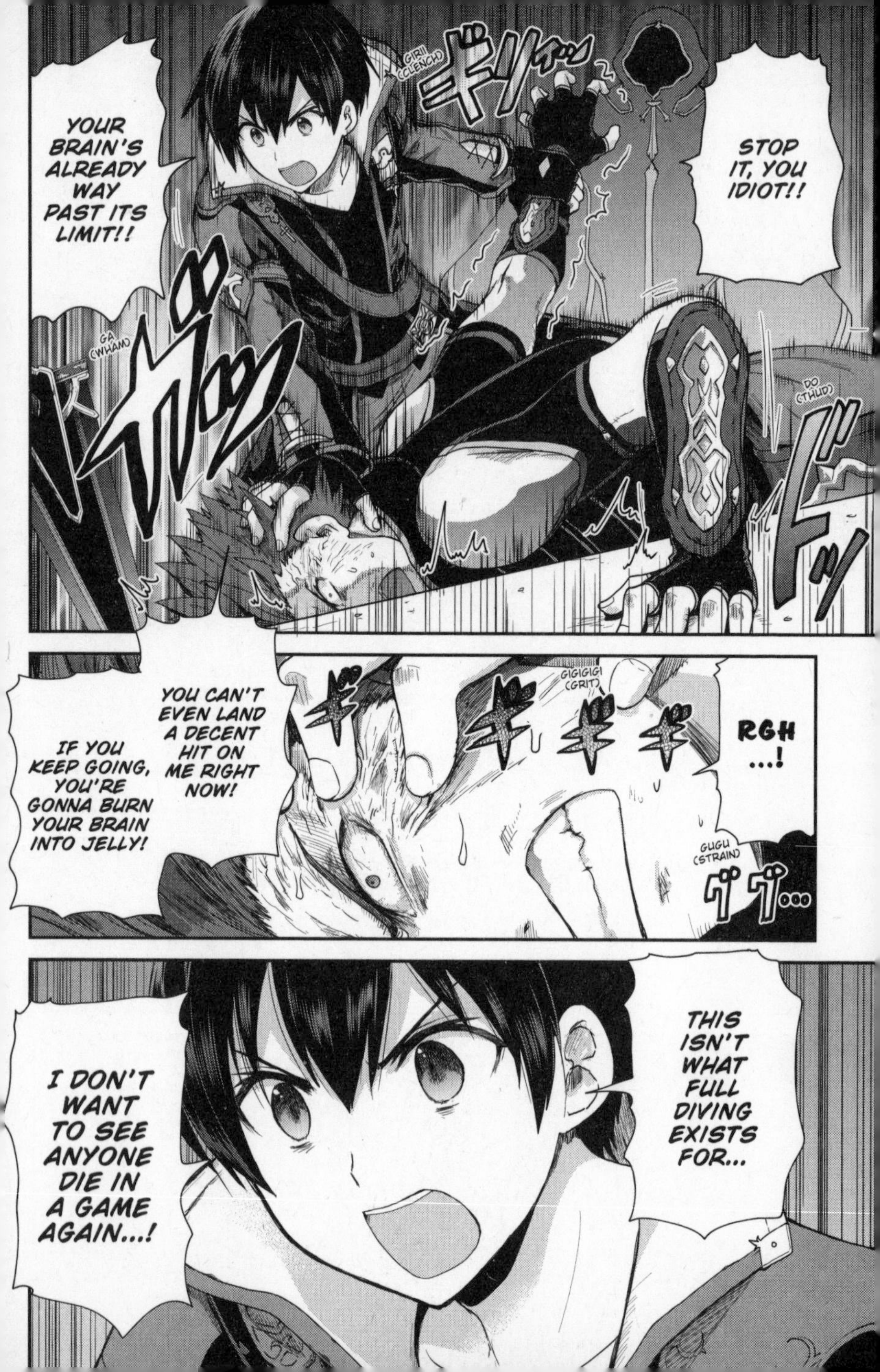
STOP IT, YOU IDIOT!!
GIRI (CLENCH)
YOUR BRAIN'S ALREADY WAY PAST ITS LIMIT!!
DO (THUD)
GA (WHAM)
RGH ...!
GIGIGIGI (GRIT)
YOU CAN'T EVEN LAND A DECENT HIT ON ME RIGHT NOW!
IF YOU KEEP GOING, YOU'RE GONNA BURN YOUR BRAIN INTO JELLY!
GUGU (STRAIN)
THIS ISN'T WHAT FULL DIVING EXISTS FOR...
I DON'T WANT TO SEE ANYONE DIE IN A GAME AGAIN...!

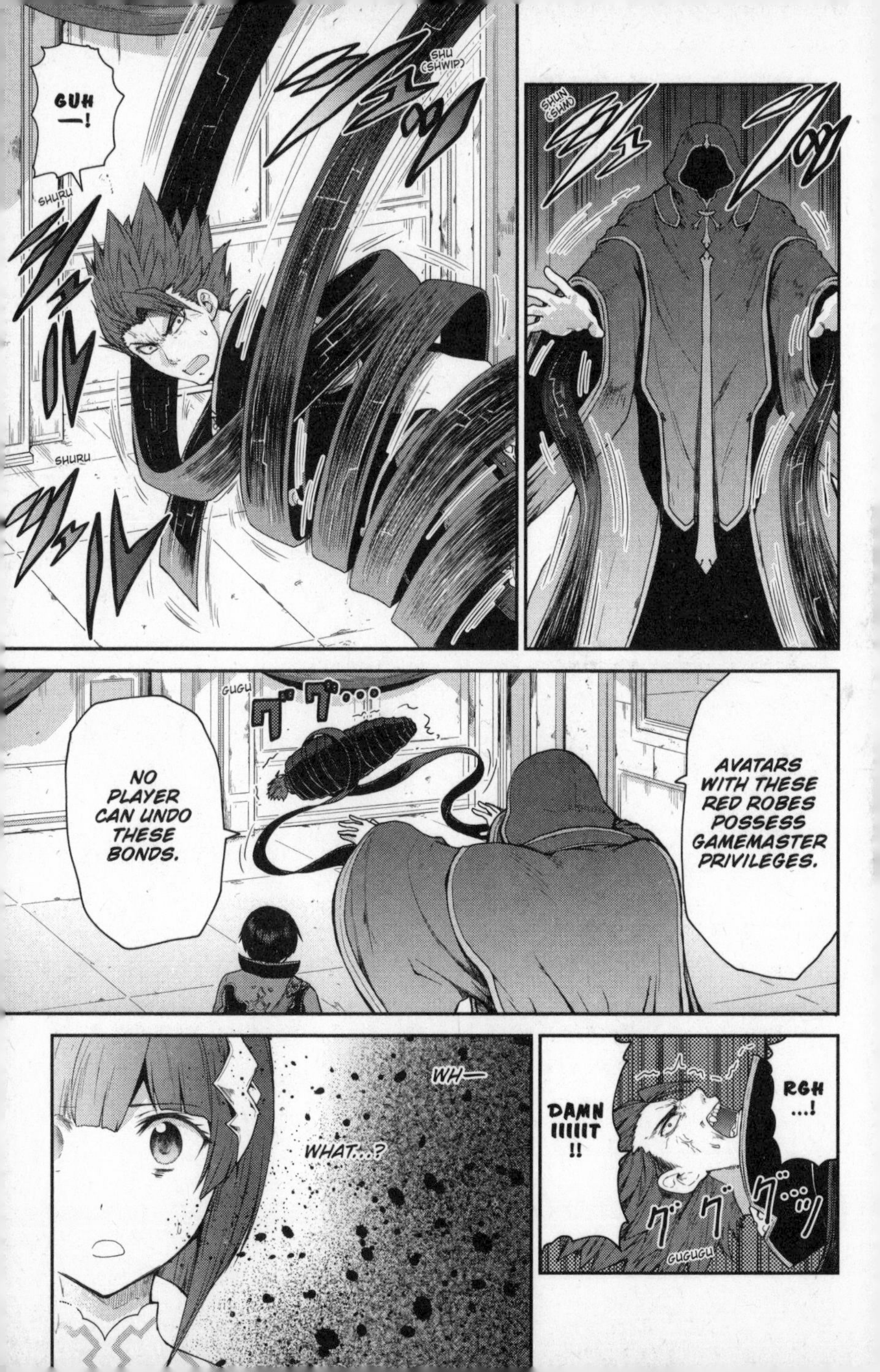

SHUN (SHN)
SHU (SHWIP)
GUH—!
SHURU
SHURU
AVATARS WITH THESE RED ROBES POSSESS GAMEMASTER PRIVILEGES.
GUGU
NO PLAYER CAN UNDO THESE BONDS.
RGH ...!
DAMN IIIIIT !!
GUGUGU
WH—
WHAT...?

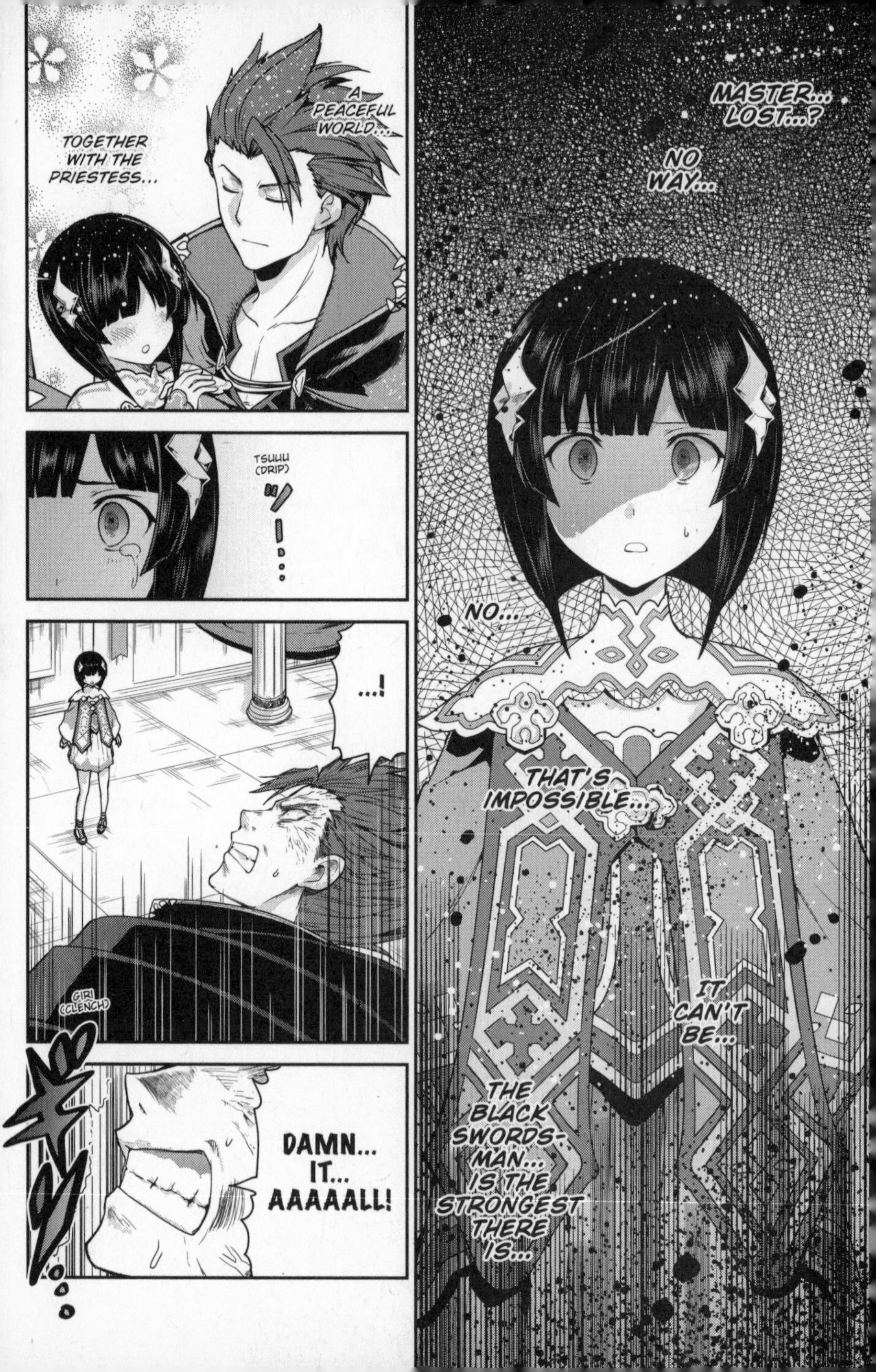
MASTER... LOST...?
NO WAY...
NO...
THAT'S IMPOSSIBLE...
IT CAN'T BE...
THE BLACK SWORDS-MAN... IS THE STRONGEST THERE IS...
A PEACEFUL WORLD...
TOGETHER WITH THE PRIESTESS...
TSUUU (DRIP)
...!
GIRI (CLENCH)
DAMN... IT... AAAAALL!

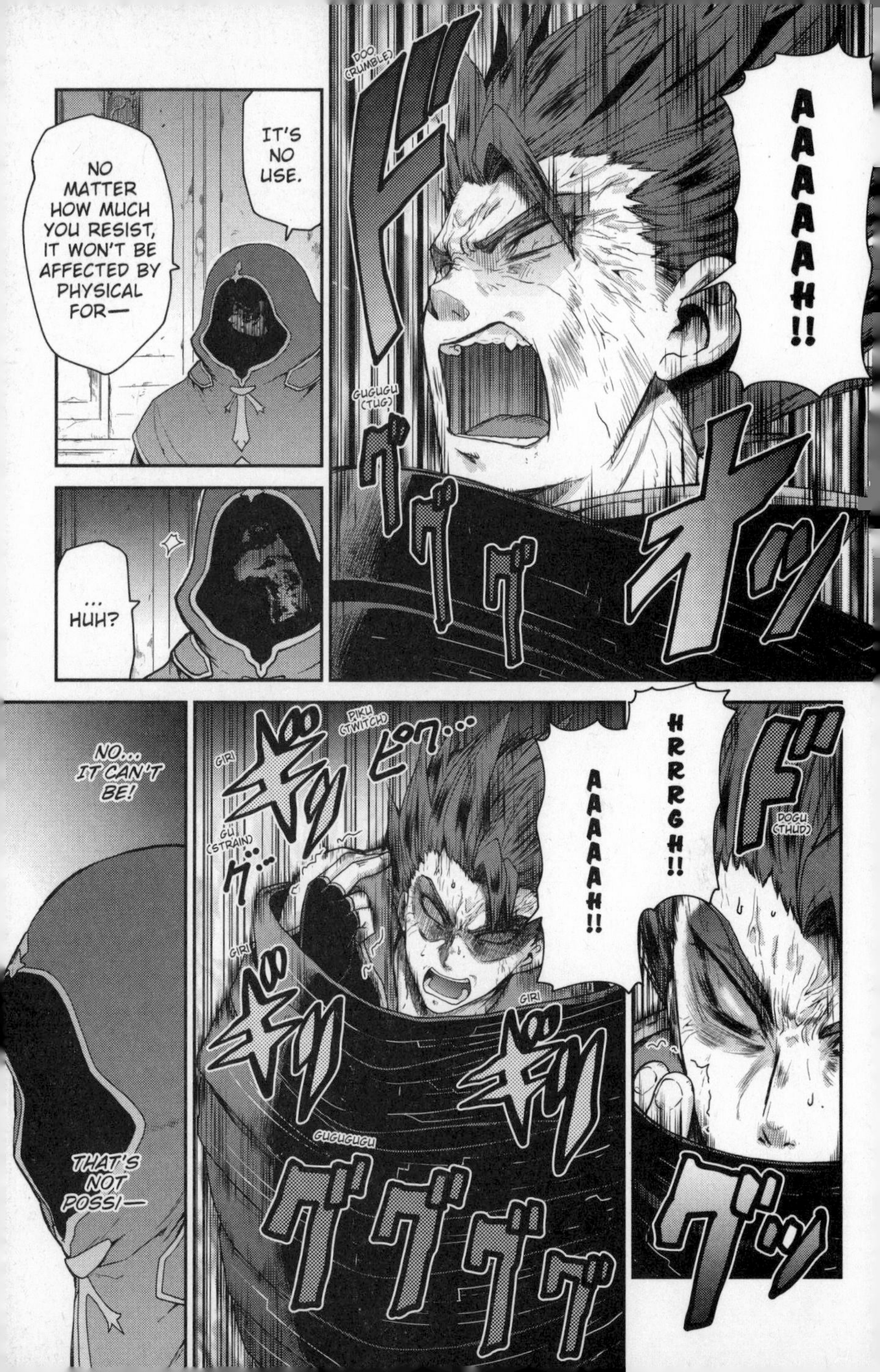
DOO (RUMBLE)
AAAAAAH!!
GUGUGU (TUG)
IT'S NO USE.
NO MATTER HOW MUCH YOU RESIST, IT WON'T BE AFFECTED BY PHYSICAL FOR—
... HUH?
DOGU (THUD)
HRRRGH!! AAAAAAH!!
PIKU (TWITCH)
GIRI
GU (STRAIN)
GIRI
GIRI
GUGUGUGU
NO... IT CAN'T BE!
THAT'S NOT POSSI—

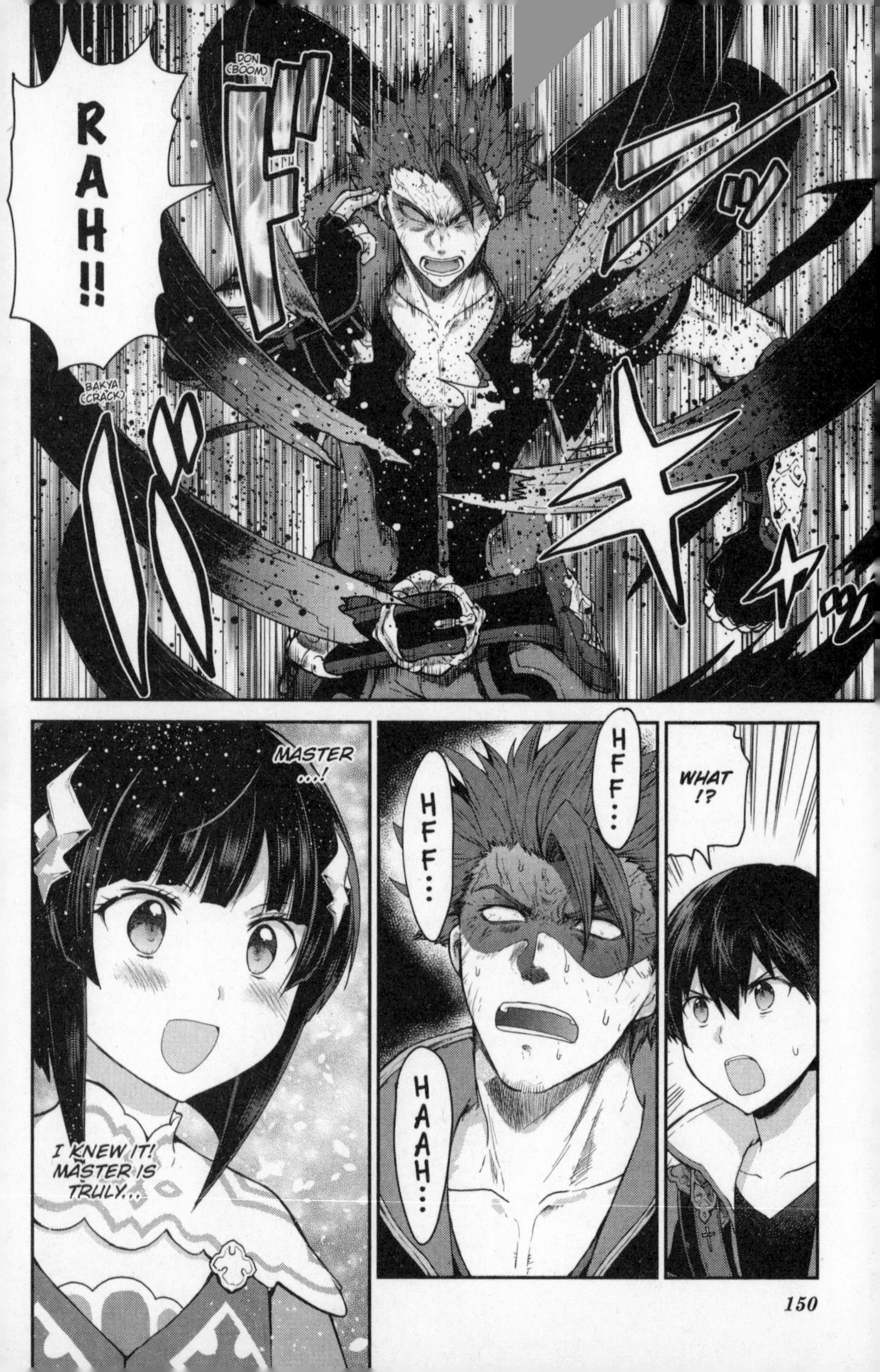
DON (BOOM)
RAH!!
BAKYA (CRACK)
WHAT!?
HFF... HFF...
HAAH...
MASTER...!
I KNEW IT! MASTER IS TRULY...

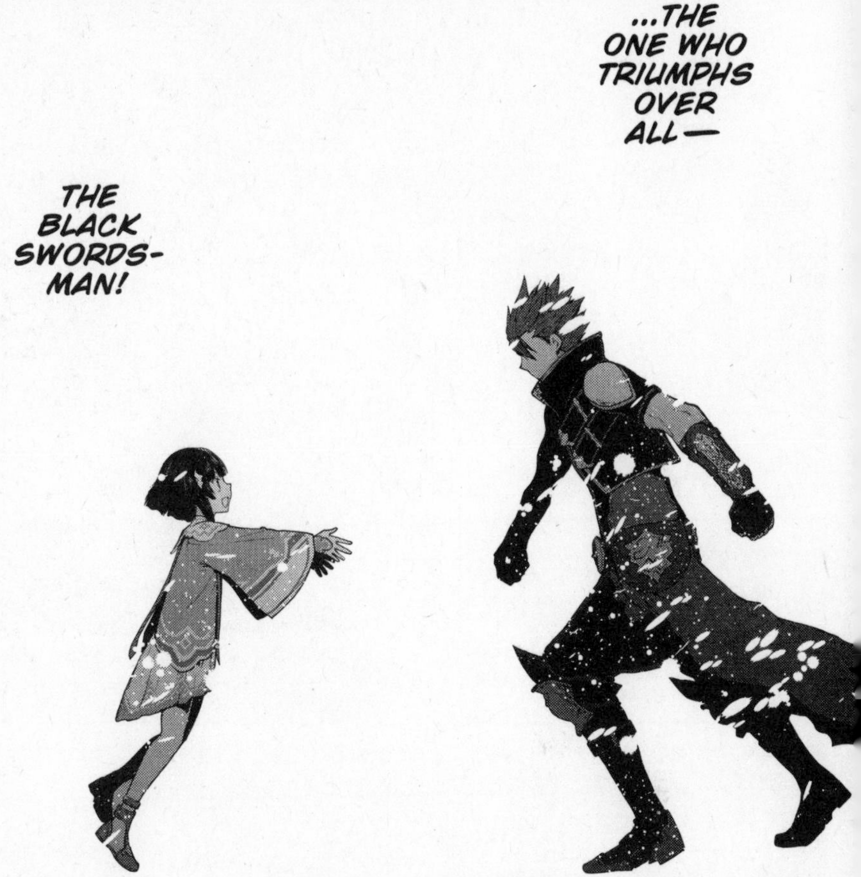
...THE ONE WHO TRIUMPHS OVER ALL—
THE BLACK SWORDS-MAN!

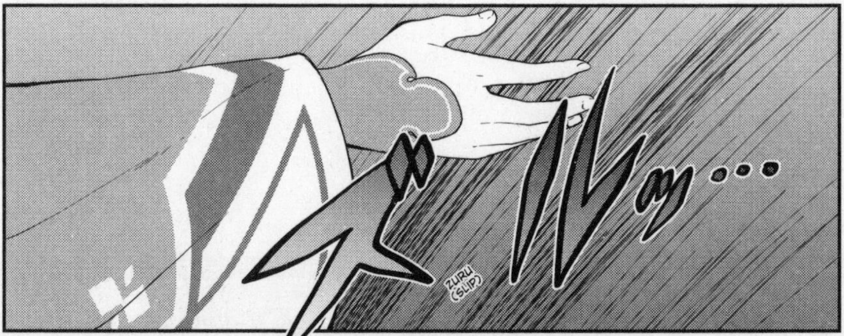
ZURU (SLIP)

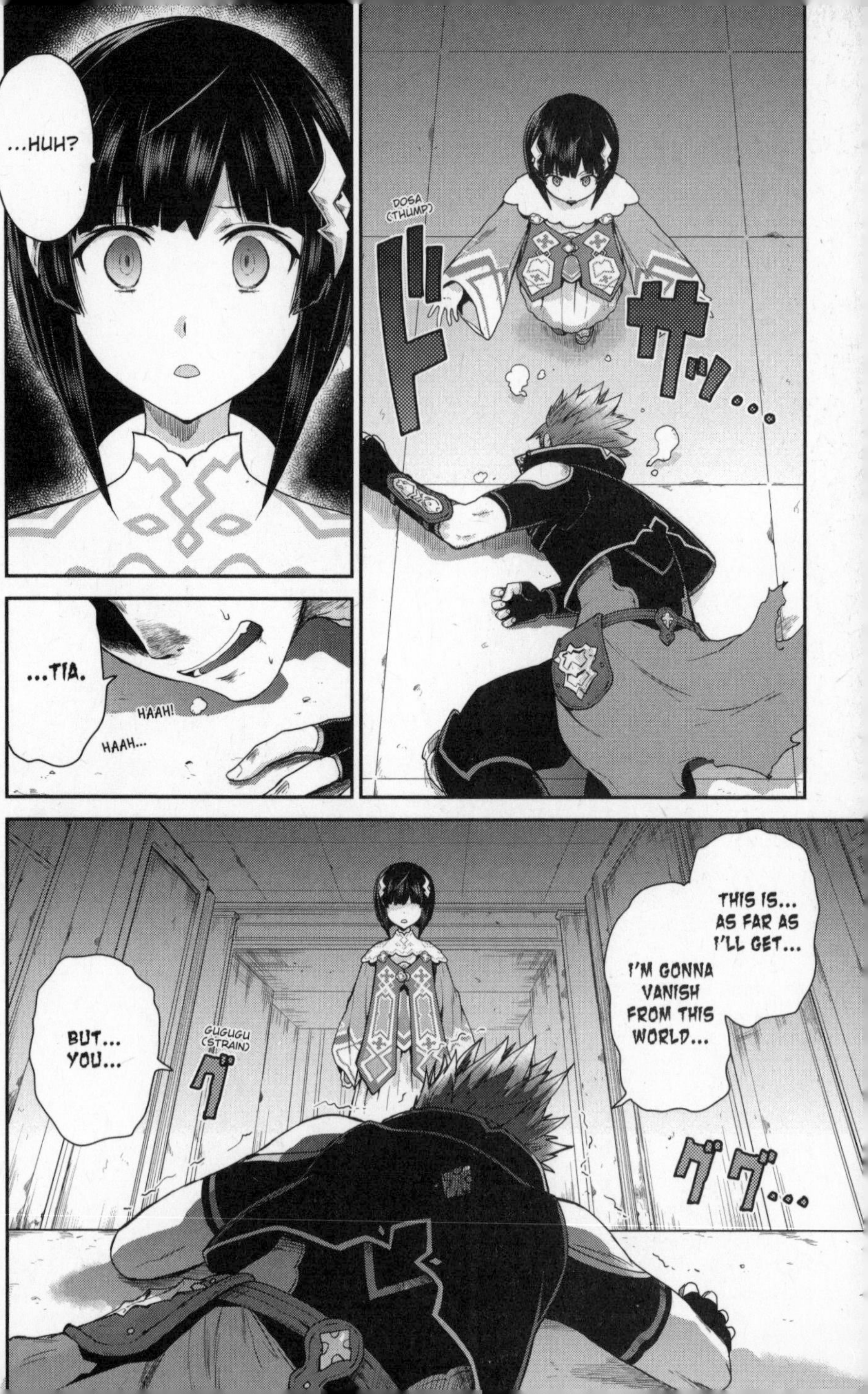
DOSA (THUMP)
...HUH?
...TIA.
HAAH!
HAAH...
THIS IS... AS FAR AS I'LL GET...
I'M GONNA VANISH FROM THIS WORLD...
GUGUGU (STRAIN)
BUT... YOU...

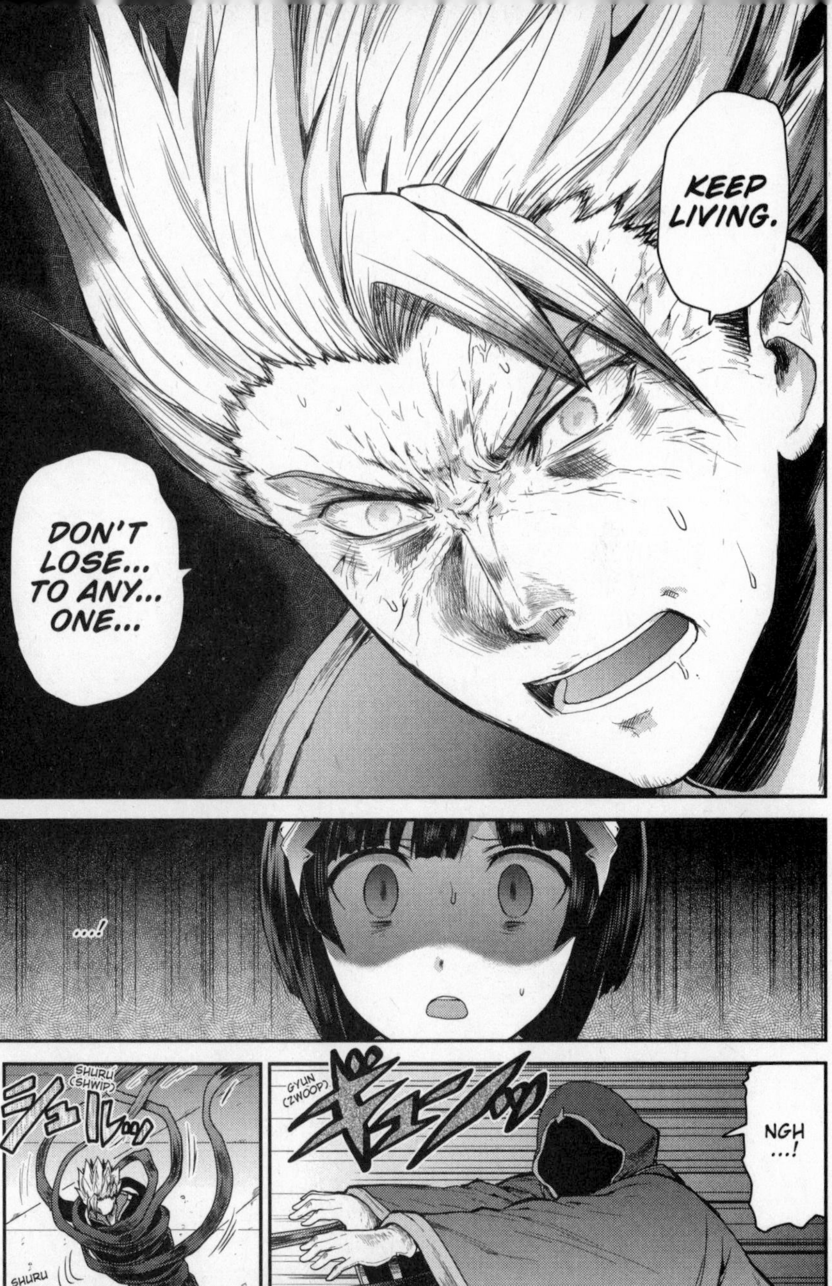
KEEP LIVING.
DON'T LOSE... TO ANY... ONE...
...!
GYUN (ZWOOP)
NGH ...!
SHURU (SHWIP)
SHURU

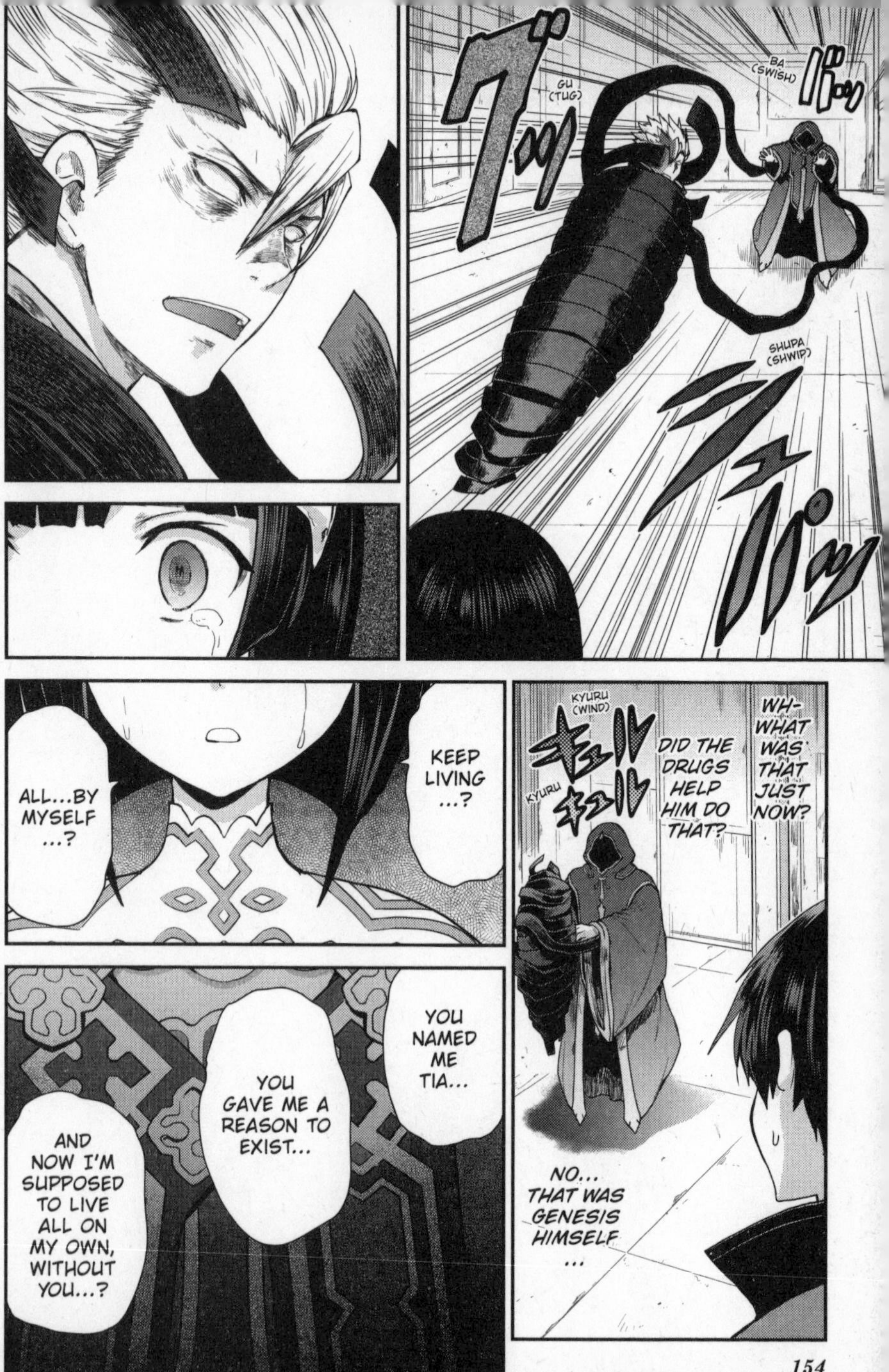
BA (SWISH)
GU (TUG)
SHUPA (SHWIP)
WH-WHAT WAS THAT JUST NOW?
DID THE DRUGS HELP HIM DO THAT?
KYURU (WIND)
KYURU
NO... THAT WAS GENESIS HIMSELF...
KEEP LIVING...?
ALL...BY MYSELF...?
YOU NAMED ME TIA...
YOU GAVE ME A REASON TO EXIST...
AND NOW I'M SUPPOSED TO LIVE ALL ON MY OWN, WITHOUT YOU...?

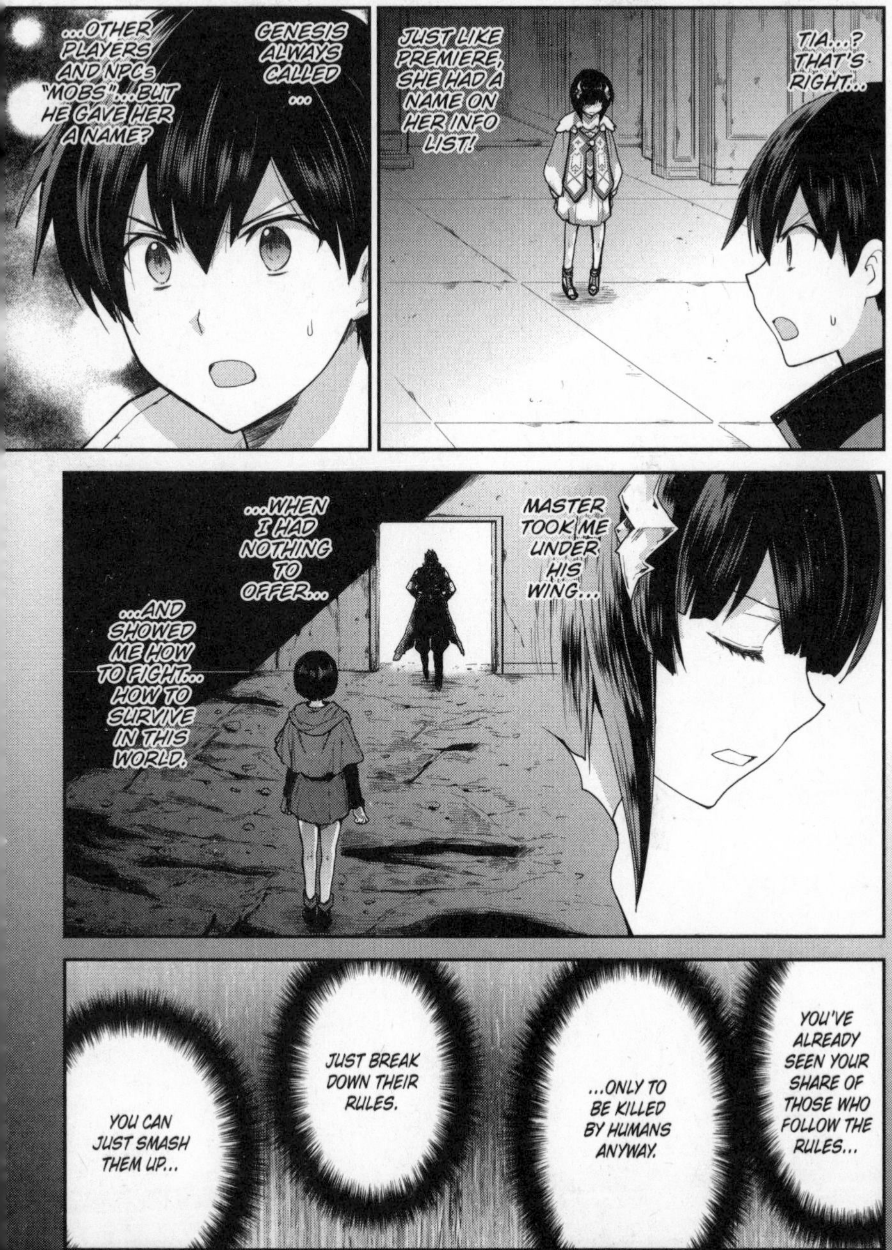
TIA...? THAT'S RIGHT...
JUST LIKE PREMIERE, SHE HAD A NAME ON HER INFO LIST!
GENESIS ALWAYS CALLED ...
...OTHER PLAYERS AND NPCs "MOBS"...BUT HE GAVE HER A NAME?
MASTER TOOK ME UNDER HIS WING...
...WHEN I HAD NOTHING TO OFFER...
...AND SHOWED ME HOW TO FIGHT... HOW TO SURVIVE IN THIS WORLD.
YOU'VE ALREADY SEEN YOUR SHARE OF THOSE WHO FOLLOW THE RULES...
...ONLY TO BE KILLED BY HUMANS ANYWAY.
JUST BREAK DOWN THEIR RULES.
YOU CAN JUST SMASH THEM UP...

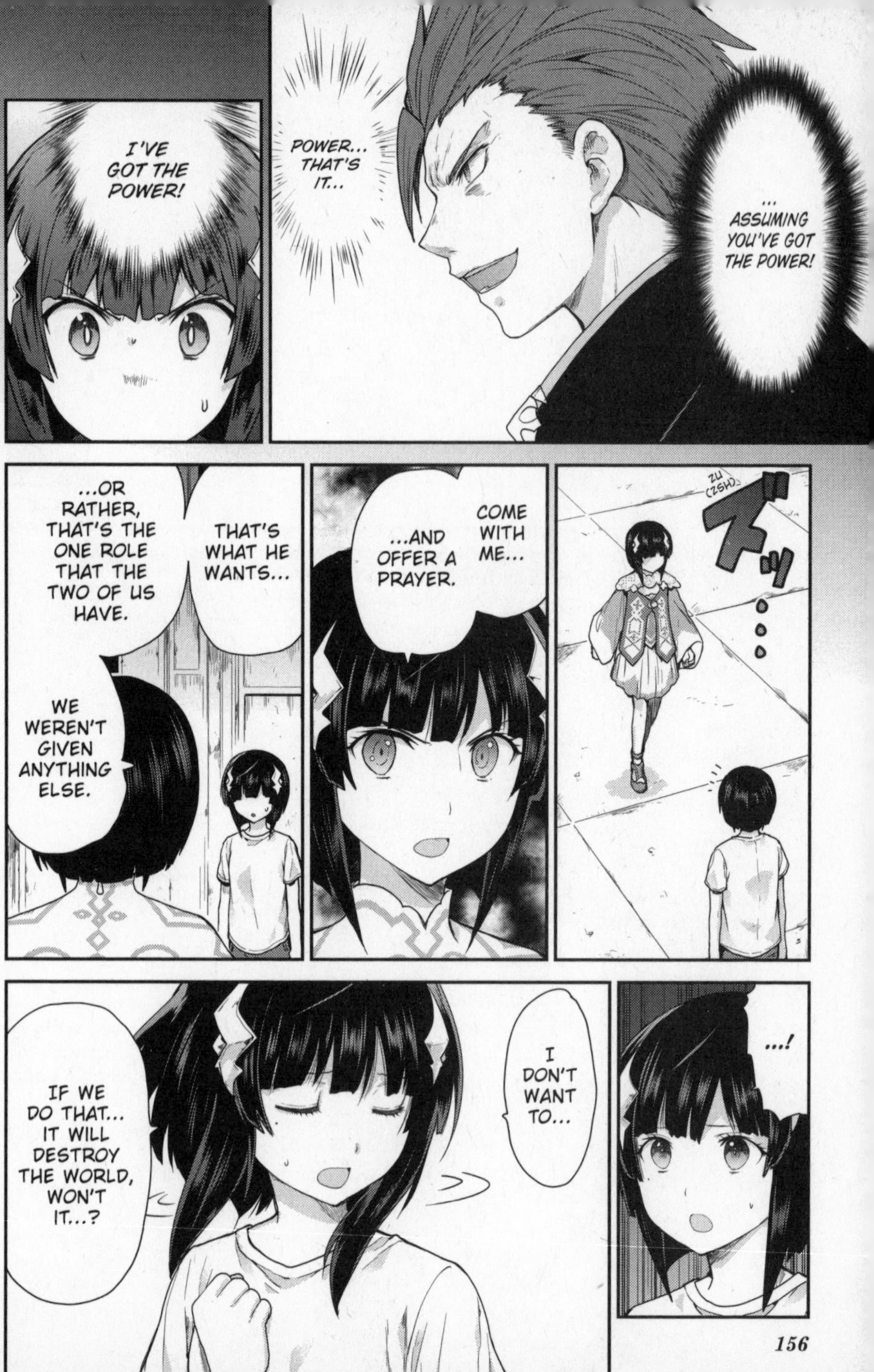
...ASSUMING YOU'VE GOT THE POWER!
POWER... THAT'S IT...
I'VE GOT THE POWER!
ZU (ZSH)
...
COME WITH ME...
...AND OFFER A PRAYER.
THAT'S WHAT HE WANTS...
...OR RATHER, THAT'S THE ONE ROLE THAT THE TWO OF US HAVE.
WE WEREN'T GIVEN ANYTHING ELSE.
...!
I DON'T WANT TO...
IF WE DO THAT... IT WILL DESTROY THE WORLD, WON'T IT...?

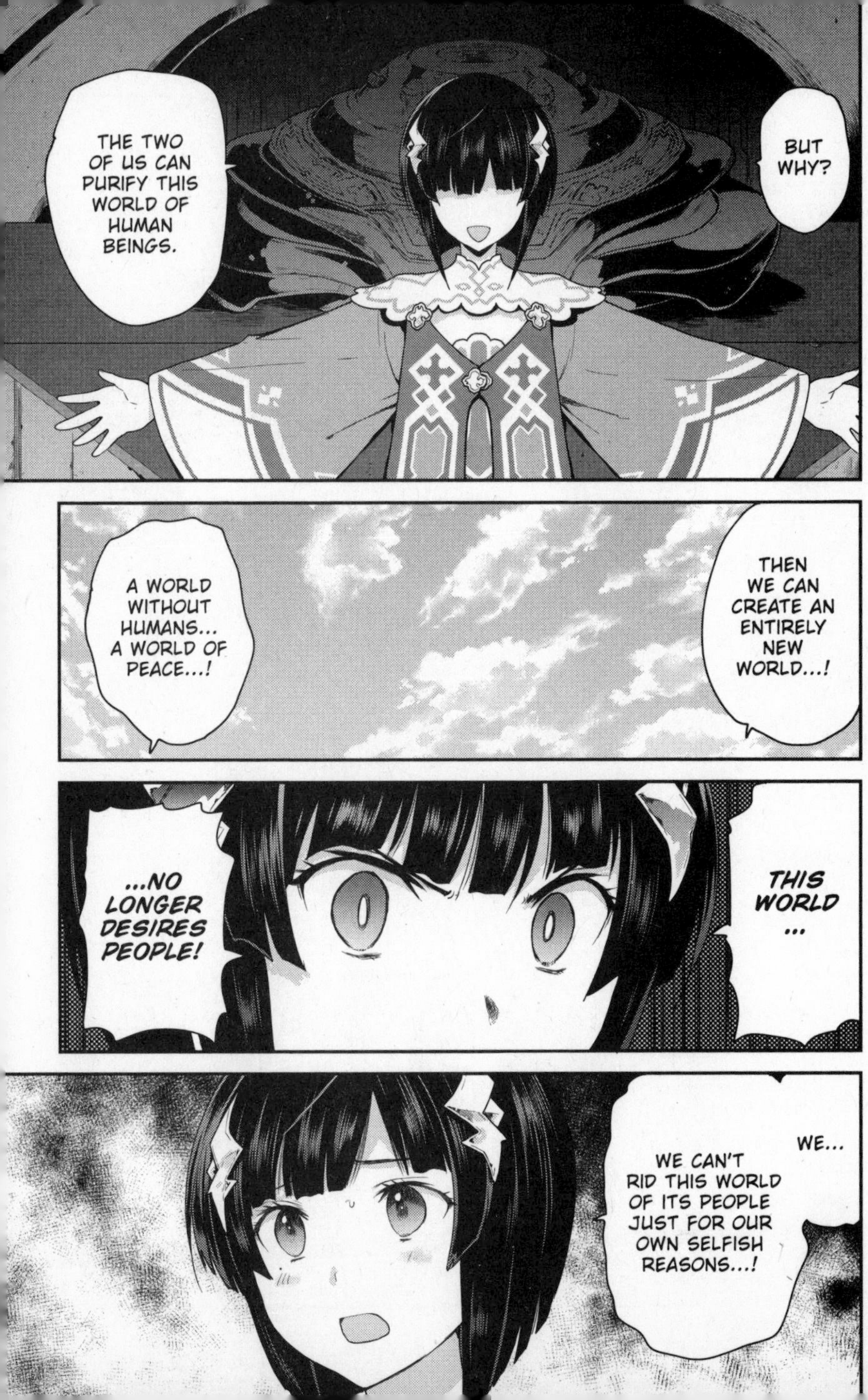
BUT WHY?
THE TWO OF US CAN PURIFY THIS WORLD OF HUMAN BEINGS.
THEN WE CAN CREATE AN ENTIRELY NEW WORLD...!
A WORLD WITHOUT HUMANS... A WORLD OF PEACE...!
THIS WORLD...
...NO LONGER DESIRES PEOPLE!
WE...
WE CAN'T RID THIS WORLD OF ITS PEOPLE JUST FOR OUR OWN SELFISH REASONS...!

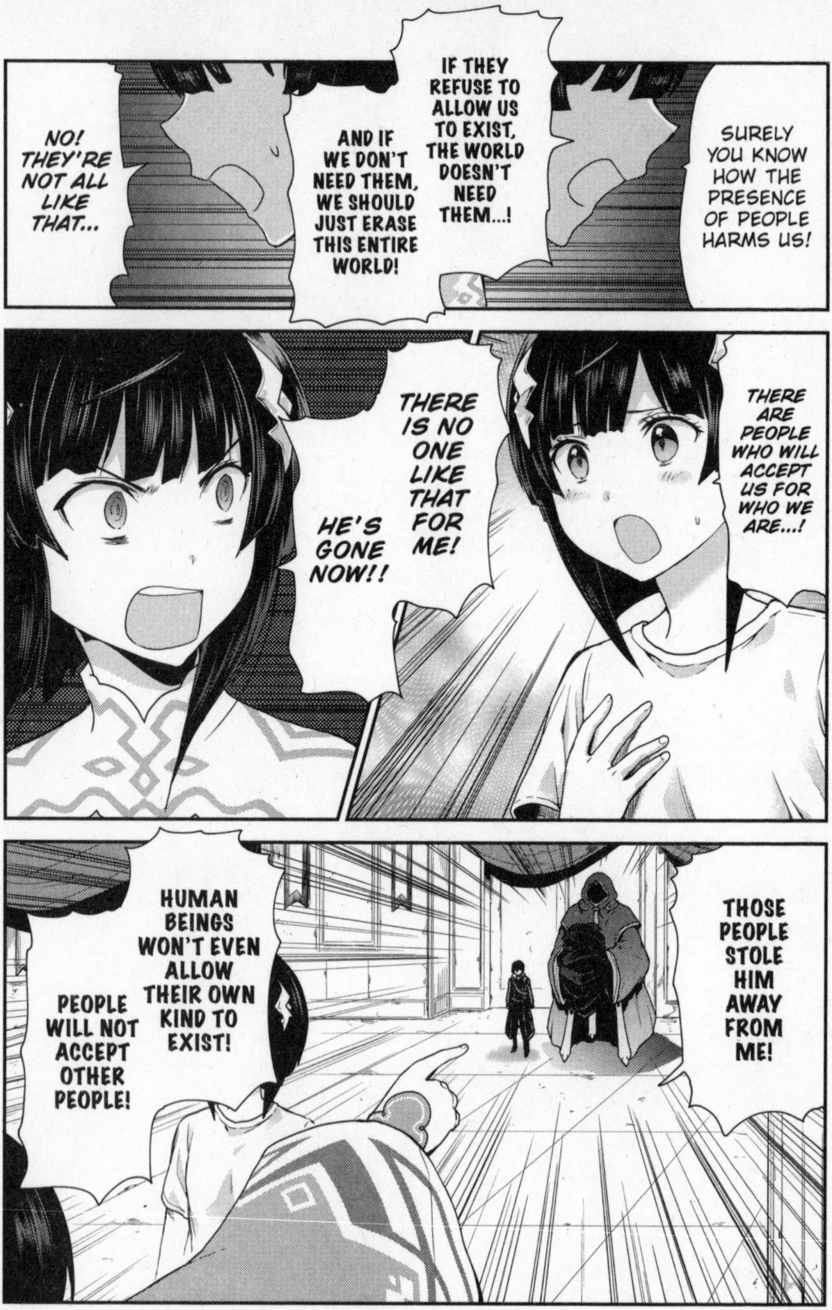
SURELY YOU KNOW HOW THE PRESENCE OF PEOPLE HARMS US!
IF THEY REFUSE TO ALLOW US TO EXIST, THE WORLD DOESN'T NEED THEM...!
AND IF WE DON'T NEED THEM, WE SHOULD JUST ERASE THIS ENTIRE WORLD!
NO! THEY'RE NOT ALL LIKE THAT...
THERE ARE PEOPLE WHO WILL ACCEPT US FOR WHO WE ARE...!
THERE IS NO ONE LIKE THAT FOR ME!
HE'S GONE NOW!!
THOSE PEOPLE STOLE HIM AWAY FROM ME!
HUMAN BEINGS WON'T EVEN ALLOW THEIR OWN KIND TO EXIST!
PEOPLE WILL NOT ACCEPT OTHER PEOPLE!

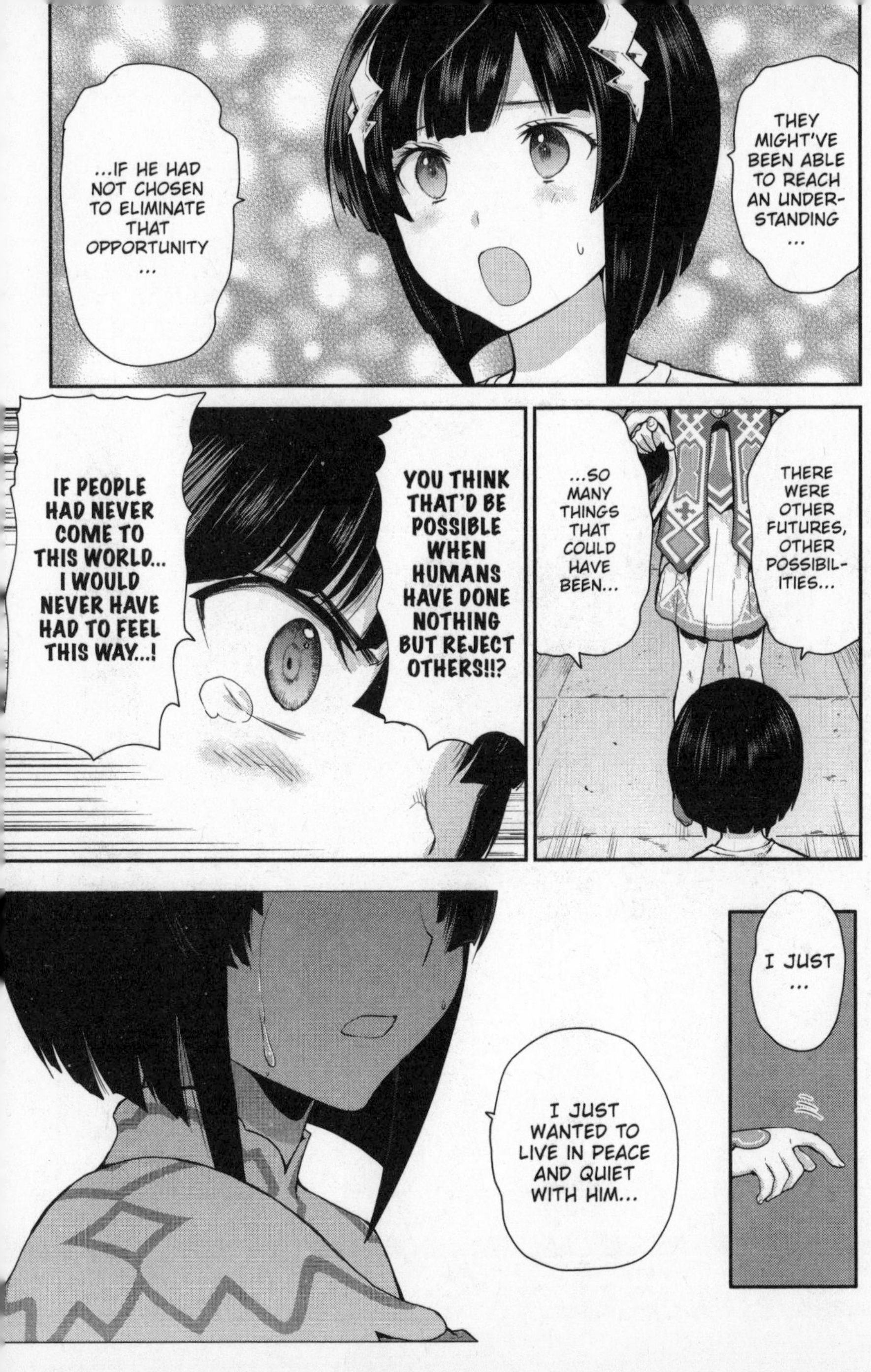
THEY MIGHT'VE BEEN ABLE TO REACH AN UNDER-STANDING ...
...IF HE HAD NOT CHOSEN TO ELIMINATE THAT OPPORTUNITY ...
THERE WERE OTHER FUTURES, OTHER POSSIBIL-ITIES...
...SO MANY THINGS THAT COULD HAVE BEEN...
YOU THINK THAT'D BE POSSIBLE WHEN HUMANS HAVE DONE NOTHING BUT REJECT OTHERS!!?
IF PEOPLE HAD NEVER COME TO THIS WORLD... I WOULD NEVER HAVE HAD TO FEEL THIS WAY...!
I JUST ...
I JUST WANTED TO LIVE IN PEACE AND QUIET WITH HIM...

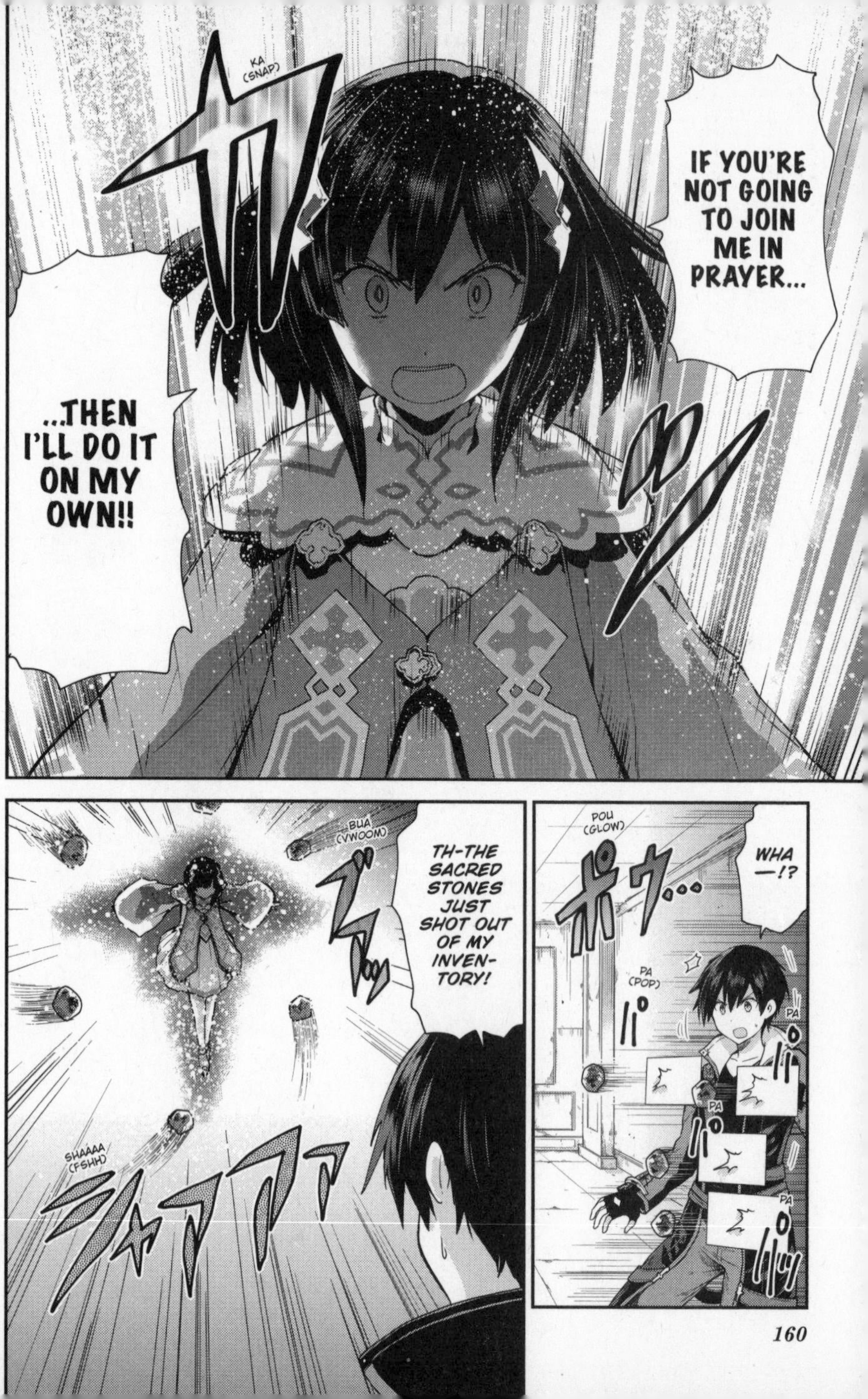
KA (SNAP)
IF YOU'RE NOT GOING TO JOIN ME IN PRAYER...
...THEN I'LL DO IT ON MY OWN!!
POU (GLOW)
WHA—!?
PA (POP)
PA
PA
PA
BUA (VWOOM)
TH-THE SACRED STONES JUST SHOT OUT OF MY INVENTORY!
SHAAAA (FSHH)

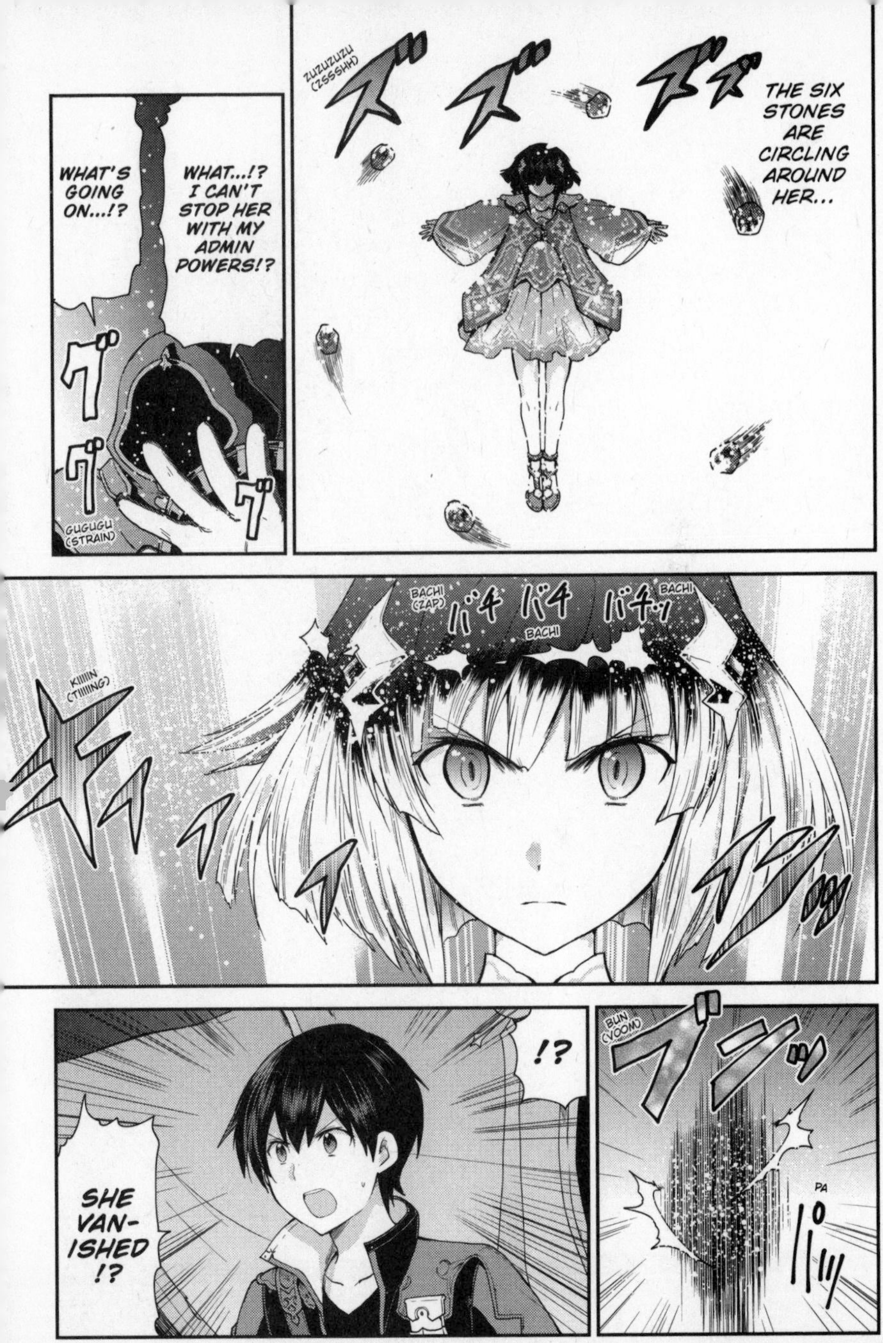
ZUZUZUZU (ZZSSSHH)
THE SIX STONES ARE CIRCLING AROUND HER...
WHAT...!? I CAN'T STOP HER WITH MY ADMIN POWERS!?
WHAT'S GOING ON...!?
GUGUGU (STRAIN)
BACHI BACHI (ZAP) BACHI
BACHI
KIIIIN (TIIIIING)
BUN (VOOM)
PA
!?
SHE VAN-ISHED !?

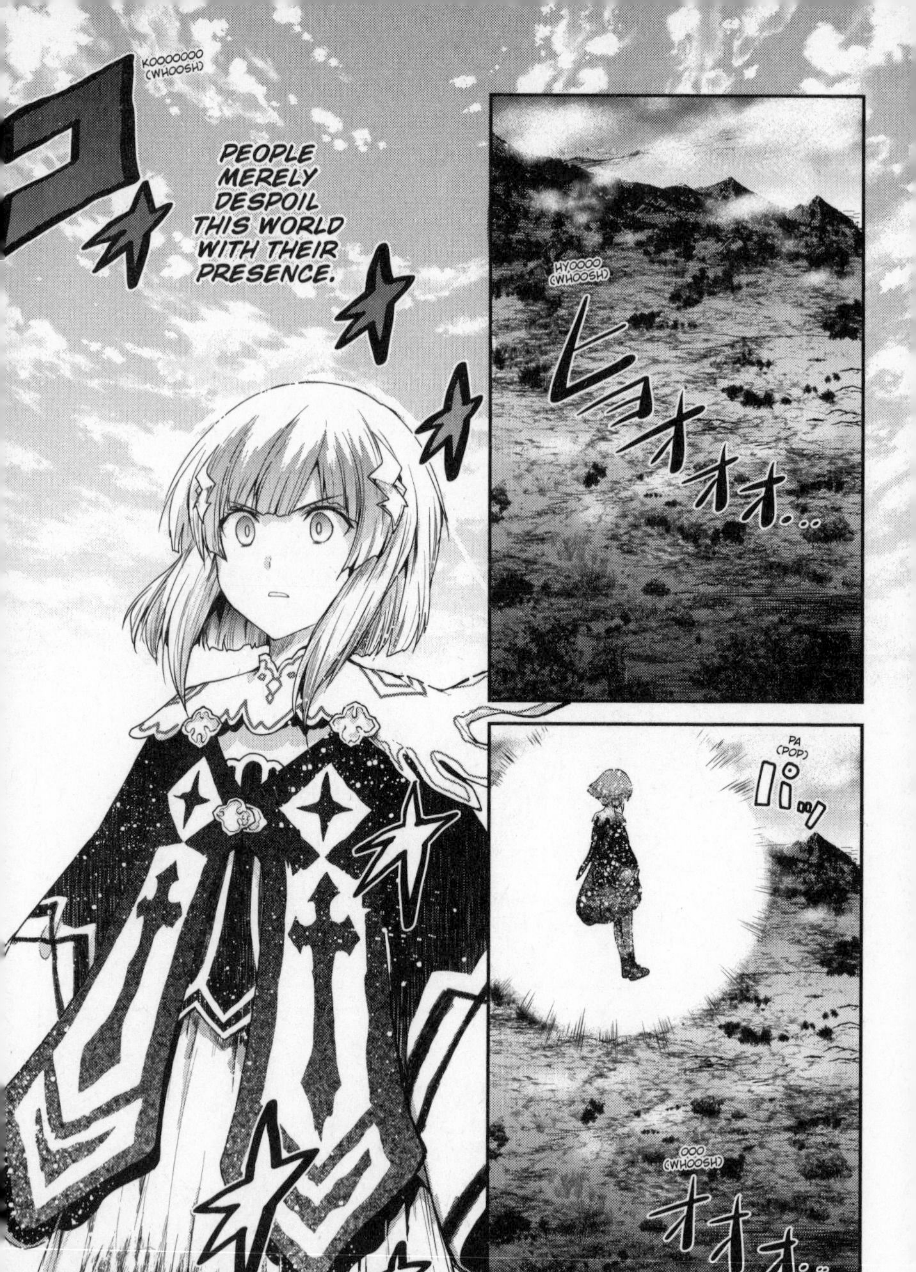
HYOOOO (WHOOSH)
ヒョオオオ...
PA (POP)
パッ
OOO (WHOOSH)
オオオ..
KOOOOOOO (WHOOSH)
コ
PEOPLE MERELY DESPOIL THIS WORLD WITH THEIR PRESENCE.

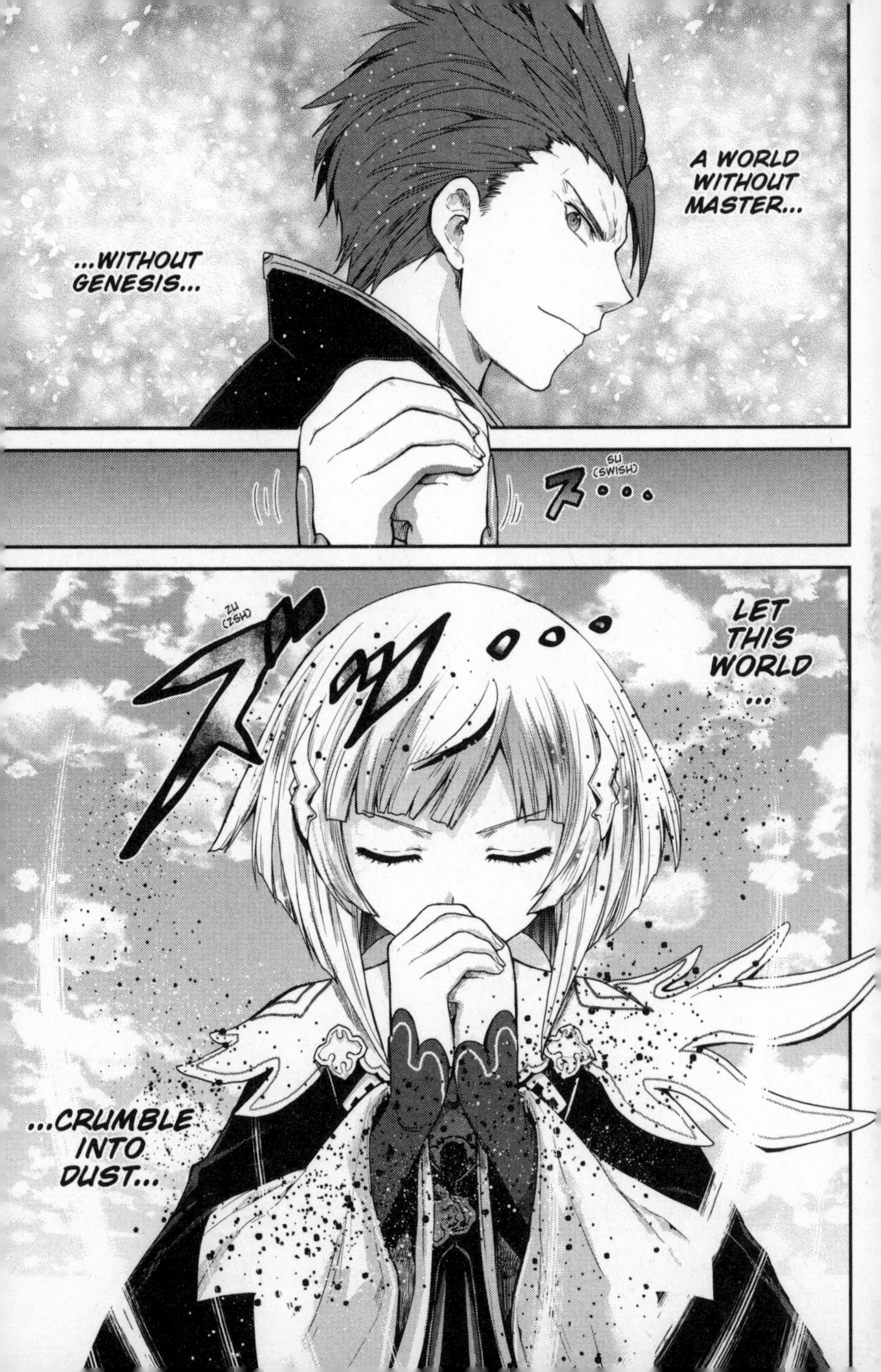
A WORLD WITHOUT MASTER...
...WITHOUT GENESIS...
SU (SWISH)
LET THIS WORLD ...
ZU (ZSH)
...CRUMBLE INTO DUST...

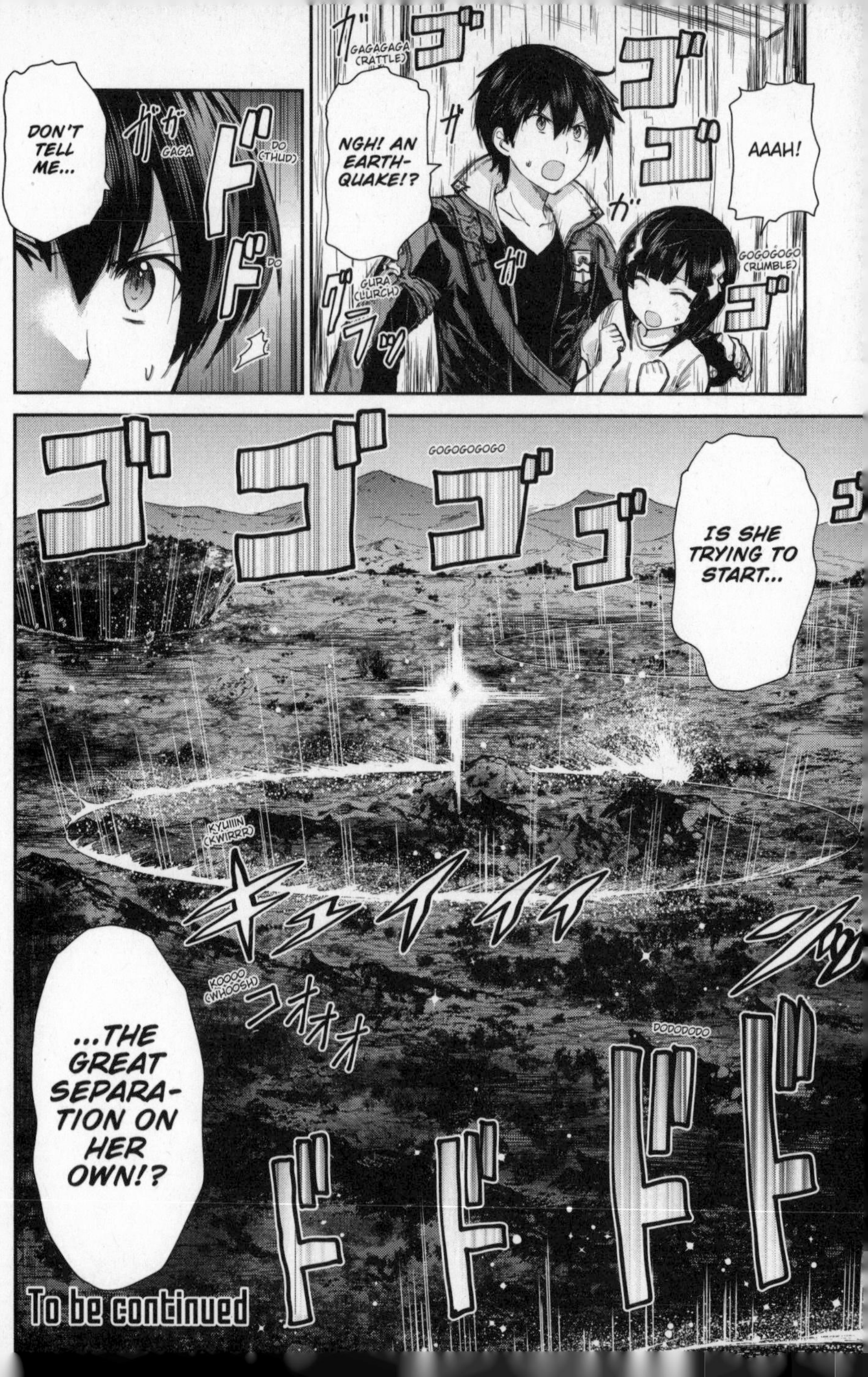
AAAH!
GAGAGAGA (RATTLE)
NGH! AN EARTHQUAKE!?
GOGOGOGO (RUMBLE)
GURA (LURCH)
DON'T TELL ME...
DO (THUD)
GAGA
DO
GOGOGOGOGO
IS SHE TRYING TO START...
KYUIIIN (KWIRRR)
KOOOO (WHOOSH)
DODODODO
...THE GREAT SEPARATION ON HER OWN!?
To be continued

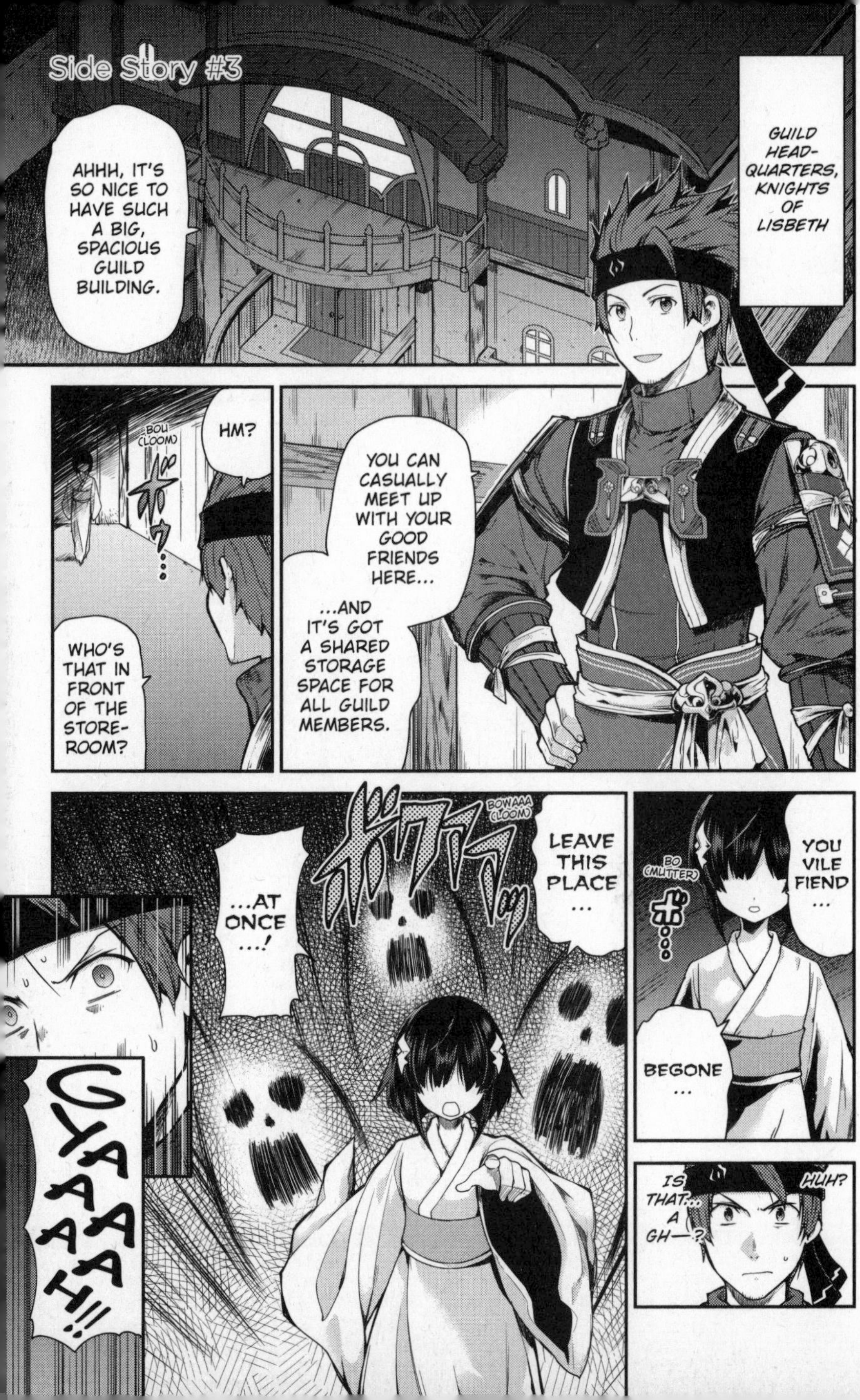

Side Story #3
GUILD HEAD-QUARTERS, KNIGHTS OF LISBETH
AHHH, IT'S SO NICE TO HAVE SUCH A BIG, SPACIOUS GUILD BUILDING.
YOU CAN CASUALLY MEET UP WITH YOUR GOOD FRIENDS HERE...
...AND IT'S GOT A SHARED STORAGE SPACE FOR ALL GUILD MEMBERS.
HM?
BOU (LOOM)
WHO'S THAT IN FRONT OF THE STORE-ROOM?
YOU VILE FIEND ...
BO (MUTTER)
BEGONE ...
HUH?
IS THAT... A GH—?
LEAVE THIS PLACE ...
BOWAAA (LOOM)
...AT ONCE ...!
GYAAAAH!!!

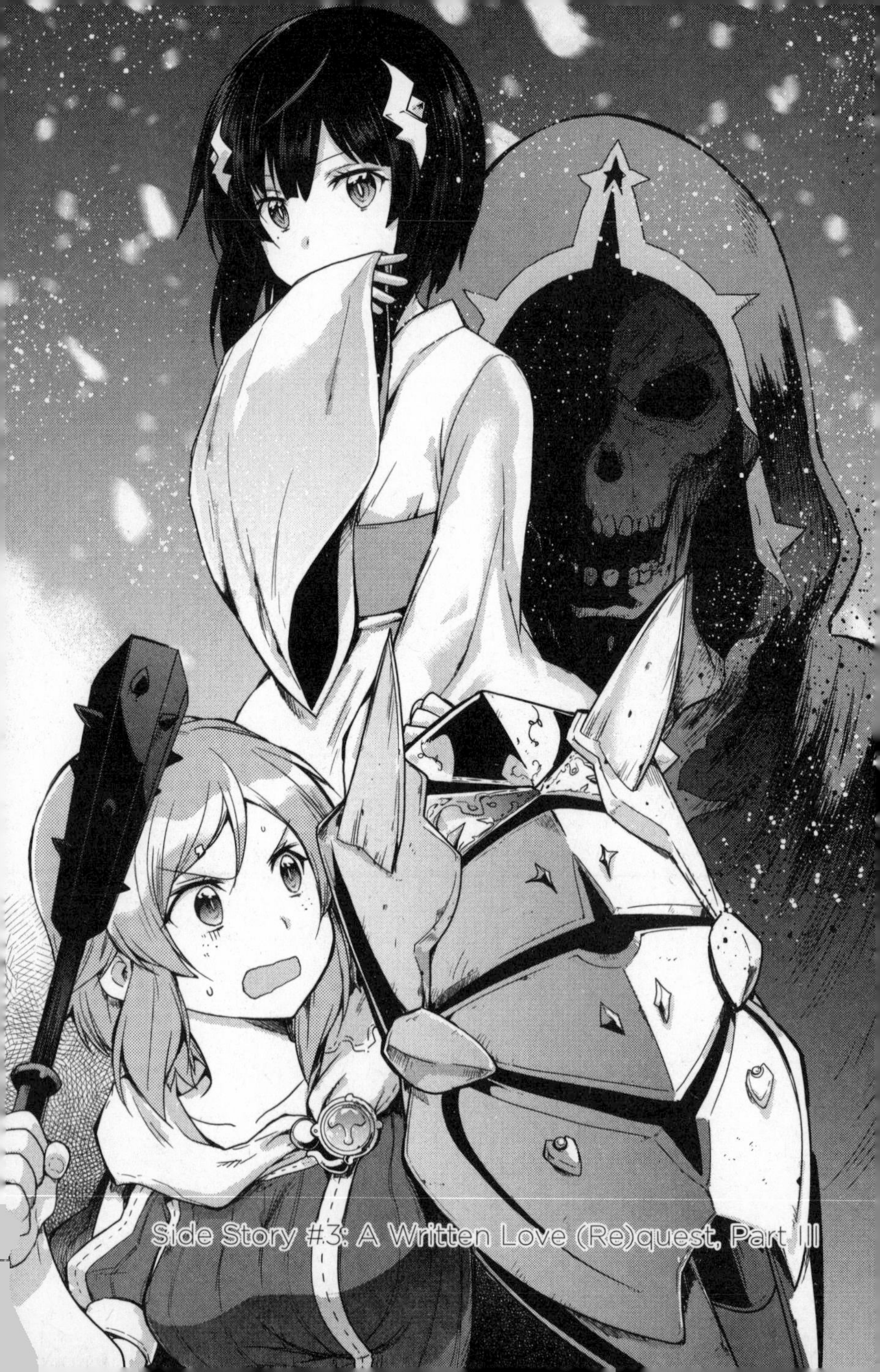

Side Story #3: A Written Love (Re)quest, Part III

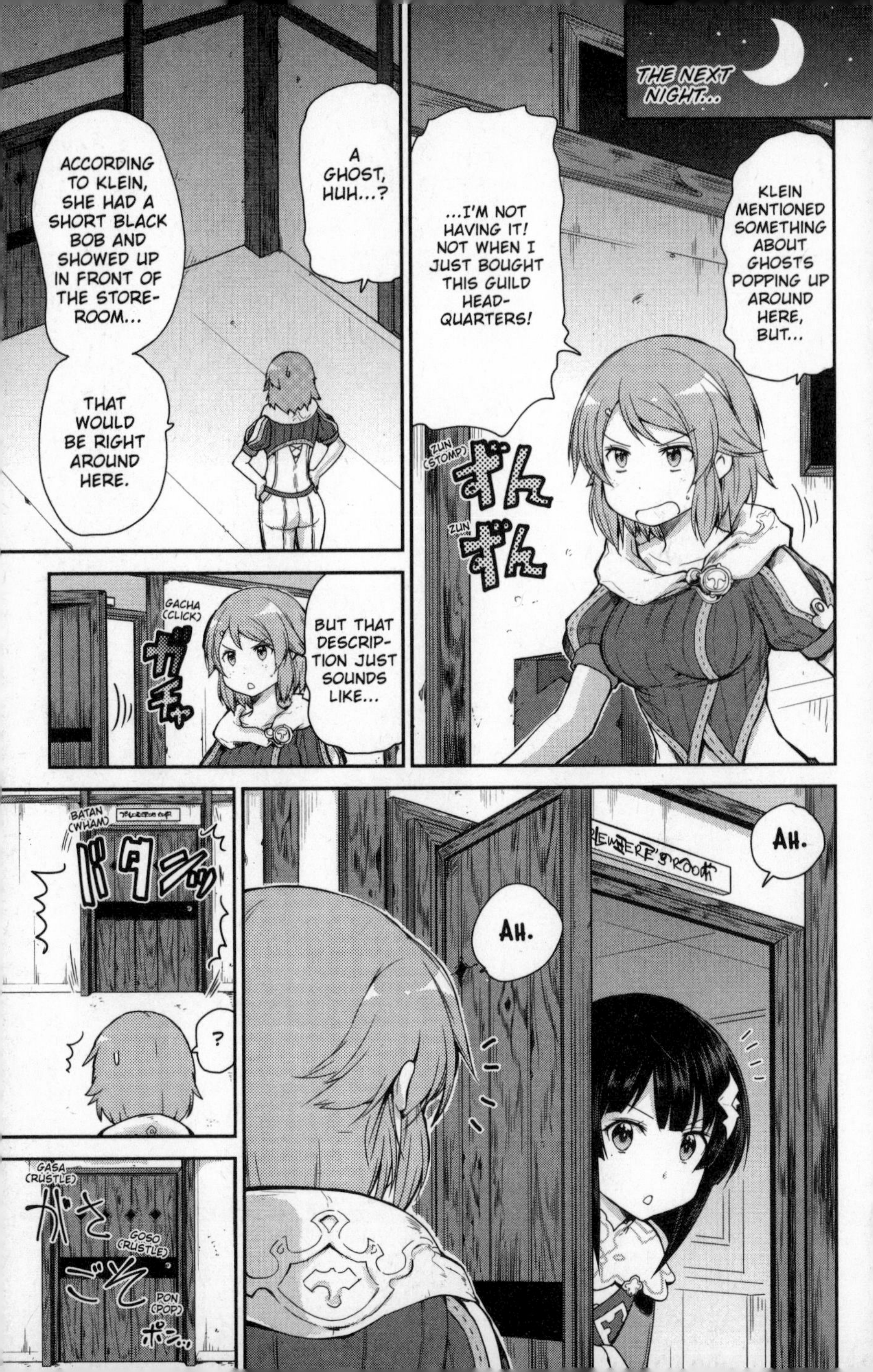

THE NEXT NIGHT...
KLEIN MENTIONED SOMETHING ABOUT GHOSTS POPPING UP AROUND HERE, BUT...
...I'M NOT HAVING IT! NOT WHEN I JUST BOUGHT THIS GUILD HEAD-QUARTERS!
ZUN (STOMP)
ずん
ZUN
ずん
A GHOST, HUH...?
ACCORDING TO KLEIN, SHE HAD A SHORT BLACK BOB AND SHOWED UP IN FRONT OF THE STORE-ROOM...
THAT WOULD BE RIGHT AROUND HERE.
GACHA (CLICK)
ガチャ
BUT THAT DESCRIPTION JUST SOUNDS LIKE...
AH.
AH.
BATAN (WHAM)
バタンッ
?
GASA (RUSTLE)
がさ
GOSO (RUSTLE)
ごそ
PON (POP)
ポン

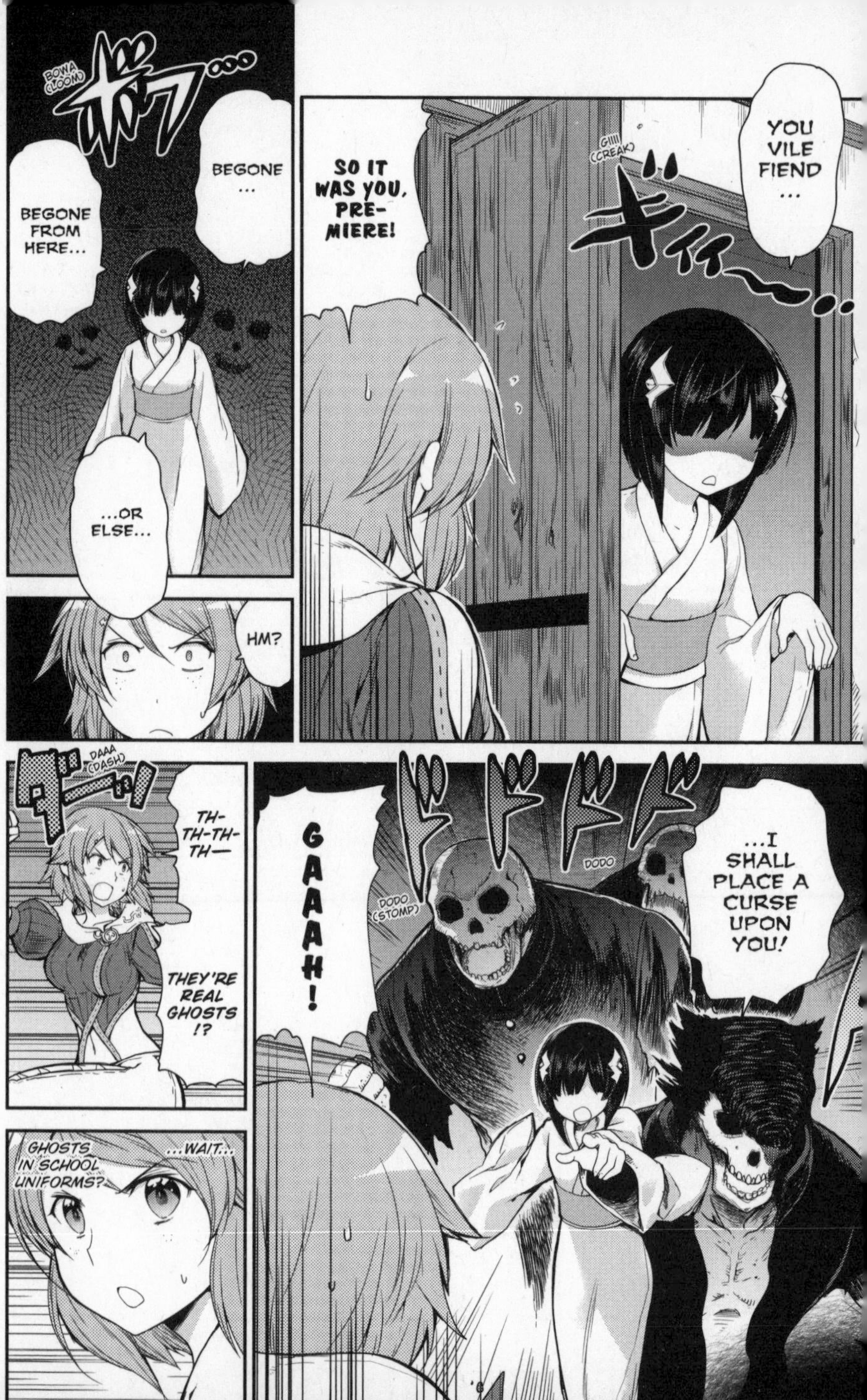
YOU VILE FIEND ...
GIIII (CREAK)
SO IT WAS YOU, PRE- MIERE!
BOWA (LOOM)
BEGONE ...
BEGONE FROM HERE...
...OR ELSE...
HM?
...I SHALL PLACE A CURSE UPON YOU!
DODO
DODO (STOMP)
GAAAAH!
DAAA (DASH)
TH-TH-TH-TH—
THEY'RE REAL GHOSTS !?
...WAIT...
GHOSTS IN SCHOOL UNIFORMS?

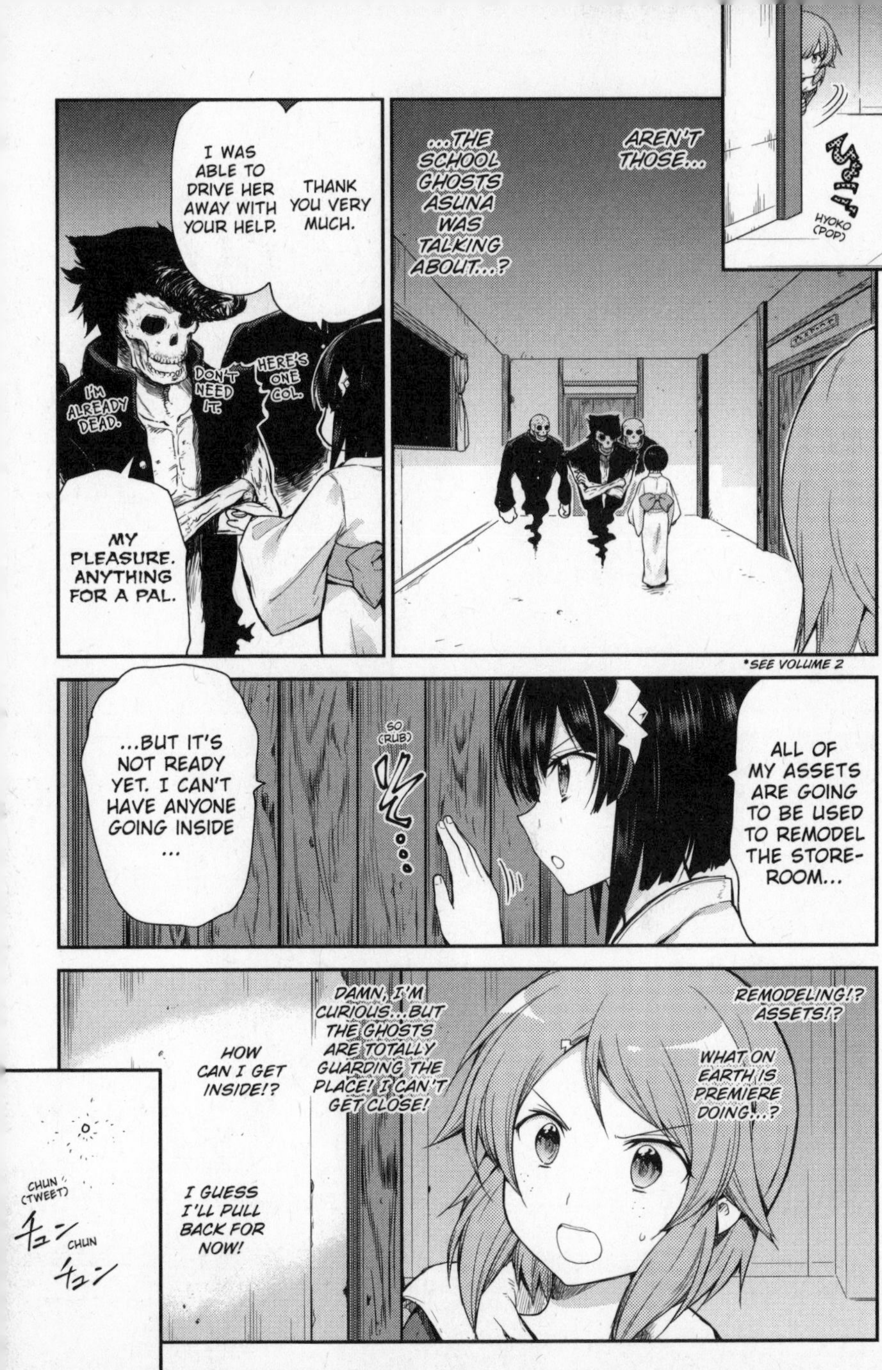
HYOKO (POP)
AREN'T THOSE...
...THE SCHOOL GHOSTS ASUNA WAS TALKING ABOUT...?
THANK YOU VERY MUCH.
I WAS ABLE TO DRIVE HER AWAY WITH YOUR HELP.
HERE'S ONE COL.
DON'T NEED IT.
I'M ALREADY DEAD.
MY PLEASURE. ANYTHING FOR A PAL.
ALL OF MY ASSETS ARE GOING TO BE USED TO REMODEL THE STORE-ROOM...
SO (RUB)
...BUT IT'S NOT READY YET. I CAN'T HAVE ANYONE GOING INSIDE ...
REMODELING!? ASSETS!?
WHAT ON EARTH IS PREMIERE DOING...?
DAMN, I'M CURIOUS...BUT THE GHOSTS ARE TOTALLY GUARDING THE PLACE! I CAN'T GET CLOSE!
HOW CAN I GET INSIDE!?
I GUESS I'LL PULL BACK FOR NOW!
CHUN (TWEET)
チュン
CHUN
チュン

*SEE VOLUME 2

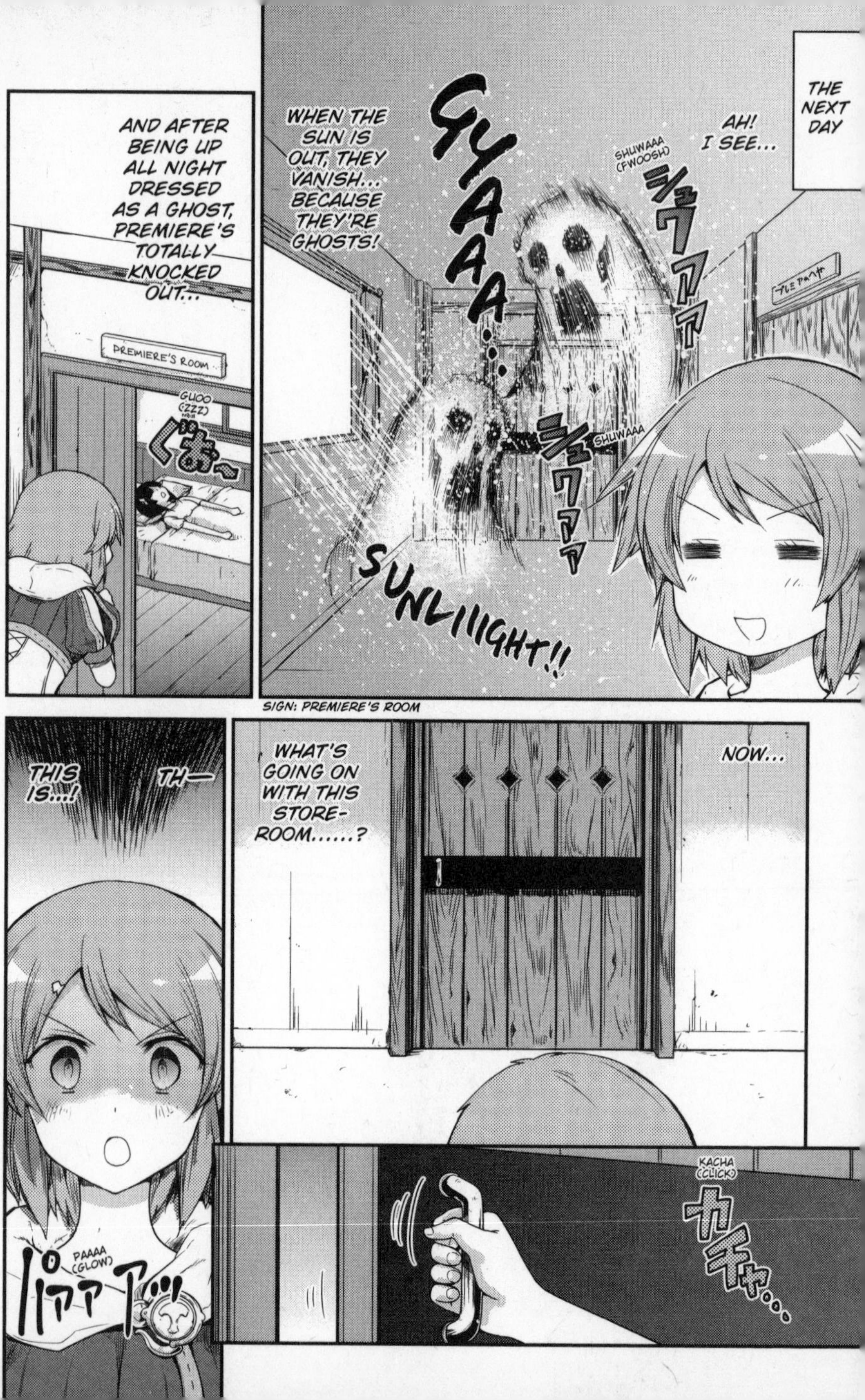
THE NEXT DAY
AH! I SEE...
SHUWAAA (FWOOSH)
GYAAAA...
WHEN THE SUN IS OUT, THEY VANISH... BECAUSE THEY'RE GHOSTS!
SHUWAAA
SUNLIIIGHT!!
AND AFTER BEING UP ALL NIGHT DRESSED AS A GHOST, PREMIERE'S TOTALLY KNOCKED OUT...
PREMIERE'S ROOM
GUOO (ZZZ)
SIGN: PREMIERE'S ROOM
NOW...
WHAT'S GOING ON WITH THIS STORE-ROOM......?
KACHA (CLICK)
THIS IS...!
TH—
PAAAA (GLOW)

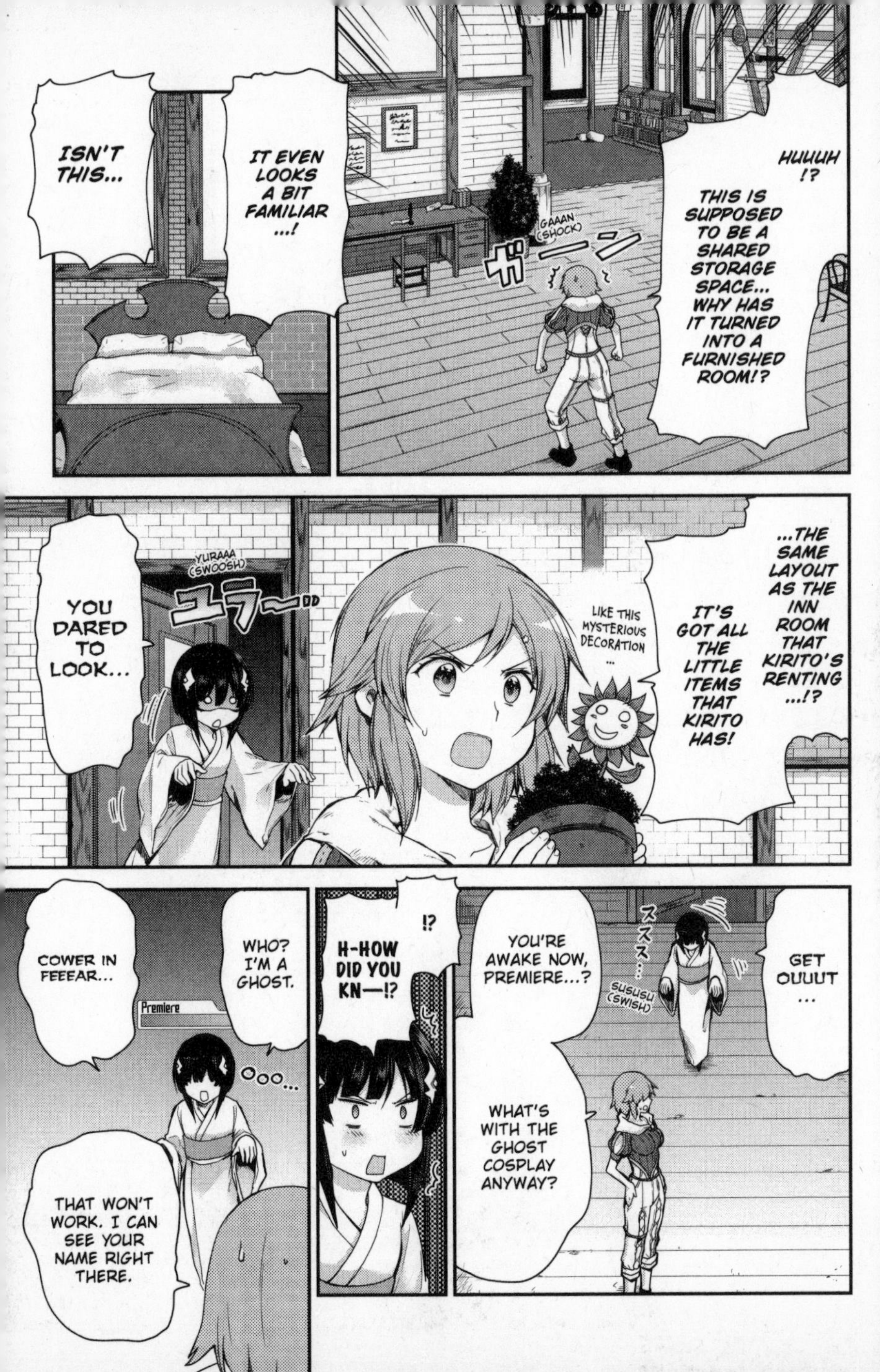
HUUUH !?
THIS IS SUPPOSED TO BE A SHARED STORAGE SPACE... WHY HAS IT TURNED INTO A FURNISHED ROOM!?
GAAAN (SHOCK)
IT EVEN LOOKS A BIT FAMILIAR ...!
ISN'T THIS...
...THE SAME LAYOUT AS THE INN ROOM THAT KIRITO'S RENTING ...!?
IT'S GOT ALL THE LITTLE ITEMS THAT KIRITO HAS!
LIKE THIS MYSTERIOUS DECORATION ...
YURAAA (SWOOSH)
YOU DARED TO LOOK...
GET OUUUT ...
SUSUSU (SWISH)
YOU'RE AWAKE NOW, PREMIERE...?
WHAT'S WITH THE GHOST COSPLAY ANYWAY?
!?
H-HOW DID YOU KN—!?
WHO? I'M A GHOST.
COWER IN FEEEAR...
Premiere
OOO...
THAT WON'T WORK. I CAN SEE YOUR NAME RIGHT THERE.

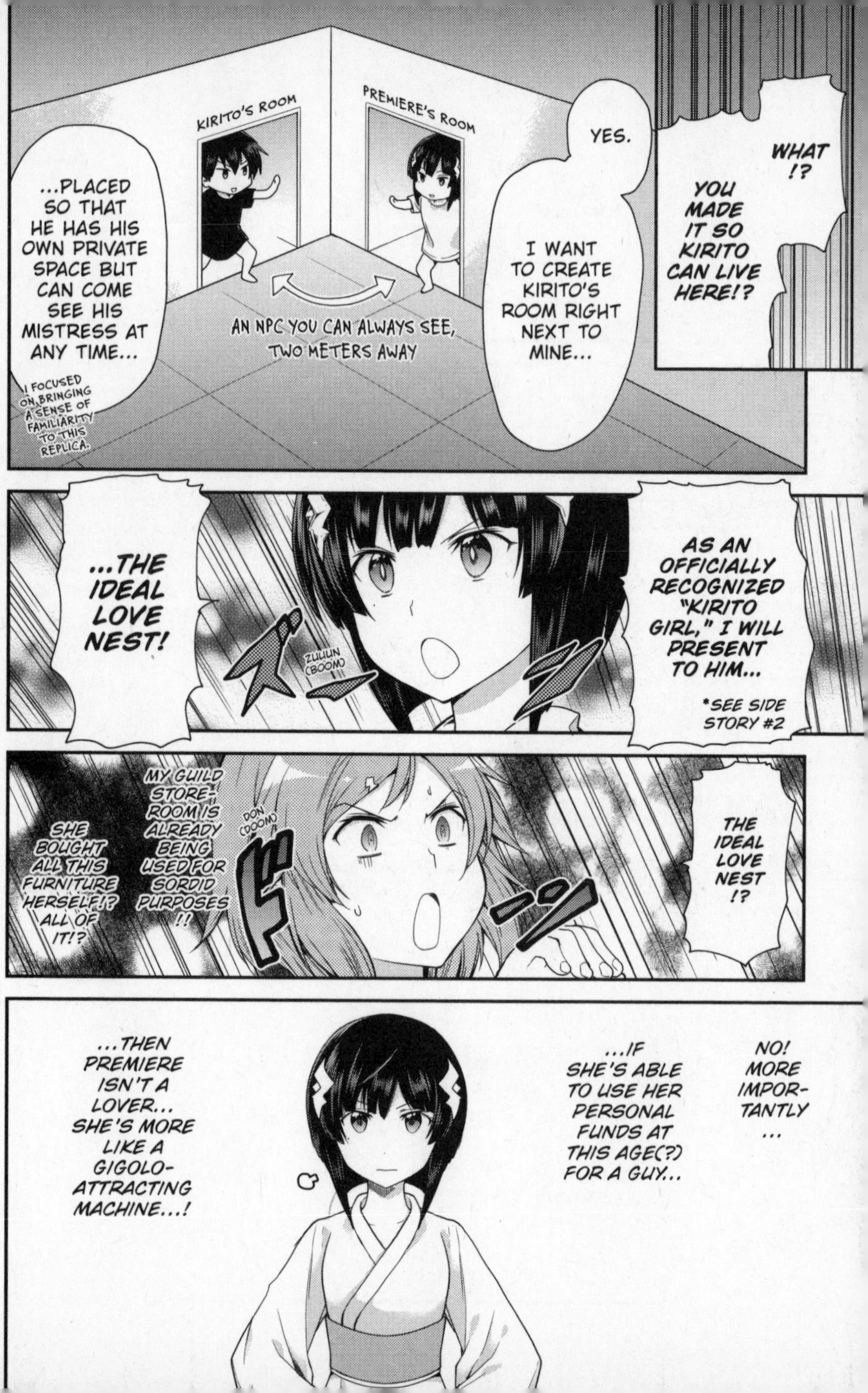
WHAT!?
YOU MADE IT SO KIRITO CAN LIVE HERE!?
YES.
I WANT TO CREATE KIRITO'S ROOM RIGHT NEXT TO MINE...
PREMIERE'S ROOM
KIRITO'S ROOM
...PLACED SO THAT HE HAS HIS OWN PRIVATE SPACE BUT CAN COME SEE HIS MISTRESS AT ANY TIME...
AN NPC YOU CAN ALWAYS SEE, TWO METERS AWAY
I FOCUSED ON BRINGING A SENSE OF FAMILIARITY TO THIS REPLICA.
AS AN OFFICIALLY RECOGNIZED "KIRITO GIRL," I WILL PRESENT TO HIM...
*SEE SIDE STORY #2
ZUUUN (BOOM)
...THE IDEAL LOVE NEST!
THE IDEAL LOVE NEST!?
DON (DOOM)
MY GUILD STORE-ROOM IS ALREADY BEING USED FOR SORDID PURPOSES!!
SHE BOUGHT ALL THIS FURNITURE HERSELF!? ALL OF IT!?
NO! MORE IMPOR-TANTLY...
...IF SHE'S ABLE TO USE HER PERSONAL FUNDS AT THIS AGE(?) FOR A GUY...
...THEN PREMIERE ISN'T A LOVER... SHE'S MORE LIKE A GIGOLO-ATTRACTING MACHINE...!

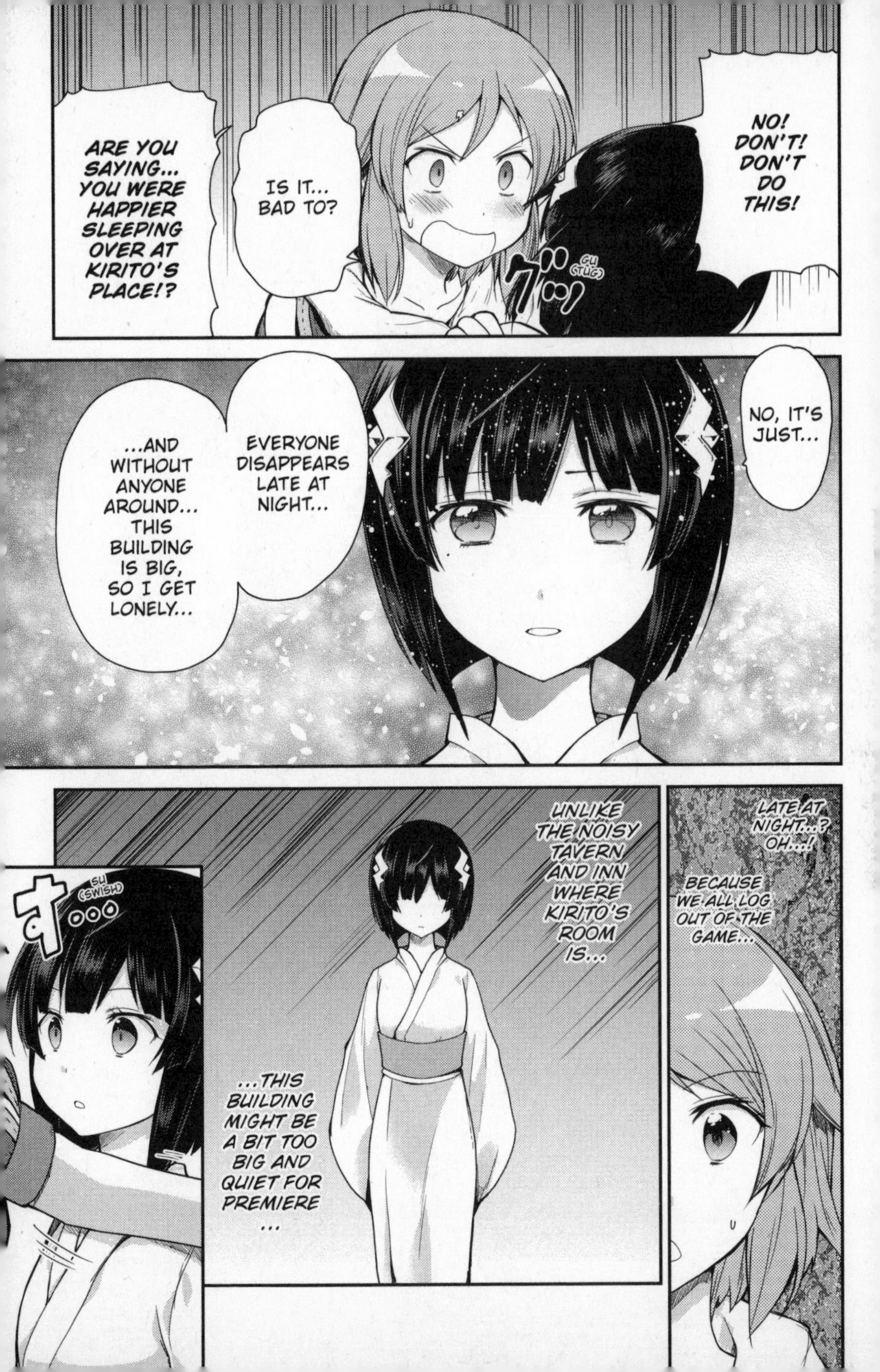
NO! DON'T! DON'T DO THIS!
GU (TUG)
IS IT... BAD TO?
ARE YOU SAYING... YOU WERE HAPPIER SLEEPING OVER AT KIRITO'S PLACE!?
NO, IT'S JUST...
EVERYONE DISAPPEARS LATE AT NIGHT...
...AND WITHOUT ANYONE AROUND... THIS BUILDING IS BIG, SO I GET LONELY...
LATE AT NIGHT...? OH...!
BECAUSE WE ALL LOG OUT OF THE GAME...
UNLIKE THE NOISY TAVERN AND INN WHERE KIRITO'S ROOM IS...
...THIS BUILDING MIGHT BE A BIT TOO BIG AND QUIET FOR PREMIERE...
SU (SWISH)

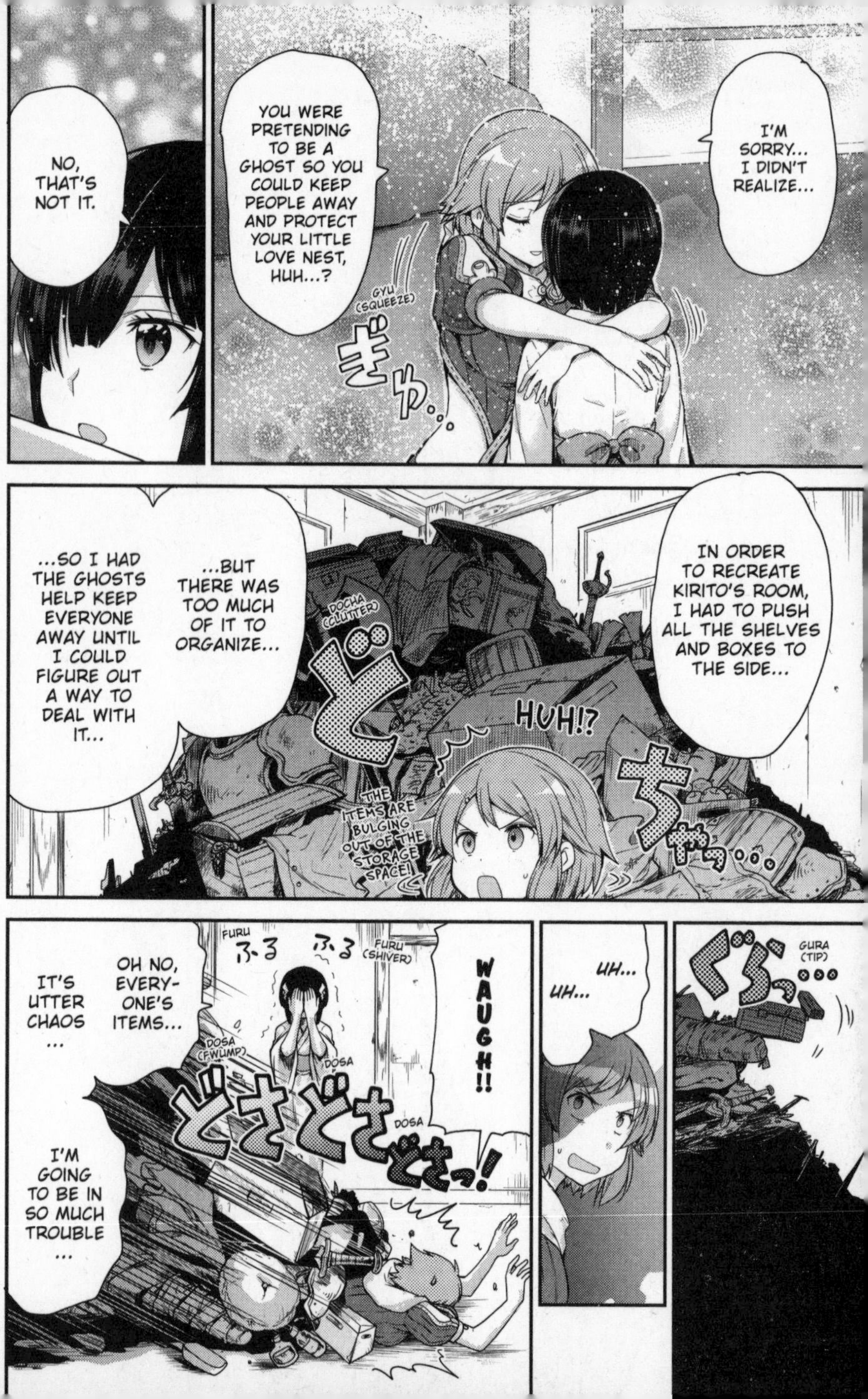
I'M SORRY... I DIDN'T REALIZE...
YOU WERE PRETENDING TO BE A GHOST SO YOU COULD KEEP PEOPLE AWAY AND PROTECT YOUR LITTLE LOVE NEST, HUH...?
GYU (SQUEEZE)
ぎゅ。。
NO, THAT'S NOT IT.
IN ORDER TO RECREATE KIRITO'S ROOM, I HAD TO PUSH ALL THE SHELVES AND BOXES TO THE SIDE...
...BUT THERE WAS TOO MUCH OF IT TO ORGANIZE...
...SO I HAD THE GHOSTS HELP KEEP EVERYONE AWAY UNTIL I COULD FIGURE OUT A WAY TO DEAL WITH IT...
DOCHA (CLUTTER)
どちゃっ。。。
HUH!?
THE ITEMS ARE BULGING OUT OF THE STORAGE SPACE!!
GURA (TIP)
ぐらっ。。。
UH... UH...
WAUGH!!
FURU FURU (SHIVER)
ふる ふる
OH NO, EVERY-ONE'S ITEMS...
IT'S UTTER CHAOS...
DOSA (FWUMP) DOSA DOSA
どさどさどさっ!
I'M GOING TO BE IN SO MUCH TROUBLE...

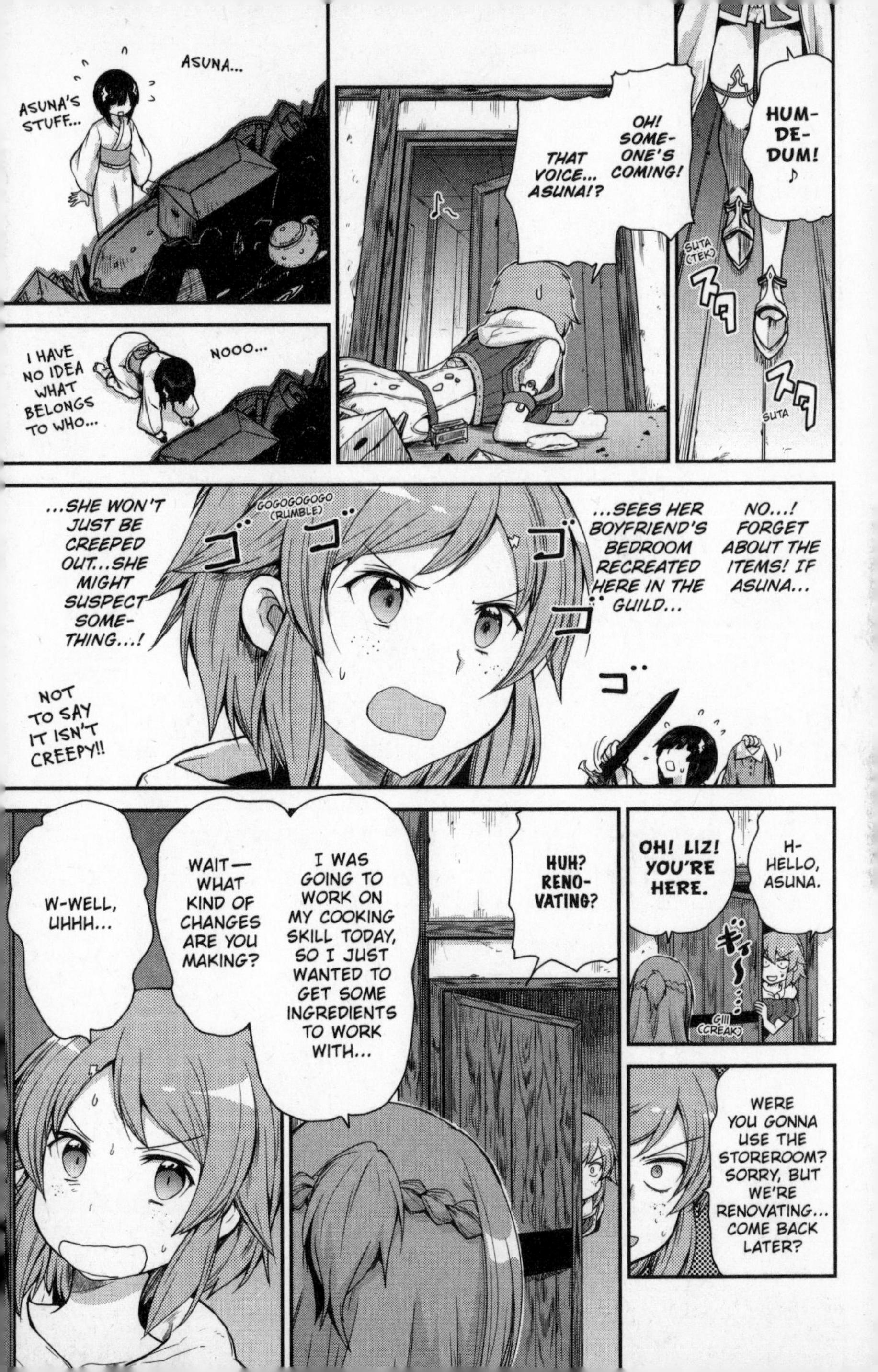
HUM-DE-DUM! ♪
SUTA (TEK)
SUTA
OH! SOMEONE'S COMING!
THAT VOICE... ASUNA!?
ASUNA...
ASUNA'S STUFF...
I HAVE NO IDEA WHAT BELONGS TO WHO...
NOOO...
NO...! FORGET ABOUT THE ITEMS! IF ASUNA...
...SEES HER BOYFRIEND'S BEDROOM RECREATED HERE IN THE GUILD...
GOGOGOGOGO (RUMBLE)
...SHE WON'T JUST BE CREEPED OUT...SHE MIGHT SUSPECT SOMETHING...!
NOT TO SAY IT ISN'T CREEPY!!
H-HELLO, ASUNA.
OH! LIZ! YOU'RE HERE.
GIII (CREAK)
WERE YOU GONNA USE THE STOREROOM? SORRY, BUT WE'RE RENOVATING... COME BACK LATER?
HUH? RENOVATING?
I WAS GOING TO WORK ON MY COOKING SKILL TODAY, SO I JUST WANTED TO GET SOME INGREDIENTS TO WORK WITH...
WAIT—WHAT KIND OF CHANGES ARE YOU MAKING?
W-WELL, UHHH...

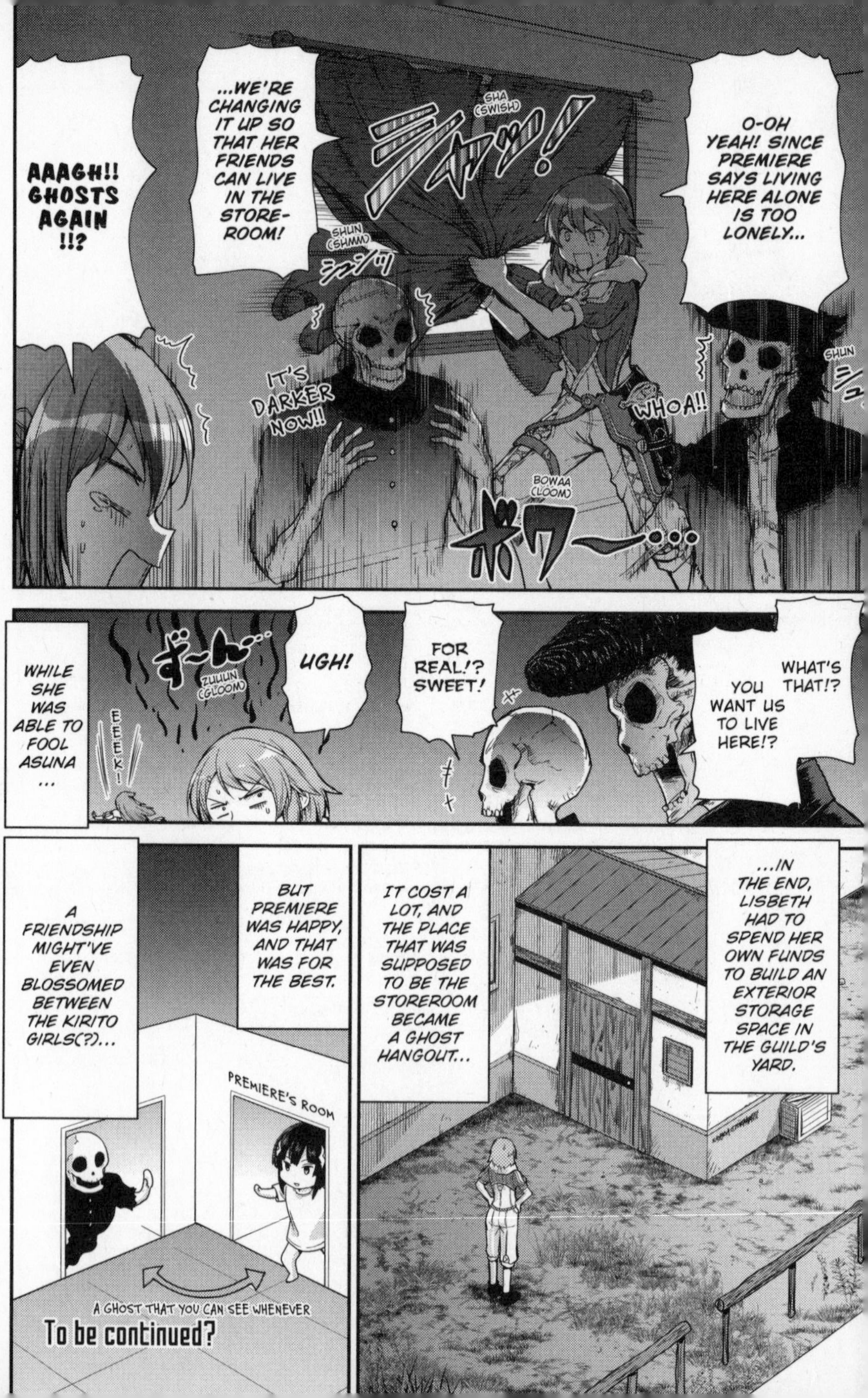
O-OH YEAH! SINCE PREMIERE SAYS LIVING HERE ALONE IS TOO LONELY...
SHA (SWISH)
...WE'RE CHANGING IT UP SO THAT HER FRIENDS CAN LIVE IN THE STOREROOM!
AAAGH!! GHOSTS AGAIN!!?
SHUN
WHOA!!
SHUN (SHMM)
IT'S DARKER NOW!!
BOWAA (LOOM)
WHAT'S THAT!? YOU WANT US TO LIVE HERE!?
FOR REAL!? SWEET!
UGH!
ZUUUN (GLOOM)
EEEEK!
WHILE SHE WAS ABLE TO FOOL ASUNA...
...IN THE END, LISBETH HAD TO SPEND HER OWN FUNDS TO BUILD AN EXTERIOR STORAGE SPACE IN THE GUILD'S YARD.
IT COST A LOT, AND THE PLACE THAT WAS SUPPOSED TO BE THE STOREROOM BECAME A GHOST HANGOUT...
BUT PREMIERE WAS HAPPY, AND THAT WAS FOR THE BEST.
A FRIENDSHIP MIGHT'VE EVEN BLOSSOMED BETWEEN THE KIRITO GIRLS(?)...
PREMIERE'S ROOM
A GHOST THAT YOU CAN SEE WHENEVER
To be continued?

VOLUME 5 AFTERWORD

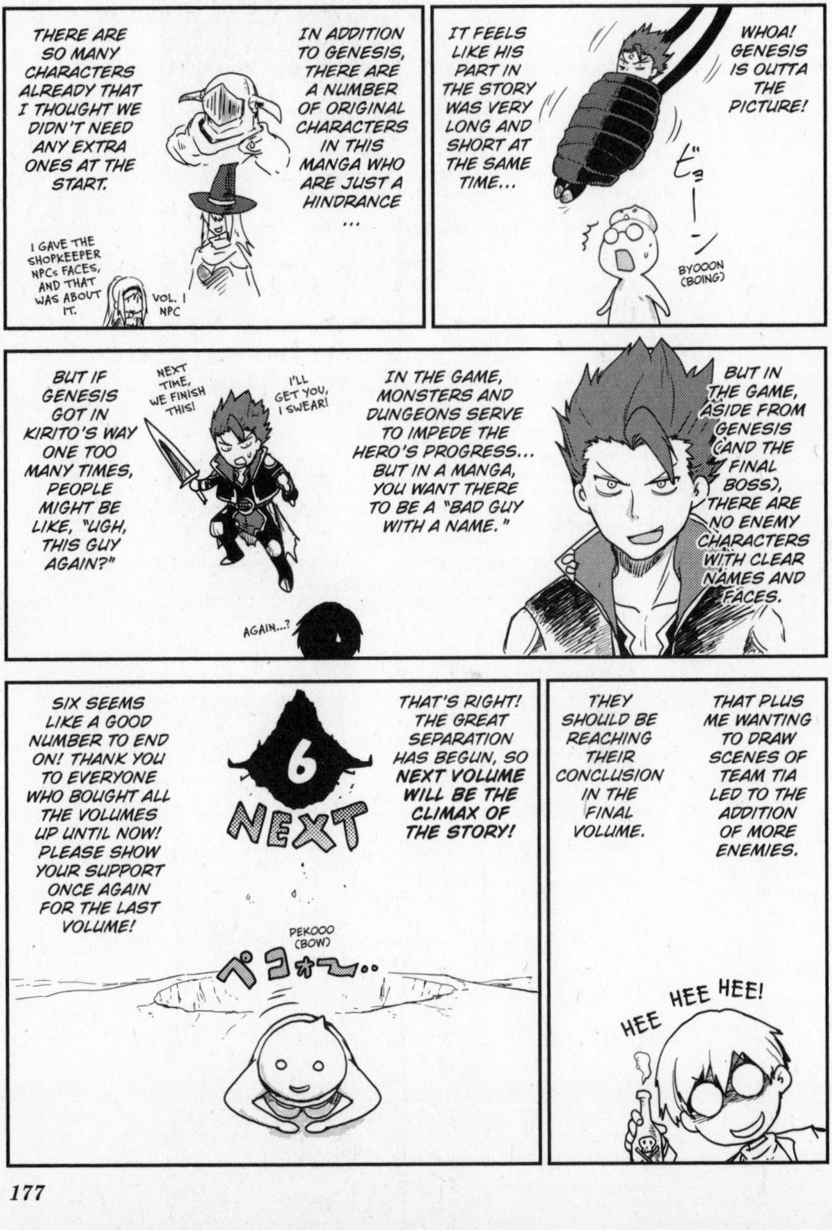
WHOA! GENESIS IS OUTTA THE PICTURE!
IT FEELS LIKE HIS PART IN THE STORY WAS VERY LONG AND SHORT AT THE SAME TIME...
ビョーン
BYOOON (BOING)
IN ADDITION TO GENESIS, THERE ARE A NUMBER OF ORIGINAL CHARACTERS IN THIS MANGA WHO ARE JUST A HINDRANCE...
THERE ARE SO MANY CHARACTERS ALREADY THAT I THOUGHT WE DIDN'T NEED ANY EXTRA ONES AT THE START.
VOL. 1 NPC
I GAVE THE SHOPKEEPER NPCs FACES, AND THAT WAS ABOUT IT.
BUT IN THE GAME, ASIDE FROM GENESIS (AND THE FINAL BOSS), THERE ARE NO ENEMY CHARACTERS WITH CLEAR NAMES AND FACES.
IN THE GAME, MONSTERS AND DUNGEONS SERVE TO IMPEDE THE HERO'S PROGRESS... BUT IN A MANGA, YOU WANT THERE TO BE A "BAD GUY WITH A NAME."
I'LL GET YOU, I SWEAR!
NEXT TIME, WE FINISH THIS!
BUT IF GENESIS GOT IN KIRITO'S WAY ONE TOO MANY TIMES, PEOPLE MIGHT BE LIKE, "UGH, THIS GUY AGAIN?"
AGAIN...?
THAT PLUS ME WANTING TO DRAW SCENES OF TEAM TIA LED TO THE ADDITION OF MORE ENEMIES.
THEY SHOULD BE REACHING THEIR CONCLUSION IN THE FINAL VOLUME.
HEE HEE HEE!
THAT'S RIGHT! THE GREAT SEPARATION HAS BEGUN, SO NEXT VOLUME WILL BE THE CLIMAX OF THE STORY!
6 NEXT
SIX SEEMS LIKE A GOOD NUMBER TO END ON! THANK YOU TO EVERYONE WHO BOUGHT ALL THE VOLUMES UP UNTIL NOW! PLEASE SHOW YOUR SUPPORT ONCE AGAIN FOR THE LAST VOLUME!
PEKOOO (BOW)
ペコォ〜..

SWORD ART ONLINE: HOLLOW REALIZATION 5

ART: TOMO HIROKAWA
ORIGINAL STORY: REKI KAWAHARA
CHARACTER DESIGN: abec
STORY SUPERVISION: BANDAI NAMCO ENTERTAINMENT

Translation: Stephen Paul   **Lettering: Phil Christie**

SWORD ART ONLINE -HOLLOW REALIZATION- Vol. 5
© REKI KAWAHARA 2019
© TOMO HIROKAWA 2019
© 2016 REKI KAWAHARA/PUBLISHED BY KADOKAWA CORPORATION
ASCII MEDIA WORKS/SAO MOVIE Project
© 2014 REKI KAWAHARA/PUBLISHED BY KADOKAWA CORPORATION
ASCII MEDIA WORKS/SAOII Project
© BANDAI NAMCO Entertainment Inc.
First published in Japan in 2019 by KADOKAWA CORPORATION, Tokyo.
English translation rights arranged with KADOKAWA CORPORATION, Tokyo, through Tuttle-Mori Agency, Inc., Tokyo.

English translation © 2019 by Yen Press, LLC

Yen Press
150 West 30th Street, 19th Floor
New York, NY 10001

Visit us at yenpress.com
facebook.com/yenpress
twitter.com/yenpress
yenpress.tumblr.com
instagram.com/yenpress

First Yen Press Edition: December 2019

Yen Press is an imprint of Yen Press, LLC.
The Yen Press name and logo are trademarks of Yen Press, LLC.

The publisher is not responsible for websites (or their content) that are not owned by the publisher.

Library of Congress Control Number: 2018950180

ISBNs: 978-1-9753-0613-7 (paperback)
          978-1-9753-0798-1 (ebook)

10 9 8 7 6 5 4 3 2 1

WOR

Printed in the United States of America